SAPPHIRE THRONE

Christopher Mitchell is the author of the epic fantasy series The Magelands. He studied in Edinburgh before living for several years in the Middle East and Greece, where he taught English. He returned to study classics and Greek tragedy and lives in Fife, Scotland with his wife and their four children.

By Christopher Mitchell

The Magelands Origins

Retreat of the Kell
The Trials of Daphne Holdfast
From the Ashes

The Magelands Epic

The Queen's Executioner
The Severed City
Needs of the Empire
Sacrifice
Fragile Empire
Storm Mage
Soulwitch Rises
Renegade Gods

The Magelands Eternal Siege

The Mortal Blade
The Dragon's Blade
The Prince's Blade
Falls of Iron
Paths of Fire
Gates of Ruin
City of Salve
Red City

City Ascendant
Dragon Eyre Badblood
Dragon Eyre Ashfall
Dragon Eyre Blackrose
Dreams of Kell
God Restrainer
Holdfast Imperium
World's End

The Magelands Dominion

Serpent Dominion
Demon Witch
Death Seer
Blood Burden
Kin Strife
Tempest's Edge
Creator of Worlds
Palace of the Almighty
Sapphire Throne
The Lost Ascendant

Masters and Makers

Fall Seldom Kings
The Making of Abigone
Whalebone King
Lies the Prince

Brigdomin Books Ltd
First Edition, March 2025
Ebook Edition © March 2025
ISBN 978-1-915978-55-4

ACKNOWLEDGEMENTS

I would like to thank the following for all their support during the writing of the Magelands Empire - my wife, Lisa Mitchell, who read every chapter as soon as it was drafted and kept me going in the right direction; my parents for their unstinting support; Marilyn Hopwood for reading the books in their early stages; James Aitken for his encouragement; and Grant and Gordon of the Film Club for their support.

Thanks also to my Advance Reader team, for all your help during the last few weeks before publication.

DRAMATIS PERSONAE

Colsbury

Karalyn Holdfast, Immortal Dream Mage

Kyra Holdfast, Karalyn's Daughter (18)

Carden Holdfast, Karalyn's Son (3)

Caitlyn Holdfast, Karalyn's Daughter (1)

Kelsey Holdfast, Unemployed Writer

Calpurnia Holdfast, Kelsey and Van's daughter (8)

Caelius Holdfast, Kelsey and Van's son (5)

Shella, Imperial Chancellor

Lucius Cardova, Imperial Constable

Olo'osso, Retired Pirate

Larron, Kyra's Friend from University

Frostback, Silver Dragon

Halfclaw, Blue/Green Dragon

Ninian Greenhold, Arrosa's Friend from University

Aila Holdfast, Purveyor of Whisky

Killop Holdfast, Corthie and Aila's Eldest Son (13)

Konna Holdfast, Corthie and Aila's Eldest Daughter (10)

Cairney Holdfast, Corthie and Aila's Son (8)

Carter Holdfast, Corthie and Aila's Son (6)

Clova Holdfast, Corthie and Aila's Daughter (4)

Carron Holdfast, Corthie and Aila's Youngest Son (2)

Ceres Holdfast, Corthie and Aila's Youngest Daughter (6 Thirds)

Lahnos Laimos, Former Commander, Imperial Army

Sigum Mon Sigel, Dragon, and Friend of Lahnos

Ora'lya, Dragon Rider

Dermot Laimos, Lahnos's Son

Corthie's Team

Corthie Holdfast, Commander

Drechtalang Fo, Sanang Hedgewitch

Wyle of Hold Liant, Army Corporal

Dominie, Kellach Marine Corporal

Jaeanna, Rahain Stone Mage

Nestorian, Banner Sergeant

Plateau City – Imperial Court

Thorn Holdfast, Empress

Naxor, Imperial Chamberlain

Brogan ae Bridget, Herald of the Empire

Slaeon, Imperial Treasurer

Bedig ae Brannig, Lord Marshal

Martius Claudian, Imperial Adjutant

Caelius Logos, Imperial Quartermaster

Jannis Holdsmith, Chief Jurist

Van Logos, Ambassador from the City of Salve

Plateau City – University

Cole Holdfast, University Student (19)

Arrosa, University Student (17)

Dazi, University Student

Elbannon, University Professor

Gallea, University Professor

Nadia, University Professor

Ravi, University Professor

Achan, Visiting Professor

Hold Fast Estate, Holdings

Celine Holdfast, Estate Manager

Ulna, Dragon Eyre

Blackrose, Queen of the Eastern Rim

Maddie Jackdaw, Blackrose's Rider

Sable Holdfast, Retired Agent

Alara'osso (Lara), Sable's Partner

Anaj'osso (Joss), Sable and Lara's Son (5)

Alindi'osso (Lindi), Sable and Lara's Daughter (1)

Edgar's Immortals

Edgar, Brother of Edmond

Allura, Daughter of Edmond

Ward, Son of Edmond

Ballatar, Grandson of Edmond

Laverne, Granddaughter of Edmond

Belfar, Son of Ballatar

Elmhirst, Ancient, and Ruler of the Doomed Worlds

Athumia

Bailey, Theodora's Brother

Bauchlie, President of Zamata

Famula Min Gahad, Queen of the Dominion

Abda Min Gahad, Famula's Sister

Saphben Mon Gahad, Famula's Brother

Konran Mon Gahad, Famula's Brother

Tirna Min Gahad, Famula's Sister

Minula Min Famula, Famula's Daughter

Sigra Min Sigmund, Sigel's Granddaughter

Sigel Mon Sagellus, Lord of Western Inopei, Sigum's Father

Amatskouri

Jazidorato, Prime Minister

Fenu, Chancellor

Others

Cael Holdfast, Marine Lieutenant, Seaborne Company

Doune, Marine Captain, Seaborne Company

Rosie Jackdaw, Munitions Expert

Gallantmorn, Eastern Rim Dragon

Annu'tila, Gallantmorn's Rider

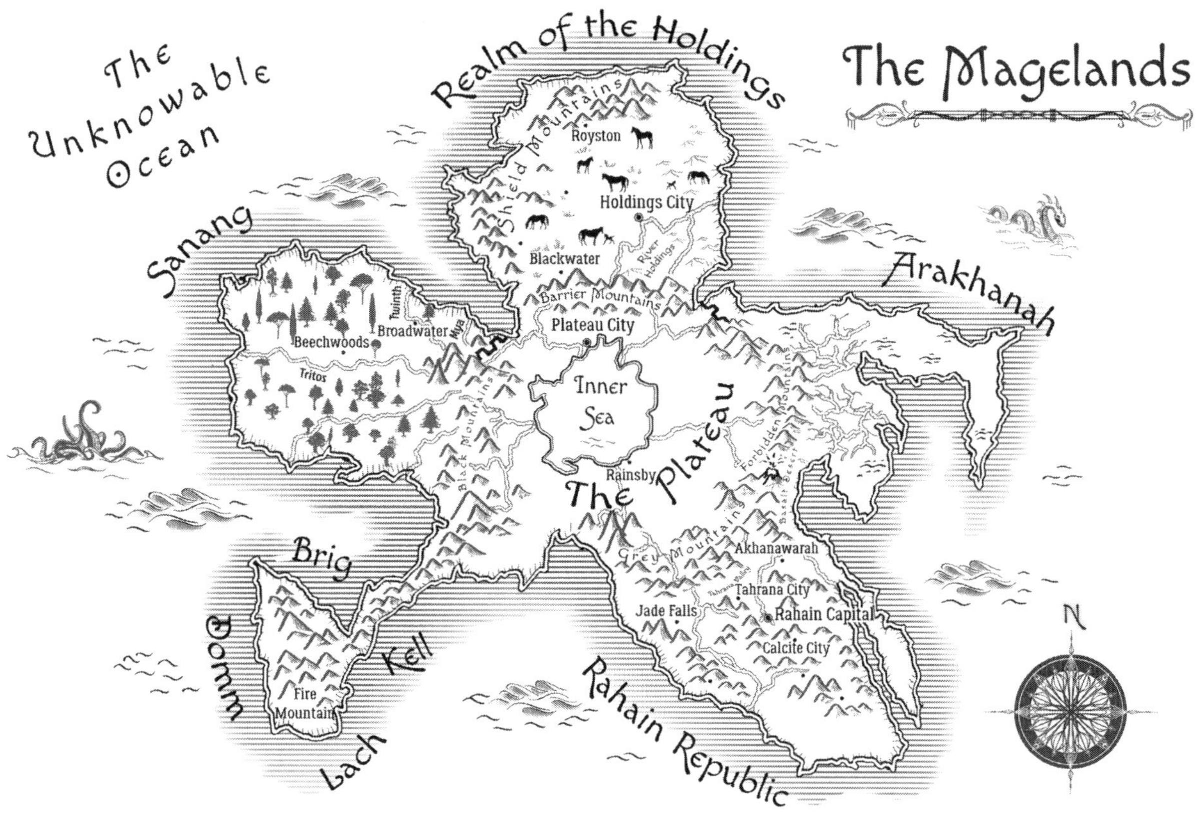
The Magelands
The Unknowable Ocean
Realm of the Holdings
Shield Mountains
Royston
Holdings City
Blackwater
River Holdings
Barrier Mountains
Plateau City
Arakhanah
Sanang
Twinth
Broadwater
Mya
Beechwoods
Tritos
Black Mountains
Inner Sea
Rainsby
The Plateau
Forbidden Mountains
Basalt Desert
Grey Mountain
Akhanawarah
Tahrana City
Rahain Capital
Jade Falls
Calcite City
Rahain Republic
Brig
Kell
Domm
Lach
Fire Mountain
N

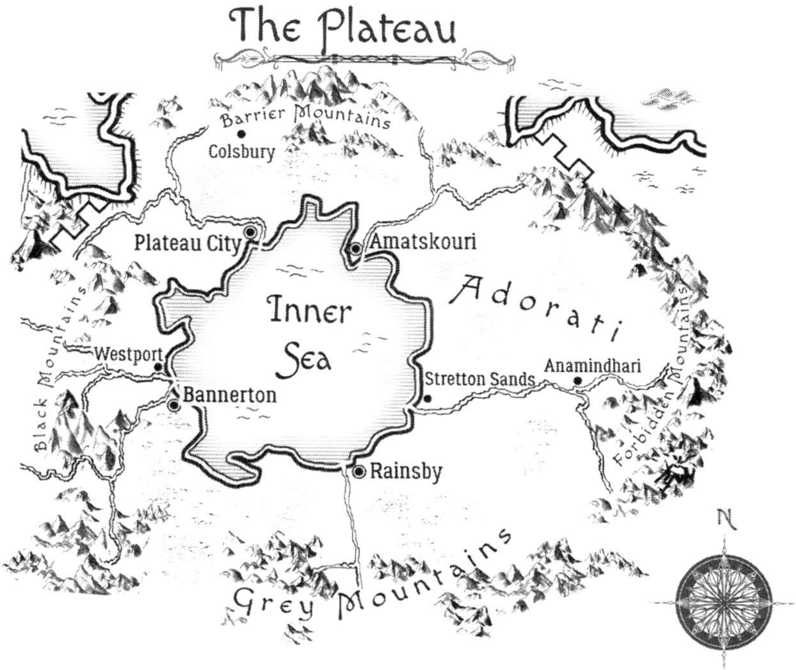
The Plateau
Barrier Mountains
Colsbury
Plateau City
Amatskouri
Adorati
Inner Sea
Black Mountains
Westport
Bannerton
Stretton Sands
Anamindhari
Forbidden Mountains
Rainsby
Grey Mountains
N

CHAPTER 1
COUNTING THE DAYS

Nom Karta, Inopei – 17th Tradinch 1597

Cael squeezed the dead bat.

Dark blood oozed from the creature's side, and dripped onto the stone floor of the cell. The hood that covered Cael's head was hot and uncomfortable, and sweat kept getting into his eyes. He had repeatedly tried to remove it, but it had been secured in place by a padlock that he had been unable to pick, and which was only unlocked when the Bullan soldiers gave him food and water. Cael didn't mind; the hood had allowed him to maintain the illusion that he was incapable of using his powers. Edgar knew much about the Holdfasts, but he didn't seem to understand that a dream mage's eyes were not necessary in order to use their vision abilities.

Cael dipped a makeshift quill into the pool of blood, then he poised it over the scrap of paper, and began to write.

To Edgar, Lord of Nom Karta,

My thanks for saving my life, and for the hospitable conditions of my confinement. I have not been starved or beaten, and I have not been unduly harassed. You have shown an honourable spirit, and so, to reciprocate, I feel obliged to let you know that I have decided to escape.

Yours,

Cael Holdfast

He laid the scrap of paper onto the pillow of his bed, then he neatened the threadbare blanket, smoothing out its creases.

Cael turned towards the barred door of his small, grimy cell. Long hours of continually using his powers had given him a pounding headache, but the intense practice had also improved his skills. For nine days, or so he had calculated, he had been imprisoned within the cramped jailhouse next to the Tempest mine on Inopei. For the previous three days, Edgar had not been present, leaving the compound and its surroundings to be defended by Lord Ballatar, who had been appointed governor of the Tempest mine. Edgar routinely wore the thin eye-shields that prevented Cael from getting into his mind, but Ballatar had not always been so careful. With the hood deemed sufficient to prevent Cael from using his powers, Ballatar had seen no need to constantly wear the uncomfortable eye guards, and he only put them on whenever any of the other gods freed from the Palace of the Almighty were in attendance. Thanks to that oversight, Cael knew the entire layout of the Dominion defences. They were awaiting a counter attack from the Empire, and had laid a trap for them; but no such attack had yet occurred.

Cael's dream powers moved out of the cell and into the dark hallway that ran through the centre of the jailhouse. Two Bullan soldiers were standing guard by a door at the end of the hallway, and a further four were in the next room. If it hadn't been for the Bullan, Cael imagined that he would have been able to make his escape far earlier, but their language was impenetrable, and he was unable to use any of his persuasion abilities on them. Fortunately, the Tempest mine was also housing several regiments of Aucterians from the Dominion army, and Cael had found their minds to be more pliable.

He sent his vision out into the main area of the camp next to the mine, and summoned the three Aucterians that he had been manipulating. Two were sergeants, and the other a lieutenant, and Cael had been working on them for days, insinuating his plan into their minds.

The three men stopped what they were doing, and dispersed, each going about the tasks that Cael had appointed them.

Ten minutes later, the lieutenant approached the jailhouse, a bag clutched in one hand.

'Orders from Lord Ballatar,' he said to the Bullan guards on duty. 'I am to question the Holdfast boy.'

The Bullan moved aside, their features unreadable, and the officer entered the jailhouse. He nodded to the other Bullan in the building, then he approached the hallway where the cells were located. Cael was the only prisoner on that floor, and he sat patiently as the officer strode up to the barred gate. The lieutenant pushed the bag through the bars, and it landed on the stone floor next to Cael.

'Tell me what you know about the Empire's plans to attack the Tempest mine,' the officer said, reciting the words that Cael had imprinted into his mind. Cael wasn't sure if the Bullan would be listening, but he had decided to take no chances.

'I'll never talk,' said Cael, as he rummaged through the contents of the bag. At the bottom, he found a small key. He lifted it to the padlock, and removed it from the chain that had been looped around his neck. As soon as it was free, he pulled the hood from his head, and wiped the sweat from his face.

'How many divisions are coming?' the officer said, as Cael unpacked the rolled-up Aucterian army uniform from the bag.

'More than enough,' said Cael.

He undressed quickly, then pulled on the uniform. A pair of boots had been included, and he crouched down to lace them up.

'When are they coming?' said the officer.

'How am I supposed to know?' said Cael.

He brushed the tangles from his hair, then he washed his hands and face in a shallow basin that had been provided for him. The Aucterian army had high standards, and he had no desire to attract any unwanted attention from one of their officers. He rolled his shoulders, and got to his feet.

Now, he said in the lieutenant's mind.

The officer began to choke and gasp.

'Help!' he cried. 'The prisoner is strangling me!'

Four armed Bullan piled through the doorway, their crossbows ready. Cael drove his powers into their minds, and scoured them clean, just as he had done to the villagers on World Three. The four Bullan tottered, then they collapsed to the floor of the hallway, their weapons and armour clattering off the smooth flag stones. The Aucterian lieutenant knelt by one, and removed a set of keys from his belt. He stood, and began trying out each key in the lock of Cael's cell door. On the fifth attempt, the key turned, and the door swung open. Cael stepped out into the hallway, his head pounding, then he helped the officer drag the bodies of the fallen Bullan into the cell. When they were all inside, Cael gazed into the eyes of the officer.

Forget everything that has happened here. Forget all you know about me. Sleep.

Cael caught the body of the officer as he fell, and then he laid him down on the floor of the cell. He walked into the passageway, locked the cell door, then he threw the keys into the dark interior.

He went into the main room of the jailhouse, and waited. A few moments later, one of the two sergeants he had been manipulating opened the main doors.

He glanced at Cael, his eyes partly glazed over. 'This way.'

Cael followed him out of the jailhouse and into the walled fortress that lay next to the Tempest mine. He glanced up at the dark sky. The dawn bell had not long sounded, but the days and nights seemed almost indistinguishable in the volcanic wasteland. Several red glows to either side marked the locations of nearby eruptions, and a steady fall of ash was swirling through the air. A mixture of Bullan and Aucterian soldiers was busy in the main courtyard in the centre of the fort, but none paid any attention to the sight of a sergeant and a trooper emerging from the jailhouse. Cael had worried a little about his Kellach stature, but there were a few among the Aucterians who were almost as tall as he was.

He sent out a message to everyone in sight.

We are beneath your notice. Ignore us.

He knew that his words would go unnoticed by the Bullan in the courtyard but, as they regarded all humans as looking much the same, he hoped it wouldn't matter. Cael and the sergeant came to a halt in the shadows of a wooden balcony that stretched round two sides of the inner courtyard. Lord Ballatar was due to make an appearance, and the second manipulated sergeant was primed and ready. Cael had spent days watching the movements of Ballatar, and had noted that he held a meeting with the senior Dominion officers every morning after the shift change on the fortress walls. True to his schedule, the young-looking god emerged from a doorway on the ground floor, flanked by two Bullan and two Aucterian soldiers. The god was wrapped in warm robes, and he had a scarf covering the lower half of his face to shield him from the ash. Cael left the side of the first sergeant, as the second walked out of the nearby barracks. The two suborned sergeants faced each other by the edge of the courtyard, then one unleashed a punch, and they began to fight, swinging their fists at each other and crying out angry insults. Cael quickened his pace as several other soldiers ran across the courtyard to prise the two brawling sergeants apart, and in the confusion, Cael followed Ballatar and the four soldiers towards the governor's quarters. One of the Aucterians unlocked a door, as Cael lingered in the shadows of the courtyard, then they escorted the governor through the entrance. The Aucterian soldier turned to close and re-lock the door, and Cael darted into his mind.

Leave it unlocked.

The soldier blinked, then his fingers came away from the handle of the door, and he disappeared into the shadows of the interior. Cael stole to the doorway, and eased himself through. The inside of the governor's quarters was the most comfortable part of the mine complex, with carpeted hallways and tapestries hanging from the walls, and it was the first place Cael had been where there was no ash in the air. Ahead of him, the god and his escort were continuing onwards in the direction of a flight of stairs, and Cael closed the door and followed them.

He got as far as three feet along the corridor before he was noticed.

'Hey!' cried one of the Bullan. 'You are not permitted in here.'

Cael raised a hand, and the four escorts fell, their minds wiped clean. Cael swayed from the effort, his headache worse than ever, and Ballatar stared at him. The god raised his own hand, and Cael felt death powers batter against his protective vision shield.

Cael smiled, then he pushed his powers into Ballatar's mind. 'No eye-guards today, Governor?'

'How did you get out of your cell, Holdfast?'

'I'm almost embarrassed by how easy it was,' Cael said. 'I am going to take your Quadrant; or should I say, my Quadrant? It was I who brought it to Athumia.'

Ballatar's right hand twitched, as though he was considering trying to grasp and activate the Quadrant before Cael could reach him.

'I wouldn't move, if I were you,' said Cael. 'I am inside your mind, Governor, and if your hand travels another inch towards the Quadrant, I will do to you what I have done to your soldiers.'

'Why are you doing this to us?' said the god. 'Why can't you leave us in peace?'

Cael laughed. 'Those who want peace do not send assassination squads to slaughter members of my family. If my Uncle Corthie and his children had been killed, we wouldn't be having this conversation – you would already be dead.'

'I am not responsible for what Ward did. He acted against Lord Edgar's express orders.'

'Is that so?' said Cael.

Ballatar's thoughts turned to escape, then his hand darted towards his robes.

Sleep.

Ballatar's eyes rolled up into his head, and he toppled to the stone floor. Cael raced forward, knowing he might have only moments to spare before more soldiers arrived. He knelt by the god, rifled through his robes, then he plucked the Quadrant free from his clothes. He moved his fingers towards its copper surface, then hesitated, his gaze going back to Ballatar. On impulse, he went back into the god's mind, and blocked up all of his powers, from death and fire, to his ability to self-heal.

Do not awaken until I command it.

A side door opened, and several Dominion officers walked into the corridor. Their eyes went to the soldiers lying on the floor, then to the sight of Cael crouching over the unconscious form of the god.

Cael smiled, tilted his head at them, then he triggered the Quadrant.

The air crackled, and he appeared in front of the marine headquarters on the quayside of Sun Ta harbour on Dragon Eyre, the unconscious body of Ballatar on the ground next to him. He got to his feet as marines emerged from the building. Cael ignored them for a moment, savouring the clean air and the blue skies of Na Sun Ka after so many days by the Tempest mine; then he raised his palms, remembering that he was wearing the uniform of the enemy.

'Who are you?' shouted a marine, a crossbow cradled in his arms.

'Second Lieutenant Holdfast of the Seaborne Company,' he said. 'I have just escaped from custody on Athumia.'

A colonel hurried forward. 'Lieutenant Holdfast?'

'Aye, sir; and I've brought a prisoner.'

The officer glanced down at the body of Ballatar, then he turned to a corporal. 'Fetch Adjutant Claudian; immediately.'

The marine corporal ran back into the headquarters building, as the other marines lowered their crossbows.

Cael kept his arms raised, the Quadrant clutched in his left hand. 'Is Captain Doune in Sun Ta, sir?'

'He is,' said the colonel; 'and he's none too pleased with you, Lieutenant. Apparently, you disobeyed orders by returning to Athumia.'

'I had good reason, sir,' said Cael, 'and I was authorised to take the initiative by the Adjutant himself.'

'Should we arrest him, sir?' said a marine sergeant.

'Not yet,' said the colonel. 'Let us hear what the Adjutant has to say first.'

More officers emerged from the building, Claudian among them.

The marines cleared a path, and they walked towards Cael. Claudian frowned, then he took a few more steps in Cael's direction.

'The Quadrant,' he said.

Cael placed the device into the Adjutant's waiting hand.

Claudian glanced down at the body. 'And this is?'

'Lord Ballatar, sir, Edgar's governor of the Tempest mine, and one of those who escaped from the Palace of the Almighty. I thought he might possess some useful intelligence.'

'Is he dangerous?'

'He will not awaken until I give the order, sir; and I took the liberty of removing all of his god powers. If you cut him, he will not heal.'

'Why are you wearing a Dominion uniform, lad?'

'I was captured by Lord Ward, sir, and then imprisoned by Lord Edgar in a jail next to the Tempest mine. It took me a few days to plan my escape. The uniform was part of my disguise to get out of the prison. I also ensured that Queen Famula has been incapacitated. She will no longer be able to play any role in the conflict.'

'Should he be placed into custody for disobeying orders, my lord?' said the colonel.

Claudian gave the officer a wry smile. 'Let us think on it. Lieutenant Holdfast has, and correct me if I am wrong, neutralised the Queen of the Dominion and captured one of Lord Edgar's chief allies, all while escaping from a Dominion prison. On top of all that, he is beloved by the Empress. All the same, he is in breach of marine regulations.'

'Apologies, sir,' said Cael, 'but did you not grant me full authority over the Quadrant? Did you not inform me that I was permitted to disregard orders concerning the use of the device?'

Claudian frowned.

'Is that true, my lord?' said the colonel.

Claudian said nothing for a moment, as the watching crowd of marines waited. Cael knew that Claudian's words had only referred to disregarding the orders of Captain Doune, not of the major who had commanded Cael to remain in Sun Ta when he had first returned.

Would the Adjutant reveal this, Cael wondered, or would he decide to play along?

'It is true,' said Claudian. 'Lieutenant Holdfast is to be commended, not punished.'

The surrounding marines started to smile, and Cael lowered his arms.

'Take Lord Ballatar inside,' said Claudian. 'Secure him in the holding cells.'

Two marines picked up the unconscious body of the god, and carried him towards the building.

Claudian extended a hand, and Cael took it.

'Well done, Lieutenant,' Claudian said. 'Excellent work.'

The marines gathered round Cael, slapping him on the back. A few comments were made about his uniform, and Cael laughed along. Claudian allowed the marines to enjoy the moment, then he gestured towards the building.

'I believe that Lieutenant Holdfast requires a full debriefing,' he said. 'Come this way.'

Cael saluted. 'Aye, sir.'

They extricated themselves from the crowd, and entered the marine headquarters, where several dozen officers and marines were lining the hallway, some applauding. Claudian maintained a polite smile on his face, then he led Cael into a private office and closed the door.

The smile vanished.

'You reckless, irresponsible fool,' he cried. 'Of all the stupid things you could have done... Do you realise that your absence had to be reported to the very highest levels? I had to stand in front of Her Majesty the Empress and explain how we had allowed you to return to Athumia alone. I thought I was going to lose my damn job. And now, to force me into colluding with your little lie regarding orders – you know fine well that I was referring to Captain Doune, and no other. The chain of command exists for a reason, Lieutenant, yet you consistently flout it.' He stared at Cael. 'Nothing to say?'

'I do have one question, sir,' he said.

'Yes?'

'What is today's date?'

Claudian blinked.

'I may have lost track of a day or two, sir,' Cael went on. 'It can be difficult at the Tempest mine to tell the difference between day and night.'

Claudian sighed and shook his head. 'Which calendar would you prefer?'

'The Holdings, sir.'

'Today is the Eighteenth Day of the Last Third of Spring.'

Cael smiled. 'I'm a day early, sir. I thought today was the nineteenth. I should have remained where I was until tomorrow.'

'You mean you timed your escape for a certain date?'

'Aye, sir. Tomorrow is my betrothed's eighteenth birthday, and I wanted to surprise her.'

'And what makes you think you will be allowed to return to the Star Continent?'

'Your words to me, sir. You said that I would be eligible for leave upon my return.'

Claudian sat down at his desk. 'If I had any hair, Lieutenant, I would be tearing it out right about now. I despair, lad. What am I to do with you? It is clear to me that you cannot be trusted to obey orders, and yet you have done more for the cause of the Empire than anyone else under my command. Is Queen Famula definitely out of action?'

'Aye, sir. The other members of her family were squabbling over who should take command in her place.'

'And Ward captured you?'

'He was wearing eye-shields, sir. He was beginning to flay the skin from me when Lord Edgar intervened. Edgar did not authorise the attack upon Clackenbaird. In fact, it seems as though Lord Edgar has expressly ordered his gods not to harm any Holdfast.'

'Were you able to take a good look at the mine's defences?'

'Aye, sir.'

'Then it is fortunate that you escaped a day early, as I will need you to write down everything you know before I will allow your leave to commence. I will also require you to assist in the interrogation of Lord Ballatar.' He gazed out of the window at the harbour of Sun Ta. 'You have one hour to get washed, shaved and clothed in a more appropriate uniform. Meet me back here, and we shall visit our captured god.'

Cael used the officers' shower room on the first floor of the headquarters to scrub nine days of ash and grime from his body, before going to the quartermaster's office to requisition a fresh uniform. Everywhere he went within the building, he was congratulated by the marines and staff for his escape; though he was also warned that Captain Doune remained livid at his behaviour. Most of the marines had heard about Cael's various exploits since joining the service and, though he sensed some disapproval from a few of the senior officers, the rest seemed to hold him in high regard.

Adjutant Claudian was waiting for him outside his office with a handful of other officers when Cael went back down to the ground floor.

'That looks much better,' said Claudian, eyeing Cael. He gestured to a major. 'To the holding cells.'

They set off along the hallway, then descended a flight of stairs into the basement of the building, where a long row of arched cellars had been converted into a prison. Unk Tannic agents were occupying the majority of the small cells, then they came to the one where Lord Ballatar was lying unconscious.

'Before you awaken him,' said Claudian, 'can you assure me that he is completely harmless, Lieutenant?'

'Aye, sir,' said Cael. 'All of his powers have been blocked.'

'Forever?'

'No, sir. Any dream mage would be able to remove the blocks with ease. I don't know if it's possible to block them forever.'

'Then proceed.'

'I will need to enter the cell, sir.'

Claudian nodded to a marine guard, who stepped forward and unlocked the cell door. Cael opened it and crouched down by the prostrate body of Ballatar. He prised open one eyelid, and sent in his powers.

When you awaken, he said in the god's mind, *you will answer our questions truthfully; otherwise, you will feel pain. Awaken.*

Cael stepped back as the god spluttered and opened his eyes. He stared around, and raised a hand. A few of the marine officers flinched, but nothing happened. Ballatar stared at his hand, his eyes widening.

'Can you sense your self-healing?' said Cael.

Ballatar turn his gaze to Cael. 'What have you done to me, Holdfast?'

'I have turned you into a mortal,' said Cael; 'a mortal with no powers; and I have compelled you to answer our questions.'

Ballatar screamed in rage and lunged at Cael, who dodged his arms and slapped the god across his face with the back of his hand.

'You felt that, didn't you?' said Cael, as the god whimpered. 'We are not here to hurt you, though we could, if we wanted to. All we want to do is ask you a few questions.' He glanced at Claudian.

'Tell us, Lord Ballatar,' said the Adjutant; 'what were your plans for the defence of the Tempest mine?'

Ballatar scowled, then his mouth opened and he began to speak.

'We were to draw the imperial forces into a trap,' he said. 'The mine is lightly defended, but legions of Dominion soldiers, supported by hundreds of dragons, and some of Lord Edgar's companions, are lying in wait, ready to ambush any invading force.'

The god frowned, as though he could not understand why he had said what he had said.

'And Dragon Eyre?' said Claudian. 'What are the plans for invading Na Sun Ka?'

'That operation has been postponed,' the god said, 'as too many of the Wystian dragons are suffering the effects of malnutrition and exhaustion after being stranded on Rigga for so long. Out of the seven thousand who travelled to Gyle, barely a few hundred are fit enough to fight. Lord Edgar has therefore decided to wait until more have recovered before launching any invasion of Na Sun Ka.'

Claudian smiled. 'What other operations are planned?'

'Lord Edgar has ordered Lady Allura to focus on Olkis until the Wystians are ready to assault Na Sun Ka,' Ballatar said, 'in order to distract the imperial forces. Lady Allura has taken a hundred dragons to Ectus, from where she intends to raid the Olkian coast and cities.'

'When will this happen?'

'I don't know. I assume that Lord Edgar will authorise it when he returns to Inopei.'

'Where is Lord Edgar now?'

'He is on the island of Zamata, holding secret discussions with Lord Bailey regarding the future.'

Claudian's eyes tensed. 'He is with Lord Bailey?'

'Yes. Lord Bailey sent Lord Edgar a message, asking to meet with him, alone. Lord Edgar accepted the invitation.'

'What exactly are they discussing?'

'I don't know. Lord Edgar speculated that Lord Bailey may be deciding to come over to our side.'

'What does Edgar want?'

'Victory over the Empire,' said Ballatar, 'followed by a peace treaty.'

'What does Ward think of this plan?' said Cael.

Ballatar turned to him. 'Lord Ward disagrees. He thinks we should annihilate the Holdfasts and assume command of the Empire, as well as the Doomed Worlds.'

'And where do you stand on this?' said Claudian.

'I am loyal to Lord Edgar.'

'I heard that Edgar tortured Bailey,' said Cael.

'It wasn't personal,' said Ballatar. 'Lord Edgar needed to lure the Holdfasts into the Palace of the Almighty in order to make his escape. Lord Bailey will understand this; they were friends for millennia.' He lowered his gaze. 'Whatever you have done to me, Holdfast, I ask that you please stop. My mind is powerless to control my own words. Were you not treated fairly during your time in prison? You were apprehended after your team carried out a series of terrorist attacks upon Nom Karta, and by rights you should have been executed. Did we not show you mercy by sparing your life?'

'I behaved no worse than the way Ward and Allura behaved by the dragon carriers,' said Cael, 'and no worse than Ward behaved when he tried to slaughter my uncle and his family.'

'Lord Ward has fled,' said Ballatar. 'Lord Edgar was going to punish him for the acts you describe; as they were expressly forbidden. Tell me, Holdfast; are you content to be compared to Lord Ward? Are you happy to be as cruel as he is?'

'Your forces slaughtered the garrison guarding the Tempest mine,' said Claudian.

'That mine belongs to the Dominion!' Ballatar cried. 'What right did the Empire have to seize it? A thief cannot complain if the rightful owners are a little rough when they reclaim their property.'

Claudian glanced at Cael. 'Release his mind from your grip.'

'Aye, sir,' said Cael.

He went into Ballatar's mind and removed the compulsion to answer their questions. Ballatar exhaled, his shoulders sagging. He raised a hand to where Cael had slapped him on the face.

'Thank you,' he muttered. 'What do you intend to do with me?'

'That will be for the Empress to decide,' said Claudian.

'I have one more question,' said Cael; 'one that you can choose to answer or not. Why did Edmond imprison you in the Palace of the Almighty?

'I rebelled against his rule,' said the god. 'Edmond was a tyrant; a bloodthirsty, rapacious tyrant, and I no longer wished to serve him.' He looked into Cael's eyes. 'Perhaps you should consider doing the same, Holdfast.'

'The Empress is not a tyrant,' he said. He turned to Claudian. 'We should send him back to Inopei, sir.'

'Absolutely not,' said the Adjutant. 'There is much we can learn about the enemy from him. Regardless, as I said, that decision belongs to the Empress alone. Let us leave Lord Ballatar to rest. Colonel, ensure that he is well fed and comfortable, but post guards around the building in case Lord Edgar decides to retaliate. As soon as I get the requisite approval, we shall transport the prisoner to a safer location.'

'Yes, sir,' said the colonel.

Cael walked out of the cell, and the door was locked.

'Now, Lieutenant Holdfast,' said Claudian, 'before I can allow you to depart on leave, there is the small matter of describing everything you did and saw while on Inopei. I have a scribe ready to write down every detail, so I hope you are ready.'

'I will be, sir,' Cael said, 'as soon as I have a coffee and a cigarette.'

CHAPTER 2
PRISONER OF CONSCIENCE

Colsbury Castle, the Holdings – 19th Day, Last Third Spring 545

'I know it's awful,' said Larron, as he and Kyra sat on the middle balcony in the sunshine; 'and I know that you are pretty much a prisoner here.'

Kyra eyed him. 'But?'

Larron smiled at her. 'But, of all the places you could be imprisoned, I think this might possibly be the best. I mean, look at the view – the mountains, the lake, the island; and the weather is perfect for this time of year. Things will be getting humid in Plateau City about now, but up here, the air is so clear and fresh. And the conversations I've overheard... Colsbury is packed full of some of the most famous people on the Star Continent – your mother, your aunt, Lahnos Laimos, the chancellor, not to mention the commander-in-chief of the entire imperial armed forces. And that old pirate guy...'

'Olo'osso?'

'Aye, him. The stories he's told me... did you know that one of his daughters lives with Sable Holdfast?'

'Of course I knew that. Listen to you; you sound like an excited child.'

Larron shrugged. 'I don't care. I had this image in my mind of what they would all be like, and I thought I was going to be intimidated by them; but, now that I've met them all, I quite like them.'

Kyra raised an eyebrow. 'I think I might leave you here when I work out how to escape, since you're clearly enjoying yourself.'

'And how are you going to be able to leave? Your mother's meddled with your mind. You can't walk, swim, sail or fly off this island; and you've lost your Quadrant.'

'I don't know how, but it needs to be before Summer's Day, when the Empress and her entire court arrive for the season.'

'But I want to be here for the gala. I've heard so much about it, Kyra. It would be cruel to deny me that.'

'You just want to get dressed up and go to a fancy ball.'

'Is that wrong of me? The Empress coming here is an opportunity for you to present your case to her. You didn't actually do anything illegal, nor did I. The law banning strikes came into force at dawn, and we were attacked during the night.'

Kyra narrowed her eyes. 'I can't believe you said that. Do you expect me to beg forgiveness from the Empress, after all that she's done? Do you think I should just forget all about the wars, massacres and atrocities? And what about my brother? No one has heard from him in several days, and it was the Empress who sent him to Athumia. Should I ignore that?'

'That's not what I'm saying. Keep true to your principles, but do so in a civilised manner. Get to work on your mother and your Aunty Kelsey before the Empress gets here; try to work out a compromise between you – a compromise that allows you to leave Colsbury.'

'And my Quadrant?'

Larron lowered his voice. 'Doesn't Elbannon make Quadrants for the Empire now? There's bound to be one in Plateau City that you could... *borrow*.'

'Elbannon's Quadrants are not as good as the real thing. They have fewer jewels, and they're missing a variety of basic commands, such as *Go back*.'

'Does that affect your ability to use them? They talk to you, Kyra.'

Kyra pondered his words for a moment. 'All right; that might be an option. Try not to think about it again, though, in case my mother reads your mind.'

'But Kelsey…'

'Aunty Kelsey only blocks regular vision powers, not my mother's. Sable's powers work in her presence, too, so be careful if she arrives.'

Larron's eyes lit up. 'Might Sable come here? Pyre's unholy jock-strap, please let me stay for that.'

The door to the balcony slid open, and Shella walked out of the palace.

'Hoi, you two,' she said.

'Aye?' said Kyra.

'You'd better not have forgotten what day it is.'

Kyra shrugged.

'What day is it, Your Highness?' said Larron.

'It's Arrosa's eighteenth birthday, laddo,' said Shella; 'so get your arses upstairs. We're having a little get-together to celebrate.'

'Am I permitted to come?' said Kyra.

'Don't give me that tone, young lady,' said Shella. 'You will come upstairs, you will be polite, and you will wish Arrosa a happy birthday. Remember how sad she is at the moment, with Cael missing on Athumia.'

'What about me?' said Kyra. 'I'm his sister. Doesn't anyone care if I'm sad?'

Shella rolled her eyes. 'If I say *Yes*, will you come upstairs?'

Kyra got to her feet, her temper rising. Larron joined her, and they followed Shella off the balcony and into the Summer Palace.

'Are you working on the gala this year, Your Highness?' said Larron.

'Drop the *Highness* crap, son,' said Shella; 'and no, the gala is Kelsey's thing.'

'Is she still organising it, even though she isn't the Herald any more?'

'Yeah.'

'Why?'

'Cause she owns the whole fucking island,' said Shella. 'Colsbury is hers, and so she takes care of the gala, and the hundred other parties that will take place over summer.'

'You're exaggerating, aye? How many parties?'

'Too many,' said Shella. 'The Imperial Court ruins my peace and quiet every damn year. Plays, music, dancing, singing, feasts; it's a complete ball-ache.'

Larron glanced at Kyra as they ascended the stairs, his eyes pleading with her. Kyra shook her head and looked in the other direction. They reached the landing, and Shella led them into a large reception room, where several tables and chairs had been laid out. Waiters and waitresses were moving among the small crowd, passing out drinks and food, while Arrosa was surrounded by others.

Karalyn glanced over, and beckoned for Kyra to join her.

'Mother,' she said.

'Thank you for coming,' said Karalyn. 'This time last year, I had to cajole Cael into wishing Arrosa a happy birthday, but I never thought I would have to do the same with you.'

'You didn't have to cajole me. I forgot, that's all.'

Karalyn eyed her, then she gestured for Kyra to approach Arrosa.

'Happy birthday,' said Kyra.

'Aye, happy birthday,' said Larron, 'and I hope there's some good news about Cael soon.'

Arrosa looked at them both, her eyes red. 'Thanks,' she said.

'How long are you here for?' said Larron. 'And what's the university been like, since... you know?'

'It's been a bit quieter,' Arrosa said. 'Over two hundred students were expelled, and all of Achan's classes have been cancelled.'

'That's because the Empress locked him up in prison,' said Kyra.

Arrosa nodded. 'I'm not really in the mood to talk about all that at the moment. I'm going back to the university tomorrow; Kelsey is taking me.'

'Kyra has told me all about Cael,' Larron said. 'He's tough, and smart. He'll be fine.'

'He disobeyed orders,' Arrosa said. 'That's what they told me. He went back to Athumia on his own; why would he do that?'

'I will find him,' said Karalyn. 'Trust me.'

Cardova looked over. He opened his mouth to say something to his wife, but seemed to think better of it.

'If you're really going to try,' said Lahnos, who was there with Ora'lya, 'then I want to help. I know Athumia.'

'You know Inopei about as well as I do,' said Karalyn; 'and that is where my son will be.'

Cardova frowned, his gaze on the entrance to the hall. 'What is Adjutant Claudian doing here? Please excuse me for a moment.'

Kyra watched as Cardova moved off through the room, stopping to talk to Claudian, who had just entered. The two men leaned in close to talk together, and Kyra shook her head.

'They're probably discussing which nation to invade next,' she said.

Cardova turned, and beckoned Karalyn to come over. 'And bring Arrosa,' he said.

'Why?' said Arrosa. 'If it's bad news...' Her voice cracked.

Karalyn took her hand and led her over to Cardova and Claudian, then all four left the room. The crowd in the chamber quietened.

'Why wasn't I called over?' said Kyra. 'If something bad has happened to my brother, then...'

The atmosphere altered in an instant as the group walked back into the room, with Cael smiling in their midst. His arm was round Arrosa's waist, and her smile matched his. The crowd moved forward to surround them, and Cael nodded to those he recognised. Kyra pushed her way to the front, and Cael embraced her.

'I hear you've been misbehaving, sister,' he said, a wide smile on his face.

'Me?' she said. 'I heard you disobeyed orders.'

'That is not technically true,' said Claudian. 'Lieutenant Holdfast's methods may have been unorthodox, but he was acting with my full permission. He was captured by the enemy, but he managed to escape from jail on Inopei. Not only that, but he took Lord Ballatar prisoner, and the god is now in our custody.'

Cardova beamed. 'Well done, Cael; truly, well done.'

'You were captured?' said Lahnos.

'Aye, for a few days,' said Cael.

'He also incapacitated Queen Famula,' Claudian went on.

'Forget about me,' he said. 'This is Arrosa's birthday, and she should be the centre of attention.'

'I thought this was going to be the worst birthday I've ever had,' Arrosa said. 'Now it might be the best.'

'Is he on leave?' said Karalyn, a hand on her son's arm.

'Yes, ma'am,' said Claudian. 'For ten days.'

'Kelsey, get over here,' Karalyn said. 'We have ten days to plan the wedding.'

'We can hold it sooner than that,' said Kelsey. 'Let's give them a few days to enjoy married life before Cael has to leave again.'

'Aye, that's a better idea,' said Karalyn.

'Could I have a word with you, sir?' Claudian said to Cardova. 'Lord Ballatar has already provided us with a wealth of intelligence, some of which you need to hear.'

Cardova nodded, then the two former Banner officers walked off together.

'Well, Arrosa?' said Karalyn. 'Cael? Do you still want to get married?'

'Aye,' said Cael, as Arrosa said 'Yes,' at the same time.

'And do you still want a Gunstian priest to officiate?'

'I do,' said Arrosa. 'Will it be possible?'

'Probably,' said Karalyn, 'though I'll have to make a few trips to Gunst in order to find out. Perhaps I should speak to Bailey first.'

'I'd be careful about that, Mother,' said Cael. 'Edgar and Bailey have been having secret talks on Zamata. That's what Adjutant Claudian is most likely telling Commander Cardova just now. Ballatar told us about it. Never mind that, though; I'm in the mood to discuss wedding plans.'

'Let's do it,' said Arrosa. 'Shall we pick a date?'

Kyra pulled back from the others as they began talking about the marriage. Larron followed her, then Lahnos and Ora'lya joined them both.

'Your brother is the luckiest man alive,' said Lahnos.

Kyra narrowed her eyes. 'Arrosa isn't that special.'

'I wasn't talking about that,' said Lahnos, 'but, while we're on the subject, he is lucky to have her.'

'What were you talking about?' said Larron.

'Cael's military record,' said Lahnos. 'What he did in Sun Ta, and then there was the Unk Tannic base in Western Na Sun Ka, the battle for the carriers, and now this? He removes Queen Famula from power, escapes from prison and captures a god? And he's still only eighteen. I'd be very surprised if the Imperial Court doesn't promote him or elevate him soon. The lad is a born leader, even if he struggles to obey orders.'

'The Adjutant said that part wasn't true,' said Larron.

'I know, but I don't believe it. Claudian was covering for him. What else could he do when faced with Cael's achievements? How can you court martial someone as successful as Cael has been?'

'Are you tempted to return to the service of the Empress?' said Kyra.

'No,' said Lahnos. 'The price was too high. At the same time, though, I'm not about to join your little band of malcontents. I feel no obligation to serve the Empire, but nor do I wish for its downfall. Believe me, the alternative could be a lot worse. Anyway, if they're all going to be discussing wedding plans, I might go downstairs and see how Aila is getting on with Dermot.'

'Can we come with you?' said Kyra. 'I feel as though I'm getting in the way here.'

'If you like,' said Lahnos, 'but prepare yourself for the noise. There are a lot of damn children down there.'

They turned for the door. Kyra glanced over her shoulder, but no one seemed to have noticed that they were leaving.

'How are you feeling about the baby, Ora'lya?' said Larron, as they started to descend the stairs.

Lahnos narrowed his eyes at the question, but Ora'lya didn't seem to mind.

'It's been difficult,' she said. 'Kelsey brought Dermot and his grandparents, I mean, Dolwyn's mother and father, to Colsbury a few days ago. Dolwyn has gone back to the army, and her parents are looking after the baby, with Aila's help. Aila is... relentless. She must have a dozen children to look after now. She has seven of her own, and everyone else just assumes that she will look after their children, too.'

They reached the bottom of the stairs, and went along a corridor. Lahnos pushed open a door, and they walked into a large room with floor to ceiling windows that faced the south. The noise inside the room hit Kyra like a wall. Children were everywhere – running across the carpets, playing on the floor, sitting by a table, and most of them seemed to be talking at the same time. Amid the chaos, Aila was moving from child to child with a baby strapped to her chest, while two elderly Kellach were sitting by a window, a small baby resting in a pram next to them.

Aila saw them enter, smiled, and walked towards them.

'How was the birthday party?' she said.

'It took an unexpected turn,' said Larron.

Aila raised an eyebrow.

'My brother is back,' said Kyra. 'Needless to say, Arrosa and my mother nearly fainted at the sight, and now they're obsessing over the wedding plans.'

'Cael's back, is he?' said Aila. 'Is he well?'

'Better than well,' said Lahnos. 'He has returned like a conquering hero.'

Larron gave a wry smile as he glanced around the room. 'I did wonder where all the children were each day. Do you look after all of them?'

'It's not so bad,' said Aila. 'If you have seven of your own, a few more doesn't make all that much difference. I have a thirteen-year-old, a ten-year-old, a nine-year-old, an eight-year-old, a six-year-old, two five-year-olds, a three-year-old, two two-year-olds, and two infants yet to reach the age of one. Eleven Holdfasts and one Laimos.'

'Pyre's cleft sweat,' said Larron. 'How do you stay sane?'

Aila shrugged. 'I've been waiting eight centuries to have children. I can hardly complain now that I have so many. My businesses in Kell are suffering though.'

'I thought you had hired a management team to look after them in your absence,' said Kyra.

'I have, but I like to be at the centre of things. I worry if they are doing everything exactly the way I want it done, you know? And, of course, I'm worried about Corthie. Malik knows what the Empress will decide to do with him.'

'I have a few ideas about that,' said Kyra; 'none of them good.'

Aila frowned, then she glared at a boy by the table. 'Cairney, put that down and leave your sister alone.'

'I'll go and see Dermot,' said Lahnos.

Aila nodded, but Kyra could see that she was too distracted by the horde of children to pay much attention. Lahnos and Ora'lya walked over to the two older Kellach and sat down next to them.

'How long will you be staying in Colsbury?' said Larron.

'What?' said Aila, blinking. 'Oh, I don't know. They keep telling me that it's not safe for us to return to Clackenbaird; but when will it be safe? They can't answer that. I can only hope that Corthie hurries up and kills everyone who is a threat.'

Kyra narrowed her eyes.

'Having been down in Kell for so long,' Aila went on, 'I'd forgotten how much Karalyn's attitude annoys me. If she was prepared to use the Sextant, she could annihilate our enemies in minutes. She could destroy the Doomed Worlds, and then remove every god from Athumia and Dragon Eyre and fling them into the abyss, along with the Wystian dragons. There. Problem solved.'

'But, Aunty,' said Kyra; 'that would result in the deaths of millions, and the extinction of the dragons as a species.'

'So? They started this fight, and they would do the same to us if they had the chance.'

'You don't know that, Aunty.'

'Two of them broke into my house and tried to murder my children. As far as I'm concerned, the sooner Corthie kills them all, the better.'

'But...'

'Maybe we should rejoin the party,' said Larron.

Kyra eyed him, then nodded.

'See you later,' said Aila.

Kyra and Larron retreated from the room and closed the door, lowering the volume of noise.

'Why did you do that?' said Kyra, as they walked away.

'I didn't want you getting into a fight with Aila,' he said. 'You can't argue with someone whose children have been threatened; and she's a demigod. They have a different moral code.'

'Aila is supposed to be one of those demigods who actually cares about mortals; she fought for their rights in the City, and yet, deep down, she's more similar to the other gods than she is to us mortals. She says she cares, but she would be happy to slaughter millions to ensure that she can continue to live a life of luxury with her family.'

'Maybe. She must have seen so much, though. Eight centuries?'

'Don't forget that she's Naxor's cousin. That family was full of unscrupulous and ruthless gods. It makes me a little worried about Corthie's children.'

They went back up the stairs. At the top, Cardova and Claudian had moved out on to the landing to continue their discussion, and Cole was standing with them. Words were exchanged, then Claudian shook Cole's hand. Cole smiled, then he saw Kyra and Larron approach, and moved away from the two older men.

'I didn't know you were in Colsbury,' said Kyra.

'I arrived with Arrosa,' Cole said, 'but I've been busy this morning, and only just got to the party. Have you seen Cael? He's back.'

'Aye, we saw him,' said Kyra. 'What were you doing this morning?'

Cole chewed his lip for a moment. 'Don't get angry with me.'

'Why would I get angry?'

'I've joined the army.'

Kyra's mouth fell open. 'What? But... You're leaving university?'

'I've done a full year,' he said, 'and I'm still not ready to go back to the Hold Fast estate.'

'Then stay on for another year in Plateau City.'

'But, Kyra, I have the same mage powers that my father had, and the Empire needs people like me to help. As a mage, I will be eligible for a commission as an officer. I have been hearing about Cael all year, mostly from Arrosa, and I started to feel that I should be doing more with my abilities.'

'The last time we spoke, you said that you didn't want to follow Cael into the marines.'

'I still don't. I have no desire to undertake six thirds of the gruelling training that the marines go through. An army commission as a mage is a lot less arduous. Basically, I will be assigned to a regiment as a staff officer, there to provide intelligence, and to use my fire powers if needed. I don't want to be a hero, but I felt obliged to do something to help.'

'Oh, Cole,' she said. 'Help who? The Empress? Do you have any idea of what she's been doing? Invading other nations is wrong.'

'I don't see it that way,' he said. 'The Empire is under attack from the Wystians and Unk Tannic on Dragon Eyre, and from Edgar and the Dominion on Athumia. If we don't defeat them, then they'll come here, to the Star Continent.' He glanced towards the open door that led towards the party. 'I want to tell Cael and Arrosa.'

Kyra nodded, then she and Larron followed Cole into the large chamber. Cole made straight for Cael, who was sitting at a table with Arrosa, Karalyn and Kelsey.

Cole grinned. 'Good to see you back in one piece, cousin,' he said.

Cael got to his feet, and the two young men embraced.

'And I have news,' Cole went on. 'Soon, there will be two Lieutenant Holdfasts.'

Cael's eyes widened. 'You enlisted? You've joined the marines?'

Cole laughed. 'Not a chance. I've joined the army as a mage.'

'Not the damn army,' Cael said, groaning. He joined in with the laughter. 'Even the navy would be better than that.'

'I've never much liked boats,' said Cole.

'I'm going to miss you next year at university,' said Arrosa, as she gave Cole a hug, 'but I can understand why you're doing this. When do you start training?'

'At the beginning of summer,' said Cole. 'I still have a couple of exams to sit in Plateau City first, then I'll be off.'

'Another Holdfast in uniform,' said Kelsey. 'I pity our enemies.'

'Maybe I should join up, too,' said Arrosa. 'I'm starting to feel a little left out.'

Kelsey smiled. 'I have a feeling that the Empress might call upon you soon, Arrosa,' she said. 'You'll be married in a few days, and that will make you one of us – a Holdfast. Be patient; your time will come.'

'Do you think so?' said Arrosa.

'What is wrong with everyone?' said Kyra. 'People are being massacred all over the Allied Worlds, and you're smiling about Cole joining the army? Can you not see what war has done to Lahnos? He lost the Bullan, his friends. How many have to die before you start taking this seriously?'

'Did you see me smile, daughter?' said Karalyn. 'Going off to war is nothing to smile about, in my opinion; but if no one joined the army, then who would protect us?' She turned to Cole. 'I hope you understand what you are getting into. As an army mage, you will be in a privileged position, but you will also be required to carry out tasks that will involve the deaths of many. How far can you range?'

'About a hundred miles, Aunty,' he said.

'And your fire powers?'

'World Three is the only place I've used them,' he said. 'I will need to practise hard. My father was able to combine the two powers; he could manipulate fire from miles away, but I'm not able to do that yet.'

'That's because you've neglected your powers,' said Kelsey. 'You know, I don't think I have ever once sensed you use them.'

'Me, neither,' said Karalyn. 'I should warn you, Cole; when you were an infant, I was in your mind every day for a while, to help your mother when you were crying. I used to soothe you to sleep. I also took the time to take a good look at your range of powers. You have some latent dream mage abilities that have never risen to the surface. But, the more you use your powers, the more likely it is that some of these other powers will reveal themselves.'

'I told him that years ago, Mother,' said Kyra. 'So did Cael, I think.'

'There is no harm in reminding him,' said Karalyn.

'I think that was one reason why I didn't want to use my powers when I discovered I had them,' said Cole. 'The other reason is that I was worried about turning into my father.'

'You are nothing like Keir,' said Kelsey. 'You are almost the opposite. I think you will do very well in the army, Cole. We need good young mages to volunteer to serve the Empire.'

'Was that a dig at me?' said Kyra.

Kelsey chuckled. 'Not everything is about you, Kyra. We all know where you stand on the subject of the Empire.'

'Why aren't there more young mages?' said Arrosa.

'The great majority of the Star Continent's mages were wiped out in two waves of fighting,' said Kelsey. 'The first was caused by Nathaniel, who, as Emperor Guilliam, killed off nearly every Rahain mage, along with many more from Rakana and the Holdings; and the second wave was caused by Edmond, who sent his Ancients all over the Star Continent to hunt down and kill any who remained. It will take generations to get back to the previous levels. It's ironic, in a way. The gods of the Doomed Worlds appear to believe that the Star Continent is full of mortals with powers, but the truth is somewhat different.'

'That is all the more reason to pursue peace,' said Kyra.

Kelsey rolled her eyes. 'Aye, because our enemies are such nice people. The Wystians would incinerate every one of us if they could.'

'They are just trying to defend themselves,' said Kyra. 'The same goes for the Dominion. We attacked them first, and now we're complaining because they are fighting back. Perhaps the Empire needs to be humbled a little.'

'Are you out of your mind, sister?' said Cael. 'Of all the things you have ever said, that has to be the craziest. Do you want us to lose the war? Do you think we should give our enemies whatever they want, and then hope they don't come back for more?'

Kyra narrowed her eyes. 'I don't think I know who you are any more, brother. The Cael I grew up with was better than this. That Cael possessed a conscience. Come on, Larron; I know when I'm not wanted.'

Larron shrugged at the others, then he followed Kyra as she walked out of the room. They went to Kyra's private quarters, and she locked the door behind them and sat on the bed.

'I hate this place,' she said. 'If I don't leave soon, I think I might throw myself from the top of the Great Keep.'

Larron said nothing for a moment, then he sat down next to her. 'What do the blocks in your head feel like?'

'Well,' she said, 'whenever I try to imagine leaving, as I am doing right now, my thoughts get all vague and hazy. If I tried to walk over the bridge, my legs would stop obeying my commands.'

'You know,' said Larron, 'it occurs to me that your mother doesn't need a Quadrant to move around.'

'Aye? So?'

'You are her daughter, and you can hear Quadrants talk to you, like she can. Maybe it's a power that you share with her. Have you ever tried to move without a Quadrant?'

'I wouldn't know where to begin.'

'How did it happen with your mother? Was it related to the Sextant? Is that how she got that ability – did the Sextant allow her to do it?'

'It started before we had ever heard of the Sextant. I know that, because she didn't use a Quadrant to take herself, Sable and Belinda to Lostwell. But she lost four years doing that.'

'But she's got the hang of it now?'

Kyra nodded. 'I think she used to have to draw upon the mage powers of others in order to do it; just as she did to King Gahad on

Athumia. I remember watching her do that. She drained the dragon of his energy, and used the power to take us all back to Kell.'

'Presumably,' he said, 'you wouldn't need as much power to take us to, say, Plateau City. That's two hundred miles away, not on another world.'

'There's one catch – I have never tried to draw anyone's power out of them. I don't want to hurt anyone.'

'If you did it to a god or demigod, then they would recover.'

Kyra peered at him. 'Is this your suggestion? Are you advising me to try this? I thought you liked it here.'

Larron smiled. 'I love it here; but, Kyra, I am your friend, and you are the only reason I am in Colsbury. I wish you could be reconciled with your family, but if that's not possible, then perhaps we should seriously consider the alternatives.'

'Do you think we should go to Plateau City?'

'Maybe. I'm not sure. I guess I would follow you wherever you decided to go.'

Kyra gazed at the floor, wondering what she had done to deserve such a friend.

'If we are going to do anything,' she said, 'then there is something I will have to do to you first.'

'Aye? What?'

She gazed into his eyes and entered his mind. Using a power that she knew Cael had lost, she began to weave a web of protection around Larron's thoughts, one strong enough to prevent her mother from penetrating without considerable effort.

'Ow,' he muttered.

'Sorry,' she said, 'but it's done.'

'What's done?'

'No god or vision mage will ever be able to read your thoughts,' she said. 'Even Cael and my mother would struggle to remove what I have done to your mind. You are now free to think whatever you like.'

'But you can…?'

'Aye. I can still read your mind, though I have never done so.'

'Never?'

'No. If I had, then I wouldn't have tried to kiss you that night. You know, I wish you had told me about that.'

'I didn't know you well enough back then.' He looked away. 'I do love you, Kyra; just not in that way. Does it bother you?'

'No. I mean, I was embarrassed for a while, but I'm over it. Would you really follow me if I found a way to leave?'

He took her hand. 'I would follow you anywhere.'

CHAPTER 3
DEVISING A STRATEGY

Sun Ta, Na Sun Ka, Western Rim – 5266 (18th Gylean Year 17)

A large crowd of Sanang warriors watched Corthie as he was led across the large plaza by Adjutant Claudian and a guard of Imperial Marines. A wagon was rolling along behind them, packed with all of Corthie's luggage, armour and weapons, but Corthie's full attention was on the enormous buildings on the far side of the plaza. They stretched out into the distance to the left and right, and each was as big as any palace.

'These are the famed temples of Sun Ta,' said Claudian. 'Some have stood for hundreds of years, but, like many aspects of Dragon Eyre history, their origins are lost. The dragons that ruled this world for millennia saw no need to record anything about past events.'

'Temples?' said Corthie. 'What gods were worshipped here?'

Claudian eyed him. 'Are you unfamiliar with the religion of this world?'

'I've never paid much attention to things like that.'

'I will try to summarise. In short, many here believe that dragons possess an immortal spirit, and that, whenever a dragon dies, its spirit not only lives on, but it joins with the spirits of every other deceased dragon. The humans of this world prayed to those spirits for help and guidance.'

'I may as well stop you there,' said Corthie. 'I'm not interested. Just point me at the enemy.'

'That is easier said than done. The next island chain to the west of here is called Gyle. It used to be the capital of Dragon Eyre, and it's where the Eighteenth Gylean lives.'

'The who?'

'The Gylean. A noble dragon of royal blood, who, some believe, represents the highest authority upon this world. Unfortunately, the current Gylean is a sickly infant, and he is surrounded by devoted Unk Tannic soldiers. He has no power of any description; think of him more as a figurehead.'

'What has this got to do with me fighting the enemy?'

'I was getting there,' said Claudian. 'I assume you know about the recent arrival of seven thousand Wystians on Gyle?'

Corthie shook his head.

'Sable Holdfast transferred them from their homes on Wyst to the remote and inaccessible islands of Rigga, where they were trapped for several years. In recent days, Edgar's gods used two Quadrants to open a portal, which allowed all seven thousand stranded dragons to reach Gyle.'

'Seven thousand dragons, eh? How am I supposed to fight seven thousand dragons?'

'We will not be asking you to take on that responsibility.'

'Then what are you asking me to do? When I knelt in front of the Empress, I imagined that I would be sent off to hunt down and kill gods – that's what I'm good at. Gods, greenhides, soldiers – let me loose on them, and I'll do what needs to be done.'

'We have brought you here in order to prepare you for such an occasion,' said Claudian, 'but first, I need to introduce you to the team with whom you shall be working.'

Corthie came to a halt in the middle of the plaza. 'What team? I work better alone. I've been given teams in the past, and... it hasn't always worked out well for them.'

'We are aware of that aspect of your military record. Nevertheless, the Imperial Court will not be sending you off to fight alone. You require support.' He gestured towards the giant building in front of them. 'There are twelve temples, one for each of the island groups on Dragon Eyre, and this is the Temple of Ulna. With Queen Blackrose's permission, the Empire has been granted authority to utilise this temple as its army headquarters.'

'I thought the headquarters was that building we passed in the harbour.'

'That is the headquarters of the Imperial Marines,' said Claudian. 'The Temple of Ulna is for the army. The Sanang divisional officers work here, along with the regular army command, logistics, and a few specialist groups. One of those specialist groups will be headed by you. You will train with them before you are deployed.'

'Why?'

Claudian's features flickered with slight irritation, which amused Corthie.

'Each member of your team will have a specific function,' the Adjutant went on; 'and they have been chosen to support you in your role. Let us go inside, and I will take you to them.'

They walked up to the massive entrance. It was high and wide enough to accommodate half a dozen dragons at once, but the enormous gates had been closed, leaving only a handful of smaller, human-sized doorways. Claudian entered through one, and Corthie ducked his head to follow him into the dark interior. Skylights ran along the tall ceiling, letting in shafts of dazzling Dragon Eyre sunshine, but the rest of the entrance hall was bathed in thick shadows. Claudian gestured to their marine escort.

'Bring in Corthie's luggage,' he said to them, 'then you may return to the harbour. Thank you for escorting us here.'

The marines saluted, then they about-turned, and began to unload the wagon. Claudian set off again, and Corthie followed him further into the building. They took a doorway to the left off the main entrance hall, and came to a suite of rooms.

'My office is around here,' Claudian said. 'I've lost count of the number of times I have used a Quadrant to travel between here and the marine headquarters in the harbour.'

'Why don't you put them both together?'

Claudian eyed him. 'Are you aware of the tension that exists between the marines and the Sanang divisions?'

Corthie shook his head.

'Well, it's real. The marines would be deeply displeased if they were forced to work alongside the Sanang. Besides, the marines need to be close to the ships of the navy; the harbour is the natural place for them.'

They carried on for a few more minutes, and came to a domed hall. The dome was open at the top to allow in the sunlight, and there were several doors leading off from the hall. Standing by one, as though they had been waiting for Corthie's arrival, were five others – three men, and two women.

'This is your new team,' Claudian said.

Corthie frowned as they approached. Out of the five, only three looked remotely like soldiers.

'Good morning,' said Claudian. 'As you can see, I have brought Corthie Holdfast. As of this moment, he is now your commanding officer.'

The five stood to attention.

'It's like a mix of every race on the Star Continent,' said Corthie.

'All except Rakanese,' said Claudian. 'There is a good reason for this, as I will explain. On the left is Drechtalang Fo, a private seconded from the Sanang divisions. On his left is Corporal Wyle of Hold Liant; followed by Corporal Dominie from the Imperial Marines. Next to her is Jaeanna, a civilian consultant from the Rahain Quarter of Plateau City, and, finally, on the right is Sergeant Nestorian from the Banner of the Sapphire Throne. With the exception of Sergeant Nestorian, all are mages.'

Corthie smiled. 'Ah, I see. Couldn't we rustle up any flow mages?'

'Unfortunately, no Rakanese mages exist within Plateau City, and Amatskouri proved unwilling to part with any of their clay mages. As for finding mages in Rakana itself, the situation there remains too volatile.' He glanced at the team. 'Step forward, one at a time, and explain to Major Holdfast what mage power or powers you possess, and detail any combat experience.'

'Wait,' said Corthie. 'Am I a major now?'

'You are,' said Claudian. He gestured to the Sanang man.

Drechtalang took a step forward, his gaze on the stone floor. 'I am a hedgewitch,' he said. 'I've fought in Rahain and in Sun Ta, and then I was put here. That's it.'

The Holdings man to his left then stepped forward. 'I possess battle-vision and line vision, sir, and I have experience of combat in Rahain. I was serving in Tahrana City when I was offered this opportunity.'

'What's line vision again?' said Corthie.

'It means I can send my vision out to a distance of one hundred yards, sir, and look around from that point.'

Corthie nodded, then the Kellach woman stepped up next to the Holdings man. 'I'm a sparker, sir. I've been a marine for six years.'

'And I am a stone mage,' said the Rahain woman.

'You're a civilian?' said Corthie.

'Yes, sir. I volunteered my services to the Empire, but have not officially joined any branch of the armed forces.'

'Thank you,' said Claudian. He turned to the Banner veteran, who looked much older than the others. 'Now, Sergeant Nestorian, please tell Major Holdfast a little about your experience.'

Nestorian stepped forward. 'Yes, sir. I have served on six different worlds, and I performed five extended tours upon Dragon Eyre when it was occupied by the forces of Implacatus. Following my transfer to the Star Continent, I served in the Banner of the Sapphire Throne, where I fought at the Battle of the Vineyards, and then in the defence of the Kell Pass. Latterly, I have been assisting Professor Ravi in the development and construction of explosive devices.'

'You fought in the Kell Pass?' said Corthie.

A hint of a smile crossed the soldier's face. 'Yes, sir. I recall seeing you when the greenhides assaulted the defences.'

'That was some day.'

'It was, indeed, sir.'

'And now you make explosives?'

'Yes, sir. I was one of the few surviving members of the Banner who worked in the explosive manufacturing facility on Ectus. Fortunately for me, I was posted elsewhere when Sable Holdfast blew the entire place to pieces.'

'The team is scheduled to receive one of Elbannon's new Quadrants,' said Claudian, 'though I understand that no one here yet has the requisite knowledge to utilise such a device. Training will be provided in due course. I want you to get to know each other first, and a programme has been devised to bind you together as a team. As far as the chain of command goes, Major Holdfast will report directly to me. You will disregard orders from any other officer of the armed forces. They have been told that you are outwith the regular hierarchy, but some may choose to ignore that. I will set the operations, and then you will be free to carry them out in any manner you see fit. Your first operation will be an attempt at assassinating Lady Allura, who is currently believed to be on Ectus; however, this will not happen until I am sure that you can work together harmoniously. Your equipment will be arriving in the next day or so, but the rooms leading off this chamber are yours. There are four bedrooms, a kitchen, a common room, and a large bathroom, and they are for your use only. Stay out of the other areas of this building for the moment, and tell no one about the others in this team. If anyone asks, tell them that you are part of a logistical detachment.' He smiled. 'Right. I will leave you to it. The kitchen has been fully stocked with food and drink, and there are no duties until dawn tomorrow, when your training regime will commence. Good day.'

Claudian nodded to Corthie, then he turned and strode away.

Corthie eyed his team. 'I guess I should say a few words. I'm bad at giving orders, and even worse at obeying them. All I really want to do is hunt down and kill the gods who tried to slaughter my family, so I'm glad our first operation will be an assassination attempt on one of the bastards. I don't work well in a team, and any teams I've had in the past invariably get themselves killed. There. That probably wasn't the rousing speech you were hoping for, but I had no idea I was being given a team until about fifteen minutes ago. Come on; let's raid the kitchen, and see if the Adjutant was kind enough to supply us with something decent to drink.'

Half an hour later, Corthie and the five members of his team were seated around a long table, eating some of the fresh bread that had been left for them, and drinking from a large barrel of ale. The Sanang hedgewitch had insisted upon smoking dreamweed, so Corthie had made him sit at the far end of the table.

'I could see the disappointment on yer face, sir,' said Dominie. 'Ye saw us standing there, and ye were told that we were all mages, and I bet ye were thinking *I've got myself a fire mage, a soulwitch, and a Holdings mage with inner vision*, and all ye ended up with was us.'

'A hedgewitch will always be useful,' Corthie said, 'as it's likely we'll be injured from time to time; and battle-vision is welcome. But, and no offence, I'm not sure what use a sparker will be.'

'How am I not meant to take offence at that, sir?' she said. 'Only kidding; I know it's pretty useless. I can always get a fire going, but, even when the rain is pishing down. To be honest, though, I'm a damn good marine, which is much more important.'

Drechtalang snorted. 'You're a woman, and women shouldn't be fighting. You should be at home making babies.'

'I can kick your arse any time, ya monkey-faced eejit.'

'And why is there a fucking Rahain woman here?' said the Sanang. 'I was fighting those lizard bastards just a few thirds ago, and now I have to be in the same team as one? The boys in my old company would laugh their asses off if they ever find out.'

'At least I am not a criminal,' said Jaeanna. 'I volunteered. You,

Mister Drechtalang Fo, were forced into the army. What was the choice given to you? Serve or be executed?'

'Is that true?' said Corthie.

The Sanang man shrugged.

'What did you do?' said Wyle, the Holdings soldier.

'I might have raided a village,' said Drechtalang. 'What's it to you? The bitch in charge of Sanang is determined to root out every real man in the country, until all that's left are piss-weak nancy-boys who shit themselves at the sight of blood.'

Nestorian eyed him. 'Do you think the same about the Empress? Her Majesty is from Sanang.'

Drechtalang shook his head. 'Thorn has a bigger set of balls on her than most of the men who are left in Sanang. It's only a pity the Matriarch isn't the same. Look; I will fight. I'm more than happy to fight, but don't come to me looking for sympathy if you twist your ankle or break a fingernail. I'm not your nursemaid.'

'Then why did you volunteer for this team?' said Corthie.

'I didn't. The commanders put out a request for hedgewitches, and I kept my damn mouth shut. Then someone – I think it was that scrawny fuckwit Lord Naxor – used his powers on us, and I was pulled out of the crowd. I've never been more embarrassed in my life.'

Corthie glanced at Nestorian. 'Why did you volunteer?'

'I think I speak for most of us when I say it was to get an opportunity to work with you, sir,' said the Banner sergeant. 'You are an Ascendant killer, and the greatest mortal warrior of all time.'

'That's why I volunteered,' said Dominie.

'And me,' said Wyle.

'I didn't know where I was going to be sent,' said Jaeanna, 'but I am happy to be here. I am the first stone mage to arise in Plateau City for over a generation. Emperor Guilliam almost completely wiped us out.'

'There were no stone mages that I saw or heard of in Tahrana City,' said Corporal Wyle, 'and there are hardly any vision mages in the Holdings. There are still quite a few with battle-vision, but precious few of any others with higher abilities. Most of the world's mages seem to be concentrated in the Holdfast family.'

'Did someone mention my infamous family?' said a voice from the kitchen door.

They turned, and Corthie saw Sable walk into the room. He got to his feet.

'Nephew,' she said.

'They make a good point, Aunty,' said Corthie. 'Why are so many of the Star Continent's mages members of the Holdfasts?'

'Two reasons,' said Sable. 'First, Daphne and her children had a habit of marrying mages, or a demigod in your case; and, secondly, we are among the few who can resist the powers of the gods.'

They embraced.

'I need to speak to you alone,' Sable said.

'Sure,' he said. He glanced at the others sitting around the table, who were staring at Sable.

'I'll bring him back soon,' said Sable, then she placed a hand into her pocket.

The air shimmered, and Corthie found himself standing next to Sable on a rocky hillside overlooking the ocean. Behind them, some of the peaks were smoking and rumbling, and lava was issuing from one, while the sun was low in the sky ahead of them.

'We are standing on the westernmost tip of Na Sun Ka,' said Sable; 'but, before I say anything else, I owe you an apology.'

'What for?'

'I might have said a few remarks that were uncalled for, back when I thought you wouldn't be helping to defend the Empire. I'm glad you changed your mind.'

'Do you know why I changed my mind?' he said. 'It wasn't for any lofty principles. Two gods invaded my home in Clackenbaird and tried to kill me and my family. We got one, but the other managed to get away.'

'To be honest, Corthie, I don't care about your motivation. The only important thing is that you're here. I have to say, though, I don't think much of your new team. Is that the best the Empire can come up with to support the famous Corthie Holdfast? A sparker? A line vision mage?'

'It seems that we've almost run out of decent mages.'

'I suppose it's been that way for a while, thanks to Nathaniel and Edmond. I wonder if Edgar knows the true extent of our weakness. Perhaps the gods of the Doomed Worlds presume that the Star Continent is overflowing with mages.'

'I hope they do,' said Corthie. 'It might make them think twice about invading.'

Sable turned to gaze out over the ocean. 'We have a more imminent invasion to worry about. Roughly five hundred miles to the west of here lies Gyle, where over seven thousand angry Wystian dragons are crying out for blood and revenge, and they have at least one of Edgar's gods assisting them.'

'Allura?'

Sable nodded. 'Do you know how many dragons are on Na Sun Ka?'

'Nope.'

'Nine. Gallantmorn is the sole survivor of Sigum's team, and Blackrose has sent eight others as reinforcements. Nine against seven thousand. Of course, many of those seven thousand will be either too young or too old to fight, so let's say that there are three thousand ready and willing to do so.'

'Not even you and I together can fight that many dragons.'

'We would need a soulwitch, or a flow mage, or a god to help us. However, what the Empire does have in great abundance are explosives. There are dozens of Forty-Eighter batteries located all along this coastline, and many more of them in the central region of the island. Sun Ta is ringed with them. Any straightforward aerial assault will result in utter carnage. The Wystians might be able to conquer Na Sun Ka through sheer weight of numbers, but they will suffer terribly in doing so, and I doubt they will want to throw away their best dragons. That leads us to Allura.'

Sable sat down on the rough slope and lit a cigarette with her metal lighter.

'Let's strip it down,' she said. 'There are three ways for the Wystians to get here. The first, and simplest, is that they all fly here. I've done this journey, though Badblood and I were going in the opposite direction. It's an exhausting ten hour flight from Gyle to Na Sun Ka, and any Wystians who attempted it would arrive too tired to fight. The Forty-Eighters would rip them apart. The second way to get here is by using a single Quadrant. Allura could transport them in batches of two to three dozen at a time, varying the locations; but it would take a tremendous effort to bring enough Wystians here, and the attrition rate would be horrific. With my vision powers, I would be able to direct the Forty-Eighters to each location in turn.'

'What's the third way?' said Corthie.

'Well, that depends upon how many Quadrants the enemy has in its possession.'

'Edgar has Bailey's Quadrant.'

'And they took another one from the garrison of the Tempest mine on Athumia,' said Sable; 'although I think that is one of Elbannon's devices, not that it matters – they do the same thing. There was also one on the Doomed Worlds, held by Lord Elmhirst; and we know that because he fled the Star Continent at the end of the war against the Ascendants. So, let's say that they have three – more than enough to open up a portal.'

Corthie sat down next to her, and they gazed out into the west in silence.

'Imagine,' she said after a while; 'imagine three thousand dragons flooding through a portal with a god at their head. We would be overwhelmed in minutes. I can control a small number of dragons at any one time, but nowhere near enough to make much of a difference, and you, my dear nephew, would be burnt to a crisp. Therefore, our priority should not be to assassinate Allura; it should be to steal her Quadrant. No Quadrant, no portal. No portal, no successful invasion.'

'She is rumoured to be on Ectus.'

'I know. Apparently, she has been ordered to initiate a diversionary attack upon Olkis.'

Corthie glanced at her. 'How's the family?'

'It's a strange time to ask that, given what we have been discussing.'

'I was just wondering how Lara is dealing with all this; with you coming out of retirement. I thought you had left all that behind to look after Joss and Lindi.'

'Believe me, Corthie; I would far rather be in Ulna. Lindi will be two in just over a month from now, and I haven't seen her for six days – that's the last time I managed to get home for a few hours. Lara understands, though; she knows what will happen if the Wystians break through our defences here and get into the Eastern Rim.'

'What have you been doing in that time?'

'Preparing. I have visited Gyle and Ectus to observe the state of the Wystians and the Unk Tannic, and I have been organising the recovery of the two stranded dragon carriers. I have enough crew assembled for one of them, but the ships are unfamiliar to the sailors on this world, so there are bound to be delays, even when I transport the sailors to the first carrier.'

'Why are you bothering with them?

'I want to open up the sea route between Alef and Wyst, so that Blackrose can send aid directly to the Olkians via the north. That would also allow oil and other goods to reach the Eastern Rim more easily. Do you think your team might be interested in helping me get one of the carriers underway?'

'Claudian told us that he will pick out our targets.'

'So?'

'Well, I'm supposed to be working for him.'

Sable nodded. 'All right. I will deal with Claudian. I'll make him think that rescuing the carriers is his idea, and then you will still be obeying orders. Do you have operational freedom once the targets have been set?'

'Aye. That's what he said.'

'Then he should have no objection to you requesting my assistance.

We might have to be on board the carriers for a few days while the sailors figure out how to sail one of them, and Allura might decide to intervene if she discovers our presence.'

'I hope she does. Things will be simpler if she comes to us, rather than having to hunt Dragon Eyre for her.'

Sable smiled. 'My thoughts exactly.'

'How did she manage to beat Cael and Lahnos?'

'She had Ward with her, for a start; and Lahnos, though powerful, is not immune to the powers of the gods. He can self-heal, but death powers can still incapacitate him. Cael is immune, but he lacks the ability to shield others. He can make those around him appear invisible, but he cannot protect them from death powers, and he, in turn, is susceptible to the Gift of Pain. Lahnos accidentally fried him. And, of course, neither have battle-vision. It was a beautifully executed operation, from the point of view of the gods; the kind of operation I would have planned, were I in their shoes.'

'All right,' said Corthie; 'so we hit the carriers. If Allura comes, good; if not, we hunt her down, kill her, and take her Quadrant. The invasion of Na Sun Ka will then be postponed, or, failing that, the Wystians will attempt it anyway, and the Forty-Eighters will destroy them. What then?'

'Then we hit them on Athumia. No mercy. We wipe the bastards out to the last god, and smash the Dominion. If they flee to the Doomed Worlds, then we follow them there, and eradicate them. Let's complete the job this time. Our end aim should be the death of every immortal whose second name isn't Holdfast or Laimos.'

'Even Bailey?'

'Bailey has been holding secret talks with Edgar.'

'How do you know that?'

'I read Claudian's mind most days. Cael captured Lord Ballatar from Athumia a few days ago, and Ballatar was forced to reveal all of his secrets. Claudian was present at the interrogation.'

'And Naxor? What about him?'

Sable shrugged. 'Does his name end in Holdfast or Laimos?'

'I know he's a devious little bastard,' said Corthie, 'but hasn't he been loyal to the Empire?'

'He has, so far, but it's only a matter of time before he decides to betray us again. That time might be a hundred years in the future, but it's inevitable, in my opinion. Do you have a problem with that?'

'There are others I think you might be forgetting about. Jade, for instance. Lydia. Doria. Maxwell. And... the other one. The one we aren't supposed to ever mention.'

Sable lowered her glance. 'I know who you're talking about,' she said, 'but his self-healing has been disabled. And anyway, he has no memory of anything he ever did as an Ascendant. We can allow him to live.'

'Fair enough, Sable. As for the rest, it seems a little... extreme.'

'You and I both have immortal children, nephew. Do you want them to have to keep fighting the old gods down the centuries? Because that is what will happen if we don't put an end to them now. Do you remember when Karalyn massacred over a thousand gods at the end of the war against the Ascendants? That was the right approach, only it didn't go far enough. Instead, we tried to pretend that the Empire could co-exist alongside the Doomed Worlds, and the presence of so many immortals who continue to loathe and fear us. Think – we could make the worlds safe for our children to inherit. Isn't that a goal worth striving for?'

'Karalyn would go mental if she knew what you were planning.'

'Do you think I care? Karalyn can be a hypocrite at times – you know it; I know it. She could intervene at any time of her choosing, yet she chooses to sit in Colsbury doing nothing, as though her inaction somehow has a nobility to it.'

Corthie stared out to sea. 'I'll need to think about it. Your idea has its merits, but it's also possibly the most ruthless thing I've ever heard you say.'

'Having children of my own has perhaps altered my perspective,' she said. 'Put it this way – I am prepared to do anything to secure Joss and Lindi's future. Unlike you, I am happy to embrace my inner demons.' She smiled at him. 'Anyway, first things first. I will implant the suggestion about the carriers into Claudian's mind. All you need to do is prepare your new team and wait for the order.'

Corthie said nothing as he gazed down at the waves crashing against the ragged cliffs. He tried to imagine the known worlds shorn of every demigod and god, the extinction of the immortals that had so often plagued the lives of those doomed to die. If such a thing were to ever happen, Lahnos and the immortal children of the Holdfasts would be free to act without ever having to worry about the existence of any other gods. Their power would be limitless, and eternal.

That was a good thing, wasn't it?

CHAPTER 4
UNITED

Colsbury Castle, the Holdings – 24th Day, Last Third Spring 545

Kelsey raised an eyebrow as Karalyn appeared in her study next to an old man in black robes. The man stared at his new surroundings and let out a shriek, then Karalyn raised a hand, and he collapsed to the carpeted floor, his eyes closed.

Kelsey chuckled as she set her pencil down onto her unfinished manuscript. 'Might I assume that you found a Gunstian priest, sister?'

'Aye,' said Karalyn, as she crouched by the man. 'I'm going to have to work on his memories and motives, as well as imprint the Holdings language into him. It's going to take a while to get him ready.'

'Where did you go?'

'Great Gunst.'

'Is that their capital? It sounds as though it should be.'

'Aye; that's right. I was there with Bailey once, when he was attempting to insert himself into their religion, so I knew where the temples were located.'

'I guess we'll need to talk about Bailey at some point, now that we know he's a traitor.'

Karalyn glanced up from the unconscious body. 'It's far too premature to call him that. Talking with one's enemy does not necessarily mean that one is a traitor. He might have been trying to reach a peaceful compromise.'

'Even so, he met Edgar without first getting permission from the Imperial Court. It looks suspicious.'

'Go back to writing your book, sister,' said Karalyn. 'I'm going to be busy for the next hour, and I could do without any distractions.'

Kelsey frowned as Karalyn prised open one of the priest's eyelids. She glanced down at the chapter she had been drafting, but her train of thought had been disturbed by Karalyn's sudden appearance.

'You can have the room,' she said, as she got to her feet.

Karalyn said nothing, her attention focussed on the priest. Kelsey shook her head and walked out of her study.

'Next time, pick your own damn room,' she muttered, as she walked along the palace hallway.

'Talking to yourself again, Miss Holdfast?' said a voice.

Kelsey glanced up, and saw Naxor leaning against a doorway.

'It's a sign of impaired mental faculties, you know,' Naxor went on; 'but then, I always knew that there was something not quite right about you.'

'How is life in the Imperial Court?' she said.

He shrugged. 'Fine.'

'Are you enjoying being able to read everyone's minds with me not there any more?'

'How dare you suggest such a thing?' he said. 'And yes, I am rather enjoying it. I was dreading coming here today, knowing that your cloying ability to nullify my powers would once again be able to vex me. Van also seems to be flourishing in your absence. Do you recall that constant frown he used to wear when he was unfortunate enough to be your husband? That has quite vanished, replaced by a smile, which has been caused by a sense of pure relief, I would imagine. He has also been seen in the company of some very attractive, younger women. I daresay he is having the time of his life.'

'Oh my sweet Naxor,' she said. 'Do you really think I give a rat's arse about your petty little jibes? If I valued your opinion, or had any respect for you whatsoever, then your words might cause me pain; but I don't, so, instead, I merely find you rather sad and pathetic.'

'Well, you would know how that feels. A mortal woman of your age, divorced with two children, and unlikely to ever find another husband – how tragic. Unless, of course, you are planning to fabricate another prophecy to ensnare some unsuspecting man. Come on; it must have crossed your mind. I mean, it worked for Van.'

Kelsey laughed.

'Does your predicament amuse you?' said Naxor.

'I was just thinking how Frostback will react when I tell her what you just said. She is in Colsbury today for the wedding, along with Halfclaw and Sigum; none of whom hold you in high regard, Lord Chamberlain. I'll be sure to sound hurt and upset when I tell them.'

Naxor eyed her.

'You can definitely survive an arm or a leg being ripped off, aye?' Kelsey went on. 'Or maybe Simon had the right idea, and I'll ask Frostback to extract your tongue. I'd have to make sure it isn't wedged halfway up the Empress's backside first.'

'Speaking of Her Imperial Majesty,' said Naxor, 'I have brought her here to Colsbury, and I know that she would be rather upset if your dragon were to harm me in any way.'

'I'll take that chance,' she said, then she opened the doors to the middle balcony.

A crowd of people were standing or sitting out on the balcony, and Kelsey walked into their midst, Naxor a pace behind her.

'Pyre's arse,' Kelsey said, 'it's like summer has begun early.' She caught the Empress's gaze, and inclined her head. 'Your Majesty.'

'Thank you for hosting the wedding on Colsbury, Kelsey,' said Thorn.

'Thank you for accepting the invitation, Your Majesty.'

'I wouldn't dream of missing it. This must be the largest gathering of Holdfasts in many years, what with Aila and her children present; along with Celine and Cole. As far as I can tell, only Corthie and Sable are missing.'

'They are both due to arrive soon, Your Majesty,' said Kelsey. 'Sable is bringing my brother from Dragon Eyre; and she's bringing Lara and their two children, too.'

'Excellent,' said Thorn. 'Adjutant Claudian has been telling me about Corthie's new team on Na Sun Ka.'

Next to them, Kyra frowned. 'Is Uncle Corthie on Dragon Eyre?'

'He is,' said the Empress; 'however, we agreed not to mention politics today, so I would be obliged if you let it pass without further comment.'

Kyra narrowed her eyes, but kept her mouth closed.

'Her companion is called Larron,' Kelsey said, gesturing for him to approach.

Larron's face flushed, and he bowed in front of the Empress. 'It is an honour to meet you, Your Majesty.'

'Thank you,' said Thorn. 'How do you know Kyra?'

'We were at university together, Your Majesty, and I was by her side when the strike… ended.'

Thorn's eyes narrowed. 'I see. Yet again, we are drifting perilously close to discussing politics.'

Larron bowed again. 'I would like to appeal to you, Your Majesty, to allow Kyra to attend university again this coming autumn, so that she may resume her studies.'

A smile re-appeared on the face of the Empress. 'What a loyal friend you are, Larron. I would be delighted to have Kyra rejoin her classes this autumn, if she is prepared to abide by the law.'

'I didn't break any laws,' said Kyra.

'That is not entirely true, is it?' said the Empress. 'You broke the law regarding the Imperial Secrets Act, when you decided to reveal private conversations to Professor Achan. Nevertheless, if you promise to remain within the law, then I see no reason why you cannot go back to university for the autumn term. I am trying to reach out to you, Kyra. If you meet me in the middle, then we can come to an arrangement that satisfies everyone.'

Kyra lowered her gaze. 'I can't; not while Achan remains in prison. If you release him, then I would be prepared to believe that you are acting in good faith.'

'Then we appear to be at an impasse,' said Thorn; 'a pity.'

'Your Majesty,' Naxor said, stepping between Kyra and the Empress, 'might I beg your attention for a few moments to go through today's schedule?'

'Certainly, Lord Chamberlain.'

Naxor led the Empress away to the far side of the balcony, and Kelsey eyed Kyra and Larron.

'You should have taken her offer,' said Kelsey. 'Do you really want to be stuck on this tiny island with me and your mother for the whole of the next academic year?'

'But what about Achan?' said Kyra. 'He's rotting in some prison cell while we're here, having a party.'

'Everyone is here for your brother's marriage to Arrosa.'

'It's still a party.' She looked around. 'Where is Mother?'

'She's currently manipulating the mind of a Gunstian priest,' said Kelsey.

'Then who is helping Arrosa to get ready?'

'Aila, I think. Shall we go to her room and find out?'

Kyra nodded. They set off, then Kelsey raised a hand to stop Larron from following them.

'Girls only,' she said. 'If you want something to do, find Cael – he's with Cole in his quarters.'

Kelsey led Kyra off the balcony, and they took a set of stairs that went up a level.

'I like that Larron lad,' Kelsey said. 'Are you two…?'

'No.'

'Fine. I was only asking.'

'Are you not sick of this, Aunty?'

'Sick of what? Be more precise.'

'Well, the Empress dumped you here because she wouldn't compromise over you looking after your children, after ten years of loyal service; and now I'm exiled here as well, along with poor Lahnos, whose only crime was to have his friends killed by a mad god. Then there's Aila and her horde of children – they are also stuck here.' She shook her head. 'And the Empress smiles and says how wonderful it is that there are so many Holdfasts on Colsbury, as if we were all here to see her.'

Kelsey laughed. 'This time last year, you were the Empress's most devoted subject, and now I think you might actually hate her.'

'There's no *might* about it, Aunty. I can't stand the sight of her.'

'And yet you still talk to me. I thought I was supposed to be a blood-thirsty warmonger; isn't that what you used to call me?'

'What you did in Rahain seems to pale next to the Empire's more recent crimes. And I heard that you often tried to restrain the Empress. I may have been a little too harsh on you.'

'Before you try to paint me as a pacifist, remember that I planned the invasion of Rahain, and the humanitarian intervention along the Rakanese border; even though it was Naxor who... never mind.'

'Naxor who did what?'

Kelsey frowned. 'I probably shouldn't be telling you this, but it was Naxor who took the decision to send the army into Rakana. I had resigned from my job as Herald the day before. That slippery demigod was looking for any excuse to expand the terms that I had set for our conduct with Rakana. I had insisted that no measures be taken upon Rakanese soil; that our sole focus was to help the starving refugees cross into the Plateau. That wasn't enough for Naxor; he wanted more.'

'And what about the Sanang divisions who killed so many in Rahain?'

'I didn't want them; neither did Lucius Cardova, but the Empress insisted.'

They came to a door and Kelsey opened it. Inside, Arrosa was sitting on a chair in front of a mirror, as a young Holdings woman styled her hair. Shella was also there, sitting close by with a glass of whisky in her hand; while Konna and Calpurnia were both wearing flowery summer dresses.

Kelsey smiled. 'Good morning, Arrosa; good morning, everyone.'

She leaned over and kissed her daughter. 'You are looking beautiful, Calpurnia; you are going to make a great flower girl today. You, too, Konna.' She nodded at Shella. 'I was expecting Aila to be here.'

'We haven't seen her,' said Shella. 'I assume she's up to her knees in nappies and baby vomit.'

Kelsey gestured to the young Holdings woman. 'Kyra, this is Ninian Greenhold – daughter of Holder Green, and Arrosa's friend from Plateau City.'

'Hello, Kyra,' said Ninian. 'I've seen you around university.'

'Ninian is going to be Arrosa's wedding maid today,' said Kelsey. She glanced at Arrosa. 'Nervous?'

'Yes,' said Arrosa. 'I'm terrified, not of getting married, but that something might go wrong at the wedding.'

'How many damn galas have I organised over the years, Arrosa?' said Kelsey. 'You're in safe hands. And that dress? You look stunning.'

Arrosa smiled. 'Thank you.'

'It must be great to be able to tell if someone's not lying, eh?'

'Most of the time.'

'I remember when Cael used to lie to you a dozen times every day,' said Kyra, 'just to give you a headache.'

'He was a right little bastard back then,' said Shella. 'Hey; I said *was*. Has the Empress arrived?'

'Aye,' said Kelsey, 'and Kyra has already managed to piss her off.'

Shella cackled.

'What happened?' said Arrosa.

'The Empress had the effrontery to offer her a compromise. All Kyra had to do was agree to obey the law, and she could have gone back to university in autumn.'

Shella eyed Kyra. 'And what did you say to that?'

'I merely asked her to release Professor Achan from prison,' said Kyra. 'Had she agreed, I would have accepted her offer.'

Ninian frowned and shook her head.

'What was that look for?' said Kyra.

'Professor Achan's behaviour bordered on treachery,' said Ninian, as she slid several pins into Arrosa's hair to keep it in place. 'He tried to bring Plateau City to its knees in the middle of a war. He deserves to be in prison.'

Kyra smiled serenely. 'I wouldn't expect a scion of the Holdings aristocracy to understand the suffering experienced by the ordinary folk of the Empire.'

Ninian rolled her eyes, but said nothing.

'No reply?' said Kyra.

'I am here for Arrosa's big day,' said Ninian; 'not to argue.'

'But...'

'That's enough,' said Kelsey. 'There will be plenty of time to debate your differences at the party after the wedding has taken place. Let's keep it civil and polite until then.'

'Have you seen Cael?' said Arrosa.

'No. I've been keeping clear of the boys this morning; letting them do their thing in peace. Lucius and Cole are with him, though.'

'And the weather?'

'Holding up beautifully.'

'And the priest? Did Karalyn...?'

'It's all in hand,' said Kelsey. 'All you have to do is enjoy yourself.'

Two hours later, Kelsey was sitting in the front row in the gardens of Colsbury. Over two hundred wooden seats had been laid out in the same location where the plays were performed every summer, and a small podium had been erected in front of them, under the spreading branches of two huge oak trees. The sun was shining down upon the island, and the crowd of guests sat in silence as the Gunstian priest conducted the ceremony. Cael was in his marine dress uniform, with Cole next to him, while Lucius and Karalyn stood a little to the side, by Ninian and the two flower girls. Arrosa was standing in front of Cael, their hands held together, as the priest talked about the blessings that Chadura would surely bestow upon the happy couple.

Whatever Karalyn had done to the priest, it had worked. His

command of the Holdings language was fluent and flawless, and he seemed cheerful and confident, a broad smile fleeting over his face as he regarded the crowd.

'And so,' he said, 'with the certain knowledge of the Blessed Chadura's love and mercy for all who follow in her divine path, and with hearts both humble and filled with devotion, let us bear witness to the joining in matrimony of Arrosa of Zamata and Cael Holdfast. May their union be blessed in the sight of the Holy Mother Chadura, and may they live their lives in the fullness of the ever-living faith. He raised his hands. 'With the vows that they have exchanged, and with the authority granted me by the holy rites of the Gunstian priesthood, I now proclaim to all that Arrosa and Cael are wife and husband, joined forever by the loving bonds of marriage.'

Cael and Arrosa kissed, then Konna and Calpurnia stepped forward, and threw pink and white petals over them from the little baskets they were carrying. To the right of the podium, a selection of musicians with stringed instruments began to play, and the guests got to their feet, led by the Empress. The guests filed forward, each congratulating the married couple, while Karalyn and Lucius stood on their right, and Ninian and Cole on their left. When Kelsey reached the front, she shook Cael's hand, then she kissed Arrosa on the cheek.

'You're one of us now, Arrosa Holdfast,' she whispered. She smiled. 'And there's no escape.'

Kelsey had organised a feast in the gardens, and the musicians kept up their playing as the guests seated themselves at long tables. Cael and Arrosa sat at the head of the main table, with Karalyn and Lucius on their left, and the Empress and Kelsey on their right. Servants from the Summer Palace served food, wine and ale, and the voices of two hundred people rose up over Colsbury. Kelsey noticed Aila sitting a few seats away next to Corthie, so she got up and crouched by her.

'Are you all right?' she said. 'I couldn't find you this morning, and I was worried that the children had thrown you into the lake or something.'

'I have a terrible headache,' Aila said, 'and I feel exhausted.'

'She's been like this all day,' said Corthie.

Kelsey frowned. 'Why isn't your self-healing taking care of it, Aila?'

'I don't know. It feels weak for some reason. Never mind me, though, that was a beautiful ceremony. And did you see Konna up there next to Calpurnia? I was so proud of them. When Corthie and I got married, all Daphne did was say a few words, and it was done. This was far better.'

'I guess Arrosa knew what she was doing when she insisted on getting a Gunstian to perform the marriage; but I agree. It made our ceremonies look a little perfunctory. Anyway, let me know if you don't feel better soon, and I'll take the children off your hands.'

'I think you are already busy enough, Kelsey,' she said, 'but thanks.'

Kelsey went back to her seat, and listened as the Empress spoke to Arrosa and Cael.

'That's the first time I've cried in a while,' Thorn said. 'It was wonderful, and I am very happy for you both.'

'Thank you, Your Majesty,' said Cael.

'And thank you for coming,' said Arrosa.

'We are all Holdfasts, and I wouldn't have wanted to be anywhere else,' said Thorn. 'Now, while I have your attention, there is something I wish to say to you, Arrosa. As you might have guessed, I have plans for your husband's future, and now that you are his wife, those plans will affect you, too. I think it is time to ask if you wish to join my side, as an apprentice member of the Imperial Court. You can say no, of course, and, if you wish, you can take some time to think about this offer. If you accept, then you would start work when I come back here to Colsbury on Summer's Day, as my personal assistant. I want you to learn the workings of government, as I suspect such skills might well be useful for your future. Naturally, I would also ask you to use your Gift of Truth to help me root out any lies that are told in my presence; but that is not the sole reason for this offer. You have shown great promise, and I believe that, one day, you will rise to become one of the most powerful women in the Empire, just as your husband will be one of its most powerful men. Together, there is no end to what you might be able to achieve.'

Arrosa stared at the Empress for a moment, then her cheeks flushed. 'I don't need any time to think about it, Your Majesty. I accept.'

Karalyn frowned slightly, but said nothing, and Kelsey was glad that her sister had decided to keep her thoughts to herself.

Thorn seemed not to notice Karalyn's expression, and she smiled at Cael and Arrosa. 'I look forward to having you by my side, Arrosa; just as I look forward to following your career in the Imperial Marines, Cael.'

'With that in mind,' said Kelsey, 'once summer is over, you can have full use of the Holdfast townhouse in Plateau City. I have a set of keys ready for you.'

'What about their honeymoon?' said Sable, who was sitting down from Lucius. 'Has anything been planned?'

'Should I have organised something?' said Karalyn. 'I was so focussed on preparing the Gunstian priest, that I might have overlooked it.'

'How long do you have before you report back for duty, Cael?' said Sable.

'Five days, Aunty,' he said.

Sable smiled. 'Would you like to spend those five days on a little island off the coast of Ulna? Palm trees, beaches, waterfalls; and you would be completely alone. It's beautiful. I can get some of Blackrose's dragons to ferry food and supplies over to you. There's a little villa that has everything you might need; and it comes with a spectacular view of the sunset. Lara and I have spent several holidays there; we had the villa built for us.'

Cael and Arrosa glanced at each other.

'That sounds great, Sable,' said Arrosa. 'Thank you so much.'

Sable nodded, then she eyed Karalyn and Cardova. 'I'll take them there this evening, and I'll bring them back here before Cael has to return to the marines. By the way, where is the Gunstian priest? I haven't seen him since the ceremony.'

'I took him back to Great Gunst,' said Karalyn, 'before he had time to get confused about why he was here. He won't remember a thing.'

The Empress turned to Kelsey. 'Would you like to take a walk with me?'

'Of course, Your Majesty,' she said.

The Empress and Kelsey got to their feet. Several others rose at the sight of Thorn standing, but she gestured for them to retake their seats. Kelsey and the Empress walked away from the tables and into a quieter part of the garden.

'Is this about me and Naxor arguing, Your Majesty?' Kelsey said.

Thorn raised an eyebrow. 'No. You and he have always had a little tension between you; that's nothing new. I wanted to ask your advice.'

Kelsey narrowed her eyes. 'Me?'

'You are no longer my Herald, but that does not mean I have forgotten how much I used to rely on you. I miss you, Kelsey; that is the truth. I miss you deeply. I think I may have made a terrible mistake in refusing to compromise with you over your children. My demands were unreasonable; I see that now.'

They walked to the shore of the lake, and gazed out over the still waters and the mountains.

'I am honoured to give you any advice I can, Your Majesty,' Kelsey said.

'By the end of this summer,' Thorn said, 'if nothing changes, the Empire will be bankrupt.'

Kelsey's mouth opened, but she remained silent.

'We have grievously over-extended ourselves and have never been more vulnerable,' the Empress went on. 'When the money runs out, we will be unable to pay the wages of those serving in the armed forces or in the government; our commitments to Rahain, Rakana and the City will not be met; we will be incapable of defending Na Sun Ka, while retaking the Tempest mine on Athumia will be beyond our abilities. If this occurs, I intend to abdicate, for the responsibility for this failure will be mine.'

'But... but... wait – what about what you just said to Arrosa about her working for you?'

'I wasn't lying to the girl. Come Summer's Day, I will take her into my service. As for the rest, I thought it best to keep up the pretence that all is well with the Empire, to avoid causing panic and instability.'

'Does the rest of the Imperial Court know all this?'

'Only Chamberlain Naxor and Treasurer Slaeon know the full extent of the truth, though the others are aware that we are facing considerable difficulties. If Naxor was being particularly rude or obnoxious towards you, it is most likely due to the intense pressure he is under. If I abdicate, then my last act will be to authorise you to organise the Council of Electors to select my replacement, and then I will fade into a shameful obscurity.' She turned to Kelsey, and a tear ran down her cheek. 'I have failed the Empire, my friend. I have tried my best, but I have made too many mistakes, and the Empire deserves better.'

'But shouldn't you stick at it, in bad times as well as good?'

'Not if the bad times came about as a result of my mistakes. I truly want the best for the people of the Empire, and if I cannot provide that, then someone better than I should.'

'Who? Who else could take on the role?'

'Well, I happen to think that you would be more than capable.'

'Me?' said Kelsey. 'No way. Not a chance. I have no desire to lead.'

'Perhaps that is what makes you well suited. I was always ambitious. I never made a secret of the fact that I wanted power, that I wanted to be Empress. From the moment I first saw Bridget sitting upon her throne, I knew that I desired the same. When I led us to victory against the Ascendants, I did so with the support of many others; many who gave their lives to defend this world. If I cannot live up to their sacrifice, then perhaps I have been deluding myself all these years.'

'No,' said Kelsey. 'You are the damn Empress, Thorn; there is no other. I had my doubts about you at first, I admit it, but it has to be you. Listen to me, Thorn – let me help you. Re-appoint me as your Herald, and give me the authority to overrule the other members of the Imperial Council. Let me fix the Empire.'

Thorn narrowed her eyes. 'Do you understand what you are saying? If you tie yourself to me, then you will fall when I fall. Stay clear of me, and pick up the pieces once I am irredeemably tainted by failure.'

'Hand me the reins,' said Kelsey, 'and neither of us will fall. Give me the summer, and I will pull us back from the brink.'

'How?'

'I don't have the answer to that just yet. I have ideas, though – plenty of them. Have Naxor bring me the accounts from Plateau City, and I'll have the rudiments of a plan worked out by the time you return here for Summer's Day.'

'I don't know, Kelsey. You are taking a tremendous risk with your own reputation.'

'With all due respect, I couldn't give a flying fuck about my reputation.'

'But if you fail...'

'I won't fail. Do you think I can't be as ruthless and bloody-minded as my mother if I have to be? She wouldn't have baulked at this challenge, and neither will I. You are the heart of this Empire, Thorn, and I will not let you down.'

Tears came to the eyes of the Empress, then she reached out and embraced Kelsey.

'Thank you,' she said. 'I came here full of despair, and you have rekindled my hope.' She pulled away a little. 'What you have asked for, I will grant you.'

'But not today, Your Majesty,' said Kelsey. 'Today belongs to Cael and Arrosa.'

'You are right,' Thorn said. 'After all, they are the future.'

CHAPTER 5
NO GOING BACK

Colsbury Castle, the Holdings – 27th Day, Last Third Spring 545

'If you aren't more careful,' said Larron, 'someone will get suspicious.'

Kyra sat down on the short pier, her legs almost reaching the surface of the lake. 'You worry too much. No one suspects a thing. Kelsey has been obsessively studying those papers Naxor brought here, and Mother is... well, she never pays much attention to what's going on around her.'

'But Aila seemed really ill, and it lasted for hours.'

'Her self-healing will recover. Do I have to remind you that it was your idea? I almost felt it last time. I'm close.'

Larron sat down next to her, and they gazed out over the lake at the mountains.

'I'm going to miss Colsbury,' said Kyra.

Larron eyed her. 'Miss it? I thought you were sick of being trapped here.'

'I am, but... well, if the plan works, then I don't think I'll be coming back for a long time. I'll be saying goodbye to more than just Colsbury. I doubt many members of my family will ever want to speak to me again.'

Larron nudged her with his elbow, and she turned to see Shella and Olo'osso entering the small harbour.

'If you want to see Lahnos and his dragon before they go,' said Shella, 'then you'd better hurry. They're about to leave.'

'Then why are you here?' said Kyra.

'We've already said our farewells to them,' Shella said. 'They're in the forecourt.'

Larron stood, then he extended a hand and helped pull Kyra to her feet.

'It's another perfect day for sailing,' said Olo'osso, as his boots reached the wooden boards of the pier. 'We can wait for you both if you hurry.'

'I'd love to, but I can't,' said Kyra.

'Ah, that's right. I had forgotten for a moment that Lady Karalyn has bewitched your mind, young Kyra. What a pity. What was it that provoked the ire of your formidable mother?'

'I tried to punch the Empress.'

Olo'osso placed a hand on Shella's shoulder and laughed out loud.

'She was lucky not to be locked up,' said Shella.

'It sounds more like youthful mischief to me, my charming princess. I've always had a soft spot for troublemakers.'

'You have your daughters for that.'

Olo'osso shook his head. 'Not any more, my darling. My beloved girls have all settled down. One can only hope that my grandchildren will be able to live up to my high standards. There is bound to be at least one pirate among them.'

They squeezed past each other on the narrow pier, and Shella stepped down into Olo'osso's yacht.

'We will see you later,' said Kyra.

'Aye, have a good time sailing around the lake,' said Larron.

Kyra and Larron walked off the pier and through the harbour. On the other side, Kyra saw Sigum's enormous bulk taking up much of the space between the Great Keep and the Summer Palace. A small group had gathered by his forelimbs, and Lahnos's horns stood out from a distance.

'I think I would quite like to have horns,' said Larron, as they walked towards the group.

Kyra eyed him. 'Each to their own.'

Karalyn and Cardova were standing next to Lahnos, Ora'lya and Dermot's grandparents, along with a few of the older children, while Aila was cradling Dermot in her arms.

'Good morning,' said Kyra.

Lord Sigum lowered his silvery-green head. 'Greetings, little Kyra, and farewell. My rider felt it would be less awkward if we departed Colsbury before the Imperial Court arrives here from Plateau City in a few days.'

'How did you get permission to leave? I thought you had been confined to Colsbury.'

'The Empress has permitted us to travel to the Hold Fast estate,' said Lahnos.

'Watch out for the heat,' Kyra said to Dermot's elderly grandparents. 'The Holdings gets very warm in summer.'

'Holder Fast is allowing us to stay in the mansion on the estate,' said Dermot's grandmother. 'We will travel back to Plateau City when Dolwyn is next on leave.'

'I am looking forward to seeing the desert,' said Sigum. 'Frostback and Halfclaw have told me how wonderful it is.'

'How are you all getting there?'

'I'm taking them,' said Karalyn. 'It's too far for a baby to travel upon a dragon's back; and this way, I can speak to Celine about the arrangements. With Cole about to join the army, Lahnos and Ora'lya have volunteered to help out on the estate.'

Kyra crinkled her nose. 'Do either of you know anything about horses?'

'Nothing at all,' said Ora'lya, 'but I'm willing to learn.'

'It will be a big change for us,' said Lahnos, 'but I would rather not have to spend the entire summer in close proximity to the Empress. I don't think she's forgiven me for resigning my commission.'

'You have a baby to look after,' said Karalyn. 'Your life has already changed.' She glanced at Aila.

The demigod gazed down at the baby in her arms. 'I'm going to miss you, little Dermot,' she said, then she passed the bundle to Lahnos.

'Thank you for your help,' said Lahnos. 'I honestly don't know how you cope with looking after so many children at the same time.'

'It might be what's been causing her all those headaches,' said Cardova.

'I'll look into that when I get back,' said Karalyn. 'You should have told me you were feeling unwell, Aila. If something's been interfering with your self-healing, then we should investigate.' She kissed Cardova. 'I will probably be back in an hour or so.'

'Take your time,' said Cardova. 'Kelsey has asked me to go over some of the imperial finances with her.'

Karalyn rolled her eyes. 'My sister has hardly left her room in days. Why is she bothering with the empire's accounts? Is it for the book she's writing?'

'Maybe; I'm not sure. I'll ask her,' said Cardova.

Karalyn gazed up at the dragon. 'Are you ready, Lord Sigum?'

'I am, Karalyn,' he said.

'Take care, Lahnos,' said Kyra, taking a few steps back. 'You, too, Ora'lya. And stay out of the midday sun.'

Kyra focussed her powers as Karalyn prepared to leave. The air shimmered, and Kyra felt it – a burst of her mother's powers detectable only to a dream mage. It was the same power that Kyra would need to harness, if she was going to be able to escape. Her mother vanished, along with Sigum, Lahnos, Ora'lya, the baby, and the baby's grandparents.

'Right,' said Cardova; 'I'd better see what Kelsey wants. Will I see you all at lunch?'

'Aye,' said Kyra.

Aila gestured to the children. 'Come on; let's get back inside.'

Kyra and Larron remained where they were as Cardova, Aila and the children walked towards the palace.

'Did you hear that?' Kyra whispered. 'My mother has finally woken up to the fact that something is affecting Aila's powers. We have to act before she gets back, or she'll work out what I've been doing.'

'But you aren't ready,' said Larron. 'None of your experiments have worked.'

'This is the only chance we have to get out of here.'

'Have you tried to remove your mother's blocks from your mind?'

'Of course I have! She's too strong for me. Every time I try to touch one of the blocks, it starts to spread and grow. Worse, she keeps checking to make sure everything is still in place.'

Larron nodded, then he glanced at the ground.

'Have you changed your mind?' she said.

'No, but I'm worried about where this will lead. Do you really want to cut yourself off from your family? Maybe, if you were patient, then you might be able to resolve your problems without... well, without breaking the law.'

Kyra snorted. 'Do you think my family ever worried about breaking the law? My mother, my grandmother, and Aunty Sable – none of them gave a shit about the law; they did whatever they felt they had to. How am I any different? We haven't got much time, Larron. If we don't do it now, we'll never get another opportunity.'

They walked towards the palace, and passed the soldiers by the entrance. Kyra led Larron up the grand stairs, and hurried towards the large chamber where Aila looked after the Holdfast children. She hesitated by the door for a moment, then pushed it open. Inside, Aila was changing Ceres's nappy on a low table, as the other ten children amused themselves. Tutors had been hired for the older children, along with a few nannies, but none of them were present.

Aila glanced up. 'Are you here to help?'

'Where are the other adults?' said Kyra.

'The tutors don't start until after lunch today, while the nannies have gone to the village to pick up a few supplies. They seem to believe that I can manage on my own.'

Kyra smiled. 'You *can* manage on your own.'

'Maybe Lucius is right; maybe I have taken on too much, and, somehow, my self-healing is suffering.'

'That sounds unlikely, to be honest,' said Kyra. 'Would you like me to take a look?'

'No offence, Kyra, but I think I'll wait until your mother gets back from the estate.'

'Do you want to play with me, Kyra?' said Calpurnia.

'Sorry, not just now,' said Kyra. 'I have things to do.'

Aila raised an eyebrow. 'Then why did you come in?'

'I, uh… I wanted to offer to help with your headaches. Come on, Larron; let's go.'

Kyra and Larron left the room and closed the door.

'That settles it,' said Larron. 'You can't go ahead; not now, not when Aila has no other adults around to look after the children when… you know, when she might be incapacitated.'

Kyra frowned, then she hurried up the next flight of stairs. She heard Larron come after her, and they both went in her room. Kyra shut and locked the door, then she dragged her packed luggage out from under the bed.

'Are you still going to try it?' said Larron. 'You can't. What if Aila is rendered unconscious? Who will take care of the children? Some of them are too young to look after themselves.'

'Killop is thirteen,' Kyra said. 'He's old enough to run and get help.'

'But…'

'Achan is rotting in a damn prison,' cried Kyra. 'The children will be fine. Have you packed?'

Larron said nothing for a moment, then he walked to a wardrobe and removed a large bag.

'Stand next to me,' she said, then she closed her eyes. She allowed her vision powers to leave her body, then she sent them downstairs to the children's room and entered Aila's mind. Every time she had experimented with draining Aila's demigod powers, she had been careful to alter Aila's memories afterwards, but she knew that she would have left traces behind that her mother would be able to detect. Kyra relaxed, and exhaled slowly, then she began to draw upon the demigod's self-healing and limited vision abilities.

In the room below, Aila swayed, then she coughed and put a hand to her head. Kyra drew more from her, and felt her own body ripple with the additional strength. She tried to match the burst of powers she had felt her mother use when she had taken Lahnos and the others to the Hold Fast estate, and then it hit her – Aila was too weak to provide what she needed. Her vision glanced around the room, and she started to think the unthinkable. Among the eleven children were nine who also possessed self-healing powers – Corthie and Aila's seven children, and Kyra's younger siblings, Carden and Caitlyn. A feeling of guilt and dread washed through her. If she carried on, then her mother would be unlikely to ever forgive her but, at the same time, the thought of remaining imprisoned upon Colsbury was too much to bear.

'I'm sorry,' she whispered, then she started to drain the life force from the children, starting with the oldest. Killop closed his eyes and slumped in his chair, the book he was reading falling to the rug, then Konna swayed and fell to her knees. Cairney cried out in alarm, as Aila slipped into unconsciousness next to them, then the nine-year-old boy felt his own powers being drained.

'No,' Cairney cried, and Kyra gasped at the boy's raw strength. Kyra pulled hard, and Cairney collapsed to the floor amid the screams of the other children.

Kyra drew back, the power drained from Aila and her three eldest children vibrating and surging within her. Once more, she tried to match the power used by her mother. It was a power she had never tapped into before, but her long experience with a Quadrant made it seem almost familiar. She heard no voice, for there was no copper device in contact with her skin, but she could sense the worlds opening up to her. She pictured the level of dungeons deep beneath the

Ministry of the Plateau in the imperial capital, and then focussed on an image of the main guard room.

Take me, Larron and our luggage to the guard room. Go.

The air in Kyra's bedroom crackled and spat, then everything went black. Kyra panicked. She had felt the void before, when her mother had tried to take them home from the City of Salve, and, instead, they had ended up being stranded next to the Tempest mine on Athumia. It was timeless, and endless, and silent. Kyra tried to breathe, but it felt as though she had no physical form, as though her consciousness had become untethered from her corporeal flesh. Terror mixed with unbounded liberation, then her vision cleared and she fell three feet and landed onto a solid stone floor.

She gasped, filling her lungs with air, then she rolled onto her knees and threw up, as four soldiers close by jumped to their feet.

'Stay where you are!' one shouted.

Kyra glanced up, her vision hazy, then she lifted an arm.

Sleep.

The four soldiers clattered to the floor of the basement room, knocking over a jug of water that shattered on the flag stones. Kyra put her hands to her head and closed her eyes, as a sharp pain went through her skull, and it took her a few moments to realise that Larron was lying on the floor next to her, unconscious. She crawled over to him, and checked that he was breathing, then she glanced around.

She had done it. They were in the room under the Ministry of the Plateau that she had pictured in her mind, and she had done it without a Quadrant. She sat up as her mind began to clear, then she noticed the large set of keys attached to one of the sleeping soldiers' belts. She reached over and unfastened them, and got to her feet. The dislocation and dizziness was fading, replaced by a surge of joy and pride at what she had achieved, then she remembered what she had done to Aila and three of her children. Colsbury would be in uproar when they had discovered that Kyra had been responsible.

It was too late for regrets, she told herself, then she walked towards the door that led to the cells. She opened it, and waited for her eyes to adjust to the dim light in the stone hallway. A dozen cells stretched out, with six on either side, and she walked down the middle of the hallway until she reached the cell where Achan was sitting on a low mattress.

'Kyra?' he said. 'Is it really you?'

He got to his feet and walked up to the bars. In the other cells, a few prisoners were staring out at Kyra, but she ignored them.

'It's really me, Professor,' she said.

'Thank you for coming to visit me,' he said. 'My trial date has been set – did you hear? The lawyer I was appointed told me to expect a ten-year sentence.' He raised an eyebrow. 'Why are you holding the keys to the cells?'

'I'm getting you out of here, Professor,' she said. 'You don't deserve to be in jail. I am here to correct the injustice that has been done to you.'

'No, Kyra,' he said. 'I'm grateful that you would even consider this, but what about your future? If you release me from prison, then you will be hunted down and arrested. Please think of everything that you will be giving up. You have your whole life ahead of you.'

'How would I be able to live with myself?' she said. 'Knowing that you were imprisoned in a filthy cell, far from the light of the sun, has hurt me every day since you were arrested.'

'But how would we get out of the building?'

'Trust me.'

She rooted through the keys, and began trying them in the lock, as the prisoners in the other cells watched with growing interest. Kyra found the correct key on her fourth attempt, and opened the cell door.

'Me next!' cried someone. 'Hey, girl; over here.'

Kyra ignored the voice, and gestured for Achan to leave the cell. Instead, he stood his ground.

'I can't,' he said. 'Lock the door and leave me here while you still have the chance.'

'Don't you want to be free, Professor?'

'Of course I want to be free, but we will never get out of the ministry undetected. All that will happen is that I will spend longer in jail and, worse, you will also be incarcerated.'

She leaned in closer to him. 'I got here without a Quadrant, Professor; all the way from Colsbury.'

His eyes widened. 'Without a Quadrant?' he whispered.

'Just like my mother can do.'

A noise came from the doorway, and she saw Larron stagger through from the guard room, their bags slung over his shoulders.

'We did it,' he groaned. 'I mean you did it.'

'Oh, Kyra,' said Achan. 'I see you have involved Larron in this, too. You are both far too young to be risking yourselves like this.'

'Just think what we could achieve if you were out of this place,' said Kyra.

'But where would we go?'

'I have an idea. Larron, get over here and stand or sit by the professor. I need to reach out again; I need more power.'

Larron swayed on his feet, then he walked over to the entrance to Achan's cell.

'What kind of power?' said Achan. 'What did you mean?'

'The kind of power Lord Naxor can provide,' she said. 'Please wait a moment or two.'

Kyra sat down on the cold stone floor with her back to the cell wall. She closed her eyes and unleashed her dream vision again. She wondered if it would get easier with time and practice. Her mother had required extra power when she had first started to travel without needing a Quadrant, but that had changed over the years, until she required nothing but her own abilities.

Kyra's vision shot through the basement levels of the ministry, and entered the upper floors. She looked into the two audience chambers, but both were empty. What would she do if Naxor happened to be away? What if he was on Dragon Eyre? He was the only immortal being that she knew of in Plateau City, and if he was absent then Achan would have been right – they would never get out of the building undetected. She cursed her lack of foresight, then she gasped in relief as she saw

Naxor hunched over a desk in his private study, a look of concern on his features as he read over some papers.

She drove her powers into Naxor's mind, and he recoiled in shock. With no time for subtlety or discretion, she immediately began to pull his life force from his body. He toppled from his chair and convulsed on the carpeted floor, foam appearing on his lips as she drew his strength from him. His skin began to shrivel and wither, and his eyes rolled up into his head. Naxor's strength was formidable next to Aila's. Not only was his self-healing stronger, but his vision powers vastly outweighed those of his cousin on Colsbury.

She waited until she had drawn enough, then she paused to see several guards and courtiers burst into Naxor's study, attracted by the noise his flailing body was making. They stared down at the demigod, their mouths opening. For a moment, Kyra was tempted to obliterate Naxor's memories, but then she decided against it. If there was no going back, then it would be better if the Empress and the rest of her family knew that she had been responsible; that way, they would begin to understand what she was capable of doing, and then, maybe, they might regret the way they had treated her, Achan, and everyone else they had wronged.

She cut the connection to Naxor's mind, and opened her eyes to see Achan and Larron staring at her.

'Larron has been explaining to me what you did to get here, Kyra,' Achan said. 'Are you sure it's the right thing to do? I don't want us to be responsible for causing pain to other people.'

'They'll recover,' said Kyra. 'They're immortal.'

'Did you find Naxor?' said Larron.

'I did, and I left him drained and empty on the floor of his study.'

Achan glanced away.

'Don't feel sorry for him, Professor,' Kyra went on. 'How many innocent people have suffered because of Naxor? And I didn't kill him.'

'Could you have killed him if you had wanted to?' said Achan.

'Aye. I could have, but I'm not a murderer.' She gazed at her hands. 'I now have enough power to take us away from here.'

Larron glanced at her with fear in his eyes. 'Will we... will we end up in that dark place again?'

'The void,' she said. 'Maybe. It might take me a lot of practice to do this smoothly.'

'It was terrifying,' he said. 'I thought I was dead.'

'If we are going to leave,' said Achan, 'then we should do so without any further delay; otherwise, all this will have been for nothing.'

'But where can we go?' said Larron. 'Won't Karalyn be able to track us down?'

'Eventually,' said Kyra, 'but we can make it difficult for her. I can shield my powers, and she will have to search everywhere. She will probably start with the Star Continent, so we should rule that out.'

'The City?' said Achan. 'We could hide in Hammer territory.'

'I don't want to hide,' she said. 'I can't live like that. We should find somewhere we can live openly. That way, even when my mother finds us, there will be little she can do. She may even decide that we're not worth the effort.'

Achan and Larron glanced at each other.

'Pass me my bag,' she said.

Larron slid it from his shoulder and handed it to her. She opened it, dug around amid the clothes, and took out the Compass.

'What's that?' said Achan.

'It can trace even the smallest amounts of Tempest,' she said. 'I have never visited the place I want to take us, and so I doubt I will be able to travel there without being able to see it first. Give me a moment.'

Kyra placed her thumb onto the Compass, and her vision clouded over. She remembered what she had done to find Cael when he had stolen the Sextant, and located the Tempest mine on Inopei within seconds. She searched the rest of Athumia and found the faint signal she had been looking for. She focussed on it, drawing upon the power she had ripped from Naxor.

Take me, Larron, Achan and our luggage to the vicinity of the Tempest signal. Go.

The air crackled and Kyra was flung back into the void. She had been prepared for it, and no sense of panic came over her. Instead, she relaxed her mind, and waited.

The air crackled again, and she opened her eyes to find herself lying next to Larron and Achan in a small courtyard halfway up a mountain-side. Behind them, a tall, many-storied building rose up the side of a cliff, with rickety wooden balconies on the upper floors. In the opposite direction, the sinewy arms of the Serpent Isle were spread out in the afternoon sunshine. Kyra staggered to her feet.

Achan rolled over on the cobbled ground, groaning and trembling.

'Believe me, Professor,' said Larron, 'that was far better than last time.'

Larron stood, then he and Kyra helped Achan get to his feet. The professor stared around at their new surroundings.

'Where are we?' he said. 'Where have you brought us, Kyra?'

'Look down at the island,' she said, pointing to the east. 'Do you see the land and water? It's the shape of the coils that are inside every Quadrant.'

'We're on Zamata?' said Larron.

Kyra smiled.

'Where in the blazes is Zamata?' said Achan. He turned, and gazed up at the tall building clinging onto the cliffside. 'Who lives here?'

'Someone who might be prepared to help us,' said Kyra.

A face appeared over the side of one of the high wooden balconies, staring down at them, then the air shimmered and Bailey walked out of the main doors of the building.

'I never bother using the stairs any more,' he said, as he placed a Quadrant into his pocket. 'So, what do we have here? Visitors? Are you here to arrest me? I have a very good explanation for my recent contact with an old friend. Are you willing to listen?'

'We're not here about that, Bailey,' said Kyra.

Bailey narrowed his eyes. 'Then, Miss Holdfast, pray tell me why you have come unannounced to my home.'

'We are in trouble,' she said. 'I was wondering if you might be willing to help us.'

Bailey gazed into Larron's eyes, then frowned again. 'I see that this young man has had his mind protected. Most inconvenient.' He turned to Achan. 'Ah. That's better. Oh, I see. Oh dear.' He folded his arms across his chest. 'Give me one good reason why I shouldn't rush off to inform the Empress of what has just occurred. If I were to hand you in, then I might be forgiven for speaking to Lord Edgar.'

Kyra smiled. 'Come on, Bailey; you know your powers are no match for mine. I could wipe your mind, or simply send you to sleep, far faster than you would be able to trigger that Quadrant. Why don't you invite us inside, and we can talk? Doesn't that sound reasonable? After all, each one of us is in trouble with the Empire right now; perhaps we could reach an agreement that would be mutually beneficial.'

Bailey said nothing for a moment, and Kyra entered his mind quietly, ready to unleash her powers if he proved uncooperative.

'Will you please stop that, Miss Holdfast?' he said. 'It is rather impertinent of you. Yes, I am able to discern your presence in my mind; do you think I was born yesterday? Tell me – how long do we have before your mother discovers that you are here?'

'A few days, perhaps. This is my first time on Zamata, and I am hoping that she will be unable to believe that I knew how to travel here.'

'Might I sit down somewhere?' said Achan. 'The experience of travelling without a Quadrant has left me a little disorientated.'

'Excuse me?' said Bailey. 'You got here without a Quadrant?'

'I willed us here,' said Kyra. 'It took a lot of power, power that I had to draw from Lord Naxor. If you refuse to help us, then I might be forced to drain you in order to travel somewhere else. Of course, I would rather we became friends. I would be very interested in hearing why you thought it necessary to talk to Lord Edgar, for instance. We may have more in common than you think.'

Bailey's frown dissipated, and a smile crept over his face.

'Very well, Miss Holdfast,' he said. 'As I am so clearly outmatched, I would like to humbly welcome you to Zamata Gataza.' He gestured towards the front gates. 'Come this way.'

CHAPTER 6
ON THE CHIN

Ulnan Waters, Eastern Rim – 18th Tradinch 5266 (18th Gylean Year 17)

Arrosa glanced at the setting sun. 'We don't have long left.'

Cael said nothing as he sat on the comfortable swing chair, his arm over Arrosa's shoulder. Behind them on the wooden veranda, their baggage was piled up in preparation for their journey back to Colsbury.

'I could happily stay here for another month,' Arrosa went on; 'and before you say *third*, remember that we're on Dragon Eyre. They use *months* here.'

'Would I ever try to correct you, my beloved wife?' said Cael.

She eyed him. 'It speaks. I thought you'd forgotten how to. You've said nothing since it started to get dark.'

'I'm just thinking.'

'I've warned you about that, husband. The last time you thought too deeply about something, you stole the Sextant.'

'Aye, but if I hadn't, then we might never have got together.'

She kissed him. 'Well, what were you thinking about?'

'A few things. First, about how you were prepared to give me a chance after the way I used to treat you. I was an arsehole, and a lot of folk wouldn't have been able to believe that I'd changed. I mean, some folk never change – once a numpty, always a numpty.'

'It was World Three,' she said. 'It changed us both. There was one time, when we thought that Cole was dead, and it was just the two of us. I was sick after eating those mushrooms, and I opened my eyes and saw you looking down on me – and that was when I knew. I knew that you were no longer the angry boy who hated me, and I knew you would never abandon me. Maybe we had to be dragged down into the depths of despair before we could realise what kind of people we really were.'

'I remember that moment,' he said. 'I would have burned down the entire world to save you; it was round about then that I was forced to admit to myself that I loved you. What I didn't expect is that you would love me in return. I still don't understand why you love me. You could have chosen any boy you wanted.'

She smiled up at him. 'I was already falling in love with you by then. Once you had shed all the bullshit, I saw what kind of man you were going to be. Since that moment, you have never once lied to me, or hurt me. I have to admit that I was wary for a while. I was watching you, to see if you would go back to your old ways once we were out of danger, but you didn't. And then the marines changed you even more, or maybe they just reinforced the changes that were already happening.'

'I would do anything for you, Arrosa; well, not anything.' He smiled. 'Sorry, I know you hate it, but I'm not going to give up smoking for you.'

'Do it when I'm not around, and don't ever kiss me after you've had a cigarette.'

'I can agree to that. The second thing I was thinking about was...'

She raised an eyebrow. 'You mean there's more?'

'Aye. I was wondering what the Empress has planned for you. I was pleased that she's recognised how smart you are, but I was disappointed about her saying that she wants to take advantage of your Gift of Truth.'

'At least she was open about it from the start. She didn't try to pretend that she wouldn't find it useful – that would have annoyed me more. Let's face it, though – she's taking advantage of both of us; but why not? I'll be glad to have a chance to prove myself. You've already done that part, and now I want to show the Empress what I can do. I don't want to be thought of as your little wife, always waiting for her husband to come home from the wars. We're partners, aren't we?'

'For sure. We're good at different things, but we have a lot in common. We both had shitty childhoods, for example, and we've both risen above it. We've seen things that no child should ever see, but it hasn't broken us. You're beautiful on the outside, Arrosa, but inside, you're as tough as a dragon's hide. I love that about you. You take no shit, and yet you still care. And, you're fucking great in bed.'

She laughed.

'I was a tiny bit worried,' he went on, 'that, you know, after waiting until we were married, that it would be awkward and weird, but it wasn't. I know it's not the most important thing in a marriage, but...'

'It is pretty important,' she said, 'and I was worried about it, too. Imagine if it had been a disappointment.' She glanced at the darkening sky. 'I wish we didn't have to leave. I'm going to miss you, Cael; I hope you know that. Where do you think you will be sent next?'

'The first thing that will happen when I get back to the marine base on Na Sun Ka is a tremendous arse-kicking. I'm going to get shouted at by every senior officer in Sun Ta, and Captain Doune is going to boot me up and down the quayside. After that, I'll be glad to get back to active duty.'

'Why did you disobey orders?'

'Because I was right and they were wrong. They know that now but, obviously, they can't admit it, so they're pretending that I didn't disregard their commands. I doubt they'll ever let me have a Quadrant again.'

'Do you regret it?'

'Not one tiny bit. I would do exactly the same. The problem is that they know that.'

'Please don't take any more stupid risks. I feel sick thinking about what that god Ward was going to do to you. What if Edgar hadn't turned up?'

'I fell asleep on the roof of a dragon palace in Nom Karta; that's why

I got captured. It was an idiotic mistake. I'm bound to make more mistakes, but I'm learning all the time. I can't promise you that I won't be putting myself in danger again; it's the nature of the job, but I will try not to do anything too stupid.'

The air shimmered a few feet away, and Sable appeared with her eyes closed.

She smiled. 'Is it safe to open my eyes?'

Cael laughed. 'Shit; get your clothes back on, Arrosa. It's Aunty Sable!'

Arrosa joined in the laughter as Sable opened one eye.

'We're all packed up, Aunty,' said Arrosa. 'Can I call you *aunty*?'

'You can call me whatever you like, Arrosa Holdfast,' said Sable. She sat down next to them and gazed at the view of the ocean. 'What did you think of my little island?'

'I'll tell you if you come back in ten days,' said Arrosa. 'You can say that you forgot to collect us.'

Sable said nothing, as though she was contemplating it.

'Did we miss anything while we were away?' said Cael.

'That is what I am deciding if I should tell you,' Sable said.

'That doesn't sound good.'

'It's not. In fact, it's quite bad.'

Cael narrowed his eyes. 'Just get it over with, Aunty.'

'All right. Your sister has gone missing. Somehow, she managed to learn how to travel without a Quadrant, and she ran away from Colsbury.'

'Fucksake,' muttered Cael.

'I hadn't finished,' said Sable. 'In order to use this new power of hers, she first nearly killed Aila and three of her children. They will recover, but she battered their self-healing into an inch of closing it down completely.'

'Which children?' said Arrosa.

'Killop, Konna and Cairney. The three oldest. Presumably, and I'm guessing, Aila didn't have enough reserves for what Kyra needed to accomplish, which was the rescue of Achan from prison in Plateau City.

After that, she vanished again, by draining poor old Naxor.' She smiled. 'That was the only positive thing to emerge from this fiasco. Naxor is beside himself with rage. Mind you, so is Karalyn, Kelsey, Lucius, the Empress... the list goes on. Kyra has done a fabulous job of pissing everyone off.'

Cael put a hand to his face.

'What about the blocks that Karalyn put in her head?' said Arrosa.

'They were too specific. They prohibited escaping Colsbury by walking, swimming, sailing, even riding off on the back of a dragon; but I guess it didn't occur to Karalyn that Kyra might be able to Quadrant without an actual Quadrant.'

'Does Corthie know?' said Cael.

'Yeah. I don't think I've ever seen the big guy so angry. His wife and three of his kids were in a poor shape when I took him back to Colsbury to see them. It's bad enough that some crazy gods want to harm us, but Kyra? I should warn you, no one is in a very forgiving mood right now.'

'I wonder how she did it,' said Arrosa. 'I mean, I wonder how she was able to access that kind of power.'

'I suppose she had watched her mother do it hundreds of times.' She glanced at Cael. 'Have you ever felt anything when your mother uses her powers to travel?'

'Not really,' he said. 'Maybe something very faint. If I had to guess, it's probably related to Kyra's ability to hear Quadrants, and to command them without having to use them like a regular person; and I've never been able to do that.'

'That's the current consensus,' said Sable. 'Of course, it seems obvious after the fact, and Karalyn is angry with herself for not having foreseen it.'

'She will be able to find her, aye?'

'In time. It depends where Kyra has gone. Karalyn is searching the Star Continent just now, scanning it from top to bottom, but I reckon Kyra would have guessed that she'd do that first. Your sister isn't stupid, clearly. She also took the Compass.'

'The what?' said Arrosa.

'It's a small device created by Elbannon. They used it last year to find you on World Three. It can track down even miniscule amounts of Tempest upon any world. In other words, if it fell into the wrong hands, then the Sextant would no longer be hidden.' She frowned. 'I wish I'd thought about stealing it first.' She got to her feet. 'Come on; the honeymoon's over.'

Cael and Arrosa stood, and Sable smiled at them.

'You look good together,' she said. 'Whatever you have, hold on to it. And listen; there is going to be a lot of pressure on you both. With Kyra leaving, you are the hope that is keeping the Holdfasts together. I know it's not fair, but that's how people are feeling right now.'

'I understand,' said Cael. 'Before we head back, I want to thank you for letting us stay on your island. It's been the best few days of my life.'

'You're very welcome,' said Sable.

She slipped a hand into her pocket, the air shimmered, then they found themselves on the middle balcony of the Summer Palace on Colsbury. Cael glanced at everyone who had been waiting for them to return. His mother approached first, then she kissed him on the cheek, and then did the same to Arrosa.

'How was your trip?' she said.

'It was great, Mother,' Cael said. 'We didn't want it to end.'

'Thank you for bringing them back, Sable,' said Karalyn. 'Did you tell them about Kyra?'

'I did,' Sable said. 'Do you want me to take Cael back to Dragon Eyre and drop him off in Na Sun Ka?'

'After dinner,' said Karalyn. She glanced at Arrosa. 'What about you? If you like, I can take you to Plateau City, but seeing as there are only two days before the Empress gets here for Summer's Day, you could always stay here.'

'All of my examinations for first year are over,' said Arrosa. 'I might as well stay here.'

'How does it feel to be a Holdfast?' said Kelsey.

Arrosa smiled. 'Pretty good, though I'm worried about Kyra.'

'Kyra has made her choice,' said Karalyn. 'It saddens me that she would run away, and it angers me how she went about it, but we have to carry on with our lives.'

Cael looked around for Aila. 'Are you feeling better, Aunty?'

'I'm almost back to normal,' Aila said. 'To be honest, I'm not too concerned about what your sister did to me; I'm nearly eight hundred years old – I can take it; but she crossed a line when she hurt three of my children.'

'Do we have any idea where Kyra might have gone?' said Arrosa.

'She's not in the Holdings or the Plateau,' said Karalyn. 'Sable seems to believe that she will have fled to another world, and I'm starting to think that she might be right.'

'Anyway,' said Kelsey, 'while you were both away on your wee island, we organised a new apartment for you both in the palace. As a married couple, you couldn't carry on living in your old rooms. It's upstairs, next to my quarters, so your view over the lake and mountains will have improved. We've moved all of your stuff in.'

'Thanks, Aunty,' said Arrosa.

Kelsey laughed. 'It's going to take a while to get used to you calling me that.'

Arrosa glanced at Cael.

He rolled his eyes. 'Fine. I won't smoke in our new apartment.'

'My mother would be outraged to know how few smokers there are among the Holdfasts these days,' said Karalyn. 'There's only Lucius, Sable and you, Cael; and Shella, if we're counting everybody in Colsbury.'

'Don't worry, Mother,' said Cael. 'There's plenty of time for you to restart.'

Karalyn smiled, then she gestured towards the balcony door. 'Let's go inside before our dinner gets cold.'

Two hours later, Cael and Arrosa were back out on the middle balcony. Cael was dressed in his Number Three marine uniform, with his bags packed beside him, as they gazed up at the clear night sky, where the seven stars were shining.

They kissed.

'I wish I knew when you were coming back,' Arrosa said. 'I can wait, but it's the uncertainty that I don't like. It could be months – no, thirds; don't say it.'

'Adjutant Claudian is always going back and forth, and he'll be reporting to the Empress when she arrives on Colsbury in a few days. I'll write, and ask him to carry the letters to you. Good luck with your new job.'

'Please don't do anything crazy.'

'I won't.' He glanced at the balcony doors, where he knew Sable was waiting out of sight. 'I'm ready.'

Sable emerged from the shadows. Cael and Arrosa embraced, then Cael stood by his luggage.

'I love you,' Arrosa said.

'I'll be back as soon as I can,' said Cael.

Sable reached into her pocket, and the air shimmered.

Cael blinked as he gazed at the long, moon-drenched stretch of cliffs. 'This isn't the harbour of Sun Ta.'

'No, it's a few miles along the coast,' said Sable. 'I wanted to have a quick word with you on your own.'

'What about?'

'Corthie is based in Sun Ta, as you might know,' Sable said, 'and he and I have been talking about our strategy. Corthie is being allowed the freedom to operate against our enemies, and I have been implanting suggestions about what those operations should be into the mind of Claudian.'

Cael smiled and shook his head. 'Yet it's me who gets into trouble about breaking the rules.'

Sable shrugged. 'What can I say? I guess I've earned the right to do as I please. Would you perhaps be interested in assisting me and Corthie in our endeavours?'

'Do you really need to ask, Aunty? I'm pretty much up for anything.'

'I felt I had to ask, seeing as how you are now a married man. Is it possible that you might have promised Arrosa that you would stay out of danger?'

'I promised I wouldn't do anything too insane.'

'You have invisibility, yeah?'

'Aye.'

'You would be exceedingly useful to us; but, some of the things we're planning might qualify as insane.'

'Aunty, I am not going to turn down the opportunity to work with two old legends.'

'Hey, less of the *old*, you little bastard. All right; one of us will be in touch. Now, I assume you know that you're about to walk into the bollocking of your life?'

'Aye, I've been expecting as much.'

'Take it on the chin. Don't talk back or try to explain yourself; it'll only make it worse. You might be the golden boy among many of the rank and file marines, but the senior officers loathe you. Many of them feel that you've made them look like idiots.'

'One or two of them are idiots.'

'Perhaps, but whatever you do, don't say that part out loud in front of them. Remember that you're a Holdfast.'

'I never forget that, Aunty. I know who I am.'

'All right. Are you ready? I won't be sticking around for this; you'll be on your own for now.'

Cael nodded. 'Bring it on.'

The air shimmered again, and they appeared on the lamplit quayside of Sun Ta harbour. Sable winked at him, then she vanished. Cael picked up his bags and walked towards the marine headquarters. A captain was standing next to the marines on duty by the entrance, and he groaned and shook his head as soon as he saw Cael.

'Pyre fucking save us,' the captain muttered. 'The spoilt wee Holdfast prick has returned.'

Cael saluted. 'Second Lieutenant Holdfast reporting for duty, sir.'

'Get yer arse inside, boy,' said the captain; 'and get ready for a fucking spanking.'

Cael walked through the doors, as the marines on duty kept their mouths closed. He went into the main office, and half a dozen officers turned to stare at him.

'Somebody fetch Captain Doune,' said one. 'Tell him the liability is back; he'll know what I mean.'

A lieutenant ran off, passing Cael by the doorway.

'Well, well,' said a major. 'I hope you enjoyed your leave, Holdfast, and I hope your little wife was accommodating, because from now on it'll be you getting shafted up the arse.'

Cael forced his mouth to remain closed. They were trying to goad him into responding angrily, and he knew it.

Captain Doune strode through the door and walked up to Cael, halting a few inches in front of him.

Cael saluted again. 'Captain, sir.'

'What is this useless piece of shit doing back here?' Doune shouted, his face reddening. 'Didn't I tell command that I never wanted to see his ugly face again? What am I supposed to do with him, eh?'

'I'm sure you'll think of something, Captain,' said the major; 'something deeply unpleasant.'

'Oh, I have a few ideas, sir. If I'm not allowed to boot him out of the marines, then we'll have to find another use for him.' He moved his face closer to Cael. 'You entitled, spoilt disgrace to the good name of the service, Holdfast, what do you have to say for yourself?'

'I am under your command, sir,' said Cael.

'That you are, boy. Someone high up may love you so much that we all have to pretend that you didn't disobey a direct order, but we know differently. People like you are worse than the fucking enemy. At least we know they're trying to kill us – with you, we all have to watch that you don't stab us in the fucking back. You glory-hunting, selfish bastard. All you care about is impressing the Holdfasts. Tell me one thing – do you regret disobeying orders?'

Cael hesitated, unsure what answer would possibly satisfy Captain Doune. There was no correct answer, he realised.

'I will obey whatever order you give me, sir,' he said.

'That's not a fucking answer!' Doune screamed in his face. He pointed at a young lieutenant, who was watching from the corner of the room. 'Take this arsehole's luggage and drop it into the fucking harbour.'

The lieutenant blinked, then she hurried forward. 'Yes, sir.'

Cael handed her his bag, and she hurried off with it.

'For irresponsibly losing your kit, Holdfast,' Doune went on, 'you will be on latrine duty for the next third. Report to the sergeant in charge of the shithouse, and get out of my fucking sight.'

Cael saluted for a third time. 'Aye, sir.'

He walked out of the office, smothering a smile. The latrines? How predictable. Didn't they know that he had spent thirds shovelling horse-shit on the Holdfast estate?

Cael lit a cigarette, and leaned back against the brick wall, his uniform drenched in urine and spattered with faeces. He eyed the three other marines who were working next to him. None were officers, and all had been convicted of various misdemeanours, from getting drunk on duty to talking back to a sergeant. They all knew who Cael was without having to ask, and they seemed amused that a lieutenant had been brought down to their level. He passed out spare cigarettes to them, and they took them without a word.

He gazed up at the stars. That morning, he had been in bed next to Arrosa, and nothing the marine command could do to him would take that away.

'You must feel humiliated, eh?' said one of the marines. 'You're one of the richest bastards in the service, and yet you're up to your elbows in shite, unblocking drains down here with us.'

Cael shrugged. 'It's not so bad.'

'It's a fucking disgrace,' said another. 'The commanders are embarrassed, because the Holdfast lad here did a better job than them, and they cannae take it.'

'I got what was coming to me,' said Cael.

'That's one way to look at it. How long will you be doing this?'

'A third.'

The three marines laughed.

'Fucksake,' said one. 'I only got four days, and this is my last shift. I'll be rejoining my company in the morning.'

'Mind ye shower first, eh?'

'Shower? I'll be shaving all my hair off and burning my uniform.'

The duty sergeant appeared from round the corner of the toilet block. 'Back to work, you lot; break's over.'

Cael walked down to the quayside when his shift had finished. He lit a cigarette, and gazed over the dark water of the harbour basin. The moon and stars were reflecting off the smooth surface, and the ships of the fleet were tied up in silence. He had been assigned a bed in a room shared with three other lieutenants within a nearby barracks, but he was reluctant to return there.

A few marines were patrolling the dark harbour, and two of them approached Cael from the left. They eyed his stinking and filthy uniform, and halted a couple of yards away.

'The harbour area is closed at this hour, sir,' said one.

Cael nodded, but said nothing.

One of the marines shook his head. 'If you are looking for your luggage, sir, it was dropped into the basin by those steps.' He pointed to their left.

'Did you see it happen?' said Cael.

'No, sir. A junior lieutenant from headquarters asked us to let you know, if you happened to come down here this evening.'

'That was good of her.'

'The senior officers may hate you, sir, but not everyone feels the same way.'

'Will you turn a blind eye for a moment if I go down to take a look?'

The two marines glanced at each other.

'We never saw you down here, sir; but we'd be obliged if you were gone by the time we pass the quayside again.'

'Thanks.'

The marines walked on, continuing with their patrol, and Cael went to the thick, stone steps that led down to a lower level of wooden piers. He descended the stairs, and and peered into the dark, still waters. He glanced over his shoulder, then dived in. The cold water surrounded him, washing away some of the raw sewage from his hair and skin, then he kicked his feet out, and swam to the bottom of the basin. He reached out in the pitch darkness, until his hands touched the stonework of the quay, then he felt around by the base of the steps. Amid the cast away rubbish and debris, his fingers found the leather handles of his pack. He gripped it in one hand, and rose back to the surface. He hauled his water-logged luggage up onto the bottom step, then he pulled himself out of the basin. He was back on shift at the toilet block from midday, and he wondered if any of his clothes would have dried out by then. Even if they hadn't, a damp, clean uniform was better than nothing. He smiled as he ascended the steps. If the senior officers of the marines thought they could break him, then they clearly had no idea who they were dealing with.

An hour later, Cael was sitting on the sloping roof of the barracks building. He had showered and then gone up to the roof, spreading out his clothes along the grey tiles so that the morning sun would begin to dry them out. Cael was sitting next to them in his shorts, a cigarette in one hand, and a bottle of Holdings rum in the other. He would thank the young lieutenant as soon as he saw her again, but he would be careful not to flaunt the fact that he had recovered his luggage in front of Captain Doune. He swigged from the bottle, then he lay back on the roof and sent his vision out from his body.

He pushed his sight high above the sprawling city of Sun Ta. With a curfew in effect, the streets were quiet, excepting a few patrols and roadblocks that were being manned by soldiers from the Sanang divisions.

He wondered why he hadn't used his powers to soften Doune's attitude. With a few tweaks to the man's thoughts and memories, he could have easily avoided any punishment; but it had seemed like the wrong thing to do. It was ironic, he thought; he had always cajoled Cole about never using his powers, but the truth was that he rarely used his full potential himself. It was a reaction to his mother's generation – they had continually employed their powers to get whatever they had wanted. People like Keir and Sable had never been shy about going into people's heads to manipulate them. Cael had also heard the stories about what his mother had done as a child; he, too, had abused his powers when he had been younger, but he was trying to be different, using his powers only when he had no other choice. Did the majority of marines even know that he could read their deepest thoughts, fears and desires? Not only that, but that he could alter their perceptions and memories? He could have made Doune forgive him in an instant, but he hadn't; instead choosing to accept whatever the captain had decided to do.

He aimed his vision towards the army headquarters in the Temple of Ulna. He entered through an open skylight, and went to the part of the building where he knew his Uncle Corthie was stationed. He found him sitting in a shallow alcove with Sable, the two of them talking together in low voices. Both had minds that were protected from ordinary vision mages, but Cael could easily read either of them, if he chose to do so. He was tempted for a moment; it would be so simple to enter Corthie's head to see what they were talking about, but he resisted. Both Sable and Corthie had been manipulated by the dream mage Daimon – Corthie had tried to attack his wife, and Sable had been forced to murder Belinda.

Cael wanted to be better than that. He was better than that. Others might mock, but Cael had no desire to take advantage of his powers to get his own way. He would do it for the Empire; to defeat their enemies, but not for personal gain. He wasn't Sable; he wasn't Keir, and he certainly wasn't Daimon. Others might not understand, but Cael was starting to realise that he didn't care what others thought of him.

He was Cael Holdfast, and he would go his own way.

CHAPTER 7
THE HUNGER RETURNS

Sun Ta, Na Sun Ka, Western Rim – 19th Tradinch 5266 (18th Gylean Year 17)

Corthie staggered out of his small bedchamber, a headache pounding behind his temples from the wine he had been drinking with Sable the previous night. Sunlight was flooding down from the skylight in the main hall, where Sergeant Nestorian was crouching by a large collection of unopened crates, reading some paperwork. Drechtalang and Dominie were watching the Banner veteran from a table next to the kitchen door, and both were drinking from mugs.

'Is that coffee?' said Corthie.

'Aye, sir,' said Dominie. 'Do you want some?'

Corthie nodded and took a seat along from them. Dominie filled a mug from a steel coffee pot and slid it across the table towards him. Corthie took it, then he glanced at Nestorian.

'What's he doing?'

'The crates arrived half an hour ago, sir,' said Dominie. 'Pyre knows what's in them.'

'They have been sent to us from the Star Continent, sir,' said Nestorian. 'New munitions.'

'Open them up,' said Corthie.

Nestorian picked up a crowbar and prised off a lid. He rummaged around amid the straw, and pulled out an orange-sized metal sphere.

'These are the bombs that go into a Forty-Eighter,' he said. 'The crate is full of them.'

'What's the point of sending us them?' muttered Drechtalang. 'We haven't got a Forty-Eighter.'

Nestorian held up the folded sheet of paper he had been reading. 'It says here that we don't need a Forty-Eighter. If we twist the top half, the device will detonate in around ten seconds.' He smiled. 'I guess we're supposed to throw them.' He glanced at Dominie. 'Like this.'

He tossed the sphere at the Kellach corporal, who caught it in her left hand.

'Are ye trying to give me a heart attack, ya eejit?' she cried.

Nestorian laughed. 'Did you see me twist it first?'

'What else have we got?' said Corthie.

The Banner sergeant prised open another couple of crates, then he knelt and began laying out two long metal pipes. They had separate flat, square bases and other attachments, and Nestorian laid them out on the floor. From another crate he withdrew several cylindrical devices, which were pointed at one end.

'Mortars,' he said, his eyes shining with a dark excitement. 'We rig up the pipes at an angle, drop in the explosive devices, and they come shooting out the end. I worked on these in Plateau City. Shall we set one up and have a go?'

'Hoi,' said a voice. 'You will *have a go* when I tell you it's safe to do so.'

Corthie and the others turned, and saw a woman enter the hall. She was dressed in civilian clothing, and Corthie smiled and got to his feet.

'Rosie?' he said.

'Hi, Corthie,' she said.

'What are you doing here?'

'I work for Ravi now,' she said, as she walked over to the pile of crates. 'I was giving lectures about salve in the university for a while, but I've been moved to Ravi's department, helping him to develop new explosive devices. It's more my area of expertise. Did you know that I once constructed a ballista...'

'...on the roof of your parent's house. Aye, I know.' He embraced her, and she laughed.

'This is Rosie Jackdaw,' he said to the others.

She glanced at Nestorian. 'How are you doing, sergeant?'

'I'm fine, ma'am,' he said. 'Did you organise these new munitions for us?'

'I certainly did. We were getting complaints about Ravi's new fuse wires, so we've come up with a brand new type of detonator.'

'Do you know her?' said Corthie.

'Of course, sir,' said Nestorian. 'I was working for Professor Ravi when Miss Jackdaw joined the team.'

'We invented a spring-loaded timer,' said Rosie; 'it's connected to a little hammer that sets off the explosion. Anyway, I'm here to give you all a lesson on how to use the new devices before you take them into combat; and then, after that, Adjutant Claudian is going to take me to Ulna so I can visit my sister. Gather your team, Corthie, and we'll get started.'

Corthie took a lungful of sea air as he entered the harbour district. Three hours had passed since Rosie had arrived to instruct them on the new devices, and Corthie's head was spinning with information. In some ways, using explosives in warfare seemed unfair to him, as it removed any aspect of martial skill, and allowed anyone with a bit of knowledge to blow the enemy to pieces. It wasn't the way that Corthie liked to fight. He imagined what life would have been like in the City, if the Blades had possessed such weapons – they could have obliterated thousands of greenhides from the safety of the Great Walls, without any need for the Rats and Wolf Packs to risk themselves. Things were changing, too fast for Corthie – salve, Tempest, Quadrants, and now explosives. Would there be any need for battle-vision if all someone had to do was throw a bomb?

Corthie reached the headquarters of the Imperial Marines and entered through the main doors, passing two marines who saluted him. He walked into a large office, where several staff officers and clerks were working, and went over to a desk.

'Hello,' he said. 'I'm looking for Lieutenant Holdfast.'

The young lieutenant glanced up from her work and her eyes widened.

'Do you know where I can find him?' Corthie went on.

A Kellach captain approached. 'Second Lieutenant Holdfast is currently performing punishment duties, sir,' he said.

Corthie smiled. 'Not any more. I'm requisitioning him.'

'I'm sorry, sir,' said the captain. 'With all due respect, you don't have the authority to requisition a marine officer. I suggest you...'

'Don't make me walk all the way back to the Temple of Ulna to fetch Claudian,' said Corthie. 'I want Lieutenant Holdfast, and I want him now. I need him for an operation. Where is he?'

A few senior officers walked over.

'What seems to be the problem?' said a marine major.

'There's no problem,' said Corthie. 'Just point me in the direction of Cael Holdfast. I have permission from Adjutant Claudian to requisition any member of the armed forces that I need – and I need Cael.'

The officers glanced at each other.

'Are you aware, sir, that Lieutenant Holdfast is being disciplined?'

'Aye? What did he do?'

'He, uh... lost his kit.'

'So?'

'He is in breach of regulations.'

'I couldn't give a rat's arse. Where is he?'

The major chewed his lip for a moment, then he exhaled. 'Try the rear of the latrine block, sir.'

Corthie laughed. 'Up to his neck in shit, is he? Well, he's now a member of my team. Write that down somewhere, in case you forget.'

Corthie turned and walked from the room. He saw the two marines standing by the main doors.

'Where's the latrine block?' he said to them.

One of the marines pointed. 'Take a right and then a left by the barracks, sir.'

'Thanks.'

Corthie walked back out into the sunshine, and turned right. He left the vicinity of the long quayside, and found the latrine block after a few minutes. He went round the back, and saw that the drains along the rear of the building had been opened, and a handful of marines were working amid the stench to free a blockage. He eyed them for a moment, then saw Cael down in the drainage pit, waist-deep in sewage.

'Get up here, nephew,' he said.

The marines looked up out of the pit at him, and Cael frowned.

'Get a move on before I throw up my breakfast,' Corthie went on.

Cael glanced at his fellow workers, then he shrugged and clambered up onto the road.

'Uncle? I mean, sir?' he said, saluting.

'I'm getting you out of here,' said Corthie. 'Sable and I have an operation, and we need you on it.'

Cael frowned. 'But I'm supposed to be here for the rest of the month, sir, and this is only my second shift.'

Corthie picked up a hose that was lying by the wall of the latrine block. 'I don't care,' he said, turning the tap on.

Water sprayed out, soaking Cael and cleaning the filth from his body and uniform. Corthie aimed the nozzle at his nephew's head, and the water soaked his face and hair. He turned the hose off and dropped it to the cobbles.

'That's a bit better,' he said.

'No disrespect, Uncle,' said Cael, 'but how will it look if you come along and get me out of punishment duties? Everyone will assume it's because we're family.'

'It's got nothing to do with that,' said Corthie. 'We need your abilities.'

Cael looked in a pocket, then he withdrew a sodden packet of cigarettes. His frown deepened.

'Do I have to order you, Lieutenant?' said Corthie.

'Can you order me, sir?' said Cael. 'You're army, and I'm not.'

'You're a stubborn little bastard is what you are. I offer you the chance to get out of a literal shithole, and you quote regulations at me? Sable said you were up for it.'

'She also told me to take my punishment without complaining about it.'

The nearby sergeant shook his head. 'For fuck's sake, lad, take the opportunity while you can, eh?'

'But the drain is still blocked, sergeant.'

'Fine,' said Corthie. 'Second Lieutenant Holdfast, I am ordering you to come with me, by the authority of Adjutant Claudian. If you wish to make a complaint, file it with the relevant office. Now, quit being a pig-headed numpty and follow me.'

Cael glanced at the marines in the pit. 'Sorry, guys.'

'I'm sure we'll manage without you, Holdfast,' said one.

Corthie set off, Cael trudging along next to him.

'So, you lost your kit?' said Corthie.

'My superior officer had someone drop it into the harbour.'

'Aye?'

'Aye. They couldn't openly admit that I'd disobeyed orders, but they needed some excuse to discipline me. Can we stop by the barracks first?'

'Why? I thought you had no kit.'

'I fished it out of the harbour last night.'

Corthie laughed.

'I thought you'd be angrier,' said Cael.

'Why? You're annoying, but you're not that annoying.'

'I was talking about what my sister did.'

Corthie's face fell. 'Oh that. You're right, Cael; I am furious with Kyra. How dare she touch my children? I moved them to Colsbury so they'd be safe, and then this happens? Did you know she could move around without a Quadrant?'

'No, and I'm not going to excuse her behaviour. I will always love her, but she went too far.'

'Do you know where she might have gone?'

'I haven't the slightest idea, Uncle. I was with Arrosa when it happened.'

They reached the entrance to the barracks.

'Give me five minutes,' said Cael, 'and then I'll be ready.'

Corthie's team was sitting by their table in the hall listening to Sable speak when he and Cael entered. Sable's gaze went to them, and she smiled.

'There he is,' she said, 'our disgraced marine.'

'He didn't want to come,' said Corthie. 'I had to give him a direct order.'

'And he obeyed it?' said Sable. 'Unusual for him. Take a seat, Cael.' She raised an eyebrow. 'Why is his uniform wet?'

'I had to hose him down,' said Corthie. 'The marines had him unblocking sewage drains.'

Sable laughed. 'I thought they might think of something like that.'

'It was no worse than being in the Hold Fast stables, Aunty,' Cael said, as he sat down between Drechtalang and Wyle of Hold Liant.

'Who is this boy?' said the Sanang hedgewitch.

'He is Second Lieutenant Cael Holdfast,' said Sable, 'and he's already done more to hurt the enemy than you could dream of.'

'Yet another fucking Holdfast,' Drechtalang muttered. 'Does he have battle-vision?'

'No,' said Sable. 'He has... other skills. Give him a taste, nephew.'

Cael nodded, then he, along with Wyle, Dominie and Jaeanna disappeared.

'Holy fuck!' Drechtalang cried, getting up out of his chair. 'Where did they go?'

They re-appeared.

'We didn't go anywhere,' said Cael.

Corthie frowned. 'Why did that work on me?'

'I can pierce your protections, Uncle,' said Cael; 'just as my mother can.'

'The boy can turn invisible?' said Drechtalang. 'What a power to possess. The things I would do...' He leered at Cael. 'How many times have you used it to spy on the girls in the marines' shower block, eh? You dirty little bastard.'

Cael narrowed his eyes.

'Ignore him, nephew,' said Sable.

'I didn't feel any different,' said Dominie. 'Was I really invisible?'

'No,' said Cael. 'All I do is persuade the eyes of others not to see you.'

'And that's not all he can do,' said Sable.

'It doesn't work on the Bullan,' Cael went on. 'You should know that. I don't understand their language.'

'No one but the Bullan knows their language,' Sable said. 'However, there will be no Bullan where we're going this evening.'

'Where are we going, ma'am?' said Wyle.

Sable smiled. 'To get our dragon carriers back.'

Another four hours had gone by before the team was equipped and ready to depart. Jaeanna had been told to stay behind, as there would be no opportunity to use her stone powers in the middle of the Inner Ocean, but the rest of them had been kitted out with new Tempest armour, while Nestorian was in charge of a mortar and a collection of explosive devices. Sable and Corthie assembled them in the centre of the hall, then Sable dipped a hand into a pocket.

'The last time I checked,' she said, 'both carriers were deserted; but that situation could change at any moment. Remember, we want Allura to turn up. If she does, then she becomes our primary target. Drop everything else and attack her – Corthie, you will lead the attack if she appears. Are you all ready?'

She gripped a Fated Blade in her right hand, and lowered her left into a pocket. The air shimmered, and they found themselves on a wide deck. Corthie gazed around, and saw a second enormous ship tied up next to the one they had appeared on.

Sable glanced at Cael.

'There's nothing,' he said. 'I detect no self-healing powers.'

Sable nodded. 'We are on the *Horned God*,' she said. 'Of the two dragon carriers, this one is in better shape, and if we can only get one underway, it'll be this one. The other carrier is the *Wondrous Light*. I warn you now, the below decks are full of the corpses of Irlanian sailors from Athumia, who died when the gods made their attack. Stay up on the flight decks, and keep watch, while I start to ferry the new crew over from the Eastern Rim. If Allura comes, it'll be by Quadrant, so keep your eyes open.'

Sable vanished.

'I have a lot of bad memories of these ships,' said Cael, as he gazed along the flight deck; 'but I'm glad we're reclaiming them. It's about time we went on the offensive.'

Corthie glanced at Nestorian. 'Set up your devices. If Allura comes, we won't have much warning.'

'Yes, sir,' said the Banner sergeant.

'Wyle,' Corthie went on. 'Use your line vision to keep watch from one of the masts. Cael, stay with me.'

Corthie walked up the middle of the flight deck of the *Horned God*. Dark patches were staining the wooden beams, but no bodies were visible. He looked over to his left, and saw the sun reach the horizon. He turned to ask Cael something, but the air shimmered before the words were out. Sable re-appeared, bringing forty sailors with her, many of whom were carrying bags of tools.

'Get to work,' she said. 'Masts, sails and anchors first; then check the rudder and steerage. I want this ship on the move as soon as possible. It doesn't have to be perfect; it just needs to sail.'

She vanished again, and the sailors got to work, fanning out over the deck.

'Do you think Allura will come?' Corthie said.

'Maybe,' said Cael. 'How often does she bother to check these ships?

She probably knows that we want them back, but she can't always be looking in this direction.' He glanced at the darkening sky. 'The night will shield us a little.'

'That's why Sable chose this time of day,' Corthie said. 'How's married life?'

'Yesterday morning, I was still enjoying it,' said Cael. 'I miss her.'

'Aye, well, I miss my family, too; but how can I sit at home when those bastards are trying to kill us? If I get my hands on Edgar, I'll rip his damn head off.'

'Edgar didn't authorise the attack on your family, Uncle.'

'Does it matter? It was Edgar who released Ward, Allura and the others from captivity in the Palace of the Almighty. He has to take responsibility for that.' He glanced at his nephew. 'You know, Cael, I missed you last winter when you didn't come down to Kell. I used to enjoy having you stay with us every year, even though I knew you hated the weather, and being moved around each season. When you first came, you were only sixteen, and look at you now – you've changed so much.'

'In a good way, I hope?'

'Well, you've ditched the whining. Do you know who you remind me of now? – and don't take this the wrong way, but I see my mother in you. You're a stubborn little bastard who doesn't give a shit what anyone else thinks; and you're a proper Holdfast. Your grandmother would be proud.'

Cael gazed out towards the dark ocean. 'She gave her life to save mine,' he said. 'Bastion was going to kill me, and she stopped him. She killed him. In all the chaos that happened in Clackenbaird that day, I think that sometimes gets forgotten, but I will never forget it. I want to be worthy of her sacrifice; I want it to mean something.'

Corthie put a hand on his shoulder. 'Just keep doing what you're doing, Cael; you'll get there.'

. . .

By the time the sky was beginning to lighten again, Sable had transported over five hundred sailors and several tons of supplies to the *Horned God.* Boatswains and carpenters had declared the *Wondrous Light* to be in need of repairs too serious to be carried out at sea, so Sable had ordered them to concentrate their efforts on the other carrier, and work had gone on all night. Sable had also brought food, coffee and cigarettes for the sailors and the members of Corthie's small team, and Cael had stayed awake, scanning the flight decks for any sign of Edgar's gods. Corthie had prowled the deck with his Clawhammer, while the rest of the team had taken it in turns to catch small periods of rest.

'Happy Summer's Day,' said Sable, as she handed Corthie another mug of hot coffee.

'Is that today's date?' he said. 'I'd lost track.'

Someone rang a bell as the sun appeared over the eastern horizon, and Sable turned towards the crew.

'Clear the flight deck!' she shouted. 'Dawn is the most likely time for an attack. Get below!'

Cael joined Corthie and Sable as they watched the workers scramble for the hatches. Sable hovered her hand over the hilt of her black-bladed sword, her eyes tight.

Corthie frowned. 'Why is dawn the most likely...?'

The air shimmered by the bow of the great ship, and four enormous ironhides appeared, accompanied by a woman in grey robes.

'What the fuck are those things?' Sable cried, drawing her sword. 'Nestorian! Bring them down!'

Corthie pushed Cael behind him as the four huge ironhides bounded across the deck. Most of the sailors had disappeared down one of the several hatches, but a few stragglers were ripped to shreds by the long claws of the beasts. One ironhide tried to break into a hatch, but the opening was too narrow. It began ripping the wooden beams apart as Corthie and Sable raced forward.

Something shot over Corthie's head, then it impacted into an ironhide with a tremendous explosion, tearing its right limbs off. The ironhide collapsed to the deck, still alive as it writhed around. The robed figure raised her hand at the three Holdfasts, but her powers were useless against them. Sable reached an ironhide, and she rolled across the deck as claws passed inches over her head. Corthie was right behind her. He leapt through the air, the Clawhammer held aloft in both hands, and then he brought the weapon down onto the creature's head, gouging through its skull and ripping its brain to pieces.

Corthie glanced over his shoulder, but Cael had gone, then another ironhide was upon him. It lunged out with its claws, but the Tempest armour deflected them. Corthie fell backwards, and Sable jumped over him, her Fated Blade carving its way through the ironhide's chest. She moved on to the next beast, as the ironhide she had injured healed itself.

'They can self-heal, Sable!' Corthie cried.

Sable glanced back, as the ironhide swung for her head. Cael re-appeared at that moment, an orange-sized metal sphere in his hand as he dodged an out-stretched claw. He rammed the sphere into the iron-hide's open mouth as the beast's limb changed direction, swinging for him rather than Sable. The extended forelimb batted Cael away, sending him flying across the deck, and he landed next to the lift at the rear of the flight deck. Sable backed away as the ironhide came for her, then its head exploded. Corthie reached the last upright ironhide, Drechtalang and Wyle by his side as they rushed forward. They fended off the ironhide's wild lunges, then Wyle was sliced in half by a long talon. Drechtalang swung his axe, but it rebounded off the ironhide's skin. Corthie charged ahead. The three talons of the Clawhammer became lodged in the ironhide's chest, and Corthie pulled it upwards, ripping through the beast's head.

Corthie's battle-vision took in everything happening on the deck. Three ironhides were dead, while the fourth was writhing, its right limbs obliterated by Nestorian's mortar attack. Over by the deck of the *Wondrous Light*, Sable was charging at the woman in grey robes; while Cael was lying motionless by the rear of the *Horned God's* flight deck. On the *Wondrous Light*, Sable swung her Fated Blade, but it passed through nothing but air as the women in grey robes vanished.

Corthie walked up to the writhing and screaming ironhide, then he removed its head with a blow from the Clawhammer, and the flight deck fell into silence.

'Remain on alert!' Sable cried. 'Allura could return at any moment.'

Corthie grabbed Drechtalang by the shoulder, and pulled him over to where Cael was lying.

'Heal him,' Corthie said.

Drechtalang knelt by Cael's side. 'Did you see what the young Holdfast lad did, boss?'

'I saw it. Heal him.'

The hedgewitch placed a hand onto Cael's forehead. 'Seventeen broken bones; internal bleeding... There we go.'

Cael opened his eyes and coughed up blood.

'It's a pity I can't do the same for Wyle and Dominie, eh, boss?' Drechtalang said.

'Dominie?' said Corthie.

'The god's death powers got her,' said Cael, as he sat up. 'She was standing right behind us.'

Corthie turned, and saw Nestorian crouching by the withered body of the Kellach marine.

'Shit,' said Corthie. 'We lost two.'

'But we killed four of those... monsters,' said Drechtalang. 'What the fuck were they, boss?'

'Good question,' said Sable, as she approached. She helped Cael get to his feet and turned to face Corthie. 'Well?'

'They're called ironhides,' said Corthie. 'I didn't know there were any on Dragon Eyre.'

'I couldn't get into their heads like I can with greenhides,' said Cael; 'and my invisibility didn't work on them.' He tilted his head to Drechtalang. 'Thanks for healing me.'

'No problem, lad,' said the hedgewitch. 'I saw what you did. You threw a fucking bomb down one of those thing's throats. I take back what I said about you – you're all right.'

'We will not be mentioning what Cael did to his young wife; understood?' said Sable. She shook her head. 'My two idiot nephews. One almost got himself killed, and the other forgot to mention the existence of ironhides. Blind, self-healing greenhides that move as though they have battle-vision?'

'They do have battle-vision,' said Corthie. 'Edgar released them from the Palace of the Almighty, and then he took them with him when he fled. But, how was I to know that they were here?'

'Allura must have brought them for the planned Ectus raid,' said Sable. 'How many are there?'

'Two dozen. I think.'

'Four fewer now, eh?' said Drechtalang. 'That was fucking amazing. I haven't had that much fun in years. Did you see the way my war axe just bounced off the bastard's thick hide? I'll be needing one of those Tempest weapons for the next operation.'

Nestorian walked over, his eyes dark.

'Good work, sergeant,' said Sable. 'Next time, though, aim the mortar at the god. We let her get away.'

'Dominie's dead,' the Banner soldier said, 'and Wyle was cut in two. Neither corporal stood a chance.'

'We need to tighten up,' said Sable, 'and we'll need to replace our casualties. Nestorian, get back to your post and reload the mortar. Cael, resume your scan of the ocean, and if the ironhides return, stay back – you have no battle-vision.'

Cael frowned. 'If I hadn't killed that ironhide, it would have killed you, Aunty.'

'Then learn how to fucking throw,' said Sable. 'You don't need to be standing next to the enemy in order to blow its brains out. Corthie – we will be having words about this later – for now, call up the sailors from below decks; we have work to do.'

Sable walked away, her sword still grasped in her right hand.

Cael lit a cigarette and passed one to Drechtalang.

The Sanang man took it and eyed Corthie. 'She's pissed off at you, boss,' he said. 'Those things took her by surprise, and I don't think she likes surprises.'

'I had no idea any of them were on Dragon Eyre,' Corthie said, 'but she's right. I should have told her about them; and now we've lost two of our team. Didn't I warn you all? Didn't I try to tell you what happens to folk who join any team of mine? I'll understand if you want to leave when we get back to Sun Ta.'

Drechtalang laughed. 'Are you joking, boss? I was the first to complain about being assigned to you, but now I've seen what it's like, there's no fucking way I'm leaving.'

'You're not getting rid of me, either,' said Cael. 'I'll replace Corporal Wyle, and we'll find someone else to replace Corporal Dominie.'

Drechtalang slapped Cael on the back. 'That's the spirit, lad. Fuck me; we are going to cause some mayhem together.'

Corthie remained where he was as Cael and Drechtalang walked away. His gaze went to the ripped-apart bodies of Wyle, the four iron-hides, and the unfortunate sailors who had still been on deck when the attack had begun; then he looked over at the withered corpse of Dominie.

He should be feeling guilty, he realised. Two of his team had been killed on their first operation together, and yet the words of the Sanang hedgewitch were ringing through his mind. As soon as the battle had started, and as soon as Corthie had summoned his battle-vision, he had felt the old joy of killing return. Lost in the haze of his powers, he had felt more alive than he had done for years, as though the struggles by the Palace of the Almighty had been nothing but practice for the real event.

The monster within him had returned, and it was hungry.

CHAPTER 8
BACK AT THE HELM

Plateau City, The Plateau – Summer's Day 545

'I really enjoyed it,' said Van. 'I wasn't sure I would, but you're a good writer.'

'Thanks,' said Kelsey. 'I don't know when I'll get around to finishing the last few chapters, but I'll pass them over to you if you want to read them.'

'I definitely want to read them,' he said. 'How is this year's gala?'

'It's going according to plan, so far. The play went down well; at least, the Empress found it highly amusing.' She glanced down at their two children, who were standing close by. 'I appreciate you not kicking up a fuss about me keeping Calpurnia and Caelius for an extra day so they could go.'

'It's no problem,' said Van.

Kelsey glanced at the entrance to the Ministry of the Plateau. At any moment, Marshal Bedig would emerge into the afternoon sunshine to open up the portal to the City.

'So,' Van went on, 'how have you been?'

Kelsey shrugged. 'Fine.'

'It would be good to catch up with you at some point.'

'Would it?'

'It would. Perhaps we could sit down and talk when I get back from the City with the children.'

'Why?'

Van looked away. 'Well, you know, it's been, what – nine months since our divorce? And I was... well...'

'Do you want to change our schedule again? To be honest, Van, I'm quite happy with the way things are at the moment – five days with me, two days with you. The children have settled into it.'

'No, it wasn't that. Shit, Kelsey, I'm just going to say it – I miss you. I miss talking to you; I miss being with you, and I wonder if there is any way, seeing that you're not as busy as you used to be, that maybe we could...'

Kelsey's eyes widened. 'Whoa; stop right there, Van. Did you bang your head? Have you forgotten the raging arguments?'

'But the reasons we split up no longer apply. When you were Herald, you had no time for anything, but now you do. And the children have asked me a dozen times if we would get back together; shouldn't we at least consider doing it for them?'

Kelsey noticed Calpurnia's ears prick up at Van's words, and she smothered her immediate reaction. She lowered her gaze.

'Naxor said that you had been seeing other women.'

'Did he?' said Van. 'That blasted liar. It's not true, Kelsey; I swear. I haven't seen anyone since we broke up.' He paused. 'Have you?'

'Of course not. I have no desire to get involved with anyone right now, and that includes you, Van. Do you think it would be easy for me to forgive what you did? You basically abducted the children and wouldn't let me see them.'

'I'm sorry about that,' he said. 'At the time, I felt I had no other choice.'

'You had a choice, Van.'

'I made a mistake.'

'Aye. Look; as far as I'm concerned, it's over between us.'

'So you're not even willing to give it another try?'

'It was you who forced the damn divorce papers down my throat; do you think that's what I wanted? You dumped me. But, I think I know why you did it. You accused me of caring more about my job than you; and you were right.'

'But you don't have that job any more.'

Kelsey eyed the entrance to the ministry again. 'We've been doing well at being civil recently,' she said, 'and I want that to continue; but I don't think it would be a good idea to throw ourselves back into a relationship that made both of us miserable.'

Van opened his mouth to say something, then Bedig emerged from the Ministry of the Plateau, flanked by soldiers and officials. Van closed his mouth again.

'Let's talk when you get back with the children,' Kelsey said.

Van broke off eye contact. He nodded, then he took the hands of Calpurnia and Caelius and walked over to where the portal would open. Calpurnia glanced over her shoulder and waved at her mother, and Kelsey blew her a kiss.

Kelsey waited until the portal to the City had been opened, then she watched Van lead the children through to Ooste. Her shoulders sagged as soon as they were out of sight, and she turned and walked away.

What had Van been thinking? Did he really believe that, after all he had done, Kelsey would be willing to get back together with him? She knew that some of the blame for their divorce was hers; she had neglected her marriage, and he had a right to be angry about that, but did he think he was still in love with her? She considered what it would feel like to be intimate with him again – would it be so bad? It was true that she had been lonely in Colsbury, despite the fact that Karalyn's family was there, along with her own children for most of the time; but loneliness did not equal a desire to be back in Van's arms. Besides, he believed that she had no job, except for writing her book and looking after Calpurnia and Caelius for five days out of seven – would he have made his offer if he had known she had secretly agreed to become Herald again?

She gave a wry smile. She knew the answer to that.

She moved into the shadows of the ministry building, took her

Quadrant out of her shoulder bag, and activated it. In an instant, she was standing on the middle balcony of the Summer Palace on Colsbury. Cardova glanced up from a table, where he was sitting with Carden and Caitlyn.

'How did it go?' he said. 'Did the children get away on time?'

'Aye,' she said. 'Lucius, why aren't you at the dinner banquet?'

'Caitlyn was crying like a wounded greenhide, so I brought her and her brother up here to give everyone some peace. Of course, she quietened down as soon as I did that.'

Kelsey sat down next to them.

'Could you do me a favour?' he said.

'Sure.'

'A meeting of the Imperial Court is due to start soon; could you look after these two for me?'

Kelsey chewed her lip for a moment. 'Sorry. I can't.'

'Fair enough; I thought you might be too busy with Summer's Day. You've done another great job of organising everything this year. It's no problem; I'll see if Aila can take them.'

'What about Karalyn?'

'She's still searching for Kyra.'

'With no luck, I assume?'

'None so far. Are you going down to the gardens to get something to eat?'

'I have some work I need to take care of first,' she said. She got to her feet. 'I guess I'll see you soon.'

Kelsey walked off the balcony and ascended a flight of stairs to her quarters. She went inside and walked to her study. Her desk was covered in heaps of documents that Naxor had delivered for her a few days before, and she sat down, her eyes roaming over a few of the pages. Her nerves jangled at the prospect of facing one of the most important moments of her life. What if the Empress decided to go back on her word; or what if she refused to accept the policies that Kelsey had chosen? When she had previously served as Herald, she had always carried out the wishes of the Empress, but, if Thorn had meant what she had said, then she would soon have almost unfettered authority over the Empire.

She picked up the sheet of paper upon which she had written down her immediate decisions. Others in the Imperial Court would no doubt object to some of her counter-intuitive suggestions; and Kelsey had to face the fact that she might be wrong about the assumptions that had underpinned her ideas for the future of the Empire. It was a colossal gamble, and she knew it.

The minutes dragged by as she waited, then she jumped as her front door was knocked. She folded the sheet of paper in two and walked to the entrance of her apartment. She opened the door and a courtier bowed.

'Her Majesty requests your presence in the teal reception room, my lady.'

'Thank you,' said Kelsey.

She stepped out into the hallway, closed her door, and followed the courtier through the palace. The teal reception room was just large enough to fit the entire Imperial Court. Marshal Bedig was remaining in Plateau City for the summer, but the other members would all be present.

The courtier knocked upon the door and opened it.

'Holder Fast is here as requested, Your Majesty,' he said, bowing; then he stood aside to allow Kelsey to enter.

Kelsey walked into the room. Thorn was seated upon a throne at the head of the table. On the right of the Empress were Brogan, Cardova, Claudian and Caelius; while, on her left were Shella, Naxor, Slaeon and Janis Holdsmith. With an effort, Kelsey kept her features expressionless as they all turned to look in her direction.

'Thank you for arranging a most delightful day, Kelsey,' said Thorn. 'Your organisational skills are second to none.'

Kelsey tilted her head. 'You are very welcome, Your Majesty, and I'm glad you have been enjoying your birthday.'

Naxor smirked, but kept his mouth shut.

'I am aware that it is unusual to hold a full meeting of the Imperial Court on Summer's Day,' Thorn went on, 'but I have an important announcement to make. As of this moment, Brogan ae Bridget is no longer my Herald.' She glanced at the Kellach woman. 'I wish to thank you for your service, and I would like to offer you a position as Imperial Legate. If you accept, you will remain as a full member of my court; if you decline, then I would ask that you leave this chamber.'

Brogan stared at the Empress, her mouth open slightly, as the others in the room gasped.

'Holder Fast is once again my Herald,' Thorn went on; 'and I am granting her full authority over all areas of policy. Everyone else in the Imperial Court now reports directly to her. Well, Brogan, what is your decision?'

'Have I… have I offended you, Your Majesty?' Brogan said.

'You have not,' said Thorn. 'I erred by giving you duties beyond your capabilities; and the fault is mine. However, I still value your contribution, and, as legate, you would be performing a vital role in the governance of the Empire.'

'I would be an imperial messenger, with Kelsey as my boss.'

'The Empire is on the edge of outright bankruptcy,' said Thorn, 'and this emergency calls for radical action.'

'But, Your Majesty,' said Naxor, 'didn't Holder Fast prove that she valued spending time with her children over her duty to the Empire?'

'I was wrong to give her an ultimatum,' said Thorn, 'when a compromise was so easily in reach. My decision has been made, but before my new Herald gives us her advice, I need to know if Brogan accepts my offer.'

Brogan got to her feet. 'I do not, Your Majesty,' she said. 'This feels like a coup. I have served the Empire for over a decade, and this is nothing less than a shameful humiliation.'

'I am sorry you feel that way, but if that is your decision, then please leave this chamber.'

'Shouldn't the Imperial Court hold a vote on this, Your Majesty?' said Naxor.

'A vote will not be necessary,' said Thorn. 'My will is the will of the Empire. If anyone disagrees, they can leave with Brogan.'

Brogan glanced at the faces of the others, but none of them moved from their seats. She cast a look of disdain and contempt towards Kelsey, then she strode from the room, shutting the door behind her.

'Take your place at the table, Herald,' said Thorn.

Kelsey tilted her head, then she sat down in the seat where Brogan had been, at the right hand of the Empress.

'Present your proposals,' said Thorn.

'Aye, Your Majesty,' said Kelsey. She glanced at the folded sheet of paper in her left hand, but knew she didn't need it. She had memorised every word.

'My first act will be to repeal four-fifths of the recent tax rises,' she said. 'All duties on trade, imports, exports, and the sales tax are to be abolished.'

'This is economic illiteracy,' cried Naxor. 'We are running out of money, and you want to reduce our source of income?'

'The taxes are doing nothing but stoking discontent and stifling trade,' Kelsey said. 'They have been counter-productive. The black market is booming, and tax avoidance is higher than ever. The strike was caused by anger at these taxes, and this measure will reduce tension in the Empire. It will show the people that we are on their side. In the long term, this will increase revenue.'

Naxor snorted.

'Be patient, Lord Chamberlain,' snapped Slaeon. 'Some of us wish to hear what else the Herald has to say.'

'Thank you, Lord Treasurer,' said Kelsey. 'The problem with the Empire isn't wealth. The Empire is exceedingly wealthy; yet the government is poor. Raising taxes by imperial decree is not the solution. Instead, we need two things if we wish to avoid bankruptcy – an imperial bank, and the consent of the governed. For the first, I propose legislation that will transform the Imperial Mint into a bank capable of lending and issuing debt; and for the second, I propose that we establish a representative body of citizens, freely elected from all corners of the Empire. This body will assume responsibility for all domestic policy, leaving only the new bank, defence, and foreign affairs under the control of the Imperial Court.'

'Now we have it!' cried Naxor. 'Kyra would be so proud of her aunt, as she wants to turn the Empire into a damn democracy. She wants a squabbling band of ignorant know-nothings to dictate how the Empire should be run. I have heard enough. If this is accepted, it will be the end of everything we have strived to achieve.'

Kelsey smiled. 'Have you finished? My proposed body shall sit in the old senate building, where Bridget's advisory council sat before it was closed down after Belinda's attempted coup. As for the rules under which this body will operate, I propose setting up a constitutional convention along the lines of that trialled by King Daniel of the City several years ago.'

'And we all know how that worked out,' said Naxor. 'It was an abject failure.'

'Was it?' said Kelsey. 'King Daniel was certainly wrong when he tried to push through too many changes at once, but were you aware that almost every part of his original proposals have been passed since then, piece by piece? I am not suggesting that we try to force the representative body to adopt any of our policies – they will be free to legislate whatever they wish, as long as it remains within the law.'

'You wish to sell the Empire to a mob,' said Naxor.

'Hold your tongue, Naxor,' said Cardova. 'Kelsey is right. It may have taken ten years, but the City finally has the constitution that Daniel fought for.'

'But we don't have ten years, Lord Constable,' said Slaeon. 'Everything the Herald has so far suggested will cost the treasury dear. For the mint to become a bank, it will first need a large injection of capital, while establishing a parliament of the nature being proposed will be extremely expensive. I want to hear how the Herald intends to pay for it all.'

Kelsey glanced round the table. 'In the short term, as Holder Fast, I shall loan the Empire all that it needs; enough to cover all foreseeable expenditure for one year.'

'And in the long term?' said Slaeon.

'That depends upon the outcome of a few negotiations I intend to undertake.'

'Negotiations?' said Caelius. 'With whom?'

'I will reveal everything in due course,' she said. 'To do so now could jeopardise the success of those negotiations.'

'Let me get this straight, Herald,' said Janis Holdsmith; 'you mean to reduce income, increase expenditure, pass authority to an elected body, and place the Empire in debt to your family, and yet you are unwilling to tell us what will happen one year hence? Tell me, what rate of interest do you intend to charge the Empire for this loan?'

'There will be no interest charged,' said Kelsey. 'My family will not profit from this.'

'This is akin to a revolution,' said Naxor.

'A bloodless revolution,' said Kelsey. 'A revolution that will be gradual and incremental. The new representative body will take years to find its feet, while the addition of banking powers to the Imperial Mint will pass unnoticed by most of the citizenry. The one thing that will not escape their attention is the reduction in taxes. If the new parliament wishes to raise income, they will have to implement taxes of their own. The difference will be that the people will have freely chosen to do so. The wealth of the Empire is considerable; and, in my view, this is the best way to harness it.'

'I want to hear everyone's opinion on this,' said Thorn. 'We shall work our way round the table, starting with the Imperial Constable.'

Cardova frowned. 'I'm not opposed in principle to giving the people a say in the decisions of the Empire,' he said. 'It works in the Holdings. However, I worry that the Empire is too large, with too many disparate regions, for Kelsey's vision to operate effectively. Is she suggesting that the area of the Empire might have to contract?'

'All areas of the Empire would have representatives in the new body,' said Kelsey, 'including Rahain, Rakana, the City and Na Sun Ka. There will be no retreat from any territory currently held by our forces.'

Cardova glanced down. 'If we do nothing, the Empire is facing collapse. I have a lot of questions, and I need more information, but, for now, I say we cautiously support Kelsey's plans. Claudian?'

The Adjutant glanced up. 'What will happen if the Empire is unable to repay the loan granted by the Holdfasts?'

'Then my family will go down with the Empire,' said Kelsey.

Claudian nodded. 'I acquiesce with the proposals. The Herald's plan appears to be the least worst option facing us. Caelius?'

'I am a quartermaster,' said Caelius, 'and I'm not going to pretend that I understand how to fix the broken finances of the Empire. What I do know, however, is that I trust Kelsey. This sounds like a gamble, but the loan from the Holdfasts will buy us another year of muddling through.'

'I am opposed,' said Janis Holdsmith. 'I'll be honest with you all – I abhor the democracy instituted in my homeland by Daphne Holdfast during her time as First Holder of the Republic. I am a monarchist at heart, and I believe in strong leadership. The new Herald's plans will not deliver that.'

The Rahain treasurer sitting to Janis's right furrowed her brow, and her forked tongue flickered out for a brief second, as the others waited for her to speak.

'I abstain,' she said. 'Without knowing the substance of the new Herald's secret negotiations, I am unable to come to a sensible conclusion. I do welcome her offer of a loan with no added interest. It will keep the government functioning, and, as the Imperial Quartermaster has stated, it will give us another year.'

'She is attempting to use her family's great fortune to bribe us,' said Naxor. 'I believe that this has been her aim all along – to blackmail the Empire into submission. How dare she suggest that a mere collection of citizens might know better than Her Imperial Majesty? It smacks of treason. The Empress was chosen according to the law of succession, and yet Kelsey wants to discard that. What power will Her

Majesty hold if this repellent idea is brought into force? The Empress will become a mere figurehead – nice to look at during official ceremonies, but lacking the ability to govern. Kelsey Holdfast should be arrested. She can occupy the cell so recently vacated by Professor Achan.'

Shella started to laugh. 'You really are a twat, Naxor,' she said. 'Kelsey makes a few sensible suggestions, and you call her a traitor? Rakana used to be well run, back when it was a democracy, and look at how it was ruled when the autocrats took over. The Holdings is indisputably the richest province of the Empire, and it elects its leaders. Even the mud-eating Kellach have a say in how their province is run. There are a few details that bother me – for instance, would each province have an equal number of representatives, or would it be weighted by population levels? Will there be one chamber, or two? Will ultimate sovereignty still remain with the Empress?'

'All of these decisions would be taken by the constitutional convention,' said Kelsey. 'Personally, I think you would be the best person to oversee the workings of the convention, Shella. If the Empress accedes to my plan, I was intending to place you in charge of it.'

Shella rolled her eyes. 'So I get stuck with the details, eh? I might have guessed.'

'I can tell by the look on your face that you would relish the prospect,' said Kelsey. 'You kept the Empire running during its darkest days in Clackenbaird, Shella, precisely because you understood the details.'

'You know me too well, Kelsey,' Shella said. 'You're damn right that I would enjoy implementing democracy across the Empire.' She smiled at Naxor and Janis Holdsmith. 'It would piss off all the right people.'

'I am bringing this meeting to an end,' said the Empress. 'Thank you all for your contributions. I will now take some time to consider these proposals.'

Naxor smiled at Kelsey as he got to his feet. 'That was the polite way to say that your plan is the most stupid idea Her Majesty has ever heard.'

'Do not put words into my mouth, Chamberlain,' said Thorn. 'A decision of this magnitude requires some reflection.'

Naxor bowed. 'My humble apologies, Your Majesty.'

A courtier opened the door, and the members of the Imperial court filed out. Cardova caught up with Kelsey in the hallway outside.

'So that was why you couldn't look after Carden and Caitlyn, eh?' he said. 'How long have you and the Empress been cooking this up?'

'A few days,' said Kelsey, then she turned and walked away.

'And did the Empress know the gist of your plan?' Cardova said, as he hurried along next to her.

'Not until I presented it just now.'

'Gods above, Kelsey. If this fails, then not only will the Empire collapse, but your family will be in ruins. Our family. We could lose Colsbury, not to mention the countless businesses sustaining the Holdfast wealth.

'I know,' she said. 'Have you got a cigarette?'

He eyed her as she stepped out on to the middle balcony. She walked up to the railings, and gazed over the island and lake. The forecourt below them was busy with hundreds of people who had come to Colsbury for the gala, and the market stalls selling food, wine and ale were seeing brisk business. Cardova joined her by the railings, and lit a cigarette.

'Don't I get one?' said Kelsey.

'You gave up years ago,' said Cardova.

'My nerves are stretched so tightly that I think I might be sick.'

'It was no coincidence that the three former Banner officers supported you in there,' he said. 'After all, we work in the military, and if defence is left untouched by your plan, then we won't be affected. And Shella's approval was a certainty; I could see her grinning as you made your proposals. All the same, you are asking the Empress to give up much of her power.'

'We will soon see what Her Majesty prefers,' said Kelsey. 'Does she want to retain full control of the Empire, even if it leads to its destruction; or is she willing to let go of some of her authority, in order to save it?'

'If she agrees, are you going to sack Naxor?'

'No. I'd rather have him criticise me to my face, than see him run into the arms of Edgar.'

'Do you really think he would defect to our enemies?'

Kelsey laughed. 'Of course he would. Where's my cigarette?'

'I'm not giving you one,' he said. 'If you want one so desperately, walk down to the village and buy some.'

She glared at him. 'I might just do that.'

A courtier approached them, and bowed. 'Madam Herald,' he said, 'Her Imperial Majesty wishes to speak to you in her private chambers.'

Kelsey nodded.

'Good luck up there,' said Cardova.

Kelsey followed the courtier into the palace, and they ascended two flights of stairs to reach the personal quarters of the Empress. A soldier by the entrance opened the door for Kelsey, and she entered a large sitting room, where Thorn was reclining on a couch with a glass of red wine in her hand.

'Your Majesty,' said Kelsey, bowing.

'Come closer,' said Thorn.

Kelsey approached the Empress, then halted a couple of yards away. 'I would be happy to answer any questions you have about my proposals, Your Majesty,' she said.

'I don't have any questions,' said Thorn. 'It is quite clear where your plan will lead. Am I so inept at governing that you wish to strip me of my authority?'

'It is not a question of competence,' said Kelsey. 'You are not ruling a unified state; the Empire consists of a dozen different forms of government, and my plan will give them all a chance to have their voices heard.'

'At the expense of my own?'

'Aye. You would be voluntarily diluting some of your power in order to stabilise the Empire. It would be the most far-reaching decision you could ever take.'

Thorn shook her head. 'As it was I who asked you to come up with a set of proposals, I can hardly blame you for their contents. But I insist that you tell me one thing – what is the nature of the negotiations you intend to hold?'

Kelsey hesitated. 'Secrecy in this matter is paramount, Your Majesty.'

Thorn narrowed her eyes. 'I will make it simple for you – tell me, or I will reject your proposals in their entirety. Your loan will last a single year – I need to know what happens after that. You can be assured that I will not repeat your words to another person.'

'Very well, Your Majesty,' said Kelsey. 'Chancellor Shella might be clever, but she was mistaken about one thing.'

'Yes?'

'She claimed that the Holdings is the wealthiest province of the Empire, but that is not true, by any objective measurement. There exists another place that is richer than almost the rest of the Empire put together.'

Thorn raised an eyebrow.

'The trick will be to persuade this place to part with a large portion of its wealth,' Kelsey went on, 'by the means of offering them something they lack; something they greatly desire, and something that is in our power to give them.'

'What place?'

Kelsey smiled. 'Amatskouri, Your Majesty; and I know exactly what they want.'

CHAPTER 9
THE USEFUL INSECT

Western Coast of Inopei – 6th Abrinch 1597

Eroded by centuries of the ocean's waves battering against its enormous stone walls, the ancient castle was in ruins. Half of it had collapsed into the ocean, and the other half looked set to join it. On its eastern edge, the side furthest from the coast, a few buildings remained, their roofs long gone, and their walls covered in damp and ivy. Inside one of those buildings was a suite of rooms so luxurious that they seemed to belong to another world, and it was there that Kyra, Achan and Larron sat, awaiting the return of Bailey.

Larron poured himself a brandy from a crystal decanter. 'It's almost as though Bailey knew that he would have to go into hiding one day,' he said. 'Why else would he have set up a place like this?'

'It might be because he's so paranoid,' said Kyra. 'Thousands of years in a restrainer mask has done something permanent to his mind. He's always making sure that he has an escape plan.'

'Do either of you want a drink?' said Larron.

'It's too early for me,' said Kyra.

'Bailey could be gone for days,' Larron said, sipping from his glass. 'Have you seen his wardrobe? If he was a little taller, I'd be trying on his clothes.'

'I'll take a small brandy, thank you,' said Achan.

Kyra glanced at the professor. 'I know that this isn't what you were expecting,' she said.

'I wasn't sure what to expect,' he said, as Larron handed him a glass. 'But you are right, Kyra; what are we doing here? I know very little about Athumia, except that half of it is ruled by dragons, while the other half detests dragons. I fail to see how we can reform the Empire from here.'

'We have to trust that Bailey knows what he's doing,' she said.

'And do you? Trust him, I mean?'

'I want to. With his eye-shields always on, I can't read what he's thinking. I almost wish Arrosa was here; she would be able to tell if he has been lying to us.'

'I want to understand his motives,' said Achan, 'but is it possible to comprehend a being who has been alive for so long? He must have seen nations rise and fall over and over; whole civilisations throughout every stage of their development, from creation to destruction. Compared to him, the gods who ruled the City were mere children; and if that is so, then what is his opinion regarding us? To him, mortals must seem practically ephemeral.'

'My mother trusts him,' said Kyra. 'He helped her defeat a couple of gods from Elidus; though, I get the feeling he did that out of a desire to stay alive, rather than for any noble purpose. My mother told me that he hated the Ascendants, excepting Theodora, of course.'

'I'm afraid that hating the Ascendants doesn't count for much,' said Achan. 'Who doesn't hate the Ascendants? Even the Empress fought against them, and you know how much I loathe what she has done to the Empire.'

'Bailey took a huge risk to meet with Edgar,' said Larron. 'He must have known that word of it would eventually reach the Imperial Court, and yet he did it all the same. He had a very comfortable life on Zamata, and he was close to those who rule the Empire. Why would he throw all that away, unless he had a very good reason?'

'But what was his reason?' said Achan.

'He and Edgar were friends for a long time,' said Kyra. 'That means more to him than an Empire that has only been in existence for a few decades.' She got to her feet. 'I need some fresh air; we've been stuck in here for far too long.

'Bailey told us to remain indoors,' said Achan.

'I know he did, but I want to feel the wind on my face for a moment, and I want to see the sun again.'

'But won't your mother be looking for you?' said Larron.

'She would have to be gazing upon the battlements of the ruins at the precise moment I'm standing there,' said Kyra. 'She can't just walk up to the Sextant and ask it to find her daughter; that's not how it works.'

Achan frowned. 'Be careful. Maybe Larron should go with you.'

'I'll be fine,' said Kyra. 'I'll be back in five minutes.'

She walked to the door of the room and left it. Bailey had set up a few other chambers within the ancient keep – there were bedrooms, a large bathroom with running water, a kitchen, and several storerooms packed with supplies. She came to a thick wooden door that had been barred from the inside. She lifted the heavy beam and leaned it against the wall, then she pushed the door open. Sunlight flooded into the dimly-lit corridor, and Kyra savoured the fresh air. She eased through the gap, leaving the door a foot open, then she walked across a ragged, crumbling courtyard. It was surrounded on three sides by the ruined walls of the old castle buildings, and Kyra gazed at the lost grandeur. For the first time, she saw the scale of the complex – some of the ruins were enormous, and she realised that they had been built to accommodate not only humans, but dragons, too. That made sense, as the Dominion was ruled by dragons, and it was natural that castles would have been constructed for them.

Kyra wandered among the ruins for a while, as she made her way to the jagged wall that lay next to the ocean. She found a set of worn steps that ran up the side of the wall, and ascended to the battlements. Twenty feet below her, the waves of the ocean were crashing into the foundations of the wall, and the wind sent saltwater spraying up into

Kyra's face. She shivered, despite the warmth coming from the sun. On an impulse, she removed the Compass from her pocket. They were on the westernmost tip of Inopei, or so Bailey had told them. The god still had one of Elbannon's Quadrants in his possession, and the small amount of Tempest within it should be visible to her.

She turned to what she presumed was the east, and placed her thumb onto the Compass. Her vision blurred and clouded over, then she began to scan the countryside for Tempest. There was none in the immediate vicinity, so she shot her powers off into the east, traversing the length of Inopei until she saw the bright glow of the Tempest mine. She tracked back to the west, and discovered two tiny pinpricks of light within a large city. The two lights were next to each other, situated within what Kyra assumed to be a palace.

One of the lights could be Bailey's Quadrant, and if it was, then the other light might be emanating from the Tempest within the Quadrant taken by Edgar, or one of the other gods who had been released from the Palace of the Almighty. It occurred to her that the Compass could be used to track down every Quadrant in existence, and she was glad she had taken the device from Colsbury. If Sable or one of the other bloodthirsty members of her family had it, then they could do untold damage to the enemies of the Empire.

Kyra frowned. Was she now an enemy of the Empire? If she was, then did that make the Dominion her potential friend? She knew very little about the politics of the Dominion, except that it was governed by dragons who believed themselves to be gods. It was true that they had been wronged by the Empire, but she needed to be careful when it came to choosing her new allies.

'You are trespassing, insect,' growled a low voice.

Kyra took her thumb off the Compass, and glanced up to see an enormous purple dragon hovering above her.

'What is your business in my grandfather's lands, insect?' said the dragon. 'Tell me, or I will rip your head off.'

'I didn't know I was trespassing,' said Kyra. 'I apologise. I am hiding here; hiding from the agents of the Empire.'

The dragon's eyes burned. Kyra sent out a tendril of her powers and entered the dragon's mind. She had little experience of using her vision on dragons, excepting a few occasions when she had gone into the minds of Frostback and Halfclaw when she had been younger. The purple dragon frowned, as though it sensed something unusual, and Kyra hoped that no one in that part of Athumia would believe that a mere mortal could possess the powers of the gods. The dragon was female, Kyra discovered as she scanned the dragon's emotions, and she held a strong contempt for all humans. They were dreadful little creatures, useful only for cleaning and repairing the grand castles and palaces of the dragon gods. She felt the dragon considering the possibility that Kyra might make a good meal. First though, she would need to find out if the human had any powerful friends who might miss her.

'Why are you hiding?' said the dragon. 'Of which empire do you speak?'

'The Empire that stole the Tempest mine in the east of Inopei,' said Kyra.

'Oh, them. They are an irrelevance to my family; a minor irritation. Kneel and bow your head in my presence, and I shall perhaps allow you to serve me.'

'I shall not,' said Kyra.

'Then you should make your peace with the false gods you worship, for you are about to die.'

'Do you intend to burn me?'

'I intend to savour your raw flesh, human; one cannot eat a pile of ash.'

Kyra rooted through the dragon's memories for something she could use.

She smiled. 'I know where your uncle lives – your father's brother Lord Sigum Mon Sigel.'

The purple dragon backed away a few yards. 'How do you know my family?'

'Lord Sigel's fame is known even upon my world,' said Kyra. 'Would the noble lord of these lands wish to know the fate of his son?'

'Sigum is dead to us. He betrayed the Dominion after a long life of abject failure.'

'You didn't answer my question, Lady Sigra Min Sigmund, granddaughter of Lord Sigel Mon Sagellus.'

'You know things that you should not know, insect,' said Sigra. 'How? I do not believe that my grandfather's name is known upon other worlds. You are lying to me.'

'Lord Sigum is a friend of the Empress, and he has mentioned his father many times.'

The dragon stared at her, then a great purple forelimb lunged down and gripped hold of Kyra. Sigra extended her wings and ascended into the air, Kyra clutched tightly in her grasp. The dragon banked over the vast complex of ruins, then she soared away to the south, following the ragged coastline of high cliffs. Kyra gasped for breath as the air whipped past her face, and her eyes streamed. The dragon's grip was constricting her chest, while her legs were dangling above the waves as Sigra flew low over the shoreline. After several minutes of flying, a promontory rose up into the sky ahead of them, and on its summit was a great castle. To Kyra's eyes, it looked similar to the layout of ruins where she had been hiding with Larron and Achan, except that it was in a far better condition. A grey dragon was perched upon a high eyrie attached to a tower, and it rose into the air as Sigra approached.

The two dragons circled each other as they banked over the crashing waves.

'Where did you find that insect, sister?' said the grey dragon. 'Is it one of ours? Did it escape?'

'It is not one of ours, brother,' said Sigra. 'I found it in the ruins of Castle Munda, up on the battlements. It knows things about us, and I wish to ask our grandfather to perform his truth spell upon it.'

The grey dragon moved in closer to stare at Kyra.

'What does it know, sister?'

'Our names,' said Sigra. 'It claims to have spoken to Sigum.'

'That will not please our grandfather,' said the grey dragon. 'You know his feelings regarding our disgraced uncle.'

'Nevertheless, I think we should discover the truth about this insect before we eat it.'

Sigra dived low, and alighted in a grand courtyard, set in the centre of the castle amid tall towers and keeps. The grey dragon landed next to her, and they walked through a huge entrance into a vast hall, lit by dozens of narrow slit-like windows that ran down the side walls. At the end of the huge hall were three other dragons, including the oldest that Kyra had ever seen – a dark green male with silver flashes, who was sitting upon a great mound of cushions and embroidered blankets. There were also several humans in the hall. Most were dressed in rags, and they were keeping to the thick shadows. Sigra walked through the hall, then she tilted her head in the direction of the elderly dragon, and held up her forelimb.

'Why are you bothering me with an insect, Sigra?' said the old dragon.

'It bears news, noble grandfather,' said the purple dragon. 'It claims to come from the world that sent soldiers to the Tempest mine; and it says that it knows the fate of Sigum.'

The elderly dragon's eyes narrowed and glowed red.

'I wished to eat it, noble grandfather,' Sigra went on, 'but I thought I should check with you first. Perhaps you might wish to use your powers upon it, to learn if it speaks the truth.'

'I care not what happened to my former son,' said the old dragon. 'Sigum's entire life was nothing but a bitter disappointment. I hope rats are feasting on his putrid remains.'

'He is still alive, Lord Sigel,' cried Kyra. 'Your son lives.'

Sigra squeezed a little tighter, and Kyra grimaced and choked.

'What a pity,' said Sigel. 'I had hoped he would have met his death by now.'

'Shall I kill her, noble grandfather?' said Sigra.

'Wait; this insect amuses me.' Sigel gazed into Kyra's eyes, and she felt his powers try in vain to penetrate her mind. 'You will speak only the truth, insect,' he said; 'your lips can utter no falsehood.'

Kyra decided to play along, while pushing her own powers into the mind of the old dragon. Within his consciousness, Sigel was trying not to appear too interested in the fate of his son, but Kyra could see that it was a façade. The old dragon loathed Sigum, but he was curious all the same. Kyra examined her options. Despite her powers, she knew that Sigra could snap her spine in two without too much effort. If Cael had been in her position, then he would have been able to use his powers of persuasion, but Kyra's ability to make others do as she commanded had withered in her teens. All that was keeping her alive was Sigel's desire to learn more about his son, and so Kyra decided to stoke his anger.

'Let us begin,' said the old dragon. 'Where is the foul Sigum?'

'He is living upon my family's estate in luxury, wealth and privilege,' said Kyra. 'He has allied himself to your enemies. Your enemies, my lord, are my enemies.'

'That makes little sense,' said Sigel. 'You say your family is hosting him, and yet he is with your enemies? Have you turned against your kin, insect?'

'As Sigum is dead to you, my lord, so I am dead to my family.'

'I see. I have also heard rumours that Sigum flies with a horned human upon his shoulders. Can it be true?'

'It's true, my lord,' said Kyra. 'His name is Lahnos Laimos, and he has the Gift of Pain. Together, he and Sigum have slain many of the Empire's enemies. They have slaughtered countless thousands with fire and pain. The Empress herself counts your son as a friend.'

Sigel roared in rage. 'My son is now also a traitor?' he cried. 'For shame! Our family's name shall be in ruins if the Royal Court in Nom Karta discovers this. I will be held accountable for my son's crimes. I should have dashed out his brains upon a rock as soon as he emerged from his hatching. How I wish he was dead.'

'One of Lord Edgar's friends almost killed him, my lord. Do you know of Lord Edgar?'

Sigel calmed a little, and he glanced at his granddaughter.

'Lord Edgar is a mighty god, noble grandfather,' said Sigra. 'He is in alliance with the Dominion. It was Edgar who helped our forces re-take the Tempest mine.'

'Yes, yes; I remember him now. This makes things considerably worse. If one of Edgar's companions fought my son, then all will soon know of his infamy. What am I to do? How can I redeem the good name of our family? Lady Famula will demand a price.'

Sigra tilted her head. 'Noble grandfather – recall that Her Majesty Queen Famula was grievously wounded a short time ago. Lord Saphben Mon Gahad and Lady Abda Min Gahad have formed a regency to govern the Dominion until the Queen recovers.'

'I knew that!' Sigel cried. 'Do you think me mired in my dotage, granddaughter? My mind is as sharp as it has ever been.'

Sigra lowered her head. 'Of course, my noble grandfather.'

'Release the insect,' said Sigel.

Sigra opened her grip, and Kyra tumbled down onto the flag stones. She clutched her bruised chest and gasped for breath.

'Tell me more, insect,' said Sigel. 'Does my miserable son bow before this Empress?'

'He does, my lord,' said Kyra. 'He has pledged his allegiance to the enemies of the Dominion. I was cast out for speaking up against the wickedness of the Empire, and exile was my punishment.'

'Where did you find her, granddaughter?'

'Castle Munda, noble grandfather. She claims she was hiding there.'

'Those ruins lie within my domains, insect,' said Sigel.

'I had no knowledge of that, my lord,' said Kyra, as she struggled to her feet, 'but it seems that fate has brought us together.'

'And do you know the precise location where my son is living?'

'I do, my lord.'

'Are you willing to help me kill him?'

'I am, my lord.'

Sigel's expressions softened slightly. His presumption that Kyra was being forced into speaking only the truth had allowed her to lie effortlessly to the old dragon. She remembered that her mother was probably the most despised person in the entire Dominion – the infamous Demon Witch who had killed King Gahad and sparked off a series of catastrophic wars. If Sigel discovered this, he would kill her in an instant.

She pretended to cower. 'I would be honoured to help you, my lord.'

'Of course you would, little insect,' said Sigel. He turned to Sigra. 'Granddaughter, as you were the one to bring this insect girl here, I am giving you a task. Find Sigum, and destroy him.'

Sigra's eyes glowed. 'Me, my noble grandfather?'

'Yes, you. You are in your prime, granddaughter, and you are a credit to the family. You will take this insect to Nom Karta and present her to the Royal Court, and there you will swear to never rest until you bring them Sigum's head.'

'But Sigum is on another world, noble grandfather; how am I to...?'

'The gods have the ability to move between worlds, or so I am told,' said Sigel.

Sigra glared down at Kyra. 'I should have eaten you when I had the chance.'

'You were wise not to,' said Sigel. 'You shall be the instrument of this family's redemption, granddaughter. You will save our good name, by destroying the one who has betrayed us.'

The air shimmered in the vast hall, and a man appeared, holding a Quadrant in his right hand. He was tall and broad-shouldered, and he looked to be the same age as Kyra, or perhaps a little older. She narrowed her eyes at him, as the dragons in the hall reared up, sparks flashing across their jaws; then he shot Kyra a smile.

'Who are you?' cried Sigel.

'I am not here to harm anyone, Lord Sigel,' said the young, unarmed man, 'but this girl is under my friend's protection. You will leave her unharmed, or there will be consequences.'

'I had no intention of harming her,' said Sigel. His eyes were flickering with rage, but there was fear there, too, Kyra noticed. 'This little insect has proved most useful to me,' the old dragon went on. 'I was, at this very moment, charging my granddaughter with delivering her to Nom Karta. There is no need to unleash your god powers upon us.'

Kyra frowned, then she sensed the man's self-healing powers.

The young man glanced at her. 'Are you all right?' he said.

'Aye; I'm fine,' said Kyra. 'How did you know I was here?'

'I knew that Lord Sigel's home was only thirty miles south of Castle Munda,' said the young-looking god; 'so it was the first place I looked. I thought Bailey told you to remain indoors?'

'You know Bailey?' she said.

'I am here on behalf of Bailey,' he said, 'and I am at your service.' He smiled again. 'Though, I count it a privilege to come to the aid of one as beautiful as you.'

Kyra felt her cheeks flush slightly. He was handsome, there was no denying it, but, despite his confident air, she thought she sensed a deeper pain in his eyes.

'I shall now remove this girl from your presence, Lord Sigel,' he said. 'You have my thanks that she remains in one piece.'

'If you are leaving,' said Sigel, 'then you will be taking my granddaughter with you. She has been charged by me to fulfil my desires regarding my traitorous son.'

The young god narrowed his eyes and glanced at Kyra.

'He's talking about Lord Sigum,' she said. 'Sigum works for the Empire. He was one of the dragons attacked by Lady Allura on Dragon Eyre.'

Sigel groaned aloud. 'Does everyone have to know of my vile son's ignominy? You will tear out his throat, granddaughter; make him suffer.'

Sigra tilted her head. 'I will do everything in my power to see it done, noble grandfather.'

The god eyed the purple dragon, then he nodded. 'I acquiesce, Lord Sigel. I shall transport your granddaughter to Nom Karta, after we have collected two of Lord Bailey's other companions. Farewell, and may your line last forever.'

He glided his fingers over the Quadrant in his right hand, and they appeared in the ruins of Castle Munda. Sigra gazed around, then her eyes narrowed as Bailey emerged from the shadows of the keep.

The young god handed the Quadrant to Bailey.

'I see it is true,' said the purple dragon; 'the gods can move from place to place.' She stared down at the two immortals. 'You look like a god,' she said to the young man; 'but you do not,' she said to Bailey.

'I often get that,' said Bailey.

The young god chewed his lip for a moment. 'I did as you asked, Bailey,' he said; 'and I have retrieved your friend. Will you now tell me who she is?'

'If you're a god,' said Kyra. 'Why don't you just read his mind?'

The young god tapped a finger to the side of his head. 'I am wearing eye-guards.'

Kyra frowned. 'All the time?'

'What is the alternative?' he said. 'Some of my enemies have the power to enter the minds of gods and manipulate them. Such a thing happened to my friend Lord Ballatar, and he was captured as a consequence.'

'Wait,' said Kyra; 'who are you?'

'I am Edgar,' he said, 'brother of Edmond. Who are you?'

Kyra's face fell. The handsome, young-looking god who had fetched her from the dragons was the millennia-old brother of the Second Ascendant?

Getting no response from Kyra, Edgar turned to Bailey. 'I'm waiting.'

Bailey smiled nervously. 'Promise me that you won't get angry,' he said.

'Why would I get angry?' said Edgar.

'Well,' said Bailey, 'the name of the fellow who captured Lord Ballatar was one Cael Holdfast, was it not? My friend, let me introduce you to his twin sister – Kyra Holdfast.'

Edgar moved faster than Kyra could grasp and, in a moment, the tip of a Tempest-edged knife was an inch from Kyra's throat.

'Hold!' cried Sigra. 'I need this insect alive; she knows where I can find Sigum.'

'You brought a Holdfast to Inopei, Bailey?' cried Edgar.

'My family have cast me out,' said Kyra, her eyes on the black blade pointed at her throat.

'It's true,' said Bailey. 'Please don't kill her.'

Sigra swept a forelimb through the air, battering it into Edgar, who was thrown back forty yards. He crashed against a ruined wall and disappeared from view.

'I don't think that was very wise,' said Bailey.

'God or no god,' said Sigra, 'I shall not allow anyone to kill my insect; not until I have fulfilled my grandfather's command.'

Kyra moved closer to the dragon. 'Thank you,' she said; 'and my name is Kyra, not *insect*.'

The dragon ignored her. Over to their right, Achan and Larron emerged from the shadows. Achan's eyes widened at the sight of the huge purple dragon, and she turned her head to regard them.

'More vile little insects?'

'My friends,' said Kyra.

'Are you truly one of the Holdfasts, girl-insect?' the dragon went on.

'Have you heard of us?

'I have heard only what has been reported from Nom Karta. My noble grandfather's castle lies many miles from the centre of Inopei, and we seldom get news quickly; even so, yes, I am aware that your family is powerful; so powerful that even the gods fear them.'

'Everyone fears them,' said Achan. 'That family rules the Empire. They steal the land of others, and slaughter all who stand in their way. Isn't that right, Kyra?'

Kyra frowned. 'Not all of them are bad.'

Edgar appeared through the ruins, his clothes a little torn and bedraggled, but otherwise unharmed.

Sigra peered down at him. 'I regret nothing, god. You shall not harm the Holdfast insect.'

'I will do what I must, dragon,' said Edgar. 'If I wished it, I could kill you in a moment; but I do not wish it. Bailey, I am displeased with you this day. You have brought a powerful enemy into my presence.'

'I have a very good reason for that, my friend,' said Bailey.

'Be warned, gods,' said Sigra; 'I will defend the Kyra insect with my life.'

'I wasn't going to kill her, dragon,' said Edgar. 'I do not kill unarmed girls; but she remains dangerous.' He regarded Kyra, his eyes narrow. 'She is now my hostage. I will barter her life for that of Lord Ballatar's.'

'Good luck with that,' said Kyra, folding her arms across her chest. 'My family wouldn't be interested in doing any deal to save me. My brother might be loyal to the Empire, but I am not.'

'I can vouch for that, sir,' said Achan. 'By rescuing me from prison, Kyra is now wanted by the imperial authorities as a criminal.'

Edgar said nothing.

'We don't need her as a hostage, my friend,' said Bailey. 'Imagine how things will change for the better if we have our own Holdfast working for us. You have told me many times that the Holdfasts are the only thing you fear.'

Sigra glanced at Kyra. 'Didn't I tell you this? – the gods are scared of you, Kyra-insect. Why? What is it that they fear from one so puny and fragile?'

'She is one of the most powerful mages on any of the known worlds,' said Bailey; 'a dream mage, like her mother.'

'A what?' said Sigra. 'What is a mage?'

'A mage is a mortal human with the powers of the gods,' said Bailey. 'Just as this world contains the Gifted in Gunst, Kyra's world has mortals who can emulate the feats of the gods. Kyra's mother was the Demon Witch, and…'

Sigra roared out in fury and stepped back a few paces.

'Why did you tell her that?' said Kyra.

'Your mother slew King Gahad?' bellowed Sigra. 'You are a witch?'

'Aye. I was there. I saw Gahad die.'

'And could you do the same to me?' cried Sigra.

Kyra nodded. 'Aye, if I wanted to.'

'So, your grovelling performance in my father's house was nothing but an act?'

'The truth spell has no effect on me,' she said. 'I just wanted to stay alive.'

'But you could have killed us.'

Kyra shook her head. 'Violence is wrong.'

The dragon stared at her in disbelief.

Bailey nudged Edgar. 'Do you see what I mean? Kyra doesn't seem to fit in with the other Holdfasts.'

Kyra glared at him. 'Why are you doing this, Bailey? I thought my mother was your friend; and yet, here you are, consorting with Edgar.'

'Your mother is my friend, Kyra,' Bailey said; 'but since she refuses to act, I felt I had to try to find a peaceful solution to our problems. I loathe war and conflict, but neither side seems willing to sit down and talk to each other.'

Kyra turned to Edgar. 'And you imprisoned my brother.'

'What choice did I have?' said Edgar. 'Your brother led a band of terrorists into Nom Karta, and they blew up several palaces; then he destroyed the mind of Queen Famula. By rights, I should have executed him, but in my folly I spared his life, in order to use him to broker a settlement with the Empire. It has never been my intention to kill any of your family. Why would I do that? If I had hanged Cael, then Sable, Karalyn, Corthie and the others would never accept any peace treaty; they would slaughter everyone on Inopei to get to me.'

'Aye, you're probably right,' said Kyra. 'It's your own fault, though; you sent gods to kill my Uncle Corthie and his family. I'm not surprised that Corthie took it badly.'

Edgar glared at her. 'I did not order that attack; in fact, I expressly forbade it, and yet Ward decided to disregard my words. I also stopped Ward from flaying your brother.'

Achan frowned. 'Where is this Ward now, sir?'

'He has fled from my control,' said Edgar. 'He stole Lord Elmhirst's Quadrant and has not been seen since.'

Kyra said nothing for a moment as she gazed at Edgar. Despite his great age, his youthful features made Bailey seem middle-aged in comparison.

'What do you want?' she said. 'Why are you fighting the Empire?'

'The Empire understands nothing but violence,' he said; 'and so, with violence I shall defeat them, and force them to the negotiating table. I will make them suffer until they realise that they cannot win, and then I shall forge a peace that shall allow every surviving god and demigod on the Doomed Worlds to flourish in safety. Now it is your turn, Kyra Holdfast – what does the Empire want?'

'To conquer and rule every world,' she said; 'and to kill every immortal who stands in their way.'

'And do you agree with their aims?'

'I most certainly do not.'

'Do you see, my friend?' said Bailey. 'Our own Holdfast.'

'I am not *your* Holdfast,' said Kyra.

Bailey smiled. 'But you will help us?'

Kyra looked at the two gods, then she gazed up at the dragon.

She shrugged. 'I might.'

CHAPTER 10
BENDING THE RULES

Hold Fast, Republic of the Holdings – 5th Day, First Third Summer 545

Cael and Lahnos sat in the shade of the rear porch of the Hold Fast mansion, as a heat haze descended over the endless plains. A servant had brought them a jug of iced tea, and Cael was sweating into his marine uniform as he smoked a cigarette.

'If I had known it was going to be this hot,' said Lahnos, 'I might have reconsidered Kelsey's offer. Dermot's grandparents are refusing to step outside between dawn and dusk, and I'm not surprised.'

'What about Ora'lya?' said Cael. 'Is she settling in?'

'It's too hot even for her, and she's used to Dragon Eyre weather.' He sipped from his glass of iced tea. 'You retrieved the dragon carriers, eh? Good work.'

'We retrieved one of them,' said Cael. 'When I left the *Horned God*, it was sailing north-east towards Ulna, and then I think it's moving into the gap between Wyst and Alef. That's what Sable told me. The other carrier was in no condition to sail, so we sabotaged its rudder, so that no one else can use it.'

Lahnos nodded. 'I'm glad to be out of all that.'

'Are you? I was hoping that you might be ready to return to the service. You could join Uncle Corthie's team; you and Sigum. Aunty Sable has a lot more planned for us.'

'I'll bet she does. So, is it Corthie's team or Sable's team?'

Cael smiled. 'Corthie is in charge, but he takes Sable's advice on pretty much everything. Why wouldn't he? My uncle is a great warrior, but Sable knows more about tactics. How about it? You would be a great help to the Empire.'

Lahnos gazed out into the distance. 'Do you know why I agreed to serve the Empire in the first place? It was because the Bullan never shut up about it. They were always telling me that I had a duty to use my abilities to assist the Empress. Eventually, they wore me down, and I knelt before Thorn. Things have changed since those days. The Bullan are dead, and I have a son to look after.'

'Dermot's grandparents are looking after him.'

'Yes, all right; but I'm here. I help out. Dolwyn might be away for months and, when she does get back, it'll probably only be for a few days before she has to leave again. I promised her I would be here for Dermot. Besides, I think I've done enough for the Empire, and now I deserve a little time to be with my son.'

'A *little* time? That sounds encouraging. Does that mean you might come back to work in the near future?'

'Don't push your luck, Cael. I'm happy to see you, but you can quit the recruitment talk. A *little time* for me could mean a decade or two. When Dermot is an old man, I will still look the same as I do now. It leaves a bitter taste in my mouth, but what choice do I have? I dread seeing my own son grow old, but should I just pretend that he doesn't exist?'

Cael picked up his glass and said nothing. It would be simple to go into Lahnos's mind and force him to agree to whatever Cael suggested, but he wanted Lahnos's willing acceptance, not his slavish obedience to Cael's dream powers.

Ora'lya walked out onto the porch. She kissed Lahnos and sat down next to him, then she eyed Cael with suspicion.

'I tried my best,' Cael said, 'but Lahnos wants to stay here.'

'I knew you were going to try to persuade him to go back to the wars,' she said. 'This peace and quiet is his reward for everything he's done for the Empress, and yet she refuses to accept his resignation.'

'Her Majesty has her reasons,' said Cael.

'What reasons?' said Ora'lya.

Cael smiled. 'I have no idea. Perhaps, like me, she is hoping that he changes his mind.'

'It's never going to happen,' said Lahnos. He glanced at Ora'lya. 'I thought you were going to fly with Sigum this morning?'

'Sigum says it's too hot for him to fly today,' she said. 'You have to remember that he's quite an old dragon, relatively speaking; and I think the extreme heat is sapping his energy. At the moment, he's bathing his head in the fountain to cool down.'

'Frostback and Halfclaw love it here in summer,' said Cael.

'Yes, but they are still child-dragons,' said Ora'lya. 'Neither will be considered adult until they reach their hundredth year. Well, those are the rules on Dragon Eyre. Is Kelsey Holdfast still Frostback's rider? I barely saw them together when we were on Colsbury.'

'My aunt is still her rider,' said Cael, 'but they have a looser relationship, compared to the bond between dragon and rider on your world. They love each other, but they don't feel the need to always be in each other's company.'

Ora'lya rolled her eyes. 'Excuse me for saying this, but your aunt is a fool. If I had a dragon like Frostback, I'd never leave her side.'

'I'm going to Colsbury next; I'll tell her.'

Cael took out his Quadrant.

'Where did you get that?' said Lahnos.

'It used to belong to my sister,' he said. 'She had it since she was little, but my mother confiscated it when she was expelled from university. Besides, she doesn't need it any more, does she?'

'Clearly not,' said Lahnos. 'Is there any news on her location?'

'None,' said Cael. 'My mother is still searching, but if Kyra doesn't want to be found, then she could remain hidden forever. She's much better at hiding her powers than I am, and she is able to shield other people from powers, too. I can't do that, as you saw on the dragon carrier. I can protect myself, but not others.' He got to his feet. 'It was good to see you both. If you change your mind, Lahnos, come and find me.'

'Don't do anything too stupid, Second Lieutenant,' said Lahnos.

Cael smiled, then he moved his fingers over the surface of the Quadrant. The air shimmered, and he appeared in the forecourt of Colsbury Castle, between the twin keeps and the Summer Palace. The island had started to quieten a little after the opening flurry of summer, but it was still busy with people who were either working for the government, or who wanted the government to do something for them. Cael eased through the crowds, then he took the tunnel that went under the two keeps. He emerged into the gardens on the far side of the island, and walked along a path. His mother was exactly where he thought she would be, tending the flowers by the grave of Cael's father.

'Mother,' he said.

Karalyn turned, and smiled at her son. 'When did you get here?'

'About a minute ago.'

Karalyn shook her head as she got to her feet. 'And you came to see me before visiting your wife?'

'I was hoping she would be here with you.'

'Arrosa will be with the Empress,' said Karalyn. 'She has started her new job, and Thorn is keeping her by her side. Did you know that Kelsey is the Herald again?'

Cael raised an eyebrow. 'Is she? That's a good thing, I assume?'

'Good for the Empire; not so much for Kelsey's family life.'

'What happened to Brogan?'

'Thorn relieved her of her position. She offered her a lesser role, but Brogan was having none of it. The last I saw of her, Claudian was taking her back to Plateau City, where she will no doubt be telling everyone she meets how badly she was treated.'

Cael smiled. 'I would have made Brogan chamberlain and sacked Naxor instead.'

'And that is why Kelsey is Herald and not you, son. Can you imagine the trouble Naxor could cause if he was stripped of his power and position? The only reason he is loyal to the Empire is because the Empire gives him everything he needs. Take that away, and he would look for another patron to support.' She gestured to a path, and they began to walk between the apple trees. 'Naxor is not intrinsically evil,' she went on; 'I learned that when he killed Daemon.'

'You forced him to kill Daemon, Mother.'

'No, I encouraged him, but I didn't force him. Try to see him as fundamentally amoral. There is only one person whose approval he craves, and that's his cousin Aila. Apart from that, he will always seek out the most advantageous position for himself.'

'How is Aunty Aila?'

'She has fully recovered, but she is still furious with your sister.'

'I can't say I blame her.'

'It's my fault.'

Cael frowned. 'Why do you think that?'

'I didn't consider the possibility that Kyra could learn to do something that I've been able to do for years. I should have made the blocks I placed into her head broader in scope; instead, I tried to be too clever by specifying all the ways to leave I thought she might try – all the ways except for the one she used.'

They came to the open part of the gardens where the plays and feasts were held. Tables and chairs were stacked up in neat rows, awaiting the next party, while gardeners were busy weeding the flowerbeds.

'I'm going to find Arrosa,' Cael said, taking out his Quadrant.

Karalyn glanced at him, then the air shimmered and they appeared inside the palace, next to a large door.

'She's in there,' said Karalyn. 'I thought I'd save you some time. Are you staying on Colsbury for long?'

'Sable will be coming here at dawn tomorrow, so we can discuss our plans.'

Karalyn frowned. 'As much as I love Sable, she has a tendency to always choose the most ruthless and bloody methods available to her. I thought having children would have dulled that aspect of her personality, but it seems to have had the opposite effect. Dinner tonight?'

'Unless Arrosa has other ideas.'

'Make sure you see me again before you leave.'

'I will, Mother.'

Karalyn vanished, and Cael knocked on the door. A courtier answered it.

'How can I help you, sir?' she said.

'I am looking for Arrosa Holdfast,' said Cael. 'Is she in there?'

'She is, but she is with the Empress, and they are in the middle of a private meeting with the Imperial Court.'

'Who is it?' said Kelsey's voice from inside.

The courtier turned her head. 'Cael Holdfast, ma'am.'

'Let him in.'

'Yes, ma'am.'

The courtier gestured towards the doorway, and Cael entered the chamber. His eyes went over the members of the Imperial Court, then they settled on Arrosa, who was sitting in a low chair to the left of the Empress's throne, and he smiled.

'Good morning, Cael,' said the Empress.

Cael bowed. 'Good morning, Your Majesty. Apologies for interrupting; I was looking for my wife.'

'We'll be another twenty minutes or so,' said Kelsey, who was seated on the Empress's right.

Thorn smiled. 'I have a feeling it might take longer than that. Why don't we pause for ten minutes, and then re-convene?'

The members of the court got to their feet. The three former Banner soldiers approached Cael on their way to the door, and he stepped aside to allow them to pass.

'I hope you are keeping out of trouble, Lieutenant,' said Claudian.

'Of course, sir,' said Cael.

Claudian rolled his eyes, while Cardova laughed.

'The lad attracts trouble like flies to honey,' said Caelius.

Kelsey was the next to walk past Cael, and she caught his glance.

'Congratulations for getting one of our dragon carriers back into service,' she said.

Cael smiled. 'Congratulations on becoming Herald again, Aunty.'

'Tell Sable that I have given my approval for tomorrow's operation,' Kelsey went on. 'When will she be here?'

'At dawn, ma'am.'

'Then I might have a chance to tell her myself.'

Cael waited until Arrosa approached, then he took her hand, bowed to the Empress, and they walked out of the chamber, and on to the middle balcony.

They kissed in the summer sunshine.

'I wasn't expecting to see you for another third,' she said.

'Things are more informal in Uncle Corthie's team,' he said, his hands round her waist. 'He and Aunty Sable are more than happy to allow us a few days of leave after each operation. It helps that they both have children they want to see.'

'I like this new arrangement.'

'What about you? When did you start sitting next to the Empress during meetings of the Imperial Court?'

'A few days ago. We've worked out a few subtle gestures that I can use whenever anyone utters a lie.'

'Have there been many lies?'

'Hardly any,' she said. 'A few exaggerations, and a couple of white lies regarding unimportant matters. I suspect that most of the people in there know about my Gift. Naxor has a skill of using very long-winded ways of saying nothing.'

'He's had lots of practice.'

'Did I hear you say that Aunty Sable is coming for you at dawn?'

'Aye.'

'So, we'll have the entire night together?'

'Aye. How busy are you going to be today?'

'That's hard to say, but I should be completely finished by late afternoon, and then we can have dinner.' She glanced over her shoulder. 'I'd better go back.'

'I'll wait for you out here.'

She kissed him, then he released her, and watched as she walked back into the building. He turned away when she was out of sight, and saw Aila sitting at a table with a few children at the far end of the balcony. He was a little wary of approaching them after what his sister had done, but Aila caught his eye and waved him over.

He joined them at the table and sat down.

'How is life in the marines?' she said.

'I work for your husband now,' he said.

'Corthie will be coming down from our quarters soon,' she said. 'Is Arrosa working?'

'Aye.'

Aila smiled. 'That means you're free to look after the children for a while. I haven't had much time alone with Corthie since he decided to fight for the Empire, and I'd appreciate a break.'

Cael smiled. 'Of course, ma'am. I am at your service.'

The following morning, once the team had reassembled within the Temple of Ulna in Sun Ta, Sable ordered them to put on their Tempest armour.

'The bad news first,' she said; 'Lahnos has declined our offer – he will not be returning to active duty in the near future. And now the good news – I spoke to the Herald of the Empire while I was on the Star Continent, and I'm pleased to announce that Lieutenant Cael Holdfast is now a permanent member of the team. The Herald also said that he can keep the Quadrant that used to belong to his sister, so we now have two. That widens our options. We can open portals, for example, or we can divide the team and appear in two places at once. Corthie will now go over today's operation.'

'We'll be hitting a place called Teros City,' Corthie said, his black breastplate gleaming in the shafts of sunlight. 'It's the capital of Aucteran, a large continent south of Inopei. Our aim is to raid the Dominion gold bullion deposits held inside the palace-fortress complex, the home of the dragon governor of Western Aucteran. With any luck, we won't be confronting the dragon in person; instead, we shall be in the cellars. Cael, Drechtalang and I will clear the area and secure it, while Sable, Nestorian and Jaeanna open the vault and transport the bullion back to Sun Ta.'

'The dragon's name is Lord Tarsun Mon Gahad,' said Sable. 'He's a relatively young dragon, the youngest of Gahad's children, and he has managed to stay in power by refusing to pick sides during the recent civil war over the succession. As Corthie stated, the bullion is being stored beneath a palace-fortress complex, but it is much more than that. It is also the military headquarters for Aucteran, and the seat of the government that rules the humans who live there. There are no Bullan, which is good news for those of us with the ability to read minds, but the complex is heavily guarded. To get into the vault, we shall be using a combination of Nestorian's explosives and Jaeanna's stone powers. Any questions?'

'Is this what we are?' said Drechtalang. 'Thieves and brigands? Terrorists?'

'Our job is to hurt the enemy,' said Sable, 'by whatever means we have to hand. This raid will show the Dominion that even their safest territories and assets are vulnerable.'

'But don't they also have Quadrants and gods?' said the hedgewitch. 'What's stopping them from retaliating? Is Plateau City at risk?'

'The gods started these tactics, not us,' said Corthie. 'They attacked my home in Kell, which I had assumed was possibly the safest place on the Star Continent.'

'I assume we won't be fighting civilians?' said Cael.

'Tarsun's palace is staffed by members of the Dominion's armed forces,' said Sable. 'Civilians are not our target. But we are at war, and bad things can happen.' She gestured to an open crate. 'Stock up on Forty-Eighter bombs; take one bag each. Nestorian, bring enough explosives to break through a stone wall a yard thick. Let's get moving.'

The group gathered round the crate, and Cael slung a bag over his shoulder. He looked inside, and saw a dozen of the orange-sized metal spheres. Next to him, Drechtalang was handed a new war axe, its blade formed from Tempest, and he hefted it with a smile on his face.

'This is almost exactly what I got arrested for in Sanang,' he said to Cael; 'carrying out raids and robbing gold. But it's all right if you do it when you're working for the Holdfasts, eh? Have you got yourself a new Tempest weapon, lad?'

Cael patted his waist, where a knife had been attached to his belt.

'Is that all you're taking?' said Drechtalang.

'It's all I'll need,' said Cael.

Sable clapped her hands. 'Gather round. Be on guard from the moment we appear in the basement, as it is likely we'll have soldiers to deal with as soon as we arrive. Jaeanna and Nestorian will follow me, while Corthie and the others secure the area.'

The team gripped their weapons, and Corthie pulled his Clawhammer from over his shoulder.

Drechtalang laughed. 'I fucking love this job!'

The air shimmered, and they appeared in the middle of a well-lit, marble-lined chamber that stretched away on both sides. Over a dozen armed Dominion soldiers were in the chamber, along with several staff in civilian clothing. Cael raised his hand, and swept it from left to right.

Sleep.

The soldiers and civilians collapsed to the marble floor, and Drechtalang cursed.

'Why did you have to do that, lad?' he cried.

'The vault is through here,' Sable said, pointing to a door. 'Keep everyone out, Corthie, while we break in.'

Sable ran off with Jaeanna and Nestorian, who was carrying a large pack of explosive devices.

Corthie gestured to the left. 'I'll take that side. Cael and Drechtalang, you take the right. There should be stairs at the end of the chamber; hold them.'

Cael and Drechtalang moved off to the right, stepping over the bodies of those rendered unconscious. A soldier ran out of a side room, and Drechtalang cut him down before he could reach for his weapon, the Tempest war axe slicing him through his stomach.

'I was too quick for you there, lad,' the hedgewitch shouted at Cael. 'I'm not going to let you send them all to sleep.'

They reached the bottom of the stairs. Cael and Drechtalang edged along the smooth wall, then they glanced up the steps. At the top, several more soldiers and civilians were walking or standing guard.

'Killing them all would have caused the alarm to be raised,' Cael whispered. 'My way was far quieter.'

'I suppose you have a point,' said Drechtalang. 'What now?'

'I'm going to make us invisible,' said Cael, 'and then we wait.'

You cannot see us.

Cael sent out his vision, and shot it towards Corthie's position, over by the stairs to the left. Corthie was doing what they were doing, keeping to the shadows by the edge of the base of the stairs, his Clawhammer ready. Cael entered his uncle's mind.

I've made me and Drechtalang invisible, he said; *so don't worry if you can't see us.*

All right, said Corthie. *Don't do anything stupid. Everyone on the floor above us will hear the explosion when Nestorian breaks into the vault; that's when things will get interesting.*

Understood, sir.

Cael withdrew from Corthie's mind, and sent his vision up the stairs where he and Drechtalang were standing. He gazed upon a huge hall, with ceilings high enough for dragons to come and go, and then he realised it was the same hall that Corthie could see. Long clerestory windows were arranged along the top of the hall, close to the painted ceiling, and the daylight was streaming in from outside. A large arched opening led off to the left, beyond which lay the private quarters of the dragon governor of Western Aucteran. The hall was packed with soldiers, and offices were dotted along the walls, where senior Dominion officers were based.

Cael frowned, as he tried to imagine what would happen as soon as the explosion in the basement went off. If every Aucterian soldier in the hall rushed down the stairs at the same time, it would be next to impossible for Cael and Drechtalang to prevent them from getting past their position. The best way to defend the vault, Cael decided, was to go on the offensive, especially while they still held the element of surprise.

He glanced at Drechtalang. 'Are you up for slightly bending the rules?'

The hedgewitch narrowed his eyes. 'Normally, I'd say yes, but do we want to risk the wrath of Sable and Corthie? I don't want to get booted off the team.'

'We were asked to make sure no one comes down these stairs to interrupt the robbery,' said Cael; 'and that is what we'll be doing, only a little more creatively.'

'Fuck it; I'm with you,' said Drechtalang. 'What's the plan?'

'Well, we're invisible, and we have two bags of throwing bombs. As soon as Nestorian sets off his explosives, we go upstairs and cause some mayhem; enough to draw the soldiers away from the basement. In fact, we should go up now, so we're in position when the bomb goes off.'

The hedgewitch nodded, and they crept up the stairs. Two soldiers were guarding the top of the stairs, but their gazes were on the crowds milling through the large chamber.

'We'll take out these two first,' whispered Cael, 'then I want to throw a few bombs into the rooms running down the left wall – they're full of officers.'

'Do I need to stay close for the invisibility to work?'

'It'll keep working until you're about ten yards from me.'

Drechtalang nodded, as Cael scanned the chamber. He selected a Dominion soldier at random, entered his mind, and began to lay down a series of implanted suggestions. He had just finished when Nestorian's bomb caused the entire basement to rumble and shake. A blast of smoke belched up and out from both stairwells, and everyone on the upper floor turned.

Cael triggered the soldier, then he reached for the knife by his belt, as Drechtalang swung his axe two handed, cutting down the soldier to their left. Cael leapt up, and slit the throat of the other soldier, then he reached into his bag. He took out a Forty-Eighter bomb, twisted the top half, then he hurled it into the centre of the crowd. On the other side of the chamber, the soldier he had manipulated drew his sword, his eyes glazed over, then he began to attack everyone around him. Cael's thrown bomb went off at the same time as screams rang out, and panic descended over the huge hall. Drechtalang charged into the crowd, his war axe as invisible to the Aucterians as he was, and he began cutting them down in a battle frenzy. Cael followed in his wake, throwing bombs to the left and right. Far to the left, his manipulated soldier was finally brought down by two crossbow bolts, but, by that time, all semblance of order had vanished. A stampede began, as hundreds of civilians tried to flee the hall to escape the war axe and the bombs. A group of senior officers emerged from an office, and Cael threw a bomb in their direction. Shrapnel from the explosion ripped through the group, shredding their flesh, and painting the nearby marble walls in blood.

Cael reached back into his bag and found it empty.

'Hey, Drechtalang,' he cried; 'pass me your bag.'

The hedgewitch dropped the bag to the floor, and kicked it over to Cael, before resuming the trail of carnage through the hall. Cael picked the bag up, and threw the metal spheres contained within until none were left. By that point, the hall was becoming deserted, and bodies lay everywhere. The head of a dragon appeared through the tall archway, and his eyes glowed bright as he gazed down upon the slaughter. Sparks flew across his jaws, then he opened his mouth and emitted a great burst of flames. Cael swept his fingers over his Quadrant as the flames filled the hall, and then he and Drechtalang appeared back in the lower basement. The hedgewitch's clothes were smoking, and his hair was singed, but all he did was laugh.

You can see us.

Cael turned, and saw Sable glaring at him. She activated her own Quadrant, and the team appeared back in their base within the Temple of Ulna on Na Sun Ka, an enormous heap of gold bullion sitting next to them.

Cael checked that all members of the team had returned with them, then he faced Sable.

'You disobeyed orders,' she said. 'Again. What's wrong with you?'

'Did anyone come down the stairs we were holding?' he said. 'We were keeping the Aucterians away from the vault. That was our objective, wasn't it?'

'Don't take that tone,' said Sable. 'You know exactly what I mean. No wonder the marine officers couldn't stand the sight of you, Cael; you can't be trusted to carry out the simplest commands. *Hold the stairs* does not mean *Go up the stairs and kill everyone in sight*. How many bombs did you set off?'

'All of them,' said Cael.

'My axe did a lot of work, too, boss,' said Drechtalang.

Cael smiled at him. 'Aye; we shouldn't forget that.' He glanced at Corthie. 'How many did you get, Uncle?'

'None,' said Corthie. 'I stayed by my post, just as we had planned. Sable's correct; you're out of control.'

Cael started to laugh. 'I can't believe I'm hearing this – do either of you have a reputation for obeying orders? Uncle Corthie, weren't you transferred several times during the war against the Ascendants because you refused to do what you were told? And you, Aunty Sable, since when did you pay any attention to the chain of command? You don't like what I did, but I'm just following the example you both set me.'

Sable and Corthie eyed each other.

'The little bastard's right,' said Sable. 'Neither of us are in a position to reprimand him, not after the careers we've had. Look at what we achieved today – we have a huge pile of Dominion gold, we suffered no casualties, and Cael and Drechtalang hit them hard. It's difficult to argue with success.'

'All the same,' said Corthie, 'how do we plan operations if we have no idea what Cael is going to do?'

'There's only one answer to that,' said Sable; 'we bring him into the planning process, and he tells us what he intends to do.'

'What if I want to make it up as I go along?' said Cael.

'Then that is what you tell us, nephew,' said Sable; 'in advance.'

Cael smiled. 'I can live with that.'

CHAPTER 11
BURIED

Pangba, Olkis, Western Rim – 28th Tradinch 5266 (18th Gylean Year 17)

Sable entered the small, smoky tavern and walked up to the booth where Corthie and his team were sitting.

'The Wystian assault force is sitting on Tankbar, doing nothing,' she said. 'It looks as though it was a false alarm.'

Corthie frowned. 'Was coming to Olkis a waste of time?'

Sable sat. She took out her cigarettes, lit two, and passed one to Cael.

'Maybe not,' she said. 'Perhaps by being here, we have deterred an attack. The Imperial Army have set up Forty-Eighter batteries all along this part of the coast, and the dragons from Skythorn have been patrolling the skies. You can be sure that Allura will have taken a good look at our defences.'

'Did you see her?' said Cael.

Sable shook her head. 'She doesn't appear to be on Tankbar with the Wystians. She might not even be on Dragon Eyre at the moment.'

'Edgar will know that Lord Ballatar was captured,' said Cael. 'He will assume that we've read his mind, and that we know everything that Ballatar knew about their plans. Ballatar was aware that Allura was due to lead an attack on Olkis; therefore, they will do something else, instead.'

'Aye, but what?' said Corthie.

Cael glanced at Sable. 'What would you do, Aunty, if you were Allura?'

Sable sat back in her seat. 'It depends. What are the war aims of Edgar and the Dominion? If we assume that the Dominion wants nothing but the Tempest mine and its own survival, then what would Edgar count as a victory?'

'Perhaps we should ask him,' said Cael.

'No,' said Corthie. 'We can't negotiate with the people who sent assassins to my home in Kell.'

Cael shook his head. 'I keep telling you, Uncle; Edgar didn't sanction that attack. He told me that he had forbidden it, but Ward went ahead regardless.'

'Do you believe that?' said Corthie. 'Was Edgar wearing eye-shields when he told you this?'

'He was.'

'Then he was telling you what he wanted you to hear. Of course he wasn't going to admit it in front of you; he was trying to win you over. The Empire will only be safe when Edgar and his gods are dead.'

'The gods of the Doomed Worlds did nothing to harm us for eight years,' said Cael.

'Aye, because they couldn't,' said Corthie. 'We had them hemmed up on the... what is it? – seven Doomed Worlds? Seven; is that right?'

Sable nodded.

'And each of these worlds is barely inhabitable,' Corthie went on, 'hence the name *Doomed*. The gods were trapped there, waiting for their opportunity – and Edgar has provided it. The bastards will stop at nothing to destroy us.'

'They don't seem to be doing much right now, boss,' said Drechtalang.

'The war has ground to a halt for several reasons,' said Sable. 'The Dominion doesn't have the resources or manpower to do anything but defend its territory, and the Wystians who escaped from Rigga need more time to recover. The Empire is in much the same position as the Dominion – we can defend what we hold, but we don't have enough money or reserves to go on the offensive. Things will only change when the Wystians are ready to launch a full scale invasion of Na Sun Ka. If I was Allura, I would sit tight and wait for that to happen. Why risk myself, when the biggest force at my disposal isn't ready?'

Corthie scowled. 'I want to fight the enemy – that's why I pledged to serve the Empress – and what have we done? Rescued a ship and stolen some gold. It's not enough, Sable.'

'I know you're impatient,' she said; 'and you have a point. If we do nothing but wait for the Wystians to recover, then it'll be too late. Na Sun Ka and the Eastern Rim will fall, and the Dominion will still be in charge of the Tempest mine.'

'Then why don't we go on the attack?'

'I thought we were going to be fighting today,' said Sable. 'That's why we're on Olkis; Allura was supposed to attack.' She gazed around the booth. 'All right; I want to hear your suggestions. How do we win the war before the Wystians are ready?'

'We kill Edgar,' said Corthie. 'We go straight to Inopei and hunt him down.'

'There are hundreds of dragons in Nom Karta,' said Sable. 'and it would be difficult to get close to Edgar. Still, it might be our best option.'

'Perhaps we should carry out a series of raids on Gyle first, ma'am?' said Nestorian. 'Whittle away the strength of the invasion force, and sow chaos among them.'

'Are you out of your mind?' said Drechtalang. 'Seven thousand dragons are waiting for us on Gyle; ten times more than in Nom Karta. Even if we managed to hurt them, it would make no difference.'

'We should be looking for the Sextant,' said Cael. 'If we could use it for five minutes, we could transfer the Wystians off Dragon Eyre, then we could do the same with the Dominion dragons. I'm not suggesting we kill them, just place them somewhere they can't attack us.'

'Unfortunately,' said Sable, 'your mother has hidden the Sextant. Without her help, we'd never find it. If we wish to go on the offensive, then Nom Karta might be our only choice. If we could eliminate Edgar, the war would be over.'

Cael frowned. 'I have been to Nom Karta,' he said. 'As well as dragons, there are Bullan and Aucterian soldiers everywhere. Edgar will be in Queen Famula's palace, and he'll be well-defended. If we decide to go back there, then I'm up for it, but it's likely to turn into a bloodbath.' He paused, as he gazed at the others. 'Maybe we should be thinking about approaching Edgar, to see what he wants.'

Corthie glared at his nephew. 'I'm not going to discuss this again,' he said. 'My answer is no.'

'Think it through, Cael,' said Sable. 'Why would Edgar concede anything to us when he has seven thousand Wystians on his side? Remember – all he has to do is wait until they are ready to attack, and then Dragon Eyre will fall.'

A waitress approached the booth with a large tray. She set it down onto the table, and unloaded the mugs of ale.

'A few of the regulars have been asking about you,' she said. 'Most are guessing that you're part of the Imperial Army that has been reinforcing Pangba; but if that's right, then what are you doing in a tavern getting drunk?'

'You're a nosy lot,' said Drechtalang.

The waitress shrugged. 'It's our tavern.'

'We're attached to the Imperial Army,' said Sable; 'that's all you need to know.'

The waitress nodded, picked up the empty tray, and walked away.

'Nice ass,' said Drechtalang.

'Must you be so crude?' said Jaeanna. 'You should be more like Sergeant Nestorian; he is a perfect gentleman.'

'Nestorian's a fucking Banner rat,' said Drechtalang.

'Keep your voice down,' hissed Sable. 'Do you have any idea how much the locals here hate the Banners? Olkis was occupied for twenty years.'

Corthie eyed Nestorian. 'Were you ever posted to Olkis?'

'Several times,' said the sergeant in a low voice. 'It's the posting every Banner soldier on Dragon Eyre dreaded more than any other. I lost a lot of good friends on Olkis.'

Drechtalang laughed. 'How many of them were killed by Sable?'

Nestorian clenched his fists, and Corthie extended an arm to keep the two men apart.

'You should apologise for that, Drechtalang,' said Corthie.

'Why?' said the hedgewitch. 'I'm only stating the truth that nobody else wants to talk about. Sable killed thousands of Banner soldiers on Dragon Eyre. How can you work with her, Nestorian?'

'I signed a contract,' said the Banner sergeant.

Sable got to her feet. 'I'm going out for a walk; and then you can talk about me all you like.'

She dropped some money onto the table, and walked out of the tavern.

Drechtalang nudged Nestorian with an elbow. 'You must hate her, eh?'

'No,' he said. 'We were at war. I respect her professionalism. You are the only member of the team I don't respect, Drechtalang.'

'What the fuck did you say?'

'You heard me,' said Nestorian. 'I'm ashamed to be working alongside a criminal. You're not a soldier; you're nothing but a mindless thug.'

Corthie got ready to intervene as Drechtalang and Nestorian stared at each other. At that moment, the front door of the tavern opened, and a man walked in, wearing a long, heavy overcoat. Nestorian's eyes narrowed, and his hand went to the hilt of his short sword.

'Death to the Empire!' the man shouted, then he activated the explosives strapped to his chest.

Corthie felt the explosion lift him from his seat amid a roar of noise and a flash of light, then there was nothing.

. . .

When Corthie regained consciousness, he couldn't move his body. He opened his eyes, and saw a few fires flickering in the ruins of what had been the tavern. Only the booth wall had been between the terrorist and Corthie's team, and most of that wall was in large fragments covering Corthie's legs and torso. He managed to free his right arm from the rubble, and he wiped some of the dust and blood from his face. He powered his battle-vision to dull the pain coming from his back, legs and left arm, and some of his hearing returned over the high-pitched buzzing sound in his ears. To his left lay Jaeanna. She had no visible injuries, but her yellow eyes were open, and it was clear that she was dead.

Two men approached, stepping carefully over the rubble and body parts littering the floor. Entire sections of the upper floors had collapsed, but most of one stairwell remained intact, along with the chimney stack that had sat at one end of the tavern. The two men crouched by a figure in the rubble, then one shook his head.

'Over here,' Corthie cried.

The two men looked over. They saw Corthie, and hurried towards him.

'Imperial soldiers from the harbour are on their way,' said one; 'they'll dig you out.'

'What happened?' said Corthie.

'Unk Tannic; who else? They must have heard that folk from the Empire were drinking in here.'

Another explosion went off, and Corthie flinched as the two men looked up.

'That came from the direction of the harbour,' said one. 'We haven't seen a night like this since the Banner were occupying Olkis.'

Cael and Drechtalang appeared from the left. Their uniforms were in tatters, but both seemed uninjured. They hurried over to where Corthie was half-buried by rubble.

'Thank Pyre you're all right,' said Corthie.

'Drechtalang healed me,' Cael said, as he knelt by Corthie.

'After I healed myself,' said Drechtalang.

A further two explosions roared out over the town, and flames rose up from the harbour buildings.

Cael turned, and his eyes glazed over for a moment.

'There will be no help coming for a while,' he said. 'Those last two bombs have sealed off the roads from the harbour, and the soldiers from the Imperial Army are on the other side.'

Drechtalang extended a hand in Corthie's direction. 'Anything broken, boss?'

'I can't feel my back or legs,' Corthie said.

The hedgewitch placed his hand onto Corthie's forehead. He said nothing for a moment, then Corthie felt a wave of healing and well-being surge through his body.

'That should help,' said Drechtalang, 'but I'll have to do a proper healing when we get that rubble off you, boss.'

'Where's Sable?' said Corthie.

'There's no sign of her anywhere,' said Cael.

'Nestorian?'

'He might be under the same rubble that's covering you, boss,' said Drechtalang.

'Jaeanna's dead.'

'We saw her,' said Cael.

'The gods are behind this; they must be.'

'Aye, most likely,' said Cael.

Cael glanced at the two local men, who were staring at the hedgewitch.

'Can you help us move the rubble?' he said.

The two men approached, and they helped Cael and Drechtalang pull at the fragments of stone wall that lay upon Corthie. They lifted one slab free, and dropped it to the ground. Corthie grimaced in pain as he felt the weight of the rubble press down on his legs and back. Another figure appeared through the dust-filled air, her armour silhouetted against the light from the fires. She raised a hand, and Drechtalang and the two Olkians fell, blood pouring from their eyes and noses.

She drew a sword as Cael turned.

'Stay where you are, Holdfast,' said the woman. 'You have no battle-vision, and I am wearing eye-guards. You cannot beat me.'

Cael said nothing.

Allura turned to face the side of the tavern, where a small crowd of locals was gathering.

'Stay back!' she shouted. 'Back, or you die.'

A few civilians moved away, but the rest remained where they were. Allura raised her left hand, pointed it at someone in the crowd, and his head exploded, showering the others with blood. Within seconds, the street was clear.

Allura glanced down at Corthie. 'I see two Holdfasts – where is the third?'

'Sable will be back any moment,' said Cael, his hands loose by his sides. 'She left five minutes before the bomb went off.'

'Why are you not injured?' said Allura. 'There isn't a scratch on you.'

'Was there ever going to be a dragon assault on Olkis,' said Cael, 'or were you just trying to lure us here?'

'There was going to be an attack, right up until the point when we realised that Ballatar would have been forced to reveal our plans to you.' She smiled. 'And yet you came – three Holdfasts, in all their arrogance. Edgar will be disappointed that I have snared only two of you.'

Her left hand moved towards the gap behind her breastplate, then she hesitated.

'Do you know how to activate a Quadrant one-handed?' said Cael.

'The stupid thing doesn't have a *Go Back* command,' said Allura.

'It must be one of Elbannon's,' said Cael. 'I presume you took it from the garrison commander of the Tempest mine.'

'You assume correctly, Holdfast.'

Cael tapped the pocket of his uniform jacket. 'I also have a Quadrant,' he said, 'and I will send us far from here if you reach for yours.'

'Have you checked that it wasn't damaged in the explosion? Your Quadrant is probably useless. I am going to take you both to Nom Karta, and then we will offer the Empire a simple trade – your lives for that of Lord Ballatar. What do you think your Empress will say to that?'

Corthie grimaced in pain. 'Whatever you're going to do,' he said; 'for Pyre's sake, do it quickly. Wait; are you the god who murdered millions by drowning an entire world?'

'Who told you that?'

'Bailey.'

'I might have done something like that,' said Allura. 'My time in a restrainer mask caused large holes to appear in my memory, so I can't be completely sure.' She smiled. 'It sounds like something I would do.'

Her fingers inched towards her breastplate, and Cael moved his hand towards his pocket.

'You are leaving me no choice,' said Allura. 'I am going to have to subdue you, Holdfast, if you don't raise your hands into the air.'

Cael smiled and clenched his fists. 'Try it.'

Allura sprang forwards, her speed taking Cael off guard. She swung her fist and punched him in the stomach, doubling him over, then she pushed him to the ground. She placed a boot onto his right wrist, and leaned over to check his pockets. At the same time, Cael reached in behind her breastplate with his free hand, and threw her Quadrant across the rubble-filled tavern, where it landed in the shadows. Allura slapped him, then she searched his uniform.

'Where is it?' she cried.

Cael laughed, as blood poured down from his nose. 'I left it in my luggage.'

'You were lying to me?'

'Of course I was lying.'

She stamped down onto his right hand, breaking Cael's fingers. Cael closed his eyes as his face creased in agony, but he didn't scream.

'I should kill you now,' she said.

'Why haven't you?' said Corthie.

Allura eyed him. 'Because I promised Edgar that I wouldn't. *Kill everyone who opposes you*, he said; *everyone but the Holdfasts*.'

She raised her sword, and clubbed Cael with the hilt, striking the side of his head. She got to her feet, and gazed down at Cael until she was sure that he wasn't moving, then she retreated into the rubble to search for her Quadrant. Cael groaned and opened his eyes.

'Beaten up by a girl,' he muttered.

'Beaten up by a god with battle-vision,' said Corthie. 'Get out of here if you can, Cael, before she comes back.'

Cael got to his knees, his injured right hand cradled in his left. 'I'm not leaving you here, Uncle,' he said. 'I'll be back.'

Corthie lay still as Cael staggered off through the smoke and flames. Allura returned a few moments later, a three-jewelled Quadrant in her left hand, her sword in her right. She stared at the spot on the ground where Cael had been, and cursed. A noise came from her right, and she turned. Drechtalang was softly groaning, his eyes still closed.

'That shouldn't be possible,' Allura said. 'He should be dead.' She nudged the hedgewitch with a boot, and he groaned again. 'Is he a god, Holdfast?'

'He thinks he is,' said Corthie.

Allura crouched down, and touched Drechtalang's arm. 'A mortal with healing powers? I should bring him back to Nom Karta; Edgar will want to see this.' She got back to her feet. 'Where did your nephew go, Holdfast?'

'He neglected to tell me,' said Corthie.

'He'll no doubt be rooting around in the rubble for his Quadrant,' said Allura, 'but I don't have any more time to waste; imperial soldiers are on their way. You and the healer will have to do. You fought well on the dragon carriers, Corthie Holdfast, but you will be taking no further part in this war.'

She sheathed her sword, and hovered her right hand over the Quadrant. The air shimmered behind her, and a black blade flashed down, slicing off Allura's left hand, which fell to the ground still clutching the copper device. Allura screamed as Sable barged into her, knocking her off her feet.

'Will Edgar be upset when I deliver your head to him, god?' Sable said. 'Will he weep?'

Allura cowered back against the ruins of a wall, as blood poured from the stump at the end of her left arm. Sable raised her sword.

The air shimmered again, and Allura vanished.

Sable stared, then she lowered her Fated Blade.

'There must be another god here,' said Corthie; 'who else could have rescued her?'

Sable plucked the three-jewelled Quadrant from Allura's severed hand. 'Where's Cael?'

'He's around here somewhere,' said Corthie. 'Where did you go?'

'Ectus,' she said. 'I should have stayed close, but there's a place I like to visit sometimes.' She crouched by Corthie. 'I have salve for you as soon as we clear the rubble away; just hold on for now.'

The first imperial soldiers reached the site of the bombed-out tavern. Sable signalled to them, and several squads fanned out through the ruins.

'Give some salve to the hedgewitch,' Sable said; 'then lift this rubble off my nephew.'

'Yes, ma'am,' said a lieutenant. 'Sorry we couldn't be here sooner; we took heavy casualties in the explosions down by the harbour.'

'You're here now,' said Sable, standing. 'Keep your eyes open for Lieutenant Cael Holdfast; he should be here somewhere.'

The soldiers formed up around the rubble, and began to lift several large fragments from where Corthie was buried. Sable paced up and down, her expression dark, then she watched as Drechtalang was given a small dose of salve. The hedgewitch convulsed for a moment, then he sat up, his eyes wide. He coughed, then he stared around as though in a daze.

'What the fuck happened to me?' he said.

'A god unleashed her death powers on you,' said Corthie.

'I know that, boss; I was talking about my healing. It felt… different.'

'It was salve,' said Sable.

'It was amazing,' said Drechtalang. 'Where's the rest of the team? Cael was here. And where's the god?'

'She vanished,' said Sable, 'even though I cut off the hand that was holding her Quadrant.'

More soldiers appeared, some with tools, and they got to work, removing the rubble that half-covered Corthie. Drechtalang crouched by him, and pressed his hand to Corthie's forehead now and again, to take away the pain. When the last of the rubble had been removed, Drechtalang whistled at the sight of Corthie's crushed legs.

'That's a lot of broken bones, boss,' he said, 'and your spine is fractured in several places.'

'Get on with it,' said Sable.

'Yes, ma'am,' said the hedgewitch, then he closed his eyes and sent a great burst of healing power into Corthie's body. Corthie cried out in agony, as his bones knitted themselves back together, and his spine straightened. Next to him, the soldiers continued to dig in the ruins, and they dragged Nestorian out of the rubble.

One of the soldiers leaned over his body. 'He's alive.'

Drechtalang glanced up at Sable. 'I'm out of power.'

Sable walked over to the body of the Banner sergeant, and felt for a pulse. It was faint, but there, so she took out a small vial of salve, unstoppered it, and poured some into Nestorian's mouth. Corthie got himself into a sitting position, and watched as Nestorian's broken body began to heal itself. The sergeant vomited up a pint of dark blood, then he opened his eyes.

Sable glanced at a soldier. 'Any sign of Cael Holdfast?'

'No, ma'am,' he said. 'He's not in the ruins.'

'He told me he would be back soon,' said Corthie. 'He threw Allura's Quadrant away, and escaped while she was looking for it.'

'Has he done a runner?' said Drechtalang.

'I refuse to believe that,' said Corthie, as he got to his feet and stretched his limbs. 'Pyre's arse, what a night. We lost Jaeanna. We nearly lost the entire team.'

He extended an arm, and helped Nestorian stand.

The Banner sergeant lowered his gaze towards the body of Jaeanna. 'I hate Olkis with every ounce of my being. As soon as that man walked in through the door, I knew what was going to happen. Damn the Unk Tannic. What kind of savage can blow up a tavern?'

'I was so close to getting Allura,' said Sable. 'I would have sliced her head off if she hadn't vanished.'

'We still don't know how she got away,' said Corthie.

'She would have had a Quadrant, sir,' said Nestorian.

Sable held up the three-jewelled device. 'I took it from her.' She glanced at the soldiers. 'Widen the search for Cael; he may have collapsed somewhere in the nearby streets.'

Several of the soldiers moved out of the ruins, and began to scan the narrow lanes leading towards the harbour.

'Where is that boy?' said Sable.

'I'm right here, Aunty,' said Cael, as he walked into the ruins. 'Drechtalang, could you heal my hand; it's fucking agony.'

'Sorry,' said the hedgewitch. 'I used all I had fixing up Corthie. Sable has salve.'

'Call off the search,' Sable shouted, then she handed the vial to Cael. He drank a small dose as she watched, then the bones in the fingers of his left hand healed. He flexed his fist, and threw the vial back to Sable.

'Where did you go, Cael?' she said.

'Inopei.'

Sable narrowed her eyes.

'What were you doing in Inopei?' said Corthie.

'I was saving Allura's life,' said Cael. He smiled at Nestorian. 'Good to see you alive, sergeant.'

Corthie's temper boiled over. 'You saved the life of a god who was going to kill us? A god who cut down civilians who were trying to help me?'

'This should be good,' said Drechtalang.

'We'll take this argument to Sun Ta,' said Sable, a menacing look on her face. 'Let's not air our dirty secrets in public.'

She placed a hand into her pocket, the air shimmered, and the team appeared within their quarters in the Temple of Ulna. Sable walked into a room, then she returned with a sheet, and placed it over Jaeanna's body.

'I'm not going to apologise for what I did,' said Cael.

Sable nodded, then she looked up into Cael's eyes. 'You're off the team.'

'Do you want to know why I saved her?' said Cael.

'I couldn't care less,' said Sable. 'I had a chance to kill one of Edgar's gods, and you took it from me. Every death caused by Allura from now on will be your fault.'

'She wasn't going to kill us,' said Cael. 'All she was trying to do was get hold of some hostages so that Edgar could bargain for the life of Lord Ballatar. Edgar ordered her not to harm the Holdfasts, and Allura was obeying that order. Think about the effect her death would have had on Edgar. You could forget any negotiations; he would refuse to speak to us, and we would have to fight it out to the bitter end. Now think about his reaction to us sparing his friend's life. It will show him that we are not the monsters he thinks we are, and it might make him more likely to compromise. I made a strategic decision, for the good of the Empire.'

'Why are you still talking?' said Sable. 'Why are you still here? Leave.'

'But the marines don't want me. Where am I supposed to go?'

'Do you think I give a shit? There's no space in this team for those who flinch at what has to be done. Go back to your mother, for all I care. She'll probably sympathise with your little act of mercy.'

Cael glanced at Corthie, who shrugged.

'Don't you care, Uncle?'

'I agree with Sable,' said Corthie. 'Allura is an enemy. Do you remember what she did on the dragon carriers? Lahnos lost his Bullan friends, and Ora'lya lost her dragon. The gods deserve no mercy.'

Cael stared at his aunt and uncle for a few long moments, then he nodded. He took out his Quadrant, swiped his fingers over it, and vanished.

'I can't believe Cael saved a god,' said Drechtalang. 'He seemed like a decent lad.'

'We're better off without him,' said Sable.

Corthie said nothing.

'We can't have him interfering with the plan,' Sable went on.

'What plan, ma'am?' said Nestorian.

'Corthie and I have decided that, this time, we aren't going to stop until we've killed every damn god who threatens the future of the Empire. There will be no negotiations, and no mercy. Corthie?'

He nodded. 'Aye. That's right. No mercy.'

CHAPTER 12
CALL ME JAZI

Colsbury Castle, Republic of the Holdings – 10th Day, First Third Summer 545

Kelsey gazed up at the silver dragon as she walked by the shore of the lake. Frostback was swooping, banking and diving, sometimes getting so low that the tips of her wings dipped into the surface of the still water, sending up spray into the summer sunshine.

'Do you still think dragons are demonic?' Kelsey said to Arrosa, who was walking by her side.

'I don't know,' she said. 'It's hard to keep that opinion around Frostback and Halfclaw. The dragons here are so different from the ones I knew on Athumia. Most were cruel and arrogant, apart from Sigum, of course. My Gunstian religion is more of a comfort to me these days, rather than something I take literally.'

'You've probably seen more of Frostback over the last few years than I have.'

'I find that a little strange, to be honest. When I first learned about dragon riders, I was told that they were utterly devoted to their dragons. Inseparable. You and Frostback act more like friends who see each other now and again.'

'Too many things got in the way – my job, my children; trying to keep my marriage together. Can Gunstians get divorced?'

'Gunstians are far stricter about it,' said Arrosa. 'Things have to be really bad before a divorce is granted. Here, it's as easy as signing a piece of paper. The Star Continent is more relaxed about a lot of things that are banned or forbidden in Gunst.'

'Which system do you prefer?'

'I think both have good and bad things about them.'

'The first Emperor tried to introduce stricter morality laws when he was in power.'

'Like what?'

'Well, he made it illegal for people of different races to get married, for instance. You wouldn't have been able to marry Cael under his regime.'

'That's just stupid.'

'Can Gunstians marry outwith their faith?'

Arrosa frowned. 'Yes, but it's complicated. Actually, it's not that complicated. If the Gunstian priest had known that Cael wasn't a believer, then he would have refused to conduct the ceremony. I think I know what you are trying to do, Aunty.'

Kelsey smiled. 'I'm not trying to do anything.'

'Are you worried that I'll infect Cael with ideas that you consider backward? I was mocked when I told people at university that Cael and I weren't sleeping together until we were married; did you know that?'

'I would have guessed that might be the case. Did it bother you?'

'Not in the slightest. Cael is the only man I ever intend to be with. I wish he had felt the same, when he was younger, and was going out with lots of girls, but I can't force my ideals onto others. Will you remarry?'

Kelsey glanced up as Frostback banked towards them. 'I seriously doubt it.'

'Don't you want to be happy?'

'I'm not sure it would make me happy, especially seeing as I'm the

Herald again. If I have no time for Frostback, how would I ever have time for a new husband?'

Frostback soared over their heads, then she turned and landed on the grassy slope on the other side of the road.

Kelsey smiled. 'How did it go?'

'It went very well, my rider,' said the silver dragon. She turned her head towards the small figure strapped into the harness. 'What say you, little Calpurnia? Did you enjoy the flight?'

'Yes, Frostback,' said the girl. 'Am I your rider now?'

'You are my trainee rider,' said the dragon; 'my only trainee. I will guard you with my life, as I guard your mother.' She turned back to face Kelsey. 'At what age did your blocking ability first manifest itself?'

Kelsey rubbed her chin. 'Um, well, I could always resist direct attacks,' she said, 'and no one has ever been able to read my mind. I wasn't able to block powers in the general vicinity until I was fifteen or sixteen, but. It came on slowly at first, and didn't reach a diameter of a hundred yards until I was around twenty.'

Frostback tilted her head. 'Then little Calpurnia is on the right path, as her mind is also resistant to being read.'

'We won't know for certain until she's a bit older,' said Kelsey. 'Caelius Junior is the same. No one can penetrate his mind, either.'

'I would prefer a girl as my rider,' said the dragon. 'Perhaps Halfclaw might be interested in claiming Caelius.'

'Halfclaw has never once expressed an interest in having a rider.'

'He is more than content to carry the Empress around whenever she asks.'

'Aye, but she isn't his rider. Do you think I should ask him? It would be nice for Caelius not to feel left out.'

'You are certainly free to ask him,' Frostback said. 'I cannot guarantee a favourable response.' She turned back to Calpurnia. 'I shall take us back to Colsbury. Hold on tight.'

The dragon extended her wings and soared back into the air. She circled once over Kelsey and Arrosa, then flew off in the direction of Colsbury.

'I was hoping she would carry us back, too,' said Arrosa.

'It's only a fifteen minute walk,' said Kelsey, as they set off by the side of the road. 'I wanted this chance to talk to you alone.'

Arrosa eyed her. 'Why? So you could question me about Gunstian morals?'

'Partly, but also to see if you would be a suitable companion for me today. I have something very important that I need to do; something vital to the future of the Empire. If I mess it up, we're in deep shit. How do you cope under pressure?'

'I don't panic or burst into tears, if that's what you mean.'

'You've been through a lot in your eighteen years,' Kelsey said.

'So have many Holdfasts.'

'True. What do you think about the Empire?'

'In general? I'm not sure I understand the question.'

'Say anything that pops into your head.'

'I like it,' said Arrosa. 'I like the idea of the Empire. One over-arching, sovereign government, but every province is free to decide how they want their region ruled. I like that people can move from one place to another without any rules or restrictions, and I like that people are free to learn whatever they like, and say whatever they like.'

'What don't you like about it?'

'We always seem to be at war.'

'That's a recent development,' said Kelsey. 'We've had long periods of peace; the latest one lasted ten years, and then we were hit by half a dozen conflicts that bubbled to the surface at the same time.'

'I sensed no lie, but was that really true, if we started a few of those conflicts? They didn't *bubble to the surface*: we caused them.'

'I was the architect of the Rahain strategy; and I had a hand in the original plan for Rakana. Can you fault either?'

'We shouldn't have used soldiers from Sanang to occupy the cities of Rahain.'

'I agree. I told the Empress that it would lead to trouble, but I was over-ruled. That's one thing you'll have to learn if you're going to sit in with the Imperial Court. It's all right to disagree during the meeting;

but as soon as you step outside, you have to present a united front. That sometimes involves telling people that you're in favour of a policy that you think is idiotic. Do you think you could do that?'

'I don't know.'

'It's hard; I won't deny it, but it's the price of loyalty.'

'Was it not disloyal for you to tell me that you disagreed with sending Sanang soldiers to Rahain?'

'No, because you are a junior member of the Imperial Court. It would be disloyal if you or I repeated that to Aila, for example. Or Cael.'

Arrosa winced. 'Would I be expected to lie to my husband?'

'You don't have to lie – just say nothing.'

Arrosa fell into silence as they walked along the road towards Colsbury. Kelsey thought back to all of the times she had lied to Van about her true feelings on certain imperial policies, and she wondered if he had sensed her dishonesty. They reached the little village that sat opposite the isle of Colsbury, and walked to the bridge that spanned the distance between them. Kellach soldiers from the Imperial Guard were on duty by the open gates, and they came to attention and saluted Kelsey as she and Arrosa passed through the gatehouse.

'Run up to your rooms, and get changed into something more formal,' Kelsey said; 'then meet me on the middle balcony in half an hour.'

Arrosa glanced at her. 'Does that mean I can come with you today?'

'It does, indeed,' said Kelsey.

Thirty minutes later, Kelsey was out on the middle balcony of the Summer Palace with Cardova, Aila, and a small horde of children. Frostback had dropped off Calpurnia, and the girl was sitting next to her brother, while Cardova was watching over Caitlyn and Carden at the far end of the table from Aila and her children.

'Thanks for not asking where I'm going today, Lucius,' Kelsey said.

'Would you have told me if I'd asked?' he said.

'Nope. I'm taking Arrosa.'

Cardova nodded. 'So an eighteen year old will learn your big secret before anyone else in the Imperial Court gets to hear it?'

'That's about right. If only you could detect lies, Lucius, then I'd bring you along, too.'

'Will it be dangerous?'

'I certainly hope not.'

Arrosa walked out onto the balcony wearing an elegant dark green dress, and with her hair styled.

Kelsey smiled. 'Very impressive for such a short time, Arrosa.'

'The palace is filled with courtiers who are only too happy to help,' she said. 'It would have been a shame not to have accepted their assistance.'

Naxor emerged on to the balcony from the palace. Kelsey braced herself to speak to him, but the demigod ignored her, and walked over to where Aila and her brood had gathered. He ruffled Cairney's hair and sat down, and Kelsey watched the way he laughed and smiled in the company of his cousin's children.

'Might I instruct you on the signals I'll be using?' said Arrosa.

Kelsey's attention went back to her travelling companion. 'What was that?'

'My signals,' said Arrosa. 'There are five you will need to learn. I will use three in rotation whenever I sense a lie, with a fourth in reserve, that I will only use if someone is watching me closely and starts to get suspicious about one of the first three. There will also be a fifth signal that I will use frequently, but which will be meaningless. It's designed to distract anyone who decides to look at me rather than you.'

Kelsey narrowed her eyes. 'Is this what you do with the Empress?'

'I use seven signals with Her Majesty, and I won't be repeating any of them for you, Aunty. The first three signals – the main ones – are these: if I touch my right ear, if I put my hands together or pull them apart, and if I scratch my left knee. The fourth is if I lean forward slightly; and the fifth, which signifies nothing, will be if I clear my throat. Will you remember all that?'

'Ear, hands, knee and leaning. Got it.'

'And please remember that lies physically hurt me. I will do my best not to grimace or cry out, but the pain might distract me from time to time.'

'That's grim,' said Kelsey. 'Hey – you share something with most dragons – you both hate lies.'

'The dragons on Athumia lied all the time.'

'That's why I said *most*. Are you ready? I have a couple of things I need you to carry.' She picked up a cardboard tube and a large envelope from a balcony table. 'Take these. When I first nod at you, hand me the tube, and then, the second time, hand me the envelope.'

'Like I'm your assistant?' Arrosa said, taking both into her hands.

'Aye. It will look good in front of the people we'll be talking with.'

'We? Am I expected to do any talking?'

'You can add a few comments, if you like, or you can remain silent. We won't be letting on about your Gift, so try to act as my aide.'

Arrosa smiled. 'I am your aide.'

'All right,' Kelsey said, as she removed a Quadrant from her shoulder bag. She glanced down at the etchings on the copper surface and flexed her fingers in readiness.

'Two fingers?' said Arrosa. 'So we aren't going to another world?'

Kelsey swiped the Quadrant, and they appeared next to a tree-lined river, in the middle of a different city. Arrosa gazed up at the high stone buildings on the opposite bank, then down at the large variety of boats plying the river.

Kelsey watched her. 'Where are we?' she said.

Arrosa narrowed her eyes. 'Amatskouri?'

'Well done.'

'The hundreds of Rakanese gave it away, Aunty. It's very beautiful.'

'You should see the waterfront promenade,' said Kelsey. 'Amatskouri is easily the most beautiful city on the Star Continent. It's what Rakana could be like, or close to what it used to look like. Turn around.'

Arrosa and Kelsey turned, and Kelsey gestured towards a grand stone building surrounded by a high iron fence.

'That is the prime minister's residence,' Kelsey said. 'We have an appointment to meet with him. I don't suppose you know his name?'

'He is Prime Minister Jazidorato, Aunty; elected last year. We covered the election in a politics class at university.'

'That's right, though he refers to himself as Jazi. In fact, his first words to you will be *Call me Jazi*, and I'm willing to put money on it. The Rakanese leadership of Amatskouri is less formal than the Imperial Court.'

They walked up to a set of iron gates, where four Rakanese guards were on duty. The militia soldiers recognised Kelsey, and smiled at her.

'Good morning, Herald,' said one. 'Lovely day for a visit.'

'It certainly is,' said Kelsey. 'There's nothing like summer in Amatskouri.'

'Are you here for the music festival on the beach?'

'Unfortunately not. We have an appointment with the prime minister.'

'Ah. Who's the new girl?'

'This is Arrosa Holdfast, recently married to my nephew Cael. We're training Arrosa up to help out with the Imperial Court.'

The four soldiers stuck out their hands, and Arrosa shook them in turn.

'Nice to meet you, Arrosa,' said one. 'Is this your first time in Amatskouri?'

'It is, yes,' said Arrosa. 'It's beautiful.'

'I'll take you both inside,' said another guard. 'This way, ladies.'

The guard led Kelsey and Arrosa through the gates and towards the main entrance of the grand, three-storey building. The guard chatted to a courtier by the doors for a minute, and then the courtier showed their guests into the building.

'The prime minister is upstairs, ma'am,' said the courtier. 'He is expecting you.'

'Thank you,' said Kelsey.

They were taken to a large chamber with wide, curving bay windows that looked out over the city, with a view of the Inner Sea in the distance. Two men and two women were waiting for them, and they got up from the long couches where they had been sitting. One of the men grinned and approached them.

'Kelsey!' he cried. 'So good of you to come. Apologies, of course, that I couldn't get to Colsbury for this year's gala. Did you get the flowers I sent?'

'We did, thank you,' said Kelsey; 'Her Majesty was delighted to receive them. This is my assistant, Arrosa Holdfast. Arrosa, this is the Amatskourian prime minister.'

Arrosa curtsied. 'It is an honour to meet you, Prime Minister.'

The man smiled at her. 'Call me Jazi. Take a seat, both of you. Coffee? Wine?'

'Coffee would be great, thanks,' said Kelsey.

Jazi gestured to one of the women in the room, who walked over to a table by the window. Kelsey and Arrosa sat down on a long couch, and Jazi took a seat opposite them.

'So, Kelsey,' he said, 'is this a social call, or do you want to discuss business? Your message was a little vague.'

Kelsey waited as the woman brought over two cups of coffee. She set them down on a low table, and Kelsey leaned over and added a couple of sugars to her cup.

'Thanks, Fenu,' she said.

'No problem,' said the woman, as she sat down next to the prime minister.

'It's business,' said Kelsey. 'As much as I would love to spend a few days relaxing and drinking wine down on your beach, the work of the Empire is never done.'

'That's right,' said Jazi; 'you're Herald again, yeah? Poor old Brogan got the boot. Still, and no offence to her, I much prefer dealing with you.' He laughed. 'Unless, of course, you're here to give me bad news. You're not, are you?'

'No, Jazi; we have a proposition for you. It amuses me to imagine that you woke up this morning thinking that this would be a normal day, when the offer I am about to present to you will utterly transform the prospects of Amatskouri.'

The four Rakanese glanced at each other, and each leaned a little further forward on their seats.

'I'm listening,' said Jazi.

Kelsey gave Arrosa a brief nod, and the young woman tilted her head and passed her the cardboard tube. Kelsey pulled out a rolled-up map from the tube, and laid it out onto the low table, using the coffee cups and sugar pot to weigh down the corners.

'The Plateau,' said Jazi. 'Sorry; sometimes I can't help but state the obvious. Carry on, Kelsey.'

The Herald pointed down at the map, 'Here, just as obviously, is Amatskouri. The city limits are marked in red.' She moved her finger down to the next large river to the south. 'And here is Stretton Sands on the coast, and Anamindhari, further up the river. The land in between is practically uninhabited. Well, it's not completely uninhabited – there are a few mining communities up in the Forbidden Mountains; but you get the gist.'

Kelsey looked into the prime minister's eyes. 'The Empire wishes to sell you the entire region between the two rivers. It would be Amatskourian sovereign territory, owned by your people in its entirety, to do with as you wish.'

Jazi's mouth fell open, and the three other Rakanese were stunned into silence.

'You would be able to free up spawning regulations and expand rapidly,' Kelsey went on, 'and the new sovereign territory would become a full province of the Empire, with a stake in the imperial succession, and a voice in the Imperial Court, through an ambassador. Amatskouri would become the capital of a large, new nation, completely under your control. The only part the Empire would keep is the town of Stretton Sands; the new border would run right up to its walls.'

Jazi sat back, his eyes wide. 'I... uh, well now... Fenu?'

The Rakanese woman next to him leaned forward and studied the map. She took a pencil and handed it to Kelsey.

'Draw the borders for me, Kelsey,' she said.

Kelsey traced out a thick line on to the map, following the course of the two rivers, and the frontier that went along by the edge of the Forbidden Mountains. She made a slight loop to exclude Stretton Sands from the area, then put the pencil down.

'There's a reason that region is uninhabited,' said Fenu. 'It's a wasteland. There are no major rivers between Amatskouri and Stretton Sands.'

Kelsey smiled. 'Much of the land is boggy and marshy, and there's plenty of rainfall. Ally that to the fact that the upper few yards of the Inner Sea consists of freshwater, then water shouldn't be a problem, especially for a people renowned for their water management skills. I estimate that the new country we are proposing could support up to five new cities, each with a population of around a million inhabitants. It would take time to reach that level, of course, but this is a vision of the future. Tell me; how many refugees from Rakana are you currently supporting within this city?'

'Over two hundred thousand,' said Jazi. 'We're cramming them in everywhere.'

'And Amatskouri already has a population of four hundred thousand,' said Kelsey. 'Imagine, you could send out citizens and refugees as pioneers, to settle your new lands. Think of the business opportunities, and think of your legacy.'

'My personal legacy is not important to me.'

'Of course it isn't, Jazi,' said Kelsey. 'According to your naming conventions, the new country would be called... let me see... Adorato? From Jazidorato, your name.'

'Adorati,' said Fenu. 'You forgot to change the ending.'

'Sorry. Adorati.'

'What's the catch?' said Jazi. 'There has to be a catch.'

'You will pay for this land by means of a twenty-year mortgage,' said

Kelsey. 'No interest will be charged. The first payment will be due by the end of summer.'

'That doesn't give us much time to get it passed through parliament.'

Kelsey smiled. 'I'm sure you'll manage.' She nodded to Arrosa, who passed her the thick envelope. Kelsey began to remove sheets of paper from the envelope, laying them out on the low table next to the coffee cups. 'Here are a few statistics – total land area, which is in the vicinity of half a million square miles, not including the Forbidden Mountains. Another sheet lists the natural resources to be found on the terrain – gold, silver, lead, iron, coal. As I mentioned, the majority of the lowlands are boggy marshes, ideal for draining into irrigation channels. You could dig a canal all the way from the Inner Sea to the heart of the new nation. And this,' she said, holding up a final sheet, 'is what it will all cost.'

The eyes of the four Rakanese went to the sheet in Kelsey's hand, then she passed it to Jazi, and they leaned in to read.

'We can't afford this,' said Fenu, and Arrosa scratched her left knee.

'What a pity,' said Kelsey. 'Oh well, it was worth a try. Would you like to go down to the beach, Arrosa, to see some of the music festival? I'll buy you an ice cream. Our business here is over.'

'Hold on a moment,' said Jazi. He glanced at Fenu and the two others, then he stared at the costings on the sheet of paper. 'Is there any wiggle room?'

'None,' said Kelsey. 'We're not here to haggle.'

'I see that you intend to raise the Imperial Levy upon the new territory,' said Fenu, 'from five per cent to ten per cent.'

'That's right,' said Kelsey. 'That's what proper provinces pay; Amatskouri is not a province, so it currently pays the lower tariff. That's the price of becoming a full member of the Empire.'

'Who came up with this valuation, Herald?' said Fenu. 'How was it calculated?'

'The workings are on the reverse side of the sheet of paper.'

Jazi turned it over, and the four Rakanese pored over the details.

'Shellakanawara had a hand in the calculations,' Kelsey went on. 'Apart from the Empress and Arrosa Holdfast, she is the only other person who knows the purpose of my visit here. If you turn down my proposal, I intend to never mention it again.'

'This is very expensive,' said Jazi. 'In order to make these annual payments, and the new ten percent levy, we would be restricted in how quickly we would be able to develop the new territory.'

'All right,' said Kelsey. 'What if we delay the start of the ten per cent levy until the twenty-year mortgage period has elapsed?'

'That would be a very generous concession,' said Jazi.

'And one the Herald intended to offer right from the start,' said Fenu.

'Of course,' said Kelsey. 'This isn't my first negotiation.'

Jazi set down the sheet of paper and got to his feet. He walked over to the large bay windows and gazed out over the city, his hands trembling.

'The people here are straining to break free of the spawning restrictions,' he said. 'We reached the territorial limits set by the founders of Amatskouri some years ago, and overcrowding is starting to become a serious problem, especially with the arrival of so many refugees from Rakana. The citizens will weep for joy if we accept.'

'Your re-election would be assured, Prime Minister,' said Fenu; 'and your name would live on forever.'

Jazi started to cry, his hand raised to his face. Arrosa glanced at Kelsey, her eyebrow slightly raised.

'We are making history,' said Kelsey. 'The Republic of Adorati will be a mighty and prosperous nation, at the forefront of the Empire. I'd also like to offer you a little gift to sweeten the deal.'

Jazi turned, unashamed of his tears. 'There's more?'

'I will give your government full access to the entire contents of the Aurelian Papers,' said Kelsey. 'I am certain that the inventive and creative minds of your citizenry would greatly benefit from the advances held in those documents. I shall, of course, also pass on to you the improvements and developments that we have made at the university in Plateau City. All that we have learned will be yours.'

'Why?' said Fenu. 'Why are you doing this?'

'In my opinion,' said Kelsey, 'Amatskouri's achievements have been somewhat overlooked in the higher chambers of power within the Empire. Your prosperity, freedom, democracy and spirit for life is an example to us all. Granting you a nation of your own in the Plateau would recognise this.' She smiled. 'Plus, we're broke.'

Fenu nodded. 'How broke?'

'Not broke enough to walk away from this deal if you choose to reject it,' said Kelsey.

'And has the Empress given her approval to what is, I assume, your idea, Herald?'

'She has,' said Kelsey. 'The Empire will lose control over what amounts to almost a quarter of the landmass of the Plateau.'

'But not Stretton Sands?'

'No. That town remains with us.'

Jazi sat down, and Fenu handed him a handkerchief.

'Do you need some time, Prime Minister?' said Kelsey.

'I will need to take this before the entire cabinet,' Jazi said, 'and then put it before parliament. I cannot guarantee that it will be passed.'

'I get that,' said Kelsey; 'but will you advocate for its acceptance?'

'I'm not sure you fully understand what this means to us, Kelsey,' said Jazi. 'Back in the old country, space was the problem that fixated the minds of everyone who lived in Arakhanah City; not enough space; not enough land – it was the problem that caused the great disaster of the Migration. And here, in Amatskouri, and in Anamindhari, space has once again become our biggest issue. We have to reject thousands of spawning licences every year, and it breaks my heart to see so many childless young couples. Of course I will advocate for this to become law; I will give every last ounce of my political capital to ensure that it happens; you can count on that.'

'That pleases me, Jazi; thank you.'

'No, thank you, Herald. This shall be a new beginning for the people of this city; a great adventure… our own country, at last…' He started to cry again, and Fenu put an arm over his shoulder.

'You may keep the map and the papers,' said Kelsey. 'Arrosa and I will see ourselves out. I would like to hear from you by the end of this third, if possible, so we can put this plan into action. The land will become yours the moment we sign the agreement.'

The four Rakanese got to their feet. Three of them shook hands with Kelsey and Arrosa, then Jazi embraced both women.

'You were right,' he said to Kelsey, 'when I woke up this morning, I thought today was just going to be another day.'

'The Empire's friendship with this city and your people will last forever, Jazi,' she said.

Kelsey led Arrosa from the room, and two guards escorted them down the stairs to the ground floor.

'Can we go to the beach?' said Arrosa, as they approached the main gates.

'You're not exactly dressed for a paddle,' said Kelsey, 'but we have plenty of time. All right – let's see the sights.'

The guards waved goodbye to them at the main gates of the residence, and they took the road by the river that ran to the sea.

'What did you think of Jazi?' said Kelsey.

'The prime minister was more… emotional than I had been expecting.'

'You should see him when it's election time. Hand him a baby, and the tears flow. It's genuine, though; that's why the people vote for him. Jazi might not be an expert on some matters, but he's honest, and he surrounds himself with tough and clever people, who allow him to get on with the arduous job of being adored by the masses.'

'There was only the one lie,' Arrosa said, 'and it didn't come from Jazi's lips.'

'Chancellor Fenu has the brains that got Jazi elected in the first place. She was bound to poke our proposal, to see if she could extract any concessions. She was doing her job.'

'But what does it all mean?'

Kelsey eyed her. 'If the Amatskourian parliament votes to accept my offer, it means that the financial problems of the Empire are over. The annual payments will cover much of our budget, and we shall avoid bankruptcy. All for half a million square miles of grass and swamps.'

'And when they fill that up? I have heard stories about how rapidly the Rakanese population can grow if left unchecked.'

'Then we'll have Karalyn use the Sextant to make them an entire world of their own.'

Kelsey gazed around at the bustling city. The river was busy with traffic, and hundreds of Rakanese were out on the streets. They crossed an elegant bridge, and came to the promenade. One side was filled with cafes, restaurants and taverns, while the beach on the opposite side of the wide road was full of people out enjoying the music that was being played from several wooden stages. Small stalls were doing excellent business, selling everything from cold beer and ice cream, to spicy insect-based snacks.

'What a sight,' said Arrosa.

'This is what we're fighting for,' said Kelsey. 'Take a good long look, Arrosa. This is it. Peace, freedom, and the right to drink cold beer in the sunshine.'

CHAPTER 13
EDGAR'S GODS

Western Coast of Inopei – 13th Abrinch 1597

'And then Uncle Sigum returned home from Nom Karta,' said Sigra, as Kyra and Larron sat outside in the sunshine. 'Naturally, my grandfather asked him why he had come back so soon after joining Lady Minula Min Famula at the Royal Court; and that was when Sigum announced that he had broken off the betrothal. I was a young dragon at the time, but I can recall the scene with precision. My grandfather had to be restrained from killing Sigum on the spot. My own father, Sigmund, took a long blow to his face, which scarred him for life, as he held my grandfather back. Sigum was severely beaten for the shame he had brought to the family, and then he was ordered never to leave the castle again.'

'I don't understand why it caused so much anger,' said Larron. 'Aren't dragons free to decide who they marry?'

'Lady Minula was a granddaughter of the mighty King Gahad,' said Sigra. 'Her children would have inherited Gahad's long life, and it would have tied our family to the Royal Court forever. With those prizes on offer, my grandfather was determined to force Sigum into agreeing. Truth be told, Lady Minula had an arrogant, spoilt character, and she would have made Sigum's life miserable, but my grandfather cared nought for that. Family honour was at stake, and Sigum let us all down.'

'He is still without a mate,' said Kyra.

'And now he is probably too old to ever find one,' said Sigra. 'Good. He deserves to be alone and unhappy. I am looking forward to ripping out his throat, if those blasted gods ever return from Nom Karta. Why are they taking so long?'

'I think Edgar is trying to decide what to do with me,' said Kyra. 'My family is his sworn enemy.'

The dragon's eyes glowed. 'I dislike traitors, and you, insect-girl, are a traitor to your kin. Right or wrong, you should be by their side, not flirting with the foe.'

'Maybe, but I wouldn't be standing by my family's side if I went home,' Kyra said; 'I would be in prison.'

'Your aunt is the Empress; another aunt is the Herald of the Empire, and your mother is the Demon Witch. Are you not ashamed to have sloughed off so many powerful kin? I would rather throw myself into the raging ocean than betray my blood.'

'Did the dragons of the Dominion not fight a civil war?' said Larron. 'Brother against brother; sister against sister?'

'That is true, insect-Larron, but the kin of Gahad are different from the other dragons. Their spirits have a divine quality.'

'You could say the same about the Holdfasts.'

'Nonsense,' said Sigra. 'Insect-Kyra is clearly mortal; there is nothing divine about her.'

'I have immortal cousins, and two immortal half-siblings,' said Kyra. 'Some of my family are definitely divine, though I wouldn't call them that to their faces.'

'How is that possible?' said the purple dragon.

'My uncle married a demigod,' said Kyra, 'and my mother... became immortal.'

'What lies you tell, insect, as a spider spins its web. Do you think me gullible? I have lived for over two centuries, and I have witnessed countless humans telling countless lies; but that lie might be the biggest I have ever heard. *Your mother became immortal*. Pah.'

Kyra shrugged. 'That's how she became the Demon Witch. She didn't need a body any more.'

Sigra laughed. 'At least you amuse me, insect-girl.' She turned to Larron. 'You should make more of an effort to entertain me, insect-boy, lest I grow hungry and eat you.'

'Would you like me to sing for you?' said Larron, an eyebrow arched.

'I would not. Singing would only hasten your demise.'

They fell into silence, and Kyra closed her eyes, feeling the warmth of the sun's rays on her face and neck. For the hundredth time since she had met Lord Edgar, she wondered if she was doing the right thing. Opposing the policies of the Empire had made her a dissident, but aiding the enemy would turn her into a traitor. What was the alternative? She had burned her bridges as soon as she had used Aila and her children to power her escape, and, if she ruled out hiding indefinitely, then what course was available other than to see if Edgar and his allies could prove reasonable? If she was right, and Ward was the sole wicked god to have emerged from the Palace of the Almighty, then might she be able to assist Edgar and the others in the creation of a lasting peace?

She felt the air shift around her, and she opened her eyes to see Bailey appear in the ruined forecourt next to them.

'Good day,' he said.

'Is it?' said the purple dragon. 'It may prove to be good if you are here to take us to Nom Karta. I could have flown there in the time you and Edgar have been absent.'

Bailey bowed low. 'My humble apologies. It took Lord Edgar some time to gather his friends, and then to convince them not to kill Kyra Holdfast on sight.'

The dragon growled. 'She must not die until she has led me to my dishonourable uncle.'

'Don't worry about that,' said Bailey. 'Edgar managed to persuade the others to swear an oath not to harm her. But, as I said, it took time. Are you ready to depart? Where is Professor Achan?'

'The sunlight was too strong for him,' said Larron. 'He's indoors. Do you want me to fetch him?'

'Yes, please,' said Bailey, 'and pack away any things you brought with you. Oh, wait, you didn't bring anything, did you? Pack a few bottles of my finest brandy instead.'

Larron got to his feet and disappeared into the half-ruined stone keep where Bailey's lair was hidden.

Kyra caught Bailey's eye. 'Please tell Sigra how my mother became immortal,' she said. 'The dragon doesn't believe me.'

Bailey glanced up at the purple dragon. 'I don't really understand how it happened,' he said. 'It was something to do with the Sextant, I think, mixed with Karalyn's odd dream powers. She was mortal; she was killed, but her... soul? Spirit? Whatever you wish to call it – it lived on and took over the body of someone else.'

'Lies,' said the dragon.

'I saw it happen with my own eyes,' said Bailey. 'Well, with one eye. Albany had gouged the other one out by that point.'

'Then, to be charitable,' said the dragon, 'I would suggest that you were delirious with pain, and mistook what you think you witnessed.'

'I'm not going to argue with you,' said Bailey. 'But, I will add one other detail. Karalyn Holdfast is not the only mortal to have recently shed their mortality. There exists a man from this world – a native of the Serpent Isle amidst the ocean – who has also ascended to immortality. His path to godhood was somewhat different, however. He is Gifted, and used his Gift to drain the self-healing powers out of a real god.'

The dragon laughed again. 'You are almost as amusing as the insect-girl.'

Bailey gave a low bow. 'I aim to please.'

Larron emerged from the building with a pack over his broad shoulders, and then Achan followed him outside, his neck and forehead burnt pink from when he had sat out in the sun on the previous day.

'Ouch,' said Bailey. 'That sunburn looks sore, Achan. Let me fix it for you.' He raised a hand, but nothing happened.

'Sorry,' said Kyra. 'That was me.' She relaxed her protective powers. 'Try it now.'

Bailey frowned, then he lifted his hand again and Achan's sunburn healed in an instant.

Achan panted in relief. 'Thank you, Bailey, sir. That feels wonderful.'

'To be honest,' said the god, 'I am more disturbed by what Kyra did just now.'

'There's nothing to it,' said Kyra. 'I usually keep my powers running at a low level; so much, in fact, that I often forget I'm doing it. It shields people in the near vicinity from being affected by any god powers that travel through the air.'

'Only a Holdfast would claim that *there's nothing to it*. What a fabulous skill, Kyra.'

Kyra smiled. 'My brother can't do it. He can protect himself, but not others. And, unlike my Aunty Kelsey, I can turn it on and off whenever I like.'

'Let's not tell anyone in Nom Karta about this,' said Bailey, 'not yet, at any rate. I wish to observe if any of the other gods try to enter your mind, or attempt to do anything malevolent towards you.'

'I thought they had sworn not to harm me?'

'Yes, they did. Perhaps I am being unfair on them, but my long life has seen more than one oath being broken. Are we all ready?'

'I have been ready since you arrived,' said Sigra.

'Wait,' said Larron. 'Can you tell us who we are about to meet?'

Bailey nodded. 'Of course. Edgar, Belfar, Allura, Laverne and Elmhirst.'

He swiped his fingers over his Quadrant, and they appeared in a vast hall, where two dozen other dragons were waiting for them, along with Edgar and a few of his gods.

Sigra bowed her head so low that it touched the stone floor.

'Your blessed Majesty, Regents, Princes and Princesses of the noble line of the mighty King Gahad,' Sigra called out, 'I prostrate myself before your divine splendour.'

A young-looking grey dragon glared at her. 'You are of Lord Sigel's brood,' she said, 'and your family was forbidden from entering this city. Why have you flouted this edict?'

'I have sworn to kill the dragon who greatly offended you, Princess Minula Min Famula,' said Sigra, her head still lowered; 'and my noble grandfather ordered me to come here to tell you this. I will hunt down and kill Sigum, and then I will lay his severed head before you, Princess Minula, as a token of the shame our family feels.' Sigra raised her head a fraction, then her eyes widened as she caught sight of the Queen of the Dominion. Famula was lying stretched out on a great mound of soft cushions. Her eyes were open but vacant, and drool and foam were issuing from her open mouth.

'The Queen!' Sigra whimpered. 'Who has done this to our beloved Queen?'

One of the gods pointed at Kyra. 'Her brother is responsible.'

'Silence, Belfar,' said Edgar, as every dragon in the hall turned to stare at Kyra. 'Hold your tongue for now.'

Kyra stepped forward. 'I possess many of the same powers as my brother,' she said. 'What he did, I might be able to undo, if you are willing to let me try.'

Edgar turned and glanced at two enormous dragons, who were flanking the queen's stricken body. 'Lady Abda, Lord Saphben – as regents, the decision is yours. I shall not interfere.'

The two dragons stared down at Kyra, as the others crowded a little closer to gaze at her.

'I propose a simple deal,' said Abda. 'Let the insect try. If she heals the Queen, she will be welcomed here; if she fails to do so, she will die.'

Sigra glanced up, but kept her mouth closed in the presence of royalty.

Abda turned to Saphben. 'Do you concur, my brother?'

'I do,' said Saphben. 'However, if this insect kills our Queen, then what shall become of the Dominion? Who shall rule?'

'Is that all you care about?' cried Abda.

'I want the Queen to recover,' said Saphben, 'but I dislike uncertainty.'

'If the Queen dies, then, after we have killed the insect, all those present here today shall vote between you and I, brother. Will that suffice?'

'It will.' The huge dragon turned to Kyra. 'You may proceed, insect. We shall be watching closely.'

Bailey and Larron walked with Kyra as she approached the still form of Famula.

'Can you really do it?' whispered Larron.

'I bloody hope so,' said Kyra. 'I was only offering to help; I didn't think it through.'

'It was a generous gesture that might cost you your life,' said Edgar, who was standing next to the mound of cushions. 'You should think before you open your mouth.'

'Piss off,' Kyra muttered.

She walked up to the fallen dragon, leaving the others behind. She clambered over a few large cushions, avoiding a pool of foam-flecked drool that had formed, and sat down next to Famula's left eye. She closed her eyes, and allowed her dream vision to rise up into the chamber. She took a slow breath, then she entered Famula's mind. At once, she saw what her brother had done to the queen's mind. Under the layers of imprinted terror and raw fear that Cael had placed there, Famula's inner core identity and memories were untouched, but they couldn't break free of the blocks that surrounded them. Kyra gasped in relief, then she stripped away the layers of panic and terror that had infected Famula's mind, dissolving them into nothing, as she freed the dragon's thoughts.

You are healed, she said in Famula's mind. *You are yourself again, Your Majesty. Come back to us; there is nothing to fear.*

Kyra toppled off the heap of cushions as Famula stretched and groaned aloud. The dragons tensed as Famula closed her eyes, then, when she re-opened them, they cried out in joy to see that life had returned to the gaze of the queen.

'My beloved Queen!' cried Abda, tilting her head. 'Are you recovered?'

'A great burden has been lifted from my thoughts,' said Famula; 'a burden that had crushed me with its weight.' She gazed around, and saw Edgar and the other gods. 'Did one of you do this? To whom do I owe my thanks?'

Bailey and Larron pulled Kyra up by the shoulders.

'It was this girl,' said Bailey. 'She did it.'

'A mortal insect?' said the Queen. 'How is this possible?'

'She has the same powers as the mortal who inflicted the damage upon you in the first place, Your Majesty,' said Edgar. 'She is his sister.'

Famula's eyes burned. 'You are the sister of the one who brought me untold suffering?'

'I am,' said Kyra.

'Did you capture her, Lord Bailey,' said Famula, 'in order to prove your loyalty to Lord Edgar?'

'She came here of her own accord,' said Edgar. 'She is the daughter of the woman you name the Demon Witch, but she has fled from her family; or so she claims.'

'Remove your eye guards and find out the truth from her mind,' said Lady Abda.

'Her mind is shielded by the same powers that healed the Queen, my lady,' said Edgar.

'Then I would imagine that the truth spell would have no effect upon her, either,' said Famula.

'That is correct.'

'Let me think this through,' said Famula, 'as I remember very little from the time I spent incapacitated. This insect is the daughter of the Demon Witch, and it was her brother who bewitched me – correct?'

'That is so, Your Majesty,' said Saphben.

'Then,' Famula went on, 'for some reason, she betrayed her kin and fled here, to Inopei, the heart of her family's enemies? Why?'

Kyra lowered her gaze. It had been easy to lie to Sigra and Sigel, but would she be able to do so in front of Gahad's kin without them knowing? She tried to work out what she wanted, and what was best, not just for her, but for the future of every world.

'I do not agree with the policies of the Empire,' Kyra said, trying to choose her words with care, 'and I refused to remain silent while the Empire invaded its neighbours. My family controls much of the Empire, and so, for opposing them, I was exiled from the imperial capital and held under house arrest. I escaped. It was not my intention to become alienated from the Holdfasts, but I had no choice.'

'You are one of the Holdfasts?' said Famula.

'Aye, Your Majesty. My name is Kyra Holdfast.'

'She could be a mighty ally,' said Bailey. 'Her powers could block those of her family, balancing them out. The Empire would lose its advantage over the Dominion.'

Famula said nothing for a moment, then she inclined her head. 'I owe you my thanks, Kyra Holdfast, but can we trust you?'

'That is what I shall determine, Your Majesty,' said Edgar. 'My friends and I shall discover her true intentions. If she can help us, then I shall put her to work; if she cannot be trusted, I will kill her myself.'

Kyra glared at him, but said nothing.

'I now require some rest,' said Famula. 'Lady Abda, please stay with me and relate all that I have missed.'

'Of course, Your Majesty,' said Abda.

Famula turned to Kyra again. 'Thank you.'

Kyra tilted her head. 'You are welcome, Your Majesty.'

Edgar gestured towards a human-sized door in the side of the hall, then he led Kyra and the others towards it. Kyra saw Sigra stare in her direction, and she felt a little sorry for the purple dragon. Sigra had been nervously waiting to swear to the Royal Court that she would hunt down and kill Lord Sigum, but few had even noticed her presence.

Kyra and the others went through the doorway and came into a well-lit, comfortable chamber, with several long couches and a small dining table by a window.

'Gods, be seated,' said Edgar; 'mortals, remain standing.'

The five gods, including Edgar, all took comfortable seats, while Kyra, Larron and Achan stood together in the centre of the room.

'Should I do some introductions?' said Bailey.

Edgar reclined into his chair and nodded.

Bailey smiled. 'Right. Well, you know me, of course, and you mortals have already met Lord Edgar. On my right is Lord Belfar, a notorious rebel who led an uprising against Edmond. He is Lord Ballatar's son, and they were imprisoned by the Ascendants for taking part in the same rebellion.'

'Where is my father?' said Belfar.

'I'll get to that,' said Bailey. 'Next to Lord Belfar is Lord Elmhirst, who led the gods of the Doomed Worlds after the Ascendants fell. It's probably quite a shock to him to see me here with Lord Edgar, as he always loathed me when I lived on Elidus.' He smiled at Elmhirst. 'Funny how things turn out, eh?'

'I've heard of you, Lord Elmhirst,' said Kyra. 'Weren't you in charge of a squad of Ancients with battle-vision during the war against the Ascendants?'

'He was,' said Bailey.

'I can speak for myself, Bailey, you imbecile,' said Elmhirst. 'Out of everyone here, I have the most experience of fighting the Holdfasts and their armies. I also know why Lord Edmond almost won that war – it was because he had a dream mage working for him; a young idiot mortal by the name of Daimon. If this Kyra can act as our Daimon, then we might actually have a chance.'

Edgar eyed Elmhirst, but kept his features impassive.

'Next to the esteemed Lord Elmhirst is Lady Laverne, a granddaughter of the Second Ascendant,' said Bailey. 'She doesn't like me much, either.'

'For good reason,' said Laverne. 'You are nothing but a vain opportunist, Bailey. Weren't you close friends with the Holdfasts until only a moment ago? Didn't you fight alongside the Demon Witch to kill Albany and Arden? You are a traitor to the gods, and Edgar should never have allowed you to get this close to us.'

'Ah, I see you have been speaking to Lord Elmhirst about me,' said Bailey. 'That explains all the dirty looks I've been getting.' He turned to Kyra, Achan and Larron. 'And that's all the gods.'

'Wasn't there another god called Allura?' said Larron. 'Where is she?'

'She is recovering from a grievous wound,' said Edgar. His eyes tightened. 'Perhaps we should fetch her. Laverne, please bring her here if she isn't sleeping.'

Laverne got to her feet, bowed her head in the direction of Edgar, then she left the room.

'Now, on to the mortals,' said Bailey.

'Wait until Laverne and Allura get here,' said Edgar.

'As you wish.'

'Why do you allow Bailey so much influence if he was a friend of my family?' said Kyra.

Edgar eyed her. 'I have known Bailey for millennia, girl. If you add up the ages of every other god in Nom Karta, then I have known Bailey for a longer period of time. I have also absorbed his memories, and I think I would have acted in the same way as he did when Karalyn Holdfast arrived on Elidus.' He glanced at Elmhirst. 'The Ascendants were wrong to have treated Bailey with such disdain, and the gods of the Doomed Worlds should not have made his life such a misery. To think that he was mocked and ridiculed for centuries does not please me.'

'We were acting under the orders of the Ascendants, my lord,' said Elmhirst.

'And yet you continued to treat my oldest friend poorly after the Ascendants were obliterated.'

Elmhirst lowered his gaze and said nothing.

The door opened and Laverne walked back into the room, another woman accompanying her.

'And here is Lady Allura,' said Bailey; 'minus one hand.'

Kyra stared at the bandaged stump at the end of Allura's left hand. The two women sat, and Allura narrowed her eyes at the sight of the three mortals.

'Tell them what happened to you on Dragon Eyre, Allura,' said Edgar.

'Yes, my lord,' said Allura, her head held high. 'I had two Holdfasts ensnared for a brief moment but, in the end, I was lucky to leave with my life. I had Corthie and Cael Holdfast within my power, then Sable appeared, and cut off my hand. She was about to kill me, when...' She took a breath. 'When Cael Holdfast triggered his Quadrant and brought me back to Nom Karta.'

'My brother saved your life from Sable?' said Kyra.

'That is so,' said Allura.

'Why?'

'He said that, as Edgar had ordered us not to kill any Holdfasts, then he would return the favour.'

'Was this Sable definitely going to kill you?' said Belfar. 'Perhaps it was a ruse.'

Bailey and Elmhirst both laughed, then they looked at each other and stopped.

'Sable is responsible for the deaths of countless numbers of gods,' said Bailey.

'She is a ruthless, pitiless killer,' said Elmhirst. 'She single-handedly drove the gods and Banner forces out of Dragon Eyre, but her worst crime was the slaughter of hundreds at the wedding of Edmond and Belinda. There can be no peace while she lives.'

'I am forced to agree,' said Bailey. 'Sable is an unstoppable force. If she has allied herself to Corthie, then the two of them could wreak utter devastation.'

'Corthie?' said Belfar.

'Another killer of gods,' said Bailey, 'and possibly the finest mortal warrior who has ever lived. Ward made a dreadful error by attacking his home, as, prior to that, it appears that Corthie had no interest in getting involved in the conflict.'

'Then it was he who killed Lord Crennic?' said Laverne.

'Corthie was defending his home and children,' said Bailey; 'and Crennic was foolish for following Ward. One on one, Corthie and Sable are a match for any of us; that is the bitter truth we must swallow. Hence, I deem it an urgent priority to open up lines of communication with the Empire. I know the people who run the Star Continent. Why don't we find out what it will take to end this futile conflict?'

'How dare you suggest that?' said Elmhirst. 'Do you wish us to submit before these vile god-killers?'

'Did I say *submit*?' said Bailey. 'There must be a compromise. Cael Holdfast was sending us a message by returning Allura here alive; perhaps he could be the conduit through which we might relay our demands to the Empress.'

Edgar glanced at Kyra. 'Is your brother favoured by Empress Thorn?'

'Cael is the golden boy,' said Kyra. 'The Empress adores him. Though, I would imagine that Sable will be pretty angry with my brother for letting Allura go.'

'Perhaps I should introduce the mortals now,' said Bailey.

'Is there any point?' said Laverne. 'One of them is a Holdfast; do we need to bother about the others? Do either of them have any interesting powers?'

'I'm a decent cook,' said Larron. 'Does that count? And Achan is a renowned professor of political science at Plateau City University.'

Laverne rolled her eyes.

'We could do with a good cook,' said Belfar. 'The locals here are only interested in preparing meals for the dragons.'

'This is irrelevant,' said Edgar. 'All we need to decide is if Kyra Holdfast can be trusted. Personally, I would not be averse to swapping her for Lord Ballatar.'

'But the Empire would throw me in prison,' said Kyra.

'That is not my concern. If we allow you to stay, what could you do for us?'

Kyra folded her arms over her chest. 'If I am to help you, then I have conditions. I want no slaughter of civilians, and no atrocities being carried out by any of the gods sitting here.'

A few of the gods rolled their eyes.

'Tell us what you can do,' said Edgar; 'we can discuss these… conditions later.'

'Well, I can use vision without fear of having my own mind read,' she said. 'In other words, I don't need eye shields to protect me. I can also…' She hesitated for a moment. 'Laverne, you don't seem to like mortals very much. Try to use your death powers on Larron and Achan.'

Laverne smiled.

'What?' cried Achan. 'But…'

'Trust me,' said Kyra.

Laverne raised her right hand, and Kyra felt a burst of death powers flow from her fingers towards both Achan and Larron. She used her own abilities to deflect them, shielding the two men.

'Do you see?' said Kyra. 'I can protect others.'

'That was you?' said Laverne.

'Aye. I could also hide us, by using the same powers. I can create a small area that cannot be penetrated by ordinary vision powers, blinding others to our presence, and to our activities. Lord Elmhirst, do you remember the vision shield that my mother created to protect Clackenbaird during the war?'

'I remember it well,' said Elmhirst. 'Can you do the same?'

'I am not as skilled as my mother, not yet; but I can create a smaller version.'

'Presumably,' said Edgar, 'your mother would be able to penetrate it?'

'Of course, but there is one thing we can count on – my mother will not lift a finger to help the Empire fight you, Lord Edgar. She will only act if she or her children are directly threatened. Therefore, this is my main piece of advice to you – do not, under any circumstances, provoke my mother to anger. If you do, she will annihilate you.'

The large room fell into silence.

'Does Ward know this?' said Elmhirst. 'What Kyra says is the truth. It was Karalyn who destroyed the thousands of gods Edmond brought over from Implacatus. If Ward attacks her, we are finished.'

'Our course seems clear to me,' said Bailey. 'Here is what I think we should do – first, we take Kyra's advice, and keep away from Karalyn. Second, we allow Kyra to join us, as her abilities will shield us from the other Holdfasts. Third, we find a way to contact Cael Holdfast, to learn if he is willing to listen to our demands and relay them to the Empress.'

'I accept the first two points, but not the third,' said Edgar. 'To force the Empire into accepting a peace treaty that is favourable to our position, we must make them feel a little pain. When they have experienced a few more defeats, then they might be ready to negotiate. Lord Belfar, take up Lady Allura's post on Dragon Eyre until she has recovered. The Wystian dragons are still not ready to launch a massive invasion of the Eastern Rim; until they are, carry out a series of raids to weaken the Empire's position in Na Sun Ka.'

Belfar bowed his head. 'Yes, my lord.'

'Lady Laverne,' Edgar went on, 'you will take over Lord Belfar's command of the Tempest mine while he is on Dragon Eyre. The mine remains the most likely target where the Empire will strike next.'

'Yes, Lord Edgar,' Laverne said.

'Lady Allura, you are relieved of all duties until you recover. Are you taking the salve I gave you?'

'I am, my lord. It's working, but I hate what it's doing to my appearance; I now look younger than any of you.'

'It will hasten the growth of your hand,' said Edgar.

'What should I do, my lord?' said Elmhirst. 'The gods and demigods of the Doomed Worlds are desperate to start evacuating to Athumia.'

'We cannot allow the evacuation to begin until the dragons of the Dominion have agreed to our proposal,' said Edgar. 'Tell the gods to be patient for a little longer.'

'How many gods live on the Doomed Worlds?' said Kyra.

'Around six dozen, or thereabouts,' said Elmhirst. 'It sounds impressive, but many are feeble demigods with paltry powers. I am the only Ancient among them.'

'Before I travel to Dragon Eyre,' said Belfar, 'I want to remind Bailey that he told us he would say more about my father.'

'There isn't much to say,' said Bailey. 'Lord Ballatar is being held in an undisclosed location, but he is alive, as far as I know. Again, I would urge making contact with Cael Holdfast – he would be able to tell us more.'

'No,' said Edgar. 'Do not initiate any dialogue with the enemy without my express permission. Before we can bargain for Ballatar's life, we shall need something to bargain with.'

'Does that mean you aren't going to use me to bargain?' said Kyra.

Edgar eyed her. 'You might be of some use to us. Bailey, show the mortals to their quarters while we finish our discussion.'

Bailey gestured to the door, and the three mortals followed him out of the room. They came to a set of stairs, and descended into the shadows.

'Not the damn basement,' said Larron. 'We had no windows in that place in the ruined castle, and now we're being put into the cellars?'

'It's temporary,' said Bailey. 'Prove yourselves useful, and I will find you somewhere better.'

He took them to a small suite of rooms. 'These were servants' quarters,' he said.

'No kidding,' said Larron, as he gazed at the damp on the walls.

'I'll leave you to it,' said Bailey, as he turned back for the stairs. 'There's a small kitchen, two bedrooms, and a bathroom.'

'Wait,' said Kyra. 'You really have turned, haven't you?'

'Haven't we both, Kyra?' he said. 'My friendship with Edgar far outweighs any loyalty I had to the Empire and your family. And you heard how often I urged negotiations over violence. I will do all I can to bring this conflict to a peaceful resolution, but Edgar is dear to me, and I will not desert him.'

Kyra watched as he hurried up the stairs, then she followed Larron and Achan into the dingy apartment.

'Can you really cook?' she said to Larron.

'Aye. I learned how to when I worked in my parents' tavern.' He smiled. 'Don't worry; I'll cook the gods something so delicious that they'll move us into the best rooms in the palace.'

'And what should I do?' said Achan. 'I feel out of place, and useless. Events have moved beyond me.'

Larron shrugged. 'Perhaps the gods will be interested in hearing you lecture on political science, Professor. Either that, or you can help me chop vegetables.'

CHAPTER 14
SWITHERING

Plateau City, The Plateau – 12th Day, First Third Summer 545

Cael stood in the thick shadows of the four-storey marine barrack block, his head aching from having made himself invisible for so many hours. In front of him stood the marine headquarters in Plateau City, a nondescript tower of grey stone.

He had travelled to Plateau City with the full intention of handing himself in. With his secondment to Corthie's team having been so abruptly severed, it was his duty to report to the commanders of the Imperial Marines. It had been four days since Sable had told him he was no longer welcome, so he was cutting it fine, but it was what would happen afterwards that had stopped him from entering the building.

He would no doubt be sent back to Na Sun Ka, to await further punishment from Captain Doune. He would surely also be asked why he had felt it necessary to travel all the way back to the Star Continent, when he could have walked the distance from the Temple of Ulna to the harbour of Sun Ta in less than an hour. They might even confiscate his Quadrant.

For once, Cael had no idea what to do. If he went back to the marines, it was likely that he would see no further active duty in the conflict against Edgar and the Dominion. The officers didn't trust him, and many thought him an entitled, arrogant liability. But, if he didn't hand himself in, he would be registered as a deserter. His family would be informed that he had abandoned his position, and Arrosa would be told that it was her duty to report him to the authorities if he appeared in Colsbury Castle. That was what the armed forces did – they visited the families of deserters and told them that they would be complicit if they didn't disclose any information they might have. Cael would bring shame to the Holdfasts. What would his mother think when not one, but both of her older children had run off rather than face up to their responsibilities?

He told himself to approach the grey tower, but his feet refused to budge. Was it pride? Did he believe that he had a role to play in the war that was so important that it overrode the oath he had sworn to the marines? What was it that he thought he could achieve if he went on the run?

He needed advice, but couldn't go to his family. He needed a friend, but his best friend was Arrosa, and he would be putting her in danger if he returned to Colsbury in the midst of summer, when the Imperial Court would be based upon the island. He turned away from the marine headquarters, and his gaze landed on the nearby army base, which was part of the same vast military compound in the southern district of Plateau City. A fence separated the two branches of the armed forces, and the gate that allowed transit between them was heavily guarded.

An idea came into his mind, but it was selfish. If he went through with it, not only would he destroy his own career, but he could wreck someone else's; someone he was close to. He bowed his head, wondering if he should have allowed Sable to kill Allura. Inaction would have made his life simpler, and his aunt would have been able to add another name to the long list of lives she had taken. In truth, he was neutral on the question of whether or not Allura *deserved* to die. The god had probably done enough evil in her long life that a reasonable case for her execution could have been established, but hadn't his Aunty Sable also done bad things – things for which she had been forgiven? By saving Allura, Cael had been trying a different approach; he had been making a measured statement to Edgar, that he respected the boundaries the god had set by refusing to allow his side to kill any Holdfast. Edgar would then be forced into the conclusion that not all Holdfasts were irredeemable god-killers; that there were some who might be prepared to talk.

He made up his mind. He would not return to the marines. He was sick of being handed orders he didn't agree with, and tired of the limitations service placed on his freedom. He had a Quadrant, and with it, he could forge his own path.

You do not see me.

Cael emerged from the shadows and walked towards the fence that separated the marine facility from the army base. He had a sharp pain developing behind his temples, which seemed worse in the bright sunshine that bathed Plateau City, but he forced himself to concentrate as he approached the guarded gate. Soldiers and marines were on duty, and they were chatting to each other, oblivious to Cael as he got closer.

Cael entered the mind of an army corporal.

You see a dragon approaching from the south, its jaws opening, flames.

The corporal stared up into the southern sky, his hand raised as he pointed.

'Look out!' he shouted. 'Get down!'

The other soldiers and marines on duty turned to see what the corporal was pointing at, and Cael slipped through the gate behind them, entering the army base.

'What are you seeing?' said a marine.

'Uh... wait,' said the corporal. 'I thought for a moment that.... Shit, never mind.'

'You dozy pillock,' said the marine.

Cael smiled to himself as he carried on. He stuck to the shadows of a line of office buildings as he walked further into the heart of the large army base. It housed the main garrison defending the capital city of the Empire, but it also contained a number of training facilities, where specialist units were prepared for combat. Cael kept his head down, sweat beginning to seep through his marine uniform from the heat and humidity. He knew where he was going, and a sense of guilt began to bite.

He reached the building he had been looking for, and gazed up at its windows. Most were open, to allow air to circulate in the classrooms that lay beyond, and Cael sent up his dream vision powers. He looked into the first room, and saw a small group of soldiers being lectured on how to defuse explosive devices; then he looked into a second chamber, and saw a larger class being taught the grammar of the Rahain language. Cael kept searching, until he reached the sixth classroom, on the second floor of the building. Inside, three junior officers were being given a lesson on leadership. They were examining how previous battles had been lost and won, and the students were giving their lecturer their full attention. The window to the classroom was open, so Cael pushed his powers inside. Two of the students were Holdings, as was the lecturer, but one was a mixture of Holdings and Kellach Brigdomin.

'Sorry, cousin,' Cael whispered, then he went into the mind of the lecturer.

As Cael had suspected, the Holdings lecturer was a vision mage, though not a particularly proficient one, his skills running from battle to range, but with no ability to read minds. Cael listened to the man speak for a few moments, then he began to implant a series of suggestions into his mind.

The lecturer smiled at his class. 'I almost forgot,' he said, interrupting his own lecture; 'there was a message I had to deliver to one of you.' He reached down to a desk, and began to write out a short note. 'This is a pass that will excuse one of you from classes and duties for the rest of the day.'

The three students sat up in their seats.

'Junior Lieutenant Cole Holdfast,' said the lecturer, 'please step forward.'

'Me, sir?' said Cole, as he got to his feet.

The lecturer nodded. 'The pass is for you. Don't get up to any mischief, and be sure to report for dinner at the usual time.'

'Why is he getting a day pass, sir?' said one of the other students.

'He has an important visitor,' said the lecturer.

Cole took the pass, his eyes narrowing. 'A visitor, sir?'

'That's right. Go down to the main entrance of the building, and you will find someone waiting for you.'

'Thank you, sir.'

'Dismissed.'

Cole walked from the room, and Cael severed his connection to the lecturer. He waited a few moments, then he walked over to the main doors of the building. Cole walked out, frowning, and glanced around.

Cael went into his cousin's mind.

Don't react; don't speak. Start walking towards the gates of the army base – the pass will get you through.

Cael? What are you doing here?

We need to talk, but I can't show my face while we're in the base. I'm standing a few yards to your right. Don't look in my direction – start walking to the gates.

There had better be a good reason for this.

There is.

Cole turned to his left and walked in the direction of a bridge that crossed the river into the northern half of the city. The south-western corner of Duncan Gardens lay on the far side of the bridge, with easy access to the Kellach Quarter and the Old Peasant District. On the near side of the bridge was a large army gatehouse, protecting the base, and controlling who was allowed to enter and leave. Cole walked up to the soldiers on the gates, and showed them the pass. They eyed it for a few moments, then waved him through. Cael stuck closely to his cousin, and followed him as he crossed the wide bridge.

What now? said Cole *Are you still in my mind?*

Aye. Keep walking. Go into the park and find a quiet place to sit.

Are you joking? The Summer Fair is taking place in the park, as it does every year. It'll be crowded with thousands of people.

That's fine. We can blend in.

Cole entered Duncan Gardens, and Cael gazed at the stalls that had been set up lining both sides of every path through the park. There was music, and hundreds of people were watching a wrestling match that was taking place on the grass to their right, while hundreds more were relaxing in the sunshine. Cole found a vacant park bench and sat down. Cael sat next to him, and relaxed his powers.

Cole shook his head at him. 'What was all that about? You look a right state, by the way – are you hungover?'

'I'm just tired from being invisible for so long. It's given me a headache.'

Cole nodded, then he gazed at the crowds. 'I suppose I should thank you for the day pass. It's nice to get out of a classroom when it's this warm.'

'How's the training?'

'It's all right. I haven't had many lessons that involve any actual fighting; it's mostly been theory about how vision mages can use their powers to assist the commanders of the army. In other words, it's all been about communication and intelligence. Are you going to tell me why you're here? I thought you were part of Uncle Corthie's detachment.'

'I was.'

'Oh. Did you quit?'

'I was booted out by Aunty Sable.'

Cole laughed. 'Sorry, I couldn't help it. She kicked you out? What could you have done that was so bad that even Aunty Sable couldn't take it?'

'She was about to kill one of Edgar's gods, and I stopped her. I took the god back to Athumia and left her there.'

Cole stared at him. 'Are you out of your mind? You rescued one of the enemy from Sable?'

'Allura could have killed me and Uncle Corthie, but she didn't. Edgar had ordered her not to kill any Holdfasts. He is playing a game with us, and I wanted to let him know that I understood the rules. Sable couldn't see that; all she could see was just another god to murder.'

'What was Allura going to do with you, if she wasn't there to kill you?'

'She was going to use us to bargain for Ballatar's life. A prisoner swap.'

'All right, so maybe you had a point; but that doesn't explain why you're here. I assume you had to report back to the marines?'

Cael looked away.

'Please tell me you reported back to the marines, Cael.'

Cael eyed the food stalls. 'You know what? I'm starving. Let's get something to eat, and maybe a cold ale. I have money.'

He got to his feet, and eyed Cole, who had remained where he was on the bench.

'I'm going to get my arse kicked for this, aye?' Cole said. 'As soon as I get back to base, I'll be asked what I was doing, and who I was meeting. You did something to the lecturer's mind.'

'Aye.'

'I should return to the base right now, and tell them everything.'

'I won't stop you, Cole.'

'But then the authorities will be looking for you.'

'I have a Quadrant; I can take care of myself.'

'You stole a Quadrant?'

'It was Kyra's. I didn't steal it, but I won't be handing it over.'

'Just answer me this, with a yes or no response – have you deserted?'

'I refuse to answer.'

Cole shook his head. 'That is an answer.'

'Tell them I interfered with your mind; they'll believe it. Tell them I gave you no choice.'

'What do you want from me, cousin?'

'Your company. Your advice.'

'My advice? All right, turn around and walk back to the base and hand yourself in.'

'I can't do it, Cole.'

'Why not?'

'Because I am due a third of punishment duties, and I'll be taken off active operations. I think I can end this war, cousin; but I won't be able to do that if I'm unblocking latrine ditches all summer.'

'You think you can end the war? How?'

'I sent Edgar a message by saving Allura.'

'You're an idiot.'

'Aye, maybe; but I'm also right. I'm going to do things my way from now on.' His stomach rumbled. 'Did you hear that? I'm getting some food.'

He walked away, and made for a row of stalls, from where a rich aroma of roasting meat and spices was coming. He gazed at the stalls. There were representatives from each of the different peoples who lived in Plateau City – sausages and blood pudding from a Kellach stall, next to deep-fried spicy insects being sold at a Rakanese stall. Chicken and rice was on offer at a counter run by two old Rahain men, while huge slabs of roasted pork were hanging from the Sanang stall. Cael's mouth watered at the sight, then he approached the Kellach stall.

'You hungry, marine?' said an old woman.

Cael smiled. 'Aye. I'll take a square sausage and a blood pudding, both on bread rolls with plenty of butter. And a cold ale.' He eyed Cole approach. 'Make it two ales.'

'Nae bother, lad,' said the woman.

Cole eyed the food on offer. 'I think I'll get something from the Rahain stall.'

'Suit yourself,' said Cael.

They paid for the food and drinks, and wandered on to the grass, where a group of Holdings singers were serenading a small crowd. Cael and Cole sat on the grass, eating while they listened to the songs lilting over the park.

'Pyre's arse, that feels good,' Cael said as he ate. He gazed around the park. 'Is this what we miss every year by staying on Colsbury all summer?'

'Colsbury has its own attractions,' said Cole. 'Aunty Kelsey puts on plays and singing, and feasts. Perhaps she knows what goes on here every year, and doesn't want the Imperial Court to think they're missing out.' He eyed Cael. 'Speak to me. Unburden yourself, and then I will tell my superiors that you used your powers to trick me into leaving the base.'

'The war seems so distant here,' said Cael, 'and the truth is that very little is happening. We're not strong enough to launch a big invasion of Inopei to reclaim the Tempest mine, while both sides on Dragon Eyre are sitting around, waiting.'

'Waiting for what?'

'Waiting for enough rescued Wystian dragons to be ready to invade Na Sun Ka. When that occurs, not even Aunty Sable and Uncle Corthie will be able to prevent what happens next. Without the Sextant, thousands of Wystians will roll across Na Sun Ka, and then they will sweep up the Eastern Rim. Queen Blackrose's realm will fall, and we will have lost Dragon Eyre to the Wystians and Unk Tannic. That means we have only a short time in which to act.'

'We?'

'Me. I meant me. *I* have only a short time to act. That's why I can't go back to the marines. By the time my punishment duties are over, the war will have been lost. The Empire will be forced to negotiate from a position of weakness, and Edgar will get what he wants.'

'What does he want?'

Cael smiled. 'Good question. You would think that someone in the Imperial Court might be interested in finding out the answer to that, but they are adamantly refusing to talk to the enemy, as if to do so would be treasonous rather than sensible. The Empire is walking into a catastrophe. Killing Allura would have done nothing to help; it would have made things worse, because then Edgar would have been convinced that there was no use in discussing anything with us.'

'So you intend to not only be a deserter, but also a traitor? Interesting approach.'

'I don't care; I'm right.'

'What if you're wrong?'

'I'm not.'

Cole half-smiled. 'Consider this for a moment – what if there is a very good reason why the Empire has chosen not to open negotiations with Edgar? What if they have tried, and been rebuffed? Would they publicise the fact? What if they know that Edgar cannot be reasoned with? It seems to me that you are making assumptions about things that you might not fully understand.'

Cael said nothing.

'Let me ask you a few questions about your theory,' Cole went on. 'What part is Bailey playing in this?'

'I don't know. The last we heard of Bailey, he had disappeared from the island of Zamata, so we can probably assume that he's gone over to Edgar's side. Doesn't that reinforce my argument? Bailey isn't a demented mortal-hating god, so why would he decide to help Edgar? Maybe he sees something in him that we don't.'

'Or maybe he's placed his loyalty with an old friend; it might be as simple as that. All right, what about Kyra?'

'What about her?'

'What might she be doing? She was bitterly opposed to the war, and she has powers that rival yours. What would she do with those powers?'

'Well, she wouldn't hurt anyone – that would go against everything she believes in. She doesn't like or trust the Empire, so I can't see her trying to act as an intermediary, which is why I have to do it.'

'All right; we're getting somewhere. How do you intend to act as an intermediary?'

Cael chewed his lip. 'I need to let both sides know that I am available to conduct secret talks.'

'And would either side pay any heed to you stepping forward?'

'Aye, I think they would.'

'You're delusional.'

'I'm not. I've met Edgar, and it was me who captured Ballatar and saved Allura; so I think his side would at least listen to what I have to say. As for the Empire...'

'No one on our side would listen to a deserter, no matter which family he belongs to.'

'I have to try.'

'They'll lock you up.'

'I'll escape.'

'You can't do this alone, cousin; you don't stand a chance.'

Cael nodded. 'Will you help me?'

'What? Wait a minute; is that why you dragged me out here? It wasn't for advice; it was to persuade me to help you?'

'Cole, if I wanted to persuade you to help me, you would be helping me right now. And no, that wasn't my original intention when I decided to meet with you; it was because I needed to talk to someone I trust.'

'Why haven't you gone to Colsbury if you have a Quadrant? Arrosa's there.'

'You know what the marines and army do when they're dealing with deserters. I can't put Arrosa into that position. She would have to lie to the investigators, or betray her husband.'

'But you're putting me into that position.'

Cael smiled. 'I'm not married to you.'

Cole laughed. 'There is that. All right; I'm going to play along with your stupidity for a moment. Let's say, hypothetically, that I were to agree to help you – what would we do?'

'I'm not going to tell you my plans. You'd have to agree first.'

Cole raised an eyebrow. 'You don't actually have a plan, do you?'

'Nope. I feel lost, cousin. I want to do the right thing, but I no longer know what that is.'

'Handing yourself over to the marines is the right thing to do.'

'I disagree. If I do that, we lose the war.'

Cole puffed out his cheeks. 'I had forgotten how bloody-minded you can be at times. Do you really believe that only you are capable of winning the war? That the hundreds of thousands of men and women serving in the armed forces of the Empire are irrelevant; that the entire officer class is incompetent; that the Imperial Court is packed with fools? That you are the only one in the Empire who truly understands what needs to be done?'

Cael shrugged. 'I can't be the only one who understands; but I'm the only one who has the power to do anything about it.'

'You were born in the wrong generation, cousin. You are like one of those Holdfasts from a few years ago – like Granny Daphne – always certain that you are right and everyone else is wrong. Stubborn, arrogant, pig-headed, unyielding.'

'Thank you.'

'It wasn't a compliment.'

'I'm taking it as one. Granny Daphne was my hero. If there was a Holdfast I'd like to emulate, it's her. She killed Bastion to save me, and I want to be worthy of her sacrifice.'

'She also pissed off the Empress, which is what you are now doing. Different Empress, same problematic Holdfasts to deal with. First Kyra, now you. Have you thought about speaking to your mother? It's unlikely that she would hand you over to the authorities.'

Cael thought about it for a moment, then he sensed something coming from a different part of the city, a few miles to the west.

Cole looked up. 'Was that death powers?' he whispered.

'I felt it, too,' said Cael.

'Somewhere near the... university,' said Cole. 'Shit. Something's happening.'

'Stand up, but don't look alarmed,' said Cael, as he got to his feet.

Cole stood next to him.

'Are you ready?' said Cael. 'I'm taking us closer to where the powers were used. There might be trouble.'

'I don't have a weapon.'

'We have our powers,' said Cael. 'We don't need weapons.'

Cael put a hand into a pocket, and triggered his Quadrant. The air shimmered, and they appeared on a wide street in the aristocratic district of the New Town. Forty yards to their right, students were running out of the arched entrance to the university quad, some screaming, as a few town guards hurried towards them.

You cannot see us.

'I've made us invisible,' said Cael; 'I'm taking us into the quad.'

He triggered the Quadrant again, and they appeared by the northern edge of the quad, close to the university canteen. Several headless bodies were lying on the cobbles, and weeping students were huddling by the walls.

'You scan left,' said Cael; 'I'll scan right.'

He sent out his vision powers, then he felt Cole do the same. Their powers entwined for a moment, before separating to begin their search of the university. Cael rushed his vision through corridors and classrooms. On the upper levels, students and teachers were gazing out of the windows down at the bodies in the quad.

Cole grabbed his cousin's arm. 'I found him.'

'Show me.'

Cole's powers shone out in Cael's mind, and he followed them to the rooms where Professor Elbannon held his classes on Tempest and Quadrants. Inside one large lecture room on the third storey, several students were lying dead on the floor, as a young man in armour ransacked a few cupboards.

Cael triggered his Quadrant, and he and Cole appeared in the room. The man turned, three of Elbannon's Quadrants clutched in his left hand, another in his right.

'Cael Holdfast?' said Ward, as he turned. 'No weapons, while I have eye-guards? That was a little foolish of you, was it not? I could kill you now.'

'You murdered those students!' Cole cried.

'They tried to stop me,' said Ward. 'What else was I supposed to do? Anyway, I have what I came for, and so it is time to leave.'

'Tell Edgar that I want to speak to him,' said Cael.

'What makes you think I am in contact with Lord Edgar?' said Ward. 'He banished me from Nom Karta after I attempted to flay the skin from your body.'

Cael smiled. 'So, all three of those stolen Quadrants are for you, aye?'

Ward smiled back at him, then he vanished.

A cupboard door opened, and Elbannon peered out from its shadows. 'Has he gone?'

Cael relaxed his invisibility powers. 'Aye,' he said. 'It's safe to come out.'

Elbannon gripped a walking stick and grunted, so Cole walked over and helped the old man climb out of the cupboard. Elbannon gazed down at the six dead students.

'I know I am a coward,' the professor said, 'but if I hadn't hidden, I would be as dead as them.' He frowned at Cael and Cole. 'Holdfasts, eh?'

'We sensed Ward use his death powers, Professor,' said Cole. 'We came as quickly as we could.'

'But not quick enough,' said Elbannon. 'How many Quadrants did he steal?'

'Three,' said Cael.

Elbannon sat down on a chair. 'Is nowhere safe? Is this what it has come to – an armed assault on a peaceful institute of learning? What manner of savages is the Empire fighting? To kill innocent students…'

Gallea entered the room. Her eyes widened at the sight of the bodies, then she hurried over to Elbannon. She crouched down and took the old man's hand.

'Soldiers are on their way,' she said.

Elbannon pointed his walking stick at Cole and Cael. 'Two are already here.'

'We should leave,' said Cael.

'Why, Cael?' said Gallea. 'Wait; are you in trouble?'

Cael said nothing, then he glanced at Cole.

'What do you want me to do?' said Cole.

'Only you can decide that, cousin,' said Cael. 'Come with me, or stay here and tell the army that I tricked you.'

Cole glanced at the two old professors, then at the bodies on the blood-spattered floor. The sound of boots echoed from the corridor outside, and Cael put his hand into his pocket, ready to trigger the Quadrant.

'I don't know what to do,' said Cole.

'Neither do I, cousin. Together, we might be able to figure it out.'

'Shit. I've been in the damn army for less than a third. I can't believe I'm doing this.'

Cael smiled. 'Then you'll come with me?'

'Aye. Someone needs to keep your feet on the ground.'

Soldiers ran into the classroom, their crossbows loaded.

Cael brushed his fingers over the Quadrant, and the two young Holdfasts disappeared.

CHAPTER 15
DECLAWED

Sun Ta, Na Sun Ka, Western Rim – 10th Abrinch 5266 (18th Gylean Year 17)

'All I am saying,' said Corthie, 'is that he might have had a point. If Edgar isn't killing any Holdfasts, then killing Allura would have made us look worse than the enemy.'

Sable lit a cigarette amid the thick shadows of the chamber.

'And the more I think about it,' Corthie went on, 'the more I'm not so sure about our *kill every last god in existence* policy. For a start, not all gods are bad – deep down, you know that. Sure, some are terrible, but all of them? What about the father of Lindi? You've never told us his name, but it's obvious that he's a god – are you going to spare him? Or, will you tell Lindi when she's older that you murdered her father?'

'Gods tried to kill you and your family, nephew,' said Sable. 'Have you forgotten?'

'I haven't forgotten; but, you know me. I don't stay angry for long; I can't maintain it. Look; I'm not saying, *let's not kill any gods*; it's more, *let's be picky*. Have you thought about Lindi's future? If we exterminate all of the gods, who would she marry, and who would my kids marry?'

'Our children don't have to marry other gods; there are plenty of mortals they will be able to choose from.'

'Aye, but then their own children would be mortal, and I don't want my kids to see their own children die in front of them. Having children with other gods would mean that their kids would be immortal, like them.'

Sable raised an eyebrow.

'These are the things I think about,' said Corthie. He sipped from his mug of coffee. 'I wonder if Cael's back to clearing sewage drains.'

'He's not,' said Sable. 'The marines are saying that he hasn't reported to them for duty. He's been officially listed as a deserter.'

Corthie groaned. 'Bollocks. We kicked him out of the team, and now he's missing? What will happen if the marines find him?'

'A court martial, I'd imagine, followed by several years in a military prison. Anyway, back to you; are you going to be ready for today's operation? It sounds as though your focus has slipped. You were different after we re-took the dragon carrier – you were full of enthusiasm for wiping out the gods; and now you're preoccupied with thinking about suitors for your children.'

'Killing those ironhides was fun,' he said, 'and I felt the old bloodlust return; but I haven't fought since then, and, like anything else, it wears off if I don't use it. I did nothing during the robbery in Teros City; I just stood there like a numpty while Cael and Drechtalang wreaked havoc.'

'You won't be standing around like a numpty today, nephew; you're going to be knee-deep in blood. If this operation is successful, then we could think about giving ourselves a longer break from action. If we can kill Edgar, Allura, and whatever other gods happen to be in Nom Karta, then that might be enough to knock the Dominion out of the war.'

'It will still leave seven thousand Wystians on Gyle.'

Sable nodded. 'That's our biggest problem. We need to talk to Karalyn again. There must be a compromise that she is willing to accept. I get that she doesn't wish to cause the extinction of the dragons as a species, but is there no middle ground? What about dumping all the Wystians onto Athumia? They might like it there; they would have plenty of humans to worship them. If we could bring those two problems to a decent resolution – Edgar in Nom Karta, and the Wystians on Gyle – then I might be persuaded that we've done enough for now. You're not the only one who wants to go back to their family, Corthie. I'll be forty-two in just over a month; I'm too old for this shit.'

Corthie shrugged. 'You're still in great shape, Aunty.'

'I'm not as fast as I used to be.'

'I haven't noticed any difference.'

'Now you're just being kind.'

'No, honestly; you fight the same as you've always done. If you're feeling older, then you're doing a good job of hiding it. Still, I agree with the gist of what you were saying. We hit Nom Karta, then we get on our knees and beg my sister to intervene with the Sextant to deal with the Wystians, and then we can go home. Do we have a deal?'

Sable eyed him, then she gave a slight nod.

'And,' Corthie went on, 'we keep an eye out for Cael. We could claim that he still works for us; would that get him out of trouble? I don't want to see the lad in jail.'

'He shouldn't have signed up for the marines if he's incapable of obeying orders.'

'He was made to join the marines, as a punishment for stealing the Sextant.'

'Yes, but the Empress offered him the chance to leave after his training was over. He should have taken it.'

'Nah. Cael did a lot of good stuff when he was on active duty. There was a reason we wanted him in the team.'

'He needs to take responsibility for his actions. If I had killed Allura, there would be one fewer god left to support Edgar, and I would be one step closer to being able to go home to my family.' She stubbed out her cigarette. 'Have you finished that coffee?'

'Aye.'

Sable got to her feet. 'Let's fetch Nestorian and Drechtalang. It's time to visit Nom Karta.'

. . .

An hour later, the four members of the team were gathered round a small table, as Sable showed them a hand-drawn map she had made of the palaces of Nom Karta.

'This is from memory,' she said, 'but I searched the city thoroughly while I was there looking for Karalyn. According to Cael, when he was captured, he was taken to the largest palace in the city, which used to belong to King Gahad. Queen Famula lives there now, with the other senior members of her family – the government of the Dominion, in other words.' She pointed at the outline of a large palace on the map. 'It's here, on the eastern edge of the city, as far from the humans of Sat Orma as it's possible to get without leaving Nom Karta. Edgar and his gods will be there, too.' She glanced at the others. 'With so many dragons around, we'll have to be quick. I can control a few at a time, but not while I'm trying to fight gods. I can transport some dragons away with the Quadrant, but then I would be absent for short periods, while you are left to fight. As far as we know, Queen Famula is currently incapacitated; perhaps she is dead. We don't know exactly what Cael did to her; it may have proved fatal. Nestorian, I want you to bring a mortar, and get ready to fire it into the dragons as soon as we arrive. Set it up here, and we'll take it fully assembled. Drechtalang, your job will be to watch Nestorian's back during the operation.'

'What?' said the hedgewitch, scowling. 'I have to watch over a Banner rat?'

'The more mortars Nestorian can loose into the dragons, the longer we'll stay alive. I've scouted the palace, and I'm going to bring us onto a narrow balcony that overlooks the main audience hall, from where Nestorian will have a perfect view of every dragon. There will be Bullan soldiers on duty for you to fight, Drechtalang; if you're up to taking them on. They can be formidable opponents.'

'Ha! I'm not afraid of a few walking cows. I'll mount their horns on the walls of the temple when we get back.'

Sable smiled. 'Corthie and I will descend to the floor of the hall and hunt down any god we can find. Our main targets are Edgar and Allura, but there will probably be other gods there. The more we kill, the better.'

'What if Bailey is there?' said Corthie.

'That depends,' said Sable. 'If Bailey is in chains with a restrainer mask on his face, we free him; but, if he is clearly working for Edgar, then he dies with the others. Nestorian, get the mortar ready. Drechtalang, you will carry a crate of ammunition.'

'I can carry two crates,' said the Sanang man.

'Great, then carry two. Bring a bag of Forty-Eighter bombs, too.'

Nestorian moved off to the side of the hall, and began to fit together the frame for the mortar, while Drechtalang carried over the wooden crates that were packed full of the explosives the weapon required.

'Is it fair to be taking two soldiers with us who can't resist the powers of the gods?' said Corthie.

'It's always the same,' said Sable. 'We never get adequate support.'

'I've lost count of the number of team members I've lost over the years.'

Nestorian attached the steel mortar to the frame, then he nodded at Sable and Corthie.

'Carry it over,' said Sable.

Drechtalang and Nestorian lifted the assembled weapon, and brought it to where the hedgewitch had stacked the two crates of ammunition and the bag of Forty-Eighter bombs. Corthie pulled the Clawhammer from over his shoulder, Drechtalang gripped his Tempest axe, and Sable drew a Fated Blade. Nestorian prised open one of the crates, and lifted out one of the bombs.

Sable nodded at them. 'Blood, death, destruction – you get the idea. If things get too sticky, I'll pull us out, so don't wander off where I won't be able to find you in a hurry. Are you ready?'

'Ready for anything, boss,' said Drechtalang.

Corthie gripped the Clawhammer as Sable dipped her left hand into the side of her Tempest breastplate. The air crackled, and they appeared on a dark balcony above a great hall, where at least twenty dragons were gathered by a vast heap of cushions. Several human-sized figures were also present, and two turned and gazed up at the balcony.

'Get to work, Nestorian!' Sable cried, and the Banner soldier dropped a projectile into the steel tube of the mortar. There was a thump, and the projectile shot out, arcing through the air, and striking the side of a huge black and white dragon. The explosion ripped off the dragon's right wing and one of its forelimbs, and the hall descended into chaos. Several squads of Bullan soldiers on another section of the balcony began running toward the mortar, and Drechtalang threw a Forty-Eighter bomb at them. Sable kept her hand in her pocket as she scanned the ground floor, then the air shimmered, and Corthie found himself down next to the dragons, Sable by his side. Another mortar projectile whistled through the air, striking an arch directly above a red dragon, showering him in rubble. A grey dragon lifted its forelimb to swipe at Corthie, and he swung the Clawhammer, its talons ripping through the grey dragon's scales, and severing half of its forelimb. Flames blasted down from another dragon, and Corthie rolled away, dodging to avoid being stamped on by another dragon. At the same time, Sable was racing across the floor of the hall towards the group of gods. A third mortar exploded in the face of a green dragon, and Sable had to dive to the side to dodge the fragments of skull and flesh that were sent flying across the hall, then she sprang at Edgar, the Fated Blade raised in her right hand.

Sable froze, then she dropped the sword and fell to her knees. Edgar raised a hand and, up on the balcony, Nestorian and Drechtalang toppled to the floor, unconscious. Three dragons surrounded Corthie, their jaws open, as sparks jumped across their fangs.

'Hold!' cried Edgar. 'We have the Holdfasts exactly where we want them.'

'They have killed one dragon and maimed three others!' growled the dragon atop the mound of cushions.

'They shall be punished, mighty Queen,' said Edgar. 'Kyra, step forward.'

'You?' said Sable, as she glanced up at her niece. 'It was you who stopped me?'

'Aye, Aunty,' said Kyra. 'What are you doing here? Are you nothing but a savage?'

'What about this one?' said one of the dragons surrounding Corthie. 'Should we render him to ash?'

'Don't kill him,' said Kyra. 'Uncle Corthie, if you want Aunty Sable to live, drop your weapon and stand by her side.'

Corthie glanced over at the kneeling figure of Sable, while trying to keep an eye on the three dragons ready to burn him.

'You fucking traitor, Kyra,' cried Sable.

'Where is Cael?' said Edgar, his white armour shining in the dim light of the hall.

'I kicked that little bastard off the team,' said Sable.

'Why, because he saved the life of Allura?'

Sable looked Edgar in the eyes. 'You would be dead right now if it wasn't for Kyra.'

'I know. Her ability to stop you saved us. I don't wish to kill you, Sable, despite the advice of my friends. Can you give me a reason to spare you?'

'No.'

'Wait,' said Corthie. He lowered the Clawhammer to the ground, and raised his hands in the air. He glanced up at the dragons surrounding him, and two parted to allow him to walk over to Sable's side. He glanced at Kyra, and she looked away, shame on her face.

'Kill them both,' said the Queen, from the mound of cushions. 'They invaded my home and brought death and misery to my kin.'

'Just as Ward did to my home,' said Corthie.

'That is true,' said Edgar. 'I do not wish to kill you, either, Corthie. Bullan, bring down the two men who were accompanying the Holdfasts.'

'Yes, sir,' said a horned warrior, and a squad of them ran for the stairs.

Corthie glanced down at Sable. 'What did Kyra do to you?'

'I placed blocks in her mind,' said Kyra; 'powerful blocks. Sable is no longer able to initiate any act of violence, unless her life, or the lives of her family, are directly threatened. She can fight back if she is attacked, but she cannot attack anyone else.'

Corthie frowned. 'How long will it last?'

'Forever, Uncle. I have also paralysed her movements, but that will wear off soon.'

'You treacherous bitch,' Sable snarled. 'You have just doomed the Empire to defeat. Is that what you wanted?'

'I want peace, Aunty,' said Kyra, 'and you were standing in the way.'

Edgar walked up to Sable, and stared down at her. 'You will never be able to kill me, Holdfast,' he said, 'as I shall never attack you. You should have stayed at home to protect your family.'

Sable's face twitched, but her arms remained by their sides.

Edgar turned to Kyra. 'Do the same to Corthie.'

Kyra narrowed her eyes as she gazed at her uncle. 'No. Corthie is not the same as Sable. He lacks... the same ruthlessness. He will not be a threat if Sable is neutralised.'

'I disagree,' said Edgar. 'Isn't he supposedly the finest mortal fighter in existence?'

'There is no doubt about that,' said Kyra. 'If we were to keep him here as our hostage, then the Empire would be very likely to offer us Ballatar in exchange.'

Edgar nodded. 'I can accept that as a compromise.'

'You are taking advice from a mortal girl?' said another god.

'I am, Lady Laverne. No one else could have stopped Sable Holdfast from killing us. We owe the girl our lives. We shall send Sable back to Na Sun Ka, without her Quadrant, and we shall keep Corthie here as our prisoner.'

Corthie glanced around. A company of Bullan soldiers were to his rear, pointing their crossbows at him, while the dragons in the hall were forming a circle round them. Nestorian and Drechtalang were dragged into their midst, and dropped to the floor next to Sable.

'That one is a healer,' said Allura, pointing at the hedgewitch with her remaining hand.

Nestorian and Drechtalang began to stir, and the Bullan kept their bows aimed at them.

'My fucking head,' groaned Drechtalang, then he opened his eyes and took in the scene. 'Oh bugger.'

'Kyra,' said Edgar, 'order Sable to hand over her Quadrant.'

Kyra nodded, then she stared into Sable's eyes. Sable's left hand moved towards the gap in her armour, and she pulled out the Quadrant.

'It's a proper one,' said Allura. 'Not one of those three-jewelled copies.'

'It used to belong to Edmond,' said Kyra.

'Did it?' said Edgar. 'This was my brother's personal Quadrant?'

He reached out to take it, but Nestorian's hand moved quicker. The Banner soldier's finger touched the copper surface, the air shimmered, and the four members of the team appeared back in the temple of Ulna in Sun Ta.

'Holy shit!' Drechtalang cried. He stared at Nestorian. 'How the fuck do you know how to operate a Quadrant?'

'I used the *Go back* command,' said Nestorian, as he struggled to his feet. 'It's the only one I know.'

Drechtalang started to laugh, his hands on his knees, then he threw up onto the floor of the hall. Corthie lowered his arms, and turned to Sable, who was kneeling, the Quadrant still clutched in her left hand.

'Don't say anything,' Sable said.

'But...'

'Please, Corthie,' she said. 'I need a moment to allow what has happened to sink in.'

Corthie nodded, then he put a hand on Nestorian's shoulder. 'Thank you, sergeant; you saved our arses.'

'No problem, sir,' said Nestorian.

They glanced at Drechtalang, who was still laughing manically as he wiped the sick from his lips.

'We lost a mortar, almost two full crates of projectiles, and most of a bag of Forty-Eighters, sir,' Nestorian went on.

'But we got back here with our lives,' said Corthie. 'Pyre's tits, we got our arses handed to us.'

'It was too mental, even for us,' cried Drechtalang. 'Dragons, Bullan, gods...'

'It was Kyra,' said Sable. 'She was the difference. Without her, I would have killed Edgar and his band of gods, and then we could have returned here in victory. Did you see Bailey hiding behind one of the hall's pillars? And I lost my Fated Blade...' She broke down in tears, as the three men gazed at her.

'You're alive, boss,' said Drechtalang.

'Without my ability to fight, I might as well be dead,' she said.

Drechtalang frowned and turned to Corthie. 'What's she talking about, boss?'

'Kyra has been inside her head,' said Corthie. 'Sable is no longer able to attack anyone. The only way she can fight is in self defence.'

'Nah,' said Drechtalang. 'That shit isn't possible.'

'It is if you're a dream mage,' said Corthie. 'It's been done to me before, and to Sable. We both know what it feels like.'

'I can sense the blocks in my mind,' said Sable; 'they are more permanent than anything Daimon was able to achieve. I was able to get rid of those, after a lot of effort, but Kyra is stronger.'

'Are your powers also blocked?' he said.

Sable shook her head. 'She left them untouched.'

'So, you aren't helpless,' he said. He extended a hand and Sable took it. He pulled her to her feet, and embraced her.

'It's over,' said Sable. 'The Wystian dragons will roll over Na Sun Ka as soon as they are fit enough to do so. This world will fall.'

'We can still talk to my sister about the Sextant.'

Sable shook her head. 'You do it. I'm going home.'

'Don't give up.'

Sable laughed, and Corthie almost flinched from the bitter sound.

'In a matter of seconds,' she said, 'Kyra stripped from me everything that made me special. Who am I if I can't kill?'

'You are Sable Holdfast,' he said. 'There's much more to you than killing.'

'I'm going to Ulna.'

'I'll come with you,' said Corthie. 'Nestorian, Drechtalang – take a couple of days off to rest. We'll be back soon.

'You might,' said Sable. 'I won't.'

Nestorian and Drechtalang stared at her in silence, then she swiped her fingers over the Quadrant, and Corthie appeared next to her by the bridge palace in Udall. The sky was clear overhead, then Corthie noticed several plumes of smoke coming from the harbour. Over a dozen dragons were circling over the tall masts, and hundreds of civilians were out on the streets, rushing back and forth.

'What's going on?' said Corthie. 'Have we arrived in the middle of something?'

Sable stared towards the ships in the harbour, then she started to run. Corthie went after her, weaving through the crowds as Sable sprinted towards a long pier that jutted out into the waters of the harbour. A fire was raging in one of the buildings along the quayside, and bodies were being carried out and laid by the side of the road. Sable ran up a gangway onto a sleek ship. Corthie followed her, and saw several sailors lying on the deck, their heads missing.

'Lara!' Sable cried, as she pushed her way through the crew.

'Clear a path for Sable!' shouted a man. 'This way, ma'am.'

Sable reached the man, who took her arm. 'Where are they, Topaz?' she said.

'Ma'am, they're safe,' he said; 'listen to me; your family got a fright, but they're safe.'

Topaz led Sable and Corthie to the quarter deck, and then through more crowds of sailors into a cabin behind the ship's wheel. Inside, Lara was sitting on a padded bench with one infant in her arms, and a small boy on her knee.

Lara looked up. Blood was running down one cheek from a long cut, and her eyes were red.

'Sable?' she said.

'I'm here,' Sable said, crouching by her family and holding them close. 'I'm back.'

'For how long?' said Lara.

'For good,' said Sable.

'What happened?' said Corthie.

Topaz cleared the cabin of sailors and closed the door. He turned, his expression grim.

'A god appeared out of nowhere,' Topaz said. 'We were preparing the *Giddy Gull* for a short trip down to Throscala, when we saw smoke and heard screams coming from the quayside. The god was looking for Lara. We tried to stop him getting on board the *Gull*, but he killed anyone in his way; then he broke into the cabin. I ran up here, but the god had gone by the time I arrived.'

'His name was Ward,' Lara said, her tears mingling with the blood on her cheek. 'He wanted me to know that. He said he wanted to show me how easily he could reach me and the children; how easily he could kill us, if he wanted to. He cut my face, then he left.'

'He was sending a message to Sable,' said Corthie.

'Do you think I don't realise that?' cried Lara. 'He was using Sable's own bleeding tactics to teach her a lesson.'

'I should never have left your side,' said Sable. 'When the Wystians come, I will take us somewhere safe.'

'Are the Wystians on their way?' said Topaz.

'Not yet,' said Corthie, 'but it's only a matter of time.'

'Shut up, both of you,' said Lara. 'Sable, what did you mean by *For good*? Are you really going to stay this time?'

'Yes. I... Kyra... she did something to my mind. Do you remember what Daimon did to me?'

Lara's eyes widened. 'Did Kyra force you to kill another friend?'

'It's not like that; Kyra has blocked my ability to fight, except in self defence. I can't attack anyone again, maybe forever.'

Lara stared at her, then she wiped a tear from Sable's eye. 'No more rampages?'

'No more rampages, Lara. I can defend myself, and I can defend you and the children, but I can never go off to war again.'

The two women embraced as they wept. Corthie took a step back, and eyed Topaz.

'Let's give them a moment,' Corthie said.

They walked out of the cabin and on to the quarter deck. Topaz closed the door and lit a cigarette.

'I'm Corthie, by the way,' he said, extending a hand.

'Master Topaz,' said the other man, as they shook hands.

The crowd of sailors stared at them.

'Sable is back,' said Topaz, 'as most of you probably saw. We're going to give the captain and her family some peace and quiet. Clear the bodies from the deck, and prepare them for a decent burial, then lend a hand to anyone on the quayside who needs it. Get to work.'

The sailors began to disperse.

'Is Kyra a Holdfast?' said Topaz.

'Aye,' said Corthie; 'one of Karalyn's twins.'

'Is she working for the enemy?'

Corthie nodded.

'Are we in deep shit?'

'The deepest. Today was a grim day for Dragon Eyre and the Empire; there's no doubt about it.'

'What will you do?'

Corthie said nothing, then Topaz gazed up at the sky.

'Blackrose and Maddie,' said the ship's master. 'They're coming in low.'

The great black dragon soared down from the blue sky, then she hovered over the *Giddy Gull*.

'Corthie Holdfast?' said Blackrose.

'I arrived with Sable,' said Corthie.

'And Lara? The children?'

'Safe. Edgar's gods were trying to frighten us.'

'How many humans were killed?'

'The *Gull* lost seven of its crew, Your Majesty,' said Topaz, 'and there were maybe a dozen casualties on the quayside.'

The dragon's eyes burned red. 'Vengeance calls to me. How dare the gods think they can assault my land and people with impunity? How does Sable intend to gain her revenge for this affront? Perhaps we can plan our response together.'

'Sable won't be leaving Ulna,' said Corthie.

'If she is worried about her family, she can hide them somewhere before she returns to battle.'

'No, Blackrose; she won't be going back to the war. Kyra Holdfast has blocked her ability to fight, permanently.'

The great black dragon said nothing.

'She did what?' cried Maddie, from the shoulder harness. 'Sable can't fight any more?'

'She can fight, but only in self defence,' said Corthie. 'Kyra didn't take that away from her, and she can still access her vision powers.'

'Our enemies will rejoice at this news,' said Blackrose, 'and our allies will tremble and weep. How can we win without Sable's prowess? Alas; this is a dark day for all who fight the gods; a bitter, terrible day that augurs worse to follow. Who will stop the Wystians?'

'I'm still here,' said Corthie. 'Kyra didn't block me.'

'Tell me, Corthie – where is your Clawhammer? I have never seen you in armour without it.'

Corthie lowered his gaze. 'I lost it in battle, as Sable lost her Fated Blade. Both are now in the hands of Edgar.'

'Then the end of Dragon Eyre is inevitable,' said Blackrose. 'Our hundreds cannot withstand the Wystians' thousands. They will burn their way through the Eastern Rim, and the Unk Tannic shall follow, as surely as night follows day, plunging my realm into darkness.'

'I will fight on,' said Corthie; 'alone, if necessary. I will plead with my sister to help us with the Wystians, and, if I can find Cael, then he might be able to remove the blocks that his sister put into Sable's mind.

For now, though, I need to go back to Na Sun Ka. Maddie, will you take me?'

'Uh, all right, if Blackrose agrees,' said Maddie.

'Why would you fight for this world, Corthie?' said the black dragon. 'You owe it nothing.'

'You are my friend, Blackrose; you and Maddie. We have known each other for fifteen years, ever since we met in Arrowhead Fortress on the Great Wall. Do you think I would desert you now?'

'Our bonds run deep, it is true,' said the dragon, 'but I do not want you to throw your life away. Nothing can prevent the Wystians from sweeping across Na Sun Ka, not even you, Corthie Holdfast.'

'Maybe,' said Corthie. 'Kyra made a mistake when she didn't place blocks into my head, and I can find a new weapon. It might be pointless, but I'm going to try. My own family is with Karalyn, so I know they're safe; and I won't return to them until I have given all I have to give.'

'You have a noble spirit, Corthie. So be it. Climb up onto my harness, and I shall fly to the bridge palace, where you can bathe and eat, and then my rider will take you to Na Sun Ka.'

Corthie glanced at the closed cabin door, then he reached out, grabbed hold of a dangling strap, and pulled himself up onto the harness, where Maddie was sitting. He fastened the buckles next to her, and the black dragon rose into the air.

'See you soon, Topaz, my love!' Maddie shouted down to the ship.

Topaz waved up at them, then the dragon banked, and soared off towards the palace.

CHAPTER 16
HOLDING COURT

Na Sun Ka, Western Rim – 12th Abrinch 5266 (18th Gylean Year 17)

'Have you been to see her?' said Corthie.

Kelsey shook her head. 'Not yet. I think I'll give Sable a few more days before I head up to Ulna. I came here to find out what you were going to do.'

'Why should I do anything different? I swore an oath to the Empress to serve, and I was posted to Na Sun Ka.'

Kelsey said nothing as they sat out on the roof of the enormous palace.

'I'm not going to abandon my post, sis,' Corthie went on. 'We already have one deserter in the family; let's not make it two.'

'We already have two deserters, brother. Cole vanished from the army base in Plateau City a few days back. He was last seen by Professor Gallea in the presence of Cael. The lad hadn't even completed one third of training. Do you remember how Bridget used to curse the Holdfasts? I'm starting to know how she felt. With Sable being forced to retire, and Cael and Cole buggering off, you are the only Holdfast left in the armed forces.'

Corthie glanced out over the sprawling city. 'Tell the Empress that she can depend on me. If and when the Wystians launch their invasion, I'll be here to hold them back.'

'There's no *if* about it, Corthie. They're coming.'

'But why? If Allura and the rest of them have Quadrants, and the Wystians want to go back to Wyst, then why don't the gods just take them there? Why bother with Na Sun Ka?'

'We have to assume that the gods want to hurt Queen Blackrose and the Empire.'

'But we don't know that for sure. Maybe Cael was right; perhaps we should be talking to Edgar. I'll be honest with you, sis – I want to go home. It was a mistake to have allowed myself to get so angry that I enlisted; but now that I've done it, I have to see it through. The only thing I ask is this – if there is a decent chance to end this war peacefully, then, as Herald, I hope you take it.'

'I will,' she said. She got to her feet. 'I'd better be going; there's a lot happening on Colsbury today.'

'Say hello to Aila and the kids for me.'

Kelsey nodded, then she took out the Quadrant from her shoulder bag. 'Do you have any leave arranged?'

'Claudian is coming for me in a few days,' said Corthie. 'I have a one-day pass.'

'Then I'll probably see you on Colsbury.'

She swept her fingers over the Quadrant, and appeared in the forecourt of Colsbury Castle, close to the entrance of the Great Keep. She placed the Quadrant back into her bag, and walked round the side of the keep, entering the small courtyard that separated it from the Lesser Keep. Arrosa was waiting for her in the middle of the stone plaza, in the only part that wasn't bathed in the shadows coming from the tall structures.

Arrosa smiled as Kelsey approached. 'Do you want me to go over our signals again?'

'We won't be needing them this morning,' said Kelsey. 'I didn't ask you to join me for your Gift of Truth.'

'Then why do you need me?'

'I don't need you. Think of it as a learning exercise – a bit like university, only in practice rather than theory. You were quiet in Amatskouri; this time, I want you to ask questions.'

Arrosa nodded. 'Where are we going?'

Kelsey pointed at the Lesser Keep. 'Nowhere exotic, I'm afraid.'

Arrosa turned, and glanced up at the dark, forbidding building. 'What goes on in there?'

'Routine government business,' said Kelsey. 'It lies empty for most of the year, and then fills up every summer when the court arrives from Plateau City. I've booked out several floors this year for a particular purpose, and they'll stay occupied until the job is done.'

'What job?'

'Let's go inside and see,' said Kelsey. 'The rooms I have reserved are all on the lower floors.'

They entered the stone keep. Workers were busy in the main entrance hall, and in the rooms to either side, cleaning the old stonework, and laying fresh rugs and wall-hangings. Kelsey walked into a large chamber to their right, where Shella was pacing up and down, overseeing the positioning of a long table by four Holdings staff. Kelsey and Arrosa waited at the side of the chamber, next to a narrow window of stained glass. Shella noticed them, and sent the workers away.

'I'll have this place ready in a day or two,' Shella said; 'but we'll need something to get rid of the musty old smell.'

'I thought that was coming from you,' said Kelsey.

'Ah, the smug confidence of the young,' said Shella, 'assuming that they will never get old. I noticed you reserved all the rooms on the bottom two floors – do you think I can't handle stairs any more?'

'You're confusing Arrosa,' said Kelsey; 'by referring to me as *young*, Shella.'

'You are young,' said the Rakanese woman. 'When I was your age, Kelsey, I was leading the Migration.' She walked over and took a seat by the table, then she lit a cigarette. 'Sit down, and tell me what you want.'

Kelsey and Arrosa sat down next to Shella.

'My proposals are set to be approved by the Empress this afternoon, and your position as president of the constitutional convention will be formalised,' said Kelsey. 'I need to have a rough idea of what you intend to do.'

'That's simple,' said Shella. 'I will invite several delegates to join me here, and we will thrash out the future of the Empire.'

'What kind of delegates?' said Arrosa.

Shella eyed the young Gunstian woman. 'Two types. The first will be representatives from every province within the Empire; and the second will be legal and constitutional experts. This kind of change needs support from every conceivable part of the Empire.'

Arrosa frowned.

'She doesn't know what you've been asked to do,' said Kelsey. 'Arrosa was appointed to the Imperial Court after we held the meeting on Summer's Day.'

'And you haven't told her?' said Shella.

'That's why I brought her along this morning.'

Shella nodded. 'All right. Well, Arrosa Holdfast, my latest task will probably be my last but, if it's accepted by the Empress, it will be the one I'll be most proud of. I am to draw up plans to turn the Empire into a democracy.'

'I sensed no lie,' said Arrosa, 'but it seems unbelievable. Why would the Empress agree to giving away her power over the Empire? And why would we want her to?'

'The Empress will remain the sovereign ruler,' said Kelsey, 'but there are so many problems affecting the Empire that we need the support of the citizens if it is to survive. You know how well Amatskouri is governed; imagine if the entire Empire was run in a similar manner.'

'I won't be recommending that we adopt the Amatskourian system in its entirety,' said Shella. 'It works well there because the Amatskourians are one people – united. The different population levels within the Empire need to be taken into account.' She set down her cigarette. 'A quick example – the City of Salve contains ten times the population of Kellach Brigdomin, yet the Kellach were founding members of the Empire, while the City is a new arrival. The Holdings contains even more people. We can't end up with a system where the City and the Holdings together can outvote every other province. The others would be pissed off; they'd feel less represented, rather than more. Look at what the Kellach themselves do. They have a similar problem – the Domm vastly outnumber the Kell, while the Brig and Lach lie somewhere in between. If the Domm had attempted to fill the Clan Council according to population levels, the Kell would have refused to join. So, what did they do? They came up with a council that contains eight delegates from each tribe, giving the Kell the same number of votes as the Domm. This compromise has kept the government of Kellach Brigdomin functioning efficiently for decades. Would it work over the Empire as a whole? Doubtful. The provinces with large populations would feel they were being outvoted by a bunch of much smaller ones.'

'Then what is the answer?' said Arrosa.

'That is exactly what the convention will attempt to work out,' said Shella. 'Perhaps the Herald of the Empire would like to provide some clarity on the matter?'

'Absolutely not,' said Kelsey. 'I'll be staying clear of this debate.'

'But you are not only the Herald,' said Arrosa; 'you are Holder Fast, with a stake in the Holdings democracy.'

Shella snorted. 'The Holdings isn't a proper democracy,' she said. 'Forty per cent of their delegates are directly selected by the Holders – a bunch of extremely wealthy, land-owning aristocratic buffoons with monarchist tendencies.' She smiled at Kelsey. 'No offence.'

'That is the system my mother set up,' said Kelsey.

'With help from Laodoc, who was also an extremely wealthy, land-owning aristocratic buffoon; even though I loved the guy. The constitution I will devise for the Empire will not be following that pattern. It won't be following any existing pattern. There will be a bumpy road ahead, as we're bound to make mistakes. We will also require a shitload of gold to implement the changes.'

'I'm taking care of the financial problems,' said Kelsey. 'Arrosa knows about Amatskouri.'

'Does she? You seem to be confiding all of our secrets in her these days.'

'She has the Gift of Truth,' said Kelsey. 'It would be hard to keep anything from her.'

'Will you be announcing the plan in today's meeting of the Imperial Court?'

'Aye.'

'Who else knows? I want to watch the faces of those who don't.'

'Just us three and the Empress.'

'Then my eyes will be on Naxor, as I love to see him get upset.'

Kelsey got to her feet. 'Come on, Arrosa; let's leave Shella to it. She seems to have it all under control.'

Arrosa stood. She curtsied before Shella, which made the Rakanese princess laugh, then Kelsey led her out of the Lesser Keep.

'Now you know my other secret plan,' said Kelsey. 'Do not breathe a word of it until this afternoon's meeting of the court.'

'Am I allowed to disagree with the plan?'

'The Empire doesn't belong to the Holdfasts.'

'I didn't say it did. What if I believe that the Empire needs a strong leader, one who isn't beholden to a parliament? For all of Prime Minister Jazidorato's support, if his parliament rejects your proposal, then there's nothing we can do.'

'A decision that large requires the backing of the people for it to work.'

Arrosa frowned. 'I'm also surprised that Shella didn't tease me about Cael.'

'I wondered when you would bring him up.'

'My husband has deserted from the Imperial Marines. You can understand why it might have been preying on my mind.'

Kelsey eyed her. 'I know he has a Quadrant. Has he been in contact with you?'

'Would you expect me to tell you if he had?'

'Aye.'

'I'll not betray him.'

'You misunderstand me. I want to help your wayward husband; I have no interest in throwing him in jail. If he contacts you, let him know that he can speak to me. I won't be summoning the Imperial Guard to arrest him.'

Arrosa narrowed her eyes, but said nothing.

'Was I lying?' said Kelsey.

Arrosa shook her head.

They walked into the large forecourt, where Halfclaw was standing. The green and blue dragon was leaning up to talk to the Empress, who was standing on the middle balcony.

'No Frostback today?' said Arrosa.

'She's taking Calpurnia on another flight,' said Kelsey. 'They are slowly developing a bond.'

'Does that make you jealous?'

Kelsey laughed. 'Of course not. I'd be jealous if Frostback had chosen a person at random to train, but Calpurnia's my daughter. I'm going to my study to work, so you'll have to amuse yourself until this afternoon's meeting. Remember, not a word about anything Shella told you.'

Arrosa nodded, then she walked off in the direction of the gardens. Kelsey watched her for a moment, then she turned for the palace.

The Empress had selected her grandest audience chamber for that day's meeting of the Imperial Court – the same chamber where Bridget had been forced to resume her reign as Empress. The huge curving windows looked out over the island of Colsbury, and the old wooden throne was in the same place where it always sat, its carved horses reflecting the bright sunlight. Kelsey watched as the other members of the court arrived. Arrosa took her place on a chair by the left-hand side of the empty throne, then the others sat down.

Naxor glanced over at Kelsey, his eyes tight as he sat. Kelsey smiled at him, and the demigod's frown deepened.

They all got back to their feet when the Empress walked into the hall, passing the armoured soldiers by the door. She went up to the throne, mounted the steps, and sat. The members of the court bowed their heads, and resumed their places.

'This meeting should be brief,' said the Empress, 'as there is very little I have to say.'

The others kept their eyes on her, saying nothing.

'I have considered all of my Herald's proposals,' the Empress went on, 'but before I pronounce my decision, I would like Kelsey to inform everyone about the negotiations she has recently been holding. Herald?'

Kelsey tilted her head. 'Thank you, Your Majesty. First of all, I make no apologies for the secrecy; it was essential to allow both sides in the negotiations the freedom to speak their minds.'

'Get on with it,' said Naxor. 'What have you done?'

'I have proposed the sale of a quarter of the Plateau to Amatskouri, so they can form their own sovereign nation within the Empire.'

Naxor's eyes widened. 'You have sold a quarter of the Plateau?'

'Not yet. It needs to pass through the Amatskourian parliament first. As soon as it is brought before them, the Amatskourian newspapers will be printing stories about the plan, and all secrecy will have evaporated. I have proposed that they pay for the land with a twenty-year mortgage, which will save the Empire from bankruptcy.'

'Twenty years from now,' said Naxor, 'there will be millions of Rakanese living on the Plateau – you all know how quickly they can breed. Other than that, I think it is a fine plan, and you have my congratulations, Herald.' He smirked at Shella. 'So sorry to disappoint you, Your Highness; it was clear you were hoping that I would be outraged by what is, at heart, a sensible way forward for the Empire.'

'Might I be permitted to see the financial details of the plan, Herald?' said Slaeon.

'Of course,' said Kelsey. 'The treasury will be the main beneficiary of the proposals.'

'Does anyone here disagree with my Herald's plan regarding the sale of land to Amatskouri?' said the Empress.

Janis Holdsmith raised his hand.

'Yes, Chief Jurist?' said Thorn. 'Speak your mind.'

'My objection concerns what Chamberlain Naxor just mentioned, Your Majesty,' said Janis. 'The Amatskourians will no doubt relax their rules on spawning, and their population will explode, as it always does. The Rakanese expand into any geographical area that they are given. Before we know it, Plateau City will have a dozen over-crowded cities as our neighbours, all bulging at the seams with Rakanese. They will outnumber everyone else on the Star Continent.'

'So?' said Shella.

Janis shrugged. 'It will upset the current balance among the peoples of this world.'

'Balance?' said Shella. 'Do you mean that the Holdings won't be the most populous race any more?'

'The Holdings people built this Empire, Your Highness. Built it, and fought for it. Thousands of Holdings soldiers have died to protect it. What contribution have the Rakanese ever made?'

'It is true that the Rakanese don't enlist in the imperial armed forces,' said Kelsey, 'but they contribute in other ways. Their sailors ply the Inner Sea, for example, and their wealth provides income to the Empire through taxes. Giving the Amatskourians a new nation to build will benefit everyone.'

Janis laughed. 'Yes. Just look how much Rakana has done for us all. What a well-run nation that was, before we had to intervene. The Rakanese have proved beyond doubt that they shouldn't be allowed to govern their own country.'

'What happened to Rakana is a lesson to us all,' said Shella. 'For centuries, it was a well-governed, functioning democracy, until it was turned upside down by the Migration. What went wrong? The pressure for more land destroyed institutions that had worked for generations. Selling land to Amatskouri will prevent that from happening again.'

'And what will we do next time,' said Janis, 'when the Amatskourians have filled up their new home?'

'Then we speak to Karalyn,' said Kelsey. 'The Sextant can deal with these issues if they arise in the future.'

'Are you advocating mass deportations, Herald?'

Kelsey rolled her eyes. 'That's not what I meant. The Sextant can create a new world for the Rakanese; one that could hold countless millions.'

'I have heard enough on this topic,' said the Empress. 'Chief Jurist, your objections are noted; however, due to the current state of the imperial finances, I am going to lend my support to this proposal. We must now hope that the Amatskourian parliament agrees.'

'Thank you, Your Majesty,' said Kelsey. 'The parliament should be hearing about it in the next few days, so we shouldn't have too long to wait for their decision.'

'Let us move on to your other proposals,' said the Empress. She gazed out at everyone seated before her. 'I have thought long and hard about the implications of the Herald's plan, and I have reached a decision. The Herald's proposals shall go ahead, in their entirety; so I decree.'

Kelsey found herself grinning. She glanced over at Shella, whose smile was mirroring hers. Further down from Shella, both Janis and Naxor were seething, their anger obvious.

'Might I interject, Your Majesty?' said Naxor. 'Perhaps it isn't too late to have a few amendments agreed upon?'

'That time has passed, Chamberlain,' said the Empress. 'Treasurer Slaeon, the immediate cut in taxation, and the establishment of the new bank fall under your remit. Have both put into effect as quickly as possible.'

'It shall be so, Your Majesty,' said the Rahain woman.

'Chancellor Shellakanawara,' the Empress went on, 'you are now the president of the constitutional convention. I expect your detailed proposals within the year, with progress reports every third. The entire court should be aware that I reserve the right to reject any conclusions reached by the convention. They will need my agreement before they are set into law. You may publicise this decision to the newspapers. I want the public to be aware that their future is being openly debated.'

'I understand, Your Majesty,' said Shella.

'That's it, then,' said Janis. 'The Empire is cutting its own throat. Professor Achan and the strikers would be proud.'

'Come now, old chap,' said Naxor. 'The Empress has made her decision clear. Right or wrong, we are duty bound to respect her decree.'

'You're taking this very well,' said Caelius.

'What choice do I have, Quartermaster?' said Naxor. 'My own powers as Imperial Chamberlain will be watered down, as will those of most of us sitting here; but I am resigned to it. Perhaps being immortal gives me a longer perspective on such matters – things ebb and flow. Right now, they are ebbing, but I will still be around when they start to flow again.' He glanced at Kelsey. 'Do you require my term of service in the Imperial Court to come to an end, Herald?'

'No,' said Kelsey. 'I want you to remain as Chamberlain.'

'That's very generous of you. Or is it more cautious? You would rather have me plotting within the court, than conspiring without?'

'Something like that,' said Kelsey.

'Nothing will change for the moment,' said the Empress. 'And might I remind everyone that we are in the midst of a war? We shall need to work together to defeat our enemies; otherwise these new proposals will never amount to much. Adjutant, what is the current situation on Dragon Eyre?'

'The Herald was there this morning, Your Majesty,' said Claudian. 'Her update will be more recent than mine.'

'I spoke to Corthie while I was there,' Kelsey said, 'and I toured the defences.'

'How is Corthie?' said the Empress.

'Sable's departure has hurt him; that's clear – and we are very fortunate that Kyra did nothing to my brother's powers. Corthie will do his duty.'

'I would have expected nothing less from him,' said Thorn. 'Are there any indications that...?'

Her voice tailed away as the door to the hall opened. Four soldiers walked in, including a senior officer from the Plateau City garrison, who was clutching one of Elbannon's Quadrants in his left hand.

'Many apologies for the interruption, Your Majesty,' the officer said, bowing low, 'but I have urgent news from the imperial capital.'

'Speak,' said Kelsey.

'Thank you, ma'am,' said the officer. 'Lord Ballatar was found dead in his prison cell this morning, his head severed from his body.'

The members of the court gasped.

'How were the prison's defences breached?' said Cardova. 'We had four companies of soldiers guarding that cell.'

'The assailant used a Quadrant, sir,' said the officer; 'and the killing was carried out in silence during the shift change at dawn. The body was discovered when soldiers went to deliver his breakfast.'

'It wasn't me,' said Naxor. 'I had nothing to do with it; I just want to make that clear.' He glanced at Arrosa. 'Did I lie?'

Arrosa shook her head. 'No.'

Kelsey groaned and lowered her head. 'This is a fucking calamity. Edgar will assume that we killed his friend in retaliation for one of Ward's attacks.'

Claudian narrowed his eyes. 'Do we know of Sable's whereabouts?'

'It couldn't have been Sable,' said Kelsey. 'Thanks to Kyra, she can't attack anyone. Lucius, you should go back to Plateau City with the officer, to lead the investigation.'

Cardova nodded. 'I'll leave at once.'

'Constable,' said the Empress, 'report to my Herald and me as soon as you have any information about the identity of the murderer.'

Cardova bowed as he got to his feet. 'I shall, Your Majesty.'

'Chamberlain,' the Empress went on; 'issue a statement to the newspapers that we had nothing to do with this crime; ensure that this message reaches the front pages.'

'As you will it, Your Majesty,' said Naxor.

'This meeting is over,' said the Empress. 'You are all dismissed. Until we know who was responsible for this act, have our armed forces placed on high alert. There may be another attack.'

The rest of the court stood and bowed, as the Empress strode from the hall, flanked by soldiers.

Four hours later, Kelsey was working in her study. She had passed over a large amount of paperwork to Slaeon, so that the Rahain treasurer could analyse the figures arising from the land sale to Amatskouri, and then Kelsey had turned her attention back to the war. With a large sum of money about to reach the Empire if the land sale was approved, she was prioritising spending on Ravi's explosives factory; throwing him and his assistants huge amounts of gold to develop new weapons and increase production. There was no other way to repel an invasion of Na Sun Ka by thousands of Wystians, though she doubted it would be enough.

A floorboard creaked in the shadows of her study.

'Stop lurking in the darkness, Karalyn,' she said. 'Do you want something?'

Cael stepped out from the shadows.

Kelsey put down her pencil. 'Not Karalyn, then?'

'No, Aunty.'

'Did Arrosa perhaps have a little word with you?'

Cael smiled. 'I don't know what you're talking about, Aunty.'

'Of course you don't. It's just a wild coincidence that you appear in my study after I told her I wanted to speak to you? Fair enough. Let's say I believe that; what do you want?'

'To explain myself.'

'You deserted your post in the middle of a war; what aspect needs further explanation?'

'Someone in the Imperial Court needs to start talking to Edgar,' said Cael. 'I can speak to him on your behalf. He knows me. If I reach out to him, would you support me, or disown me?'

'And what would you say to him?'

'I would ask him what he wants in order to end the war, Aunty. I would negotiate.'

Kelsey smiled. 'You have a rather high opinion of your abilities, Cael. The Empress is opposed to negotiating with Edgar and his allies.'

'That doesn't make sense. There has to be a way both sides can coexist in peace.'

'Are you aware that Kyra has defected to Edgar, along with Bailey? Are you aware that Sable's powers have been crippled, and that she has returned to her family in Ulna? And, finally, are you aware that someone entered Lord Ballatar's cell this morning and decapitated him?'

Cael's mouth opened.

Kelsey gave him a wry smile. 'You didn't happen to kill Ballatar, did you?'

'Why would I kill him? I brought him out of Inopei alive, and then I argued that he be spared. He was someone to trade. Something we could offer Edgar. And my sister is working for our enemies?'

'It was your sister who crippled Sable's powers. With Kyra on his side, Edgar is now pretty much untouchable. All right; here is what I am going to do. I want you to talk to Edgar, safely, to deliver the message that we were not responsible for Ballatar's death. Make sure he hears that loud and clear. In exchange for doing this for me, I will protect you from a court martial. We will claim that you were working for me in secret all this time, and that will grant you immunity from the marines. You will not, under any circumstances, engage in secret negotiations with Edgar. You may listen to his demands, but offer him nothing in return. You are my envoy, not my negotiator.'

Cael smiled. 'Thank you, Aunty.'

'Your timing is impeccable. Just when I needed a way to let Edgar know that we didn't kill his friend, you appear.'

'Does Cole fall under the same protection?'

'Aye.'

'And you won't hold it against Arrosa that she has spoken to me?'

Kelsey shrugged. 'As I asked her to let you know I was available to talk to you, I can hardly hold it against her now.' She leaned forward, and scribbled a few instructions onto a piece of paper. She then heated her metal seal over the flame of a candle, dripped some wax onto the paper, and pressed her seal into it. She passed the paper to Cael. 'Show that to any marines if you are caught and arrested.'

Cael read the words she had written, and smiled. 'Thanks.'

'There is one detail that might have slipped your mind, nephew,' Kelsey said.

'Aye?'

'Aye. You really do work for me now. And I will tell you this – if you disobey any of my commands, I will not be as generous as Sable was. You will not only lose your job, you will lose everything. I am prepared to give you free rein to carry out my objectives, but those objectives must be met. Is that understood?'

'Aye, Aunty.'

'Swear allegiance to me.'

Cael lowered his gaze. 'I swear to obey your orders, Herald.'

'All right,' said Kelsey. 'Now bugger off before anyone finds out you were here. Come back when you have spoken to Edgar; and try not to get yourself captured or killed.'

Cael brushed his fingers over his Quadrant and vanished.

Kelsey smiled, then she rang a small bell. Two minutes later, a palace courtier knocked at her door and entered.

'Yes, ma'am?' he said.

'Fetch me Arrosa,' Kelsey said. 'Tell her it's time for a little chat.'

CHAPTER 17
WARMONGERING

Port Edmond, Gyle, Western Rim – 14th Abrinch 1597

The air shimmered by the half-ruined palace, and three figures appeared on the street next to it. Kyra glanced at her new surroundings.

'I have been told that this city was once very beautiful,' said Edgar.

'Before Sable destroyed it?' said Kyra.

Bailey raised a finger. 'It wasn't actually Sable who burned Port Edmond to the ground. It was Wystian dragons who performed that act.'

'And who brought the Wystian dragons here?' said Edgar.

'Yes, that was Sable,' said Bailey. 'She appears to have believed that the Wystians would have restricted their attacks to Banner personnel but, alas, the Wystians were not hers to control.'

They turned, and gazed up at the magnificent ruins. The side of the building closest to a large, derelict parkland was the least damaged, and Kyra could sense its vast scale. Standing on the paved road next to an enormous entrance was a group of humans, with Lord Belfar at its centre. They saw Edgar, Bailey and Kyra, and walked forward. As they did so, three huge dragons soared overhead, coming from the direction of the parklands, then they landed in the street to Kyra's right.

Edgar eyed the dragons, then his gaze went back to Belfar.

'Greetings, my lord,' said Belfar, bowing his head. 'Welcome to Port Edmond.'

'Has Lord Elmhirst arrived yet?'

'No, my lord,' said Belfar. 'I wasn't aware that he was coming.'

'He will be here soon,' said Edgar.

'Allow me to make a few introductions, my lord,' said Belfar. 'Standing next to me are some of the leaders of the local Unk Tannic, while the brown dragon to your right is Lord Earthfire, a notable leader of the Wystian dragons.'

Edgar said nothing.

'Its, uh, nice to meet you all,' said Bailey.

Earthfire lowered his head to stare at Edgar. 'Is this the brother of the Second Ascendant?' the dragon said. 'He appears to be just another feeble human.'

Edgar eyed the brown dragon. 'If you don't want our help, then I would be happy to depart Dragon Eyre, never to return.'

'Please, my blessed lord!' cried one of the Unk Tannic to Earthfire. 'These allies will help you return home to Wyst, and they will assist us in the destruction of Blackrose's realm.'

'You pathetic specimen,' said Earthfire. 'Did the Unk Tannic not once fight against the occupation of this world by gods? And yet now you want to accept their aid?'

'We are not interested in occupying Dragon Eyre,' said Edgar. 'In fact, we have very little interest in helping those who clearly do not appreciate it. The only reason we are aiding you, dragon, is that we share the same enemies – the Holdfast Empire and Blackrose. By helping you, we hurt them. If such a deal is too sophisticated for your reptilian mind to encompass, then we would be happy to leave you to fight the Empire alone.'

Earthfire laughed. 'At last, a human who does not cower before me. The Unk Tannic make me sick. Their obsequious toadying drives me to despair.'

'We live to serve you, blessed lord,' said one of the Unk Tannic.

'Yes, yes; I know,' said the dragon. 'Edmond-brother, I accept your offer of assistance. We do not need it, but it will cause more suffering to Blackrose and her cowardly minions. Tell me, though; do you know where Sable is hiding?'

'The threat Sable represented has been neutralised,' said Edgar.

'I care not. I want revenge against the witch who imprisoned my people upon Rigga for so many years.'

'I will not help you find or kill Sable, or any of the Holdfasts. This is not a war of extermination, or one of vengeance. We have legitimate claims and grievances, and we shall seek peace once these have been addressed.'

Earthfire laughed again. 'You used many words to avoid saying that you fear the Holdfasts, god.'

'I fear no one,' said Edgar. 'The only being who ever scared me is dead – my brother Edmond. When will you be ready to strike at Na Sun Ka?'

'We could strike today, god,' said the brown dragon, 'but our invasion force would number fewer than a thousand. Allura told us that she thought two thousand would be required. Where is Allura?'

'She lost a hand to Sable,' said Edgar. 'She is recuperating on Athumia. Two thousand will be enough. When will they be ready?'

'Soon, Edmond-brother.'

The air shimmered a few yards away, and Elmhirst appeared with four others.

'You're late,' said Edgar.

'Apologies, my lord,' said Elmhirst. He gestured to the four others. 'I have brought demigod volunteers from the Doomed Worlds, as you requested.'

Edgar reached into a deep pocket and pulled out three Quadrants. 'Take these, Belfar.'

Belfar walked up to Edgar and took the devices.

'Where did you find three Quadrants, my lord?' said Elmhirst.

'I have the means,' said Edgar. 'With the addition of the Quadrant in Belfar's possession, there will now be four such devices available for the invasion of Na Sun Ka. The three new ones were fashioned upon the Star Continent, but they are able to create portals. Listen carefully, Belfar. When the time comes, open up two separate portals upon Na Sun Ka. With one, keep it in location long enough for one thousand Wystians to pass through, but vary the location of the other. Move it after every batch of two hundred dragons have entered Na Sun Ka. The imperials will be unable to respond, and their defences will be overwhelmed.'

'Which locations should I choose, my lord?'

'The Unk Tannic probably know Na Sun Ka better than anyone else – ask them for their advice. The Empire has positioned hundreds of explosive-throwing machines to protect the western coast of the island, and the city of Sun Ta. Lahnos, Sable and Cael have gone; only Corthie remains to lead the imperial armies. Do not kill him. I want Corthie brought to me, subdued but very much alive.'

'He will be powerless against the dragons, my lord,' said Belfar. 'He shall be wrapped in chains and dragged before you.'

Edgar turned to Elmhirst. 'Leave your four demigods here, under the authority of Lord Belfar. They will operate the two portals.'

Elmhirst tilted his head.

'Thank you, Edgar,' said Earthfire. 'You see, I can show gratitude. The extra Quadrants will lessen our casualties, and surprise the enemy. Will you assist us again when we begin our conquest of the Eastern Rim?'

'We will help you as far as Haurn,' said Edgar. 'I already have a plan to get past Yearning. However, after that, you will be on your own.'

'After that, we will not require any further aid. The journey from Haurn to Wyst shall be simple. Blackrose's realm will be reduced to ashes when we pass through Throscala and Ulna, and then, at last, we shall be home again.'

The dragon tilted his head as Edgar watched, then the god turned to Belfar. 'Send word to me in Nom Karta when two thousand Wystian dragons are ready to begin the invasion. Until then, carry on with individual attacks upon the imperial defences.'

Belfar bowed low.

Edgar turned to Elmhirst. 'Thank you for bringing your demigods. Bailey, the Holdfast girl and I shall now take our leave.'

Bailey triggered the Quadrant, and the three of them appeared back in Famula's palace in the city of Nom Karta. Bailey walked over to a table and began pouring brandy.

Kyra narrowed her eyes at Edgar. 'I didn't agree to help you help a bunch of fanatics and unhinged dragons,' she said. 'Thousands will die if this invasion goes ahead.'

'Can you think of any peaceful ways to stop the injustices caused by the Empire?' said Edgar. 'If you can, I'd be delighted to hear them.'

He took a glass from Bailey as Kyra stared at him.

'The Wystians were forcibly ripped from the only home they had known for thousands of years,' Edgar went on, 'then they were abandoned on a treeless wasteland in the middle of the ocean; left to slowly starve, with no hope for them or their children. All I am doing is helping them reclaim what was wrongfully stolen from them in the first place.'

'That's not what you're doing,' said Kyra. 'If you wanted to, you could open up a portal today, linking the dragons on Gyle directly to their old lands on Wyst. They could be home by this evening.'

Bailey chuckled. 'She has you there, old friend.'

'She does not *have me*,' said Edgar. 'Kyra is being naïve. She appears to believe that those who have been so cruelly wronged and abused as the Wystians do not deserve an opportunity to strike back at those who abused them.'

'You told the dragon it wasn't about revenge,' said Kyra.

'I know, but do you think Earthfire believes that? The Wystians need a measure of revenge; otherwise, they will not be satisfied. If I merely opened a portal to Wyst, then two things would happen – first, the Wystians would invade Ulna from the north; and second, the huge imperial army occupying Na Sun Ka would still be there. By giving the Wystians a little of what they desire, the imperials will have to evacuate this world, and we will ensure that the peace which follows has a chance to last.'

'You are full of shit, Edgar. What about the people who live on Wyst? Are you happy to see the Wystians slaughter them all?'

Edgar narrowed his eyes. 'What people? There are no humans native to Wyst; I was told this months ago.'

'The Riggans, Edgar,' said Kyra. 'When Sable moved the Wystians to Rigga, she also moved fifty thousand humans from Rigga to Wyst.'

Edgar said nothing.

'You mean you didn't know this?' said Kyra. 'Bailey?'

'I didn't know it, either,' said Bailey. 'The dragons and Unk Tannic we spoke to didn't mention any humans living on Wyst.'

'Those damn eye guards,' cried Kyra. 'If you weren't wearing them all the time, you would be able to find out the truth. I'm leaving. It is clear to me that neither of you possess the slightest amount of moral rectitude. You are just as bad as the Empire.'

'Wait,' said Edgar. 'What if I was to promise to save the humans living on Wyst? Let me correct this mistake – a mistake caused by ignorance, not malice. I could transfer the humans to a safe place.'

'Where?' said Bailey.

'I'm not sure,' said Edgar, 'but, together, we can think of something. Kyra, tell me what you would have me do. Imagine you were in charge – what would be your plan? Give us the accumulated wisdom of your eighteen years of life.'

'I thought you were being honest for a moment,' she said, 'until you mocked my age. I may not have thousands of years of experience, but at least I can tell the difference between right and wrong.'

She walked out of the room, and headed down the stairs towards the subterranean basement she shared with Larron and Achan.

'How was it, Kyra?' said Achan, as he sat upon a rickety chair.

'It was just wonderful,' said Kyra. 'I had to listen to Edgar and a dragon talk about slaughtering half the population of Dragon Eyre.'

Larron glanced over from the small kitchen, where he was

preparing food. 'Remember that we aren't trapped here. We're not prisoners. We could leave, any time we liked.'

'Any time Kyra chooses to go,' said Achan. 'You and I can do very little about that, Larron.'

'Do you want to leave?' said Kyra.

'Do you?' said Larron.

'I don't know. Edgar infuriates me. Sometimes, he seems intelligent and caring; other times, he can be a ruthless bastard. I still don't understand what he really wants.'

'I think it's fairly clear,' said Achan. 'He wants to squeeze the best possible terms out of the Empire, and he has calculated that the most efficient way to do that is to bludgeon Dragon Eyre out of the Empress's grasp.'

'He had three new Quadrants with him,' Kyra went on. 'Each had only three jewels – in other words, they were all made by Elbannon. Where did he get them?'

'Three more Quadrants?' said Larron.

'Aye. They're going to open up two portals when they invade Na Sun Ka. My uncle is still there. Uncle Corthie. What can he do against thousands of dragons? Edgar wants him captured alive and brought here; presumably so they can swap him for Ballatar.'

'If we leave,' said Achan, 'then Edgar will be vulnerable again. He needs you far more than you need him. Doesn't that give you a measure of influence over him? Set your boundaries. Tell him exactly what actions will gain your support, and which will cause you to walk away. You have power over him, Kyra – remind him of this fact.'

'You know,' she said, 'I think I will.'

She turned, and went back up the steps. She entered the large room where she had left Edgar and Bailey, and found Allura sitting with the two gods, her left hand covered in bandages.

They glanced over at her.

'Call off the invasion of Na Sun Ka,' Kyra said, 'or I'm leaving.'

Allura narrowed her eyes. 'Did you hear that, my lord? You are being threatened by a mortal girl.'

'I heard her,' said Edgar.

'Chain her up, if you can't bring yourself to kill her,' said Allura. 'Or torture her two friends until she promises to stay.'

'You need my willing assistance,' said Kyra. 'If you chain me up, or hurt my friends, then I will refuse to help you. My Uncle Corthie would take around two minutes to chop all three of you up into small pieces. If you really piss me off, I will visit Sable and remove the blocks I placed into her head. I could drive the dragons away, leaving none to protect you, and then watch as Sable and Corthie get to work. That would end the war. Best of all, only a small number would die, rather than the thousands you lot are planning. Well?'

Edgar said nothing.

'Do you want me to kill her?' said Allura. 'We could put her head in a box and send it to the Empress, with a note saying that we understand why she was exiled in the first place.'

'I hope that was a joke,' said Bailey. 'You mustn't forget Karalyn, Allura. If we kill her daughter, we all die.'

'You need me,' said Kyra. 'If you kill me, my mother will drop everything and make it her life's purpose to destroy you. If you imprison me or harm my friends, I will drive the Nom Karta dragons insane and refuse to help. And then I will escape. I don't need a Quadrant. Accept my terms, or pay the consequences.'

'What terms?' said Edgar.

'First, save the humans on Wyst,' she said.

'I had already agreed to that. What else?'

'Call off the invasion of Na Sun Ka.'

'Then why would I move the humans from Wyst? If there is no invasion, their lives wouldn't be in danger.'

'The girl has no idea what she wants,' said Allura.

'I want peace,' said Kyra. 'I want an end to the killing.'

'As do I,' said Edgar; 'but I don't just want a temporary cessation of hostilities. I want a stable and secure foundation of peace that will endure for centuries. You may call me arrogant, but I have experienced thousands of years of war and peace. I have studied how wars start, and how they end. Many wars begin because the previous war did not end in a way that allowed peace to flourish; did you know that? Any side that is humiliatingly beaten but not destroyed always harbours a bitter grievance, and that grievance is what fuels the next war. The most stable peace arises from only two situations – in the first, one side is utterly obliterated, so that there is no one left to reignite a conflict later on; and, in the second, it is when both sides feel that they have a good deal; when both sides get what they want. Face is saved and honour retained. Which of the two situations would you press for in your desire for a lasting peace, Kyra?'

'The second of those, obviously.'

'Then we are in agreement. I can see that you don't quite understand my strategy. It must seem to you that I am waging war to gain peace, and this is a clear contradiction. Now note what I haven't done. I haven't sent the ironhides to Plateau City, for instance. If I wanted to cause death and destruction on a vast scale, that is what I would do. But do you think the Empire would ever make peace with me if I did that? I have to defeat the Empire, while ensuring that they can negotiate a peace with honour. It's a dirty business; I'll not deny it. Both sides have resorted to underhanded tactics – us, when we stole the dragon carriers; them, when they came here to assassinate us. The crucial point is this – neither side has yet done anything that would make peace unthinkable; and we haven't done anything that would incur the implacable wrath of your mother. The invasion of Na Sun Ka, and the expulsion of imperial forces from Dragon Eyre, follow these simple rules. The Empire will have been defeated in fair and open battle, and they will have lost an important ally, but they won't have lost any of their own territory. Defeated, but not humiliated. Then, and only then, will they be ready for peace.'

Kyra narrowed her eyes, trying to think of a weakness in Edgar's words.

Bailey smiled at her. 'He's right, Kyra. If we declared that the war was over, do you believe the Empire would accept it? Wouldn't they build up their strength, and try to retake the Tempest mine as soon as they felt they had a chance to be successful?'

'And remember this,' said Edgar; 'even if I were to forbid the invasion of Na Sun Ka, the Wystians would go ahead and do it anyway. Do you honestly believe I have the power to stop them?'

'Better to help them,' said Bailey, 'and thereby retain some measure of control over their actions.'

Kyra sat down. 'I don't know what to believe.'

'I'm not surprised,' said Allura. 'You are a child.'

'She is a principled young woman,' said Edgar.

Allura snorted. 'I'm beginning to think that you have feelings for this mortal, my lord.'

'I have feelings about many people and many things, Allura.'

'You know what I meant. Did millennia in a restrainer mask addle your mind? You should sleep with a few of the servant girls in the palace – get thousands of years of enforced chastity out of your system, instead of fawning over this Holdfast.'

'We need her willing cooperation, Allura,' he said. 'With her, we will win this war; without her, there's a good chance the Holdfasts will kill us all. You may not like it, but it's the truth.'

Kyra narrowed her eyes as the gods talked about her. Allura was clearly lying, as the only feelings Edgar had displayed towards her had been contempt and condescension. She had found it hard to argue against his speech on why invading Na Sun Ka would be the best way to ensure a lasting peace, and that annoyed her.

'I'm going to give Larron a hand with dinner,' Kyra said.

'Yes, make yourself useful, child,' said Allura.

Edgar glanced up. 'And think about what I said.'

Kyra frowned, and left the room.

'That might have been your best attempt at a decent meal yet, Larron,' said Bailey, pushing his empty plate away.

'It was acceptable,' said Allura.

'I need a better range of ingredients,' said Larron. 'I can only cook what's in the kitchen. Find me some high quality meat and vegetables, and maybe a few herbs and spices, and the food will get better.'

Edgar poured himself a glass of red wine, his gaze preoccupied, as Kyra watched him. She felt a strange sensation pulsing by her temples, as if... No, that couldn't be right. She felt it again.

Cael? Is that you trying to get into my head?

Aye, it's me, sister. How are you? Might we speak for a moment?

Kyra got to her feet and walked away without saying anything. Larron eyed her from the table, then she left the dining room.

Where are you? she said in her mind.

Close. I want to speak to Edgar. I have a message from Aunty Kelsey for him, but first, I need a guarantee that I'll be able to walk out alive.

Give me the message, and I'll pass it on to him.

No, sister. I will deliver it in person or not at all.

I will stop you if you try to hurt or kill anyone.

I'm only here to talk.

Kyra came to a halt in a corridor of the palace. *All right. Give me a moment.*

She walked back to the dining room. 'Edgar? Could I speak to you alone for a moment?'

The god looked at her, then he wiped his hands on a napkin and got to his feet.

'Have you thought of more conditions, Kyra?' he said, as he reached the door.

'This way,' she said, leading him down the corridor. They went into a small storeroom, and Edgar frowned as he gazed at the shelves filled with supplies.

'A visitor wishes to talk to you,' Kyra said; 'but first you must promise not to do anything violent.'

'What visitor?' said Edgar.

'My brother.'

A hint of a smile touched Edgar's features. 'Cael Holdfast wants to talk, does he? I'll not harm him, if he does no harm to me.'

Did you hear that, Cael?

I heard it.

The air shimmered in the small room, and Cael appeared. He grinned at his sister, and extended his arms to embrace her. She took a step back, her eyes on him.

'I'm still your brother,' he said.

'Aye, Cael; I know.'

Edgar watched the two siblings, then he coughed. 'Greetings, Cael; we meet again.'

Cael tilted his head slightly at the god. 'I am unarmed.'

'That seems a little foolish,' said Edgar.

'You are an honourable man,' said Cael. 'My sister wouldn't be here if you weren't.'

'What do you want?'

'I have a message from the Herald of the Empire; I'm not here to negotiate.'

'Though I get the feeling that is what you would rather be doing.'

Cael smiled. 'Perhaps. Would you like to hear the message?'

Edgar nodded.

Cael's smile dropped. 'The Herald wants you to know that the Empire had nothing to do with Lord Ballatar's death.'

Rage and disbelief passed over Edgar's face.

'Ballatar is dead?' said Kyra.

'Didn't you know?' said Cael. 'It happened two days ago. Ballatar was found dead in his prison cell in Plateau City. He had been decapitated. I've taken a look at the cell, and I've been inside the heads of the soldiers who were on duty at the time. Someone used a Quadrant to enter the cell, as the door remained locked at all times. Whoever it was, they then killed Ballatar, and left. They wanted everyone to think it was the Empire, but it wasn't.'

Edgar put a hand to his face.

'It wasn't us, Edgar,' Cael repeated. 'We are investigating this as a crime.'

Edgar clenched his fists, as rage and grief twisted his features. He lashed out, and punched the side of a wooden shelf, splitting the beams in two, and causing tins and tubs to crash to the floor.

He stared at Cael. 'Go, before I break my word. Go.'

Cael stepped back, a hand going into a pocket. He glanced at Kyra, nodded, and vanished.

'My brother was telling the truth,' Kyra said. 'I would have sensed if he was lying, Edgar. He spoke the truth.'

'Or he believed his words to be true,' said Edgar. 'There is a difference.'

'What do you mean?' she said.

'The Herald could have lied to him, and sent him here to spread her lies. Kelsey Holdfast's mind is impenetrable, is it not?'

'Aye. No one has ever been able to read her mind, not even my mother.'

'Then she could have lied to Cael, and he wouldn't have sensed it. She could have arranged this, to try to make me believe that the Empire is innocent of murdering Ballatar. She could have done this, couldn't she?'

'I suppose so, but I doubt it.'

'Why?'

'If the Empire had murdered Ballatar, why wouldn't they want you to know that they'd done it?'

'For a hundred reasons.' Edgar sunk to his knees, as tears streamed down his face. 'Does it matter? My friend is dead. Despite everything; all the care I have taken in making sure no Holdfasts were harmed, and they murdered my friend. You were right about the Empress and her regime – they are warmongering savages.'

He got to his feet and wiped a hand across his face.

'What are you going to do?' said Kyra.

He gazed at her, his eyes dark, then he strode towards the door, saying nothing.

'Edgar,' she said. 'Please. Don't do anything stupid.'

He stared at her from the doorway, then walked away.

CHAPTER 18
MISDEEDS REMEMBERED

Port Edmond, Gyle, Western Rim – 14th Abrinch 1597

Cael appeared on the upper floor of a large, derelict apartment block, and Cole glanced up at him from where he was sitting by a hole in the wall.

'Did you deliver the message?' Cole said.

'Aye. It didn't go down too well.'

Cole turned back to glance at the collection of dragons, gods and Unk Tannic standing by the ruins of the Winter Palace.

'Did Edgar not believe you?' he said.

'He didn't know that Ballatar was dead,' said Cael, as he sat next to Cole and lit a cigarette.

'Ah. We've been assuming that Edgar must have spies everywhere, and that he knows everything that's happening, when, in reality, he's just as clueless as we are.'

Cael laughed. 'We're hardly clueless,' he said. 'Didn't we just observe Edgar's entire discussion with the Wystian dragons and the Unk Tannic? We saw the whole meeting, and none of them had the slightest idea that we were watching them.' He looked down at where Lord Belfar was speaking to the four demigods brought from the Doomed Worlds by Lord Elmhirst. 'Did I miss anything?'

'Belfar's been telling the new demigods what to do. The new arrivals aren't wearing any eye guards.'

Cael smiled.

'The dragons will sense something if you use your powers on the demigods,' Cole went on.

'I wasn't going to do anything,' said Cael. 'Not yet. This is merely an intelligence-gathering operation. Still, it's good to know. I'll be able to interfere with the invasion if they aren't wearing eye guards. I could command them to open their portals in the middle of a volcano.'

The air shimmered by the ruins, and one of the gods disappeared.

'That's Elmhirst away,' said Cole.

'Back to the Doomed Worlds, most likely,' said Cael.

'How was your sister?'

'You saw her with your own eyes,' said Cael. 'She was standing right next to Bailey and Edgar.'

'Yeah, but I didn't get a chance to speak to her.'

'Neither did I. I was in Nom Karta for less than five minutes. I did manage to get into her head, but only after she let me in. I couldn't see any of her thoughts or memories.' He paused. 'I should be telling this to Aunty Kelsey.'

'Our new boss,' said Cole.

'Better her than prison, cousin.'

Cole nodded. 'Let's go.'

They both stood, and Cael activated the Quadrant in his pocket. The air crackled, and they appeared in Kelsey's study in Colsbury Castle. Bright sunshine was coming in through an open window, and Kelsey glanced up from her desk.

'Good afternoon, boys,' she said, standing. She triggered her own Quadrant, and the three of them appeared next to a long beach, fronted by swaying palm trees.

'Your mother sensed that you were on Colsbury the last time you came,' Kelsey said. 'She arrived at my door five minutes after we had spoken. I was speaking to Arrosa at the time, and...'

'You spoke to Arrosa just after I left?' said Cael.

'Let me finish. Aye, I summoned her as soon as you'd gone, to tell her about our little agreement. Anyway, then your mother walked in, and so I had to tell her as well. She isn't going to do anything about it, though; I think she was just glad to hear that you were all right.'

'Is this Dragon Eyre?' said Cole.

'It certainly is,' said Kelsey. 'I can't have you turning up on Colsbury again, not while there's a chance that someone from the Imperial Court sees either of you. If you want to talk to me, use your powers to let Arrosa know. She will then tell me, and I'll meet you here, on this beach.'

Cael gazed around. 'I don't know where *here* is, Aunty.'

'We're on an island called Serpens, south of Ulna.'

'Can you show me on your Quadrant?'

Kelsey held up her device, and Cael watched as she traced her fingers above its copper surface.

Cael nodded. 'Got it.'

'Let's hear your report then.'

'Cole and I observed Edgar, Bailey and my sister discuss the impending invasion of Na Sun Ka with a brown Wystian dragon by the name of Earthfire.'

Kelsey raised an eyebrow. 'Where was this?'

'In Port Edmond. On Gyle.'

'You went to Gyle? You were supposed to pass on my message to Edgar.'

'Aye, but we went to Nom Karta, and he wasn't there. I read the mind of a Dominion dragon, found out where he had gone, and we followed him to Gyle. I could hardly talk to him there, so Cole and I waited until he had gone back to Inopei, and then I followed him, contacted Kyra, and passed on your message to Edgar.'

'We learned a lot about their invasion plans, Aunty,' said Cole.

'We're more than just your messenger boys,' said Cael, 'and I did exactly what you asked. We didn't disobey any orders.'

'We saw Edgar hand over three Quadrants to Belfar,' said Cole.

'And three Quadrants were stolen by Ward from the university,' said Cael. 'Therefore…'

'Ward is secretly working for Edgar?' said Kelsey. 'That hardly surprises me.'

'They are going to use the extra Quadrants to open two portals at the same time,' said Cole. 'One will be in a fixed position, and the other will move to different locations, bringing a total of two thousand Wystian dragons over to Na Sun Ka. Belfar was ordered to capture Corthie alive, and bring him to Nom Karta.'

'We can disrupt the invasion, Aunty,' said Cael; 'if you'll let us. Elmhirst brought over four demigods from the Doomed Worlds to operate the portals. The thing is – none of them were wearing eye guards. I can tinker with their plans, and send them off to open the portals in the wrong locations.'

'Stop,' said Kelsey. 'You boys are bombarding me with too much at once. Go back to my message. What did Edgar say when you told him that the Empire didn't have Ballatar executed?'

'There was a slight problem with that, as Edgar was unaware that Ballatar was dead. I could see how angry he was, and upset. I'm not sure if he believed me.'

'Were you alone with him?'

'My sister was there.'

'And what is their relationship like?' said Kelsey. 'How were they getting on?'

Cael frowned. 'Uh…'

'Think, Cael,' said Kelsey. 'If Kyra is dedicated to Edgar's cause, then she is an enormous threat to the Empire. However, if she has doubts or, better, if she is a restraining influence on Edgar, then we might have a chance to prise her away.'

'I couldn't tell,' said Cael. 'Edgar was wearing eye guards, and my sister was protecting her thoughts.'

'You need to get better at picking up little cues that don't rely on your powers,' said Kelsey. 'These things matter.'

'I could see the way Kyra was looking at the Unk Tannic and the dragons, Aunty,' said Cole. 'It was obvious to me that she was unhappy with the plan to invade Na Sun Ka.'

Kelsey smiled. 'Good lad. That's the kind of thing we can use. An unhappy Kyra will not give Edgar free rein to slaughter everyone in the Empire. He needs her to shield him from the rest of the Holdfasts; he will have to pay attention to what she says. You are both too young to remember much about that wee prick Daimon, but even the mighty Second Ascendant had to pander to him. Edmond relied upon Daimon; and Edgar will have to rely upon Kyra. Do we have any indication of when the invasion will take place?'

'They are waiting until they have two thousand dragons who are fit enough to fight,' said Cael. 'At the moment, they only have one thousand, and Earthfire was vague about when the others would be ready.'

Kelsey nodded. 'Good work, boys.'

'What's our next objective?' said Cael.

'You can get up to some mischief of your own designs for a while,' she said. 'I have nothing specific for you at the moment. Bring me more intelligence, and carry out a few acts of sabotage, but no massacres, and don't kill anyone in Nom Karta. I do need you to come with me to Ulna first, though.'

'Are we visiting Sable?' said Cole.

'How did you guess?'

'I doubt I'll be able to remove her blocks,' said Cael. 'That's Kyra's area of expertise.'

'Nevertheless, I require you to try,' said Kelsey. 'I asked your mother this morning, but she refused. She appears to believe that the worlds are safer places with Sable neutralised.'

She activated her Quadrant, and they appeared on the quayside next to the bridge palace of Udall.

'This is very nice,' said Cole, as he looked around. 'Ulna?'

Kelsey nodded. 'Your first time?'

'Yeah.'

'You need to travel more, Cole. Cael, make sure your cousin visits every region and city of importance, and show him how to use a Quadrant.'

Kelsey set off along the quayside, as the two cousins eyed each other. Kelsey halted, and turned.

'Come on,' she said. 'Keep up.'

Cael and Cole followed Kelsey as she made her way through the harbour. Gulls were squawking and circling overhead, along with a few dragons, and the basin was filled with tall masts. A few sailors nodded to Kelsey as she passed, and the cousins received several curious glances.

Kelsey stopped by a sleek ship. 'This is the *Giddy Gull*,' she said. 'Lara's vessel. If Sable isn't on board, then someone will probably know where she is.'

A sailor glanced over the side of the ship, a cigarette hanging from his lips.

'Good afternoon, Ryan,' said Kelsey. 'Is Sable on the *Gull*?'

'Who's asking?' said the sailor. 'Wait; I've met you before, I think.'

'We have met three times over the years, Ryan,' said Kelsey.

Another sailor peered over the railings, and his eyes widened.

'It's the Herald of the bleeding Empire, Ryan, you dozy twat,' the second sailor said.

Kelsey smiled. 'Thank you, Topaz; I'm glad someone remembers me. Is Sable on board?'

'Aye, ma'am,' said Topaz. 'Come on up.'

Kelsey led Cael and Cole up the gangway and onto the deck of the ship. She gestured to her nephews.

'This is my sister's son Cael; and my brother's son Cole,' she said.

'Nice to meet you, lads,' said Topaz.

'And this is Topaz, the master of the ship.'

'I remember you from a gala on Colsbury a few years ago,' said Cael. 'You're Maddie's husband.'

'That's me,' he said. 'You've grown a fair bit since then. Sable and Lara are in their cabin with the two tiddlers. Give me a moment to announce your arrival.'

Topaz walked off towards the rear of the vessel, and Ryan held out his cigarettes.

Cael took one. 'Thanks.'

'No problem,' said Ryan, striking a match.

He lit Cael's cigarette, and they gazed at the view as they waited for Topaz to return.

'You lads sail much?' said Ryan.

'I did a fair bit when I was training as a marine,' said Cael.

'A marine, eh? You look about the right size for that job.' He glanced at Cole. 'What about you, mate?'

'I'm not one for boats,' said Cole.

Ryan shook his head.

Topaz returned. 'Sable says you have five minutes. Be warned – the captain ain't best pleased with you turning up here. She thinks you're going to try to persuade Sable to go back to fighting.'

'She's not wrong,' said Kelsey, 'but we'll take the offer of five minutes.'

Topaz led them to the rear of the ship, and they mounted a few steps to the quarter deck. They passed the ship's wheel, and Topaz opened the door of the cabin. Inside, the curtains had been drawn, and the cabin was bathed in dim light. Kelsey entered, followed by Cael and Cole, and Topaz closed the door.

Lara was pacing the deck of the cabin, a small child in her arms, while Sable was seated, an infant boy sitting on her knee.

'Say what you have to say, Kelsey,' said Lara, a thin scar visible on her cheek.

'Sit,' said Sable.

Kelsey, Cael and Cole found chairs, while Lara continued to pace up and down.

'How are you feeling, Aunty?' said Kelsey.

'How do you think?' said Sable. 'Kyra's blocks weigh upon my mind like bricks.' She glanced at Cael. 'Your sister did an excellent job.'

'I don't want you to be removing those blocks,' Lara said to Cael.

'Those blocks are the reason Sable's home again. She's where she needs to be, looking after her two children.'

Cael said nothing, as he pushed out with his powers. He entered Sable's mind, and knew immediately that he would not be able to undo his sister's work. He tried to loosen some of the blocks, and Sable winced.

'Stop that!' Lara cried. 'Stop it now!'

'The blocks are too strong for me, Captain Lara,' said Cael. 'I couldn't remove them if I wanted to.'

Lara's shoulders sagged, and she fell into a chair with the baby in her arms.

'I must seem like a right bitch,' she said. 'I know that you all need Sable to do her thing; and I know that, if she doesn't, then things might turn out into a great heap of shit, not just for the Empire, but for Ulna, too; but I love her, and I need her to be here. The children need her.'

'I'm not going anywhere,' said Sable.

'I know that, but you want to go; admit it.'

'I want to defend Na Sun Ka from the Wystians,' she said. 'That's the only thing that will keep Ulna safe. If the Wystians break through, then we'll have to evacuate.'

Lara nodded. 'Yeah. I know.' She eyed Kelsey. 'I assume Karalyn refused to help?'

'Aye,' said Kelsey. She turned to Sable. 'My sister discovered your little scheme to exterminate every single god who isn't a Holdfast or a Laimos. Corthie is on Colsbury at the moment, visiting Aila and the children, and Karalyn read it from his mind. Needless to say, she does not approve.'

'You want to kill every god?' said Cael.

Sable shrugged. 'It seemed like a reasonable suggestion at the time, but Corthie managed to change my mind about it. I don't suppose Karalyn read that part. How is Corthie?'

'Fairly miserable,' said Kelsey, 'but he's determined to do his duty to defend Na Sun Ka.'

'On his own?'

'He won't be on his own. The Empire has sixty thousand soldiers, sailors and marines on Na Sun Ka and Yearning, along with hundreds of Forty-Eighters and other weapons made by Ravi's laboratory. We also have Cael and Cole.'

'Two deserters?' said Sable.

Kelsey smiled. 'They aren't deserters. They work for me. They have been working for me all along.'

'If you say so. Cael must have forgotten to mention that when he worked for me. Be careful, Kelsey, Cael has a tendency to disregard even the simplest orders.'

'Letting Allura go was the right thing to do,' said Cael.

'I happen to agree,' said Kelsey. 'That act of mercy allowed Cael to speak to Edgar earlier today. We now have an open line of communication with the leader of the enemy forces.'

Sable rolled her eyes.

'Corthie also agrees,' said Kelsey.

'Your five minutes are up,' said Lara.

'I want to talk to Karalyn,' said Sable.

'She won't remove your blocks,' said Kelsey.

'Not about that; about the Sextant. I want to plead with her to allow me to transfer the Wystian dragons somewhere off Dragon Eyre. A safe place, where they can survive without being a threat to the entire Eastern Rim.'

Kelsey narrowed her eyes for a moment. 'A meeting could be arranged,' she said, 'but we can't hold it on Colsbury, as I have neglected to inform either the Imperial Court or the military authorities about the fact that Cael and Cole are working for me.'

'Why am I not surprised?' said Sable.

'I can get my hands dirty,' said Kelsey, 'so the Empress's remain clean. Wait here. I'll see if Karalyn is willing to come on board the *Giddy Gull*.'

'I don't want her on my ship,' said Lara.

'Fine. Shall we meet in the bridge palace? I should probably say hello to Blackrose while I'm here.'

'I'll be there in five minutes,' said Sable.

Kelsey eyed her nephews. 'Stay with Sable, boys. I'll see you in the palace.'

Kelsey stood, triggered her Quadrant, and vanished.

Lara eyed the two cousins as an awkward silence grew.

'This is a very nice ship,' said Cole.

'Nice?' said Lara. 'It's the best bleeding ship in the Eastern Rim.'

'Your father is still living on Colsbury,' Cole went on.

'Yeah? Still shagging that Rakanese princess, is he?'

Cole laughed. 'I think so.'

'It keeps him out of my hair, at least. You two need to keep a close eye on that Kelsey woman. She's more ruthless and calculating than the rest of the Holdfasts put together.'

'Maybe now that Aunty Sable has been rendered harmless,' said Cael.

'You cheeky bastard,' said Sable. 'If you hadn't disobeyed orders, you would have been with us when we raided Nom Karta, and your sister wouldn't have been able to put those blocks in my head. Right now, Edgar and his gods would be dead and the war would be over. The fact that it isn't is your fault.'

'Edgar's death wouldn't stop the invasion of Na Sun Ka,' said Cael. 'He's helping the Wystians, but he doesn't control them.'

'And how would you know that?'

'Because Cole and I heard Edgar talking to the Wystians this morning on Gyle.'

Sable got to her feet, and handed the infant boy to Lara. She smiled down at her nephews, who remained seated, then she slipped a hand into her pocket. The air shimmered, and Cael and Cole fell to the floor of a large hall. Sable smiled at them as they sprawled on the ground, then she glanced up at several huge dragons.

'Good day, Your Majesty,' she said.

'Good day, Sable,' said Blackrose. 'Why are those young men lying on the floor?'

'I forgot to tell them I was about to use the Quadrant.'

Cael and Cole got to their feet.

'Greetings, Holdfasts,' said Blackrose. 'To what do we owe this pleasure?'

'Kelsey was here, too,' said Sable, 'and she'll be joining us in a moment, possibly with Karalyn.'

The huge black dragon's eyes burned red. 'What could cause the immovable Karalyn to leave Colsbury? Is the world about to end?'

'She might not come,' said Sable. 'She might refuse my invitation. If she does arrive, then you are in store for a rare treat – seeing me beg on my knees.'

'Do you intend to beg Karalyn to remove the blocks from your mind?'

'No. I already know that she would refuse to do that; I'm going to ask for something else.'

The air shimmered, and Kelsey appeared, with Karalyn by her side. Karalyn ignored Sable, Cole and the dragons, and walked forward to embrace Cael.

'Son,' she said; 'it's good to see you alive and well. Kelsey told me you saw Kyra.'

'Aye, Mother. My sister is also alive and well.'

Karalyn nodded, then she eyed Sable. 'What is she doing here, Kelsey?'

Kelsey half-smiled. 'I might have used Cael as an excuse to get you to come here, sister,' she said. 'It's Sable who wanted to speak to you.'

Karalyn moved away from Cael and faced Sable. 'I know about your plan to slaughter every god in existence, Sable. It sickens me that you would stoop so low.'

'I have abandoned that plan,' said Sable.

'Aye, now that you are incapable of carrying it out.'

Sable glared at her. 'Read my damn mind. Do it. You will see that I dropped the idea long before your daughter made me unable to commit acts of violence.'

Karalyn's eyes glazed over for a few moments, then she looked away.

'Well?' said Cael. 'Is she telling the truth, Mother?'

'She is,' said Karalyn, 'but I'm still not going to remove the blocks from her head.'

'That's not why I wanted to speak to you,' said Sable. 'I'm begging you, Karalyn – allow me or Cael to use the Sextant; allow one of us to transport the Wystians elsewhere; or do it yourself. I don't care who does it. Take them somewhere safe; somewhere they can flourish. By doing so, you will save the lives of thousands; you will save Blackrose's realm; you will save the entire Eastern Rim from death and destruction. Please, Karalyn.'

'I, too, ask you to do this, Karalyn,' said Blackrose. 'I appeal to you, as a friend and ally.'

Karalyn eyed the dragon. 'It was your scheming that lured the Empire into intervening in the affairs of Dragon Eyre in the first place, Blackrose; and now you will have to pay the consequences. As do you, Sable, as it was you who stranded the Wystians on Rigga. Your own misdeeds will be the cause of your downfall.'

'You wicked, spiteful wretch!' roared Blackrose.

Karalyn narrowed her eyes. 'Do you deny my accusation? Was it not your plan all along to draw the Empire into defending your southern borders? You tricked Thorn into sending a huge army – an army that now stands between you and thousands of vengeful Wystians. You and Sable will learn nothing if I have to save you from your own mistakes. The Wystians deserve to go home.'

'I sent them to Rigga because they were about to invade Ulna,' cried Sable. 'They had butchered hundreds on Enna and Geist, and were about to do the same to Blackrose's realm. They were lucky I didn't kill them all.'

Karalyn shook her head, then she vanished.

'Damn her!' Sable shouted.

'Her words cut deep,' said Blackrose, 'for she spoke the painful truth. I did behave dishonourably when I called for the Empire to attack Na Sun Ka, an act that led directly to the gods freeing the Wystians from Rigga. I have brought war and destruction upon us.'

'Thank you for that admission, Your Majesty,' said Kelsey; 'but you weren't to know what Edgar and his gods would do. You were trying to protect your realm; your motives were honourable.'

'I appreciate those words, Herald,' said the black dragon, 'but words will not save us from the Wystians. Nothing will, now that Karalyn has decided to withhold her aid. She has truly become a god, one who sits above us all, watching over the worlds, and judging them. She decides who gets to live, and who is made to suffer for their crimes. I will go to Na Sun Ka. I will fight to the end to repair the damage I have done. Tell me, Herald; is Corthie there?'

'He is in Colsbury Castle at the moment, Your Majesty, but he'll be returning to Na Sun Ka in the morning.'

'Then I shall ask Maddie to use her Quadrant to take me there tomorrow, as I would like to fight by his side.'

'Corthie will appreciate that, Your Majesty,' said Kelsey.

'Your Majesty,' said Cael; 'Cole and I work for Kelsey now, and we have a few ideas about how to beat the Wystians. We were in Gyle this morning, and we've found a few weaknesses in their plans.'

Blackrose gazed at him. 'And can I trust the son of Karalyn?'

'You can trust that I'll do everything in my power to win this war, Your Majesty.'

'Did you agree with what your mother decided?'

'Not one bit. If I knew the location of the Sextant, I would do exactly what Sable asked my mother to do. I have learned over many years that my mother's will is as hard and inflexible as iron. She inherited that stubbornness from Daphne Holdfast, and it has been passed down to me. I can be just as bloody-minded as my mother.'

'I can attest to that,' said Sable.

'This war is still winnable,' said Cael. 'I can't fight like Sable, but I have other abilities. We mustn't give up, and we mustn't despair. Edgar is over-confident, and the Wystians are complacent. They think the war is already as good as won. I can't wait to prove them wrong. If we can repel the invasion, Edgar's whole strategy falls apart, and we can force him to sit down with us and negotiate.'

'Negotiate?' said Blackrose. 'I was stirred by your defiant spirit, young Holdfast, right up until you uttered your last word. Why would I negotiate with a god who means to destroy my realm and my people?'

'This is why he disobeyed my orders,' said Sable, a hand on her hip. 'He freed a god I was about to kill, in the hope that Edgar's heart might be softened by his act of mercy.'

'He did the right thing,' said Kelsey. 'Cael and I are in agreement over this. Unless we intend to invade and conquer the entire Dominion on Athumia, this war will only end by negotiating with Edgar. That's the point we have to reach. Repelling the invasion of Na Sun Ka will be essential for this. Queen Blackrose, allow Cael and I to disagree with you on this matter – for all of us here want the invasion of the Eastern Rim to fail. All of us want to protect your realm from the Wystians, and all of us are determined to fight to the bitter end.'

'I see your reasoning, Herald,' said the black dragon, 'and I reluctantly concur. Squabbling over the future will be in vain if we cannot hold Na Sun Ka. We shall remain united until then, and leave our disagreements for the aftermath of that battle.'

'Thank you, Your Majesty,' said Kelsey.

Blackrose gazed down at Cole. 'What do you have to say for yourself, silent Holdfast? You watch everything, but say nothing.'

'I say little, because my mind is filled with death,' Cole said; 'the deaths of soldiers and dragons, and the deaths Cael and I shall cause. My father killed thousands during the war with Agatha; he burned entire armies of Rahain, and although I have inherited his powers, I have rarely used them. The thought of fighting thousands of Wystians terrifies me, but not because I am scared of battle. I am scared of becoming a killer, like my father.'

'You are a Holdfast,' said Blackrose; 'killing is your destiny. Strike down your enemies, so that your friends may live.'

Cole lowered his head.

'It's time to go,' said Kelsey. 'Queen Blackrose, it was a pleasure to speak with you. Sable, I will try again with Karalyn. I can also be a stubborn bugger when I want to be.'

Kelsey triggered her Quadrant, and they appeared on the beach on the island of Serpens.

Kelsey eyed the location. 'I might have to bring a few chairs if we'll be meeting here regularly; or maybe a blanket, so we can sit on the sand.' She gave the cousins a crooked smile. 'You did well today, boys; I'm proud of you both. Remember to let Arrosa know if you want to speak to me.'

'Are you going back to Colsbury?' said Cole.

'Aye. I have a shitload of paperwork to get through. Where will you two be going?'

'Gyle,' said Cael. 'Just before Edgar left to go back to Athumia, he ordered Belfar to organise a few raids into Na Sun Ka. We're going to do our best to disrupt those raids.' He glanced at Cole. 'And maybe carry out a few raids of our own.'

Cole nodded.

'Be careful, boys,' said Kelsey, then she and Cael triggered their Quadrants, and all three vanished.

CHAPTER 19
SHOULDERING THE BURDEN

Colsbury Castle, Republic of the Holdings – 25th Day, First Third Summer 545

Corthie groaned as someone poked him in the face.

'Da,' came a voice, followed by another poke. 'Da.'

Corthie opened his eyes to see Cairney looking down at him.

'Morning, son,' Corthie said.

'It's time to get up, Da,' said the nine-year-old boy.

Corthie glanced over to his left, but the other side of the bed was empty.

'Ma's already up,' said Cairney. 'She told me to come and get you. What are we doing today?'

Corthie remembered what he was going to be doing.

'Well, Da?' said Cairney. 'Can we go swimming in the lake? I saw Halfclaw from the window, and he was down by the harbour. Can we go and see him?'

Corthie sat up in bed. 'I was only back on Colsbury for one day and one night, son. I have to go back to work.'

Cairney's face fell. 'But you only got here yesterday. That's not fair. Why do you have to go?'

'I made a promise to the Empress,' said Corthie, 'but I'll be here for breakfast. Tell your mother that I'm up and getting dressed. Go on.'

Cairney's shoulders sagged and he trudged out of the room. Corthie swung his legs out of bed, grabbed a towel from the back of a chair, and walked into the small bathroom attached to Aila's quarters in the Summer Palace. He turned a tap, and warm water poured down from the showerhead. Corthie grabbed some soap and stepped under the flow of water, letting it wash away his drowsiness. After washing, he dried himself and went back into the bedroom and got dressed. He opened the shutters and gazed down on the view of the island and the lake. Frostback was wheeling and banking over the still surface of the water with Calpurnia on her shoulders, while Halfclaw was lazing by the harbour, his limbs stretched out in the sunlight. Olo'osso was reclining on the pier next to the dragon's head, the old pirate's feet resting on the narrow deck of his yacht. To the right of the harbour, past a row of storage buildings, the gardens were bathed in the morning light. Servants were moving amid the trees, setting up chairs in front of the stage. Another play was due to be performed that day, but Corthie would miss it.

He dried his hair, hung up the towel, and walked out of the bedroom. The sound of children's voices could be heard coming from another chamber, and Corthie walked in to see his wife sitting next to Kelsey. Eight children were also in the room. A few were sitting by a table eating breakfast, while Ceres, who had yet to turn one, was strapped to Aila's chest in a harness.

Corthie smiled as the two women and the children turned to look at him.

'Coffee?' said Kelsey.

'Aye, thanks,' he said, sitting as his sister got to her feet.

Kelsey walked to the table and filled a mug from the coffeepot. 'I went to see Sable yesterday,' she said.

'Aye?' said Corthie. 'How's she bearing up?'

'Not so great,' said his sister. 'Lara's trying hard not to show everyone how happy she is that Sable has to stay by her side; and Sable is pretty open about wishing she was able to join you. Here's a piece of news that might interest you – Blackrose and Maddie are going to Na Sun Ka today.' She walked over and handed the mug to Corthie.

'Did you remember the milk and sugar?' he said.

'I'm not going to dignify that with an answer,' she said, sitting.

Corthie took a sip. 'Thanks. Blackrose, eh? Is she there to visit the Eastern Rim dragons?'

'She says she wants to fight by your side.'

A few of the children looked over.

'Are you going to be fighting, Da?' said Killop.

'Maybe,' Corthie said.

'Are we in danger?' said Konna.

'No,' said Aila. 'We're perfectly safe on Colsbury. We have dragons and Karalyn here.'

'I want to go home,' said Cairney. 'I want to go back to Clackenbaird, and I want Da to come home with us.'

'Soon,' said Corthie.

'When?' said the boy.

'I don't know, exactly.'

'Who will you be fighting?' said Killop.

'There are one or two angry dragons who might try to attack our friends on Dragon Eyre,' Corthie said. 'I'll be there to stop them. And did you hear? Blackrose will be there, too; and she's the biggest, toughest dragon there is.'

'How are you supposed to fight dragons, Da?' said Konna.

'Maybe Blackrose will let me ride on her back, sweetie.'

Karalyn appeared at the door. Kelsey's eyes narrowed slightly, but she said nothing.

'Hey, sis,' said Corthie.

'Can I speak to you for a moment, Corthie?' Karalyn said.

'Aye, sure,' he said, getting back to his feet. He carried his mug of coffee out of the room, and followed Karalyn out on to a small balcony facing the village on the mainland.

Karalyn eyed him. 'This is a mistake,' she said.

'What is?'

'You, going back to Dragon Eyre. This is not a war that concerns you, and I don't think you should be involved.'

Corthie smiled. 'You say that about every war.'

'I do not. Did I hesitate when the Ascendants invaded the Star Continent? This isn't the same. The Star Continent is not being threatened; our homes and loved ones are safe.'

'My home was attacked.'

'I know, but Colsbury is impenetrable. You should be here, with your wife and children; you are under no obligation to fight a war that was caused by Blackrose and Sable.'

Corthie gazed out at the view. 'That's a bizarre way to look at it.'

'It's the truth. Who put the Wystians on to Rigga? Who enticed Thorn into sending an army to Na Sun Ka?'

'Come on, sis. Have you never made a mistake? Do you think we should watch the Wystians destroy the Eastern Rim while saying, *We told you so; you have only yourselves to blame*?'

'Why should it be up to you to fix their mistakes?'

'You seem to be forgetting which side is about to launch an invasion,' said Corthie; 'an invasion that isn't needed. If Edgar cared about getting the Wystians home, he would take them home. They don't have to rampage through the entire Eastern Rim to get there – they have Quadrants. Do the people of the Eastern Rim have to suffer because Blackrose and Sable made mistakes? You know, sis, I'm starting to think that becoming immortal has done something to your sense of empathy or compassion. What you seem to be saying is that the Eastern Rim is about to get what it deserves. Are the children who live on Ulna and Throscala responsible for this war? They are the ones who will suffer if the Wystians break through; children, old folk – civilians who are just trying to get on with their lives. I'm going back to Na Sun Ka not only because I swore an oath to serve the Empire – I'm going because it's the right thing to do. I will put myself between the invading Wystians and the civilians of the Eastern Rim because I can, and because I should. Do you remember when we first discovered that I had battle-vision?'

Karalyn said nothing.

'I remember it well,' Corthie went on. 'We spoke about it, you and I. You said that I should use my powers to defend those unable to defend themselves, and that is what I have tried to do. I defended the City from the greenhides, the Falls of Iron from the gods, and the Kell Pass from the Ascendants – and now you're telling me to stand back and do nothing to defend the people of the Eastern Rim?'

He fell silent, realising that he had raised his voice. He took a breath, and his anger subsided.

'You could help, you know,' he said. 'You have the Sextant, and you are the most powerful being alive. You could save the people of the Eastern Rim, if you wanted to.'

'There will always be wars, brother,' Karalyn said, 'and I will be alive to witness them all. Do you expect me to stop each one? I have the power to act as only a god can act – but when will it all end?'

'I can't answer that; I can only fight the next battle in front of me. I am Corthie Holdfast; it's all I've ever done, all I've ever been good at. When the Wystians and Edgar have been defeated, I will be able to go home, with Aila and the children. I will know that I did my best. What will you be able to say, sis?'

Karalyn said nothing. Corthie nodded, then he walked towards the balcony doors.

Karalyn put a hand on his arm. 'Don't fight for Na Sun Ka,' she said. 'Don't waste your powers in a war on a foreign world that means nothing to us, not when you have a family here who needs you. You can't protect every civilian in every war, no matter how well you fight. If you try, then there will always be other wars; there will always be more innocents to protect. It will never end, Corthie. It breaks my heart to see the way Thorn has twisted the goodness that lies within you. You promised that you would only fight if the Star Continent was invaded, and now the Empress is manipulating you into defending her new conquests. You say I lack empathy. You are wrong. I care about this world, and the people living upon it; and I care about you. Don't go.'

'My mind is made up, Karalyn,' he said. 'I will not desert my post.

My children look up to me, and I will not let them have a father who abandons his friends when things get tough.'

'Very well,' said Karalyn. 'You are wrong, but you are my brother, and I will always love you.'

She turned and walked away. Corthie remained out on the balcony, then he saw Aila join him, Ceres still strapped to her chest.

'The children heard every word of that,' she said in a low voice.

'Was I shouting?'

'Only at one point, but the windows of the room next door were open, and the sound came in through there.'

'What did the children say?'

'Not much. Everyone was quiet, listening, until Kelsey closed the window.'

'Do you agree with Karalyn?'

'No, but I would rather you were fighting gods than dragons. The god who tried to kill our children is still alive; in my opinion, you should be going after him.'

'There's a good chance he'll be in Na Sun Ka when the Wystians invade. I'll find him.'

He put his arm round her waist and they gazed at the view together.

Kelsey joined them.

'Sorry to interrupt,' she said, 'but Claudian is here to take you to Dragon Eyre, brother.'

Corthie nodded.

'Listen,' Kelsey went on; 'as Herald, I have the power to re-assign you. If you like, I can post you to Plateau City, where you will be placed in charge of a facility to train Holdings soldiers with battle-vision. You would still be doing your duty to the Empire.'

Corthie frowned. 'I thought you needed me on Na Sun Ka?'

Kelsey lowered her gaze. 'I just want to offer you the choice. If you think Karalyn was right, then I don't want to force you into returning to Sun Ta.'

'Karalyn was wrong,' he said. 'She thinks that because she can't stop every war, she shouldn't try to stop any; and she believes that I should act the same way. I can't protect every civilian, so therefore, I shouldn't bother protecting any. I can't accept that.'

'All right,' said Kelsey. 'This next bit is confidential, so I need Aila to agree not to mention it to anyone.'

Aila nodded.

'Cael and Cole are working for me,' Kelsey went on, 'and they will be assisting in the defence of Na Sun Ka. You won't be the only Holdfast there.'

Corthie smiled. 'My wee deserter nephews will be lending a hand?'

Kelsey shook her head. 'They are not deserters. They have been secretly working for me right from the start. Well, that's going to be the official story.'

'That makes me a little happier,' said Aila.

'That's why I thought you both should know,' said Kelsey. 'Cael is working on a whole variety of plans to foil the invasion. Cole is a little anxious about using his fire powers to incinerate the enemy, so some gentle encouragement might be in order.'

'Understood,' said Corthie.

They walked off the balcony, and went back into the room where the children were sitting. A few of the older ones glanced at Corthie with apprehension, so he made sure he was smiling. Claudian was also there, and someone had carried Corthie's luggage into the room.

Corthie nodded at the Adjutant. 'Sir.'

'Good morning, Corthie,' said Claudian. 'Are you ready to depart?'

'Aye,' he said. 'Just let me say goodbye to my wee horde first.'

He crouched down and embraced his children, kissing each one in turn; then he stood and kissed his wife.

'Hurry back,' Aila said, as Claudian took out his Quadrant.

Corthie glanced at Aila and Kelsey. 'I'll see you all soon.'

Claudian triggered the Quadrant, the air crackled, and they appeared in the hall at the centre of Corthie's quarters within the Temple of Ulna. Nestorian and Drechtalang were sitting at the table, and they stood at the sight of the Adjutant and Corthie.

'Welcome back, boss,' said Drechtalang. 'New Tempest weapons arrived for us this morning; you can take your pick.'

Corthie glanced at Claudian. 'Do you have any specific jobs for us, sir?'

'Not at the moment,' said the Adjutant. 'We shall be holding exercises on artillery tactics, and I would like your team to be present for that. It's important that we don't allow our soldiers to be hit by our own explosives. Report to my office one hour after dawn the day after tomorrow; you are free until then.'

Claudian triggered his Quadrant and vanished. Corthie picked up his luggage and walked over to the table. He opened one bag, and pulled out two bottles of whisky.

Drechtalang rubbed his hands together. 'Two bottles of Severton's finest, eh?'

'One bottle of Severton,' said Corthie, 'and one bottle of Marchbrae. Both were matured in a warehouse two hundred yards from my home in Kell.'

Nestorian raised an eyebrow as he picked up a bottle. 'Do you live next to Marchbrae Distillers, sir?'

'I own Marchbrae Distillers,' said Corthie.

The two survivors of his team stared at him.

'You own Severton?' said Drechtalang.

Corthie laughed. 'No, you numpty; my wife and I own Marchbrae. Severton isn't the only whisky; not any more. My wife runs the company, and I get to enjoy its bountiful produce. I didn't pay for these bottles. It's been many years since I've had to pay for whisky.'

'I am very familiar with Marchbrae, sir,' said Nestorian. 'There's a lovely little tavern in the Old Town that has recently started stocking a few Marchbrae whiskies. Me and a few of the old Banner lads have been trying them all.'

Corthie sat and opened one of the bottles. 'Get some glasses, Drechtalang.'

'Yes, boss,' said the hedgewitch, getting to his feet.

'What were you lads up to while I was away?'

Nestorian frowned. 'Drechtalang got a verbal warning for talking back to an officer.'

The hedgewitch shrugged as he set down three glasses onto the table. 'He was insulting the Sanang,' he said. 'What was I supposed to do?'

'Stand there and take it,' said the Banner sergeant.

'Not my style,' said Drechtalang. He pulled out a tied-up bundle of weedsticks. 'Mind if I smoke one of these, boss?'

'As long as it's not dullweed,' said Corthie.

'I don't touch that shite,' said the hedgewitch. 'Last time I did, someone robbed me, and I was too out of it to even notice.'

He lit up a weedstick as Corthie poured whisky into the three glasses.

'We'll start with the Marchbrae first,' Corthie said. 'It's called Domlach, because it's a blend of three Lach whiskies with Severton Eight-Year-Old, and it's the most expensive whisky you'll ever taste in your life.'

Drechtalang laughed. 'Then why are you wasting it on us, boss?'

Nestorian took a sip. 'Gods above, sir; this beats anything they serve in the Old Town.'

'Once this is over,' said Corthie, 'I'll give you both a tour of Marchbrae. We can drink straight from a cask.'

Nestorian smiled. 'I'm going to hold you to that, sir. How is your family?'

'All good, thanks.' He glanced at a few crates lying over by a doorway. 'I suppose I should check out the new Tempest weapons before we get too drunk.'

Cael and Cole appeared right next to the table, and the three men jumped back in shock.

'Holy fuck!' Drechtalang cried. 'It's Cael Holdfast. You little bastard, Cael.'

'Nice to see you, too, Drechtalang,' said Cael.

'I heard you had deserted.'

'That was only a rumour,' said Corthie. 'They are working as agents of the Empire. The one next to him is Cole, another nephew.'

'Cole and Cael?' said the hedgewitch. 'I'm glad their names sound so different, boss; it'll be hard to mix them up.'

Corthie smiled. 'Have you just arrived, lads?'

'We've been here for ten minutes,' said Cael. 'We were waiting for Claudian to go, and then we heard you talk about the new Tempest weapons.' He gestured towards something lying on the stone floor that hadn't been visible a moment before. 'You won't be needing any Tempest weapon, Uncle.'

Corthie stood and walked over to the object. It had a thick blanket wrapped round it, but its shape was unmistakable. Corthie removed the blanket and picked up the Clawhammer with both hands.

'We retrieved it for you,' said Cael. He patted his belt, where a sword was buckled. 'We also got the Fated Blade back.'

'You went to Inopei?'

'Aye, on a scouting expedition, to see what Edgar's lot were up to.'

'Does, uh, your new boss know you went there?'

'We weren't told that we couldn't go,' said Cael. 'We were ordered not to kill anyone in Nom Karta, but no one said we couldn't travel there.'

'We found the weapons locked up in a storeroom,' said Cole.

'Aye,' said Cael, 'and as soon as we saw them, we knew we had to steal them back. Don't worry, though, we left a note for Edgar telling him it was us.'

Drechtalang laughed, then he passed the weedstick to Cael, who took it.

'What about Kyra and the gods?' said Corthie. 'Did no one sense you? How did you get past them?'

Cael took a draw of the weedstick, then he sat down at the table. 'Normally,' he said, 'one of the gods would have sensed us using a Quadrant, but they're all wearing eye shields – they can't sense anything with those things in their eyes. As for my sister, she can only find me if she's actively searching for me in a certain location. We took the chance that she wouldn't be looking in Nom Karta. I've been there five times now, and she hasn't once sensed me. It works both ways, though – I need to be searching for her to see her. She could be lurking in Sun Ta right now.'

'She won't be,' said Cole, as he sat down. 'Edgar needs her to remain by his side. He needs her to shield him.' He glanced at Corthie. 'What's the plan, Uncle?'

'I'm flattered that you think I have a plan,' said Corthie. 'I'm here to defend Na Sun Ka when the invasion begins; my remit doesn't go any further than that.'

'Our remit allows Cole and me to do pretty much whatever we like,' said Cael, 'as long as we fulfil the objectives set by you-know-who. I'm guessing you were told about our new arrangement?'

'Aye. I was told right before I left Colsbury.'

'Did you see Arrosa?'

Corthie shook his head. 'I think she was with the Empress the whole time I was there.'

Cael nodded. 'I want to visit her, but I'm not allowed to walk openly around Colsbury. I'd sneak in to see her, but I don't want to jeopardise her new job with the Empress.'

'You could use your Quadrant to appear a few miles away from Colsbury, and then you could vision into her mind,' said Corthie.

'That's exactly what I was doing, Uncle. You-know-who still found out. That's how she got me and Cole to work for her.'

'I always said she was the smartest Holdfast.'

Nestorian frowned. 'I assume you are referring to the Herald of the Empire, sir? If you wished to keep her identity a secret, you should have given us fewer clues.'

Drechtalang shrugged. 'I had no idea who they were talking about.'

Cael offered the weedstick to his cousin.

'No thanks,' said Cole, 'but I'll take a whisky if there's any going.'

Corthie leaned the Clawhammer against the table and fetched two more glasses. He sat down, poured two measures, and slid them across the table towards his nephews. They all sat for a moment, sipping their whiskies in silence.

'It's a pity Sable's not here,' said Drechtalang.

'Cole and I saw her yesterday,' said Cael. 'I tried to remove the blocks from her head, but my sister's powers were too strong for me.'

'So she won't be coming back?' said Nestorian.

Cael shook his head.

A soldier ran into the large hall.

Drechtalang frowned. 'Who said you could come in here?'

'Sorry,' said the soldier, 'but there's a dragon outside who wants to speak to Corthie Holdfast.'

Corthie stood. 'Who?'

'Queen Blackrose of the Eastern Rim, sir.'

'Invite her in. This hall is big enough for a dragon.'

'Yes, sir.'

The soldier hurried away. Corthie turned, and saw that Cael and Cole had vanished. They re-appeared as he was looking at their empty seats, and Corthie rolled his eyes.

'We're not supposed to be seen by anyone, Uncle,' said Cole; 'but we met Queen Blackrose yesterday. She knows who we're working for.'

Blackrose walked into the large hall, her red eyes glowing. Maddie was down on the ground, walking next to the black dragon's forelimbs.

Blackrose gazed down, her eyes flitting over the men by the table. 'This is my first time in the Temple of Ulna for over two hundred years,' she said. 'I never cared much for the religion of the Unk Tannic, nor for its temples.'

'It makes an excellent army headquarters,' said Corthie.

The black dragon said nothing for a long, still moment, then she tilted her head. 'My dear Corthie, my friend – I owe you an apology. Were it not for my grievous miscalculation, you would not be here, defending my world from the foes set to overwhelm it. I lured the Empire into Na Sun Ka for selfish reasons, and now the soldiers of the Empire are facing odds that would put fear into the hearts of the bravest warriors. Can you forgive me?'

'I don't think there's anything to forgive,' said Corthie. 'Was it selfish to want to protect your realm?'

'Your sister seems to think so.'

'Who, Karalyn?' He shook his head. 'She also spoke to me about coming here. She tried to tell me that this war had nothing to do with me, and that I should stand aside.'

'And yet you came.'

'I don't abandon my friends, Blackrose.'

'Are you sitting here getting drunk?' said Maddie. 'What if the Wystians attack?'

'The Wystians aren't ready,' said Cael. 'We have a few days, at least. Cole and I have been watching their preparations on Gyle. Every day, more dragons report that they are strong enough to fight, and over a thousand of them have assembled in the fields south of Port Edmond, ready to be transported to Na Sun Ka. When that number reaches two thousand, they will come.'

'And we shall be ready,' said Blackrose. 'Na Sun Ka shall be my home until the Wystians have been vanquished. I shall prove to the Empire that I am a worthy ally, by fighting alongside its soldiers. Victory or death, there is no middle ground.'

'It will be victory,' said Cael. 'Have no doubt; we shall win.'

'Malik's ass,' said Maddie; 'I wish I shared your confidence. Is that whisky?'

'Sit down, Maddie, and join us,' said Corthie. 'Should we order food?'

'I shall not be eating here today,' said Blackrose, 'not if the Wystians remain unprepared. I sent eight dragons from the Eastern Rim to help defend this island, and Gallantmorn is among them. As their leader, I shall do my duty by visiting them. They need to know that their Queen shall be fighting by their side. Maddie, please remain here. I am sure that you will be well looked after by Corthie.'

Blackrose tilted her head again, and walked from the hall.

'I am pretty hungry,' said Maddie, 'so feel free to order some food.'

Corthie gestured to Nestorian. 'Dinner for everyone, please.'

'Yes, sir,' said the Banner sergeant, getting to his feet as Maddie sat down.

Corthie fetched another glass, and filled it for Maddie, as Nestorian left the hall.

'Blackrose is feeling terrible,' Maddie said. 'Karalyn... well, the way she spoke to Blackrose and Sable – blaming them for everything. It hurt Blackrose deeply. Why does your sister have to be like that, Corthie?'

'That's my mother you're talking about,' said Cael.

Maddie nodded. 'I know. Why don't you answer my question, then? Your mother was so harsh.'

'You weren't there,' said Cael.

'Yeah, but Blackrose recited the entire conversation to me. I've never seen her so ridden with guilt.'

'My mother was harsh,' said Cael. 'Too harsh, in my opinion.'

'But?' said Maddie. 'I know there's a but coming.'

'Put yourself in her position,' said Cael. 'Everyone expects my mother to intervene whenever there's a problem. It doesn't matter who causes the problem – everyone thinks my mother can fix it. Do I think she was right in this instance? No. Do I understand why she took the position she did? Aye, I do. Imagine going through everything my mother's been through. Imagine dying, and then being forced into another body; and now she has powers that she didn't have before. The responsibility weighs down on her as if she's shouldering the burden of every world. Now imagine that those powers were in the hands of someone who intervened all the time. We're lucky that she chooses to stay out of politics, and refuses to interfere in what's happening on all the different worlds. She could be all-powerful if she wanted to be.'

'That's a scary thought,' said Maddie, 'but it doesn't excuse her behaviour. Do you know what it reminded me of? That day in the Falls of Iron when she forced me to hand over the Quadrant, so that she could return home. Of course, it meant that Blackrose wasn't able to return home, but she didn't care about that. She was cold, mean and ruthless, and that was long before she became immortal.'

Corthie glanced from Maddie to Cael. 'Forget the past,' he said. 'All that matters is what we do with the future. Right now, we're here to defend Na Sun Ka, not bicker about my sister.'

'I thought we were here to drink whisky, boss,' said Drechtalang.

'Good point,' said Corthie, raising his glass. 'Let's save our disagreements for after we've kicked the arses of the Wystians, and sent Edgar scurrying home. Can we drink to that?'

'I can,' said Cole, raising his own glass.

'Good lad,' said Corthie. 'Come on, the rest of you; lift your glasses.'

They all did so, and Corthie smiled.

'To victory.'

CHAPTER 20
TRAGEDY IN THE GARDENS

Colsbury Castle, Republic of the Holdings – 28th Day, First Third Summer 545

'And so it is with deep regret, Your Majesty,' said Janis Holdsmith, as he bowed before the throne, 'that I must tender my immediate resignation as Chief Jurist, and surrender my position upon the Imperial Court.'

The Empress gazed down at him, while the rest of her court stood flanking the throne.

'I accept your resignation, Janis,' the Empress said, 'and I thank you for your service to the Empire. Do you require a means to travel to Plateau City?'

'No, Your Majesty,' he said, 'I have a carriage ready to take me to my estate in Hold Smith, where I shall reflect upon my future.'

'I hope you have a safe journey,' said Thorn.

Janis bowed again, then he turned and walked away. He caught Kelsey's eyes as he passed the rest of the court.

'Holder Fast,' he said.

Kelsey tilted her head slightly. 'Holder Smith.'

Naxor sighed as Janis left the grand audience hall. 'And now I shall have to find another Chief Jurist from somewhere,' he said.

'I've already found a few possible candidates for you to take a look at,' said Kelsey. 'I had a feeling that Janis was ready to go. My proposals were too much for him to stomach.'

'They have certainly given me a severe case of indigestion, Herald,' said Naxor, 'but I see no reason to resign; not yet, at any rate. I assume your new candidates are in favour of your plans?'

'The ones from Amatskouri are.' She glanced at the Empress. 'Shall we bring the prime minister in?'

Thorn nodded. 'Do so.'

'Walk with me,' Kelsey said to Arrosa as she turned for a side door.

Arrosa joined Kelsey, and they crossed the floor of the hall.

'Is Janis really going to Hold Smith?' Kelsey whispered.

'No,' Arrosa whispered back.

'That sneaky little bastard,' Kelsey said, her voice low. 'He's probably going to Holdings City, to encourage opposition to my plans among the other Holders.'

They reached the door and a guard opened it for them. On the other side, Jazidorato was pacing up and down in an anteroom, while four others from his government were sitting on comfortable chairs. Four Rakanese militia were also in the room, guarding eight large chests. Kelsey eyed the prime minister's lavish purple suit, but decided not to mention it.

'Kelsey!' Jazi cried. 'Is it time? Please tell me it's time – I don't think my heart could take any more waiting.'

Kelsey half-smiled. 'It's time.'

Jazi exhaled, a grin spreading across his face, as his colleagues got to their feet.

'This is a solemn occasion, Prime Minister,' said Fenu, his aide; 'one that requires a solemn expression.'

Jazi tried to flatten his features. 'I'll try my best.' He glanced at Arrosa. 'Nice to meet you again, Arrosa Holdfast. Are you having fun in the Imperial Court?'

'I wouldn't exactly call it fun, Prime Minister,' she said, 'but I am enjoying it.'

'I'm sure you'll do a terrific job.'

Fenu eyed Kelsey. 'What is the current mood of the Empress, Herald?'

'Sour,' said Kelsey. 'One of her court has just resigned over my proposals.'

'Someone resigned because the Empire is selling us land?' said Jazi.

'It wasn't just that,' said Kelsey. 'It was the democracy stuff, too. I assume you've heard about that?'

Jazi smiled and wagged a finger at Kelsey. 'Stealing our ideas again, eh? If you need any hints on winning elections, Kelsey, come and ask me. Actually, you'd be better off asking Fenu.'

'I won't be standing in any election, Jazi,' said Kelsey. 'I'm a Holder; I don't need to stand. I already have a permanent seat in the Holdings parliament. Come on; let's not keep the Empress waiting.'

Kelsey and Arrosa walked to the door, and the Rakanese officials lined up next to them, with Jazi in the lead.

The prime minister turned to grin at the four militia soldiers. 'Don't you be running off with all that gold, eh?' he said. 'You wouldn't get far; I can run faster than you.'

'Prime Minister, please,' whispered Fenu.

Jazi removed the grin from his face and nodded, then Kelsey led them into the grand audience hall. She walked them up to the area directly in front of the throne, and when she bowed, the Amatskourians did the same.

'Your Majesty,' said Kelsey; 'may I present to you the prime minister of Amatskouri, the honourable Jazidorato?'

Thorn gave a serene smile. 'It is a pleasure to meet you again, Prime Minister.'

'Likewise, Your Majesty,' said Jazi; 'and might I say how wonderfully regal you are looking today? Your beauty rivals that of the seven stars.'

'Thank you,' said the Empress.

'The prime minister is here to announce the decision taken by the Amatskourian parliament in yesterday's vote, Your Majesty,' said Kelsey.

'The vote was on whether to accept the planned land sale, and the rest of the package that was negotiated.'

Jazi's smile broke through. 'It was passed with a tremendous majority, Your Majesty,' he said. 'In fact, the parliament rose to give a standing ovation. It was the proudest moment of my life.'

'I am very pleased to hear that,' said the Empress.

'Shall we move to the signing ceremony, Your Majesty?' said Kelsey.

The Empress inclined her head.

Kelsey gestured to where a long table had been set out, with five chairs running down each side.

'If the Amatskourian representatives would please take their places on the left side of the table,' she said.

Fenu tilted her head, then she ushered the others to the table, where they sat, with Jazi in the centre. Cardova stepped forward, and helped the Empress step down from the throne, then he escorted her to the table, and pulled out her chair. The Empress sat. Cardova and Naxor took their places to her left, while Kelsey and Shella sat to her right. Behind them, Claudian, Slaeon and Arrosa remained standing, as the most junior members of the Imperial Court who were present.

Kelsey lifted up a single large sheet of thickened paper, upon which, in tiny script, had been written the title deeds for the expanse of land that was being sold to the Amatskourians. Kelsey set it down in front of the Empress, who studied it for a moment, before lifting a silver pen and inscribing her name at the bottom. The charter made its way round the table, until it reached Jazi, who was the last to sign. He poised the silver pen over the paper, his eyes welling, then he appended his name.

'Congratulations,' said Kelsey. 'With that final signature, the land between Amatskouri and Stretton Sands now belongs to the people of your city.'

'I shall have this charter framed and hung above the speaker's chair in parliament,' said Jazi; 'right next to the portrait of the Empress.'

Kelsey lifted another document. 'This is a copy of the law on the imperial succession,' she said. 'It has been amended to include a vote by the prime minister of the Republic of Adorati. You don't need to sign it, but I thought I'd bring it along to show you.'

She slid it over the table to Jazi, who smiled as he read it.

'It's funny to see it written down,' he said. 'The *Republic of Adorati*. I wish my father was alive to see this day.' He paused, and Kelsey could see that he was struggling to retain his composure.

'I am sure that your father would have been very proud of your achievements, Prime Minister,' said the Empress.

That was enough for Jazi, and he broke down in tears. Fenu put a hand on his shoulder, as Naxor rolled his eyes. Kelsey gave the demigod a chiding glance, then she turned to Jazi.

'We have a reception arranged for you all in the gardens,' she said; 'if you're in the mood for a party.'

'Thank you, Herald,' said Fenu; 'but first, there is the small matter of making our first payment.'

She gestured to the side door, where the four Rakanese militia had been waiting for her signal. They began carrying in the large chests two at a time, until all eight had been set down by one end of the table. Fenu got to her feet, lifted a key from a pocket, and unlocked the chests. She opened all eight, revealing a fortune's worth of gold coins.

'This is the entire payment,' Fenu said; 'the first of twenty. In the future, Herald, I was hoping that we could come to an agreement about the medium of payment. Perhaps trade bonds or credit notes might suffice, rather than bullion? Or perhaps a system of payment in kind might be negotiated?'

Kelsey glanced at Slaeon.

'That would be acceptable,' said the Imperial Treasurer. 'We can hammer out the details later.'

Jazi wiped his eyes and smiled. 'Apologies for that little outbreak of emotion.'

The Empress smiled back at him. 'Think nothing of it, Prime Minister. It is heartening to see a leader who cares so deeply about the future of his people. I wish you and your new republic well, and I offer you our eternal friendship.'

'Thank you, Your Majesty,' he said. He eyed Kelsey. 'Did someone mention a party?'

Kelsey narrowed her eyes at the theatre agent. 'A tragedy? You're kidding me, right?'

'But, ma'am,' the agent said, 'we have performed nothing but comedies and romances all summer; and my in-house playwright is starting to get a little overwrought by the situation.'

Kelsey extended her hand, and the agent passed her the script. 'How many deaths?'

'Fourteen, ma'am.'

'Fourteen?' she said, as she skimmed through the pages. 'It sounds like a bloodbath.'

'Most occur off-stage, ma'am.'

'Plot?'

'A wicked usurper from within the royal family; betrayals, treachery… he gets his comeuppance at the end, naturally.'

'Is the monarch killed?'

'Uh, yes, ma'am, but his brave son returns from exile to wreak bloody revenge upon the wicked traitors who stole his father's kingdom.'

'Songs? Surely there are some songs?'

'Four, ma'am. Mournful lamentations.'

Kelsey eyed the crowds that were starting to fill the rows of seats in front of the stage.

'It's the only script we have with us today, ma'am,' the agent went on, 'and it's the only play we have rehearsed.'

'In other words, it's this, or I have to tell everyone that the play has been cancelled?'

'Uh, yes, ma'am.'

'I ought to slap you round the face for putting me in this position, ya cheeky wee prick,' she said. 'I'm telling you now, if the Empress hates it, I won't be the only one getting their arse booted.'

'The Empress shall love it, I am sure, ma'am. It has a strong thread of loyalty to the throne running through every page, and the royal family is portrayed in a very favourable light.'

'Apart from the wicked, murdering usurper, eh? All right; go ahead. Don't be surprised if the audience throws things at you.'

She passed the script back to the agent, who bowed with a flourish. Kelsey turned, and saw Shella and Arrosa waiting close by.

'Do you need me for something?' Kelsey said.

Shella smiled. 'I'm sure you remember how much I love spending other people's money, and it's time for you to hand some over.' She gave Kelsey a scrap of paper. 'That's how much it comes to.'

Kelsey's eyes widened. 'Pyre's knackers, Shella.'

Shella shrugged. 'I have sent out invitations to one hundred delegates, who shall be living in the Lesser Keep for up to a year, maybe longer; and, on top of that, I need to hire around two hundred clerks, scribes, notaries and secretaries. That's three hundred salaries. Plus, I need a ton of paper, ink, and all manner of other bits and bobs. Lamp oil, for instance, so the convention isn't working in the dark. Wine for entertaining, and coffee for the mornings-after. Democracy doesn't come cheap, Kelsey.'

'Slaeon is going to weep when she finds out. She's had her hands on the Amatskourian gold for less than an hour, and you'll be taking a large chunk of it.'

Karalyn walked over, carrying two-year-old Caitlyn in her arms. 'What's this I've been told about the Lesser Keep, Kelsey? Apparently, it's going to be full all year round.'

'Aye,' said Kelsey. 'The constitutional convention will be living there, while they work out the detailed proposals for the transition to democracy.'

'Why do they have to stay here? You know how much I prize the peace and quiet that descends upon Colsbury when the Imperial Court leaves each Autumn's Day.'

'Colsbury is remote – far from the distractions of Plateau City. It's a good place for contemplating our constitutional future.'

'And why should I have to move?' said Shella. 'This is my home, too, Karalyn. In fact, I was living here long before you chose to make Colsbury your home.'

'How many people will be staying here when the rest leave?' said Karalyn.

'Three hundred,' said Shella.

Karalyn glared at her. 'I came to Colsbury for the peace,' she said, 'and then I had to sacrifice my summers to the Empress and her hordes of courtiers.'

'Boo hoo,' said Shella.

'I'm taking Caitlyn and Carden up to the Hold Fast estate,' said Karalyn. 'The mansion will be hot, but it will be worth it for the quiet.' She glanced at Kelsey. 'We'll be gone within the hour.'

'Woah,' said Kelsey. 'You're leaving Colsbury today? What about Aila and her kids? What about the damn Empress? Your presence here protects them.'

'I will take Aila and her children with me, if they want to come. As for the Empress, she manages to live in Plateau City for three-quarters of each year without me; I'm sure she will manage fine on Colsbury.'

Karalyn walked away, and Kelsey hurried after her.

'Wait,' said Kelsey. 'Before you go...'

Karalyn turned. 'What?'

'Please use the Sextant to move the Wystians.'

Karalyn sagged. 'Not this again. No, sister; I shall not.'

'Please. Doing this one small thing will save countless lives.'

'It wouldn't be a *small thing* for the seven thousand Wystians. I'd be uprooting them from their home world and dumping them in a place completely unknown to them. Can you imagine how much despair and pain that will cause them?'

'But they would be alive, sister. Alive, as opposed to dead. Just as thousands of imperial soldiers and Eastern Rim civilians and dragons would also be alive.'

Karalyn's expression hardened. 'I'll not be your god, Kelsey. Find someone else to pray to.'

Kelsey stared at Karalyn as she walked away.

Shella and Arrosa joined her.

'That didn't go very well,' said Shella. 'I guess we forgot to take Karalyn's feelings into account.'

'The Empire can't tiptoe around my bloody sister's idiotic notions,' said Kelsey. 'She needs everything to be arranged exactly the way she wants it, she refuses to help, and she storms off in the huff if we do something she doesn't like. You know what? – screw her. Let her roast in the heat of the Holdings summer.'

'All she wants is a quiet life, Aunty,' said Arrosa. 'It isn't that much to ask.'

'What about her responsibilities?' said Kelsey. 'Don't they matter? Where is her sense of duty? It's as though she's loyal to no one but her own children. Bridget used to complain that my mother always put her family first, and she was right; but at least Daphne put the needs of the Empire second. The Empire doesn't even get a mention on Karalyn's list of priorities. We do nothing but inconvenience her summer.' She lowered her gaze. 'Now I'm in the mood to watch a fucking tragedy. Come on; let's see how long it takes Jazi to start weeping.'

The gardens were in a sombre mood after the play had finished. Kelsey had kept an eye on the Empress's reactions to the story being performed in front of her, but Thorn hadn't shown any outward signs of displeasure, not even when the king in the play was brutally murdered by his half-brother. Their Rakanese guests had clearly been expecting to watch a comedy, and a few of them had looked queasy as the number of on and off-stage deaths rose inexorably towards the play's bloody climax.

To Kelsey's relief, the audience applauded at the end, then they dispersed into the gardens to eat and drink, as the afternoon's light began to fade. Kelsey mingled through the crowds, talking to everyone she met, then she took a glass of wine from a waiter and sat down next to Aila and her children, who were occupying a large table at the edge of the crowd. Naxor and Arrosa were also seated with them, and Naxor gave Kelsey a wry smile.

'A courageous choice of play, Herald,' he said. 'Regicide performed in front of Her Majesty? Traitors within the royal family?'

'I enjoyed it,' said Aila. 'I was getting a little tired of all the romantic comedies.'

'I liked it when the traitor got his head chopped off,' said Cairney.

'Is he really dead?' said Carter.

Naxor ruffled the hair of the six-year-old boy. 'Not at all, Carter,' he said. 'They were only pretending.' He pointed through the crowds. 'Look – there he is. He's standing next to that oak tree. He is an actor.'

The children squinted through the evening light.

'It's just like playing a game,' Naxor went on. 'No one got hurt.'

'I didn't like it,' said Clova. She reached for her mother, but Aila was already holding Carron on her knee, while Ceres was strapped to her chest. Clova turned to Arrosa, and sat on her knee, instead.

Arrosa smiled. 'I'll keep you safe, Clova,' she said.

'Next time, though, Kelsey,' Aila said, 'warn me if there are going to be multiple deaths and buckets of fake blood being thrown about. I wouldn't have brought the younger children along if I'd known.'

'The theatre guys ambushed me,' said Kelsey. 'Did, eh... Karalyn speak to you?'

Aila nodded. 'She's gone.'

'Karalyn has gone?' said Naxor. 'Where?'

'To the Hold Fast estate,' said Aila. 'She offered to take me and the children, but it's like a furnace up there at this time of year. The children would have hated it.'

Naxor frowned. 'Could someone please explain to me why we allowed the woman who protects Colsbury to leave?'

'You try and stop her,' said Kelsey. 'She was pissed off about one of the keeps being occupied all year round. I asked her to reconsider. She refused.'

'And what did her husband have to say about it?'

'I haven't seen Lucius since the signing ceremony,' said Kelsey. 'He might have gone with her for all I know.'

'I saw him at the play,' said Arrosa. 'He was sitting a few rows back from us. He didn't look very happy.'

'I assumed the play had made him miserable,' said Naxor; 'it certainly made me feel that way. So, Karalyn has walked out on us in the midst of a nasty little war. Once again, she proves how little she cares about us lesser beings.'

'We'll be fine,' said Kelsey.

Naxor raised an eyebrow. 'I am not quite as stupid as you believe me to be, Herald,' he said. 'I know that you are getting intelligence about Edgar's movements from somewhere. I have yet to discover your source, but it seems clear to me that you have a spy in your employ; someone who can get close to Edgar without being detected.'

'Did you have a point to make?' said Kelsey.

'I was coming to that,' he said. 'Here's the thing – if you have someone spying on Edgar, then mightn't Edgar have someone spying on us? If that were the case, then you would be blocking any mage or god powers from affecting us; but Karalyn would have prevented them from entering Colsbury. No spy would have been allowed to get anywhere near the Empress with Karalyn around.'

'We have three thousand soldiers, two dragons, several mages, and me,' said Kelsey. 'No one's getting close to us.'

Naxor sipped from his glass, looking unconvinced.

'Are spies coming to kill us?' said Carter.

'No,' said Aila. 'Your Uncle Naxor is just a little paranoid.'

'What does paranoid mean?'

'He's always worried that he might be in danger,' Aila said.

'I am *not* being paranoid, cousin,' he said. 'I am merely thinking about the security of our beloved Empress. Has anyone told Her Majesty that Karalyn has left Colsbury?'

Kelsey frowned, and Naxor sighed and shook his head.

He got to his feet. 'I will inform Her Majesty now,' he said. 'Is there anything else that you have neglected to tell the Empress, Kelsey?'

'Aye,' she said. 'I forget to tell her that you're a sanctimonious prick.'

Naxor smiled. 'Come now; I'm sure you've mentioned that to Her Majesty on several occasions.'

The demigod walked away in the direction of the Empress, who was seated at a table close to Jazi and his officials.

'Arsehole,' Kelsey muttered.

'I wish you two would get along,' said Aila. 'I don't like being in the middle. You know, Naxor has been very good to me and the children since Corthie enlisted in the armed forces. He's been a great help.'

'Really?'

'Yes, really. I won't lie; it's been hard living here while looking after seven children; sometimes more.'

'Was that a sly dig at me?' said Kelsey. 'I haven't dumped my own kids on you today.'

'Yes, because Van has them both in Plateau City.'

'I thought you didn't mind.'

'I know you're busy,' Aila said. 'Being the Herald again leaves you very little time for anything else; but it would be nice if you offered to help now and again.'

'Aye? Well, I'm dreadfully sorry.'

'Ow,' said Arrosa.

Kelsey eyed her. 'That was sarcasm, not a lie.'

Cairney laughed. 'Konna's head is made of poop.'

Arrosa grimaced, which made Cairney laugh even more.

'Stop that,' said Aila. 'One more lie, and it's off to bed for you, Cairney.'

Cairney frowned and muttered something under his breath.

Kelsey picked up her glass, then she noticed a handsome young man smiling at her through the crowds in the gardens. She caught his gaze, and he raised his glass in her direction.

'Who's that?' she said.

Aila shrugged, then her eyes widened.

Before the demigod could say anything, a bomb exploded by the base of the Great Keep at the edge of the gardens. Screams, smoke and debris rose into the air, then a second bomb went off by the stage where the play had been performed; then a third in the midst of a large group of guests eating dinner by a table. Kelsey was blown from her seat by the proximity of the third explosion, and she was flung to the grass. A figure stepped over her, and Kelsey raised her eyes to see the handsome young man she had noticed earlier. He approached Arrosa, who was also on the ground, her arms shielding Clova, then he, Arrosa and Clova vanished.

Soldiers flooded through the gardens. A large number of them surrounded the Empress and led her away towards the safety of the Summer Palace, while others began to search among the trees. A few civilians were stumbling around, their clothes in tatters, while others were on the ground, their features disfigured and bloody.

Kelsey wondered why she couldn't hear anything. She tried to get to her feet, but slipped on the grass. She looked over, and saw Aila with six of her children.

Aila cried out, as her eyes scanned the ground, but Kelsey was oblivious to what she had said.

Someone grabbed Kelsey's arm. She turned, and saw a soldier from the Imperial Guard shouting at her, but all she could hear was a high-pitched whine. The soldier helped her to her feet, his mouth opening and closing, then more soldiers arrived by the table and went over to Aila and her children. Kelsey glanced down. Her dress was ripped in places, and she was coated in dust. She coughed, and her hearing slowly began to return.

'Clova?' she heard Aila shout.

'She's gone,' said Kelsey.

Aila and the soldiers turned to her.

'I saw it,' said Kelsey. 'A man; that man we saw. He walked over to Arrosa and Clova, and they vanished.'

'That man was Ward,' Aila cried.

Naxor ran over, and threw his arms round Aila.

'Ward was here,' she said, sobbing. 'He took Clova.'

'And Arrosa,' said Kelsey.

Naxor held Aila close. 'We will find her, cousin; we'll find your girl.' He glanced up at Kelsey, as if to say *I told you so*, but his mouth remained closed.

'There's something down here,' said a soldier, as she crouched by the table where Arrosa and Clova had been. She picked up a white envelope, and looked at Kelsey. 'Is this yours, ma'am?'

Kelsey snatched it from the soldier's hand. The envelope was unmarked, so she ripped it open. Inside, was a small note. Kelsey took it out of the envelope, and gazed down at it.

To those who find this,

Pray we do not treat our prisoners the way the Empire treated Lord Ballatar.

Edgar

One hour later, Kelsey was sitting on a long couch in the Empress's private quarters. She had a glass of whisky in her right hand, but was saying nothing as the others debated what to do while they waited for the Empress to return. Caelius walked into the room, and raised his hand for attention.

'The Empress has healed the wounded,' he said, 'and Her Majesty will be with us in a moment or two. We also have the final tally of the dead – seventeen people lost their lives in the three explosions. A fourth device was found by soldiers close to the base of the Lesser Keep.' He paused for a moment. 'It was a bomb made by the Empire – a device used by the Forty-Eighter artillery batteries.'

'Why didn't this fourth device explode?' said Cardova.

'Faulty fuse, sir,' said Caelius. 'However, it seems clear to me that these bombs were intended to cause a distraction, rather than claim the maximum number of casualties. There were no people by the Great or Lesser Keeps, and the stage area was deserted. The bomb that inflicted by far the highest rate of deaths and injuries was the one placed by a dining table.'

'Are you trying to excuse the actions of a vile terrorist and murderer?' said Naxor.

'No, my lord,' said Caelius; 'all I am saying is that if Ward had wanted to kill hundreds, then he could have killed hundreds. None of the devices were placed next to anyone from the Imperial Court, and the members of the Amatskourian government were left untouched – why? Perhaps Ward is incompetent; however, it is my belief that the entire purpose of his mission was to capture a hostage or two.'

'Then is it likely,' said Cardova, 'that Arrosa was his primary target. ' He glanced down at Aila, who was weeping silently. 'Little Clova just happened to be in the wrong place at the wrong time.'

'She was sitting on Arrosa's knee,' said Naxor. His expression darkened. 'The Holdfasts have three dream mages who could have prevented this attack, and not one of them was present.'

The demigod's voice tailed away as the Empress walked into the room. Her features were drawn, and she looked tired.

'I have done what I can,' she said. Her eyes fell on Kelsey. 'Thank you for remaining here in the palace so that I could use my healing powers on the wounded, Herald.'

Naxor coughed gently. 'I was just saying, Your Majesty…'

'I heard what you said, Chamberlain.'

'Three dream mages, Your Majesty; and none were here to help us. All three have deserted their posts.'

'We shall need to inform Karalyn of what has occurred,' said the Empress; 'while Kyra has made her choice – her loyalty now lies with the enemy. As for Cael, I still hope that he will return to us. For now, we need to find a way to let him know that his wife is in danger.'

Kelsey looked up. 'I can find him, Your Majesty.'

All eyes turned to her.

'Do you know where that little deserter is hiding, Herald?' said Naxor.

Kelsey got to her feet. 'Cael is not a deserter; neither, for that matter, is Cole. Both have been secretly working for me. They have been providing me with vital intelligence, and they have been supporting

Corthie in Na Sun Ka. I don't know their exact locations, but I will be able to track them down.'

Thorn eyed her. 'Was there a good reason to have kept this information from me, Herald?'

'Under the circumstances, Your Majesty,' said Kelsey, 'I felt that the fewer who knew the truth, the better. However, as Edgar has recently become aware that they are my agents, I was going to tell you this evening.'

'Or so you claim,' said Naxor.

'So I claim,' said Kelsey. 'Surely you, Naxor, know the importance of keeping the identities of certain agents hidden.'

The Empress said nothing for a moment, then she gave Kelsey a slight nod. 'I understand, Herald, and I am relieved that both Cael and Cole remain loyal to the Empire. Can you please ensure that Cael is made aware of the events that have taken place here?'

'He will wish to search for Arrosa and Clova, Your Majesty.'

'Indeed,' said Thorn, 'and you shall give him free rein to do so. I want Ward hunted down and eliminated as quickly as possible. The note left behind by Ward makes it clear that he is working for Edgar. I want Cael to find Ward, kill him, and retrieve the captives. Is that understood, Herald?'

Kelsey withdrew her Quadrant from her shoulder bag.

She bowed her head. 'It shall be done, Your Majesty.'

CHAPTER 21
THE FLICKERING FLAME

Nom Karta, Inopei – 3rd Lexinch 1597

Kyra gazed at the dragons who had gathered round Queen Famula's great mound of embroidered cushions. Nine days had passed since her Aunty Sable and Uncle Corthie had attacked the palace in Nom Karta and, while the floor and walls had been scrubbed clean, the damage from the explosive devices was still apparent. Of the four dragons who had been struck by bombs, one had been killed instantly, while the other three had been healed by Edgar and his gods. One of those injured dragons – Lord Konran Mon Gahad, was present in the audience chamber, and, like the others, he was acting as though nothing had happened.

'I would quite like to meet some of these Wystians,' said Lady Abda.

Queen Famula turned her long neck to regard her half-sister. 'Why would you wish to do such a thing?'

'I am curious to see how dragons live upon another world, Your Majesty,' Abda said.

'You might find the Wystians to be a little primitive,' said Edgar, 'compared to the dragons of the Dominion. They are certainly the least sophisticated of their kind upon Dragon Eyre. It has been a challenge to weld them together into a force with enough coherence to invade Na Sun Ka.'

'Do they have a monarch?' said Famula.

'No, Your Majesty,' said Edgar. 'Their society is based around extended family groupings. There is no single Wystian in overall control.'

'How close are they to being ready to launch the invasion?' said Lord Saphben.

Edgar glanced at Belfar, who tilted his head.

'At the moment, my lord,' said Belfar, 'around one and a half thousand dragons are fit and ready. We would like that number to rise to two thousand before any invasion is launched. I would estimate another ten to twelve days.'

'How many dragons does Queen Blackrose have in position to defend Na Sun Ka?' said Abda.

'Eight, my lady,' said Belfar.

The Dominion dragons laughed.

'Eight?' said Saphben. 'It seems to me that a hundred Wystians would be able to conquer Na Sun Ka, if only eight are defending it. Waiting for two thousand strikes me as being over-cautious.'

'Na Sun Ka is being defended by more than dragons, my lord,' Belfar went on. 'The Empire has some sixty thousand soldiers stationed there, together with hundreds of artillery batteries that can loose explosive devices into the sky. A previous attack on a handful of vessels belonging to the Imperial Navy claimed the lives of dozens of Wystians in a few short minutes; and we know the effect a few such devices had upon this court when Sable Holdfast attacked.'

A few of the dragons glanced down at Kyra, but she said nothing.

'Has Corthie Holdfast returned to Na Sun Ka?' said Queen Famula.

'He has, Your Majesty,' said Belfar, 'and he has been joined there by Cael and Cole Holdfast.'

'Corthie, as we have seen, is a magnificent warrior,' said Edgar; 'the best on any world; while Cole has vision and fire powers. In my opinion, however, Cael is the greatest threat to the invasion force. He can appear invisible, and he has the power to enter and subvert the minds of dragons and humans alike.'

Famula's eyes burned. 'There is no need to remind me of what Cael can do. How do you intend to neutralise this threat?'

'We are working on a variety of tactics, Your Majesty,' said Belfar.

'In other words,' said Abda; 'you don't know? Cael could wreck everything. If we lose the war on Dragon Eyre, the Empire will attack this world.'

'You should have killed him when you had the chance,' said Famula.

'We cannot risk it,' said Edgar. 'With all due respect, Your Majesty, if we were to kill Karalyn's son, then there is a chance that Athumia would be obliterated. Karalyn Holdfast possesses the Sextant – a device with the power to destroy entire worlds. There have been occasions in the past when Karalyn has been so overwhelmed with grief and rage that she has conducted wholesale massacres of her enemies. With one hand on the Sextant, she could lift every dragon from Athumia and cast them into the abyss. We must tread very carefully. We must find a way to win that does not involve the death of any of Karalyn's close kin.'

'Curse the blasted Demon Witch,' cried Saphben. 'Even now, after all the damage she has done, she still represents the greatest peril to any world. How can she be stopped?'

'If I knew that, my lord,' said Edgar, 'I would sleep easier at night. It does not matter how many times her physical form is destroyed, her spirit endures. I know of no way to fight such power.'

'We are fortunate that my mother pays little attention to anything that happens outside Colsbury,' said Kyra. 'She doesn't care about politics or war, and she doesn't desire power. The Empire could fall, and she wouldn't lift a finger to save it. Lord Edgar is correct – we can win if we don't provoke her anger.'

'Then I must ask that you be careful, Lord Edgar,' said Famula. 'You helped us regain the Tempest mine, and for that we are grateful. We are also happy to continue our alliance with you; however, under no circumstances do I wish to see the Demon Witch upon Athumia again. Appease her; placate her, but ensure she remains out of this conflict. For now, this meeting is over. Please return to the human areas of the palace.'

The four humans – Edgar, Bailey, Belfar and Kyra – bowed their heads in the direction of the Queen of the Dominion, then they turned and left the vast audience chamber. Edgar led them into the wing of the building that had been taken over by the gods, and they entered their large common room, where Allura was sitting. The god's left hand had re-grown, and the bandages had been removed.

'Pour me some wine, Bailey,' Edgar said, as he sat down on a chair.

Bailey went over to a table and opened a bottle of Aucterian wine.

'Should I return to Gyle, my lord?' said Belfar.

'Not yet,' said Edgar. 'I want to discuss some ideas about how we can get round Cael Holdfast. I noticed that none of the demigods that Elmhirst brought over from the Doomed Worlds were wearing eye guards.'

'There are none left to give them, my lord,' said Belfar.

'That is a significant weakness in our plan,' said Edgar. 'What is to stop Cael from interfering with the thoughts of these demigods? What is to stop him from forcing them to open their portals in the wrong place? We could have a catastrophe on our hands.'

Bailey came back with a glass of wine, and Edgar took it.

'Couldn't we kill him and make it look like an accident?' said Allura.

'Maybe I should kill you and make it look like an accident,' said Kyra.

Allura glared at her.

'My brother's life is to be preserved,' Kyra went on. 'That is a condition of my staying here with you.'

'Cael is the only individual from the Empire who has tried to talk to us,' said Edgar; 'that is another reason to keep him alive. When this war ends, we shall need reasonable people to be in charge of the Empire; otherwise, with whom would we negotiate?'

'I loathe all this untidiness,' said Allura. 'In the old days, we would simply slaughter our enemies and rule as we pleased. Under your governance, Lord Edgar, we are in alliance with dragons of two varieties, and we are forbidden from killing our main foes. You aren't making it easy for us.'

'I am thinking of the long term,' he said. 'In the old days, we didn't have someone like Karalyn to worry about.' He got to his feet, the glass of wine in his left hand. 'I wish to speak to Kyra alone for a while; the rest of you – remain here.'

Kyra narrowed her eyes but followed Edgar out of the room. They walked out onto a gallery that was open on one side, and Edgar took a seat. Kyra sat down next to him, and gazed out at the view of the palaces of Nom Karta.

'Tell me more about Cael,' said Edgar. 'What are his weaknesses?'

'He can be very reckless.'

Edgar nodded. 'What else?'

Kyra frowned. 'I don't know if I should be discussing my brother with you.'

'But you heard what I said. I have no intention of harming your brother – but we still need to beat him.'

'What do you want out of this, Edgar?' she said. 'What do you actually want?'

'Peace and stability,' he said. 'There are seven Doomed Worlds, and each one is inherently unstable. Two might have to be abandoned within the next few years, and the others aren't far behind. What I would like is this – a safe, stable world onto which I can evacuate every god and mortal from the Doomed Worlds. A world that is not threatened by the Holdfast Empire. A world where I can finally relax.'

'I don't understand you,' she said. 'How long did you spend in a restrainer mask?'

'Around five thousand years, give or take.'

'That is beyond my comprehension. How can you still be sane after that?'

He gave her a wry smile. 'Am I sane? Sometimes, I doubt that. I have terrible insomnia, nightmares, memory loss, mood changes… I am not the same person I was before my brother put the mask over my face. In truth, I can only remember the first few centuries of being in the mask; after that, I think my mind retreated into a kind of hibernation. My body was shrivelled up, and only the faintest amount of self-healing was keeping me alive. Perhaps I no longer had the strength to keep my mind functioning. Regardless, it was a blessing. My nightmares come from those first few centuries. If I could remember the entire experience, I would have almost certainly lost my mind.'

Kyra eyed him. 'That's the most you've ever told me.'

'I don't like to talk about it. It took Bailey many days to revive me. He had to use a mixture of his healing powers and salve, which was a substance of which I had no prior knowledge. He slowly and gradually nursed me back to health, and he restored my youth, but my thoughts were wild and incoherent. I didn't know where I was, or how much time had elapsed; I was utterly disorientated. To my shame, I lashed out at my saviour. I subdued Bailey so that I could ransack his memories, and then I placed the mask onto his face so that I could ensnare Karalyn and Corthie long enough to make my escape. I am very lucky that Bailey forgave what I did to him. Others wouldn't have, but our friendship runs deep.'

'How do you feel now?' she said.

He looked into her eyes. 'My thoughts remain dark,' he said, 'but you, Kyra, have lit them, like a flame flickering in the shadows.'

Her mouth went dry and she looked away.

'In many ways,' he went on, 'I feel as though I am starting again. My old life was fragmented by five millennia in that mask, and my memories are in pieces. In the old days, I wouldn't have given any thought or attention to a mortal woman, except perhaps as a disposable concubine; but now? My eyes have been opened as though I am newly born. And when I look at you...'

'Don't say any more,' she said.

'Then you do not feel the same?'

'I don't know what I feel. That day when we first met, and neither of us knew who the other was, I thought I felt something. But you are who you are – an immortal god who has lived for twenty thousand years; while I am a mortal Holdfast. Nothing ever can or should happen between us, and we both know it.'

'That grieves me.'

'In a hundred years from now, I will be long gone, while you will remain exactly as you are.'

Edgar lowered his gaze.

Kyra kept her eyes on him, wishing she could think of something to say that would make him feel better, and wishing she didn't find him so attractive. It wasn't just his looks, though that was part of it; it was something about the way he carried such a tremendous burden of pain without it making him cruel and spiteful. He wanted peace, and was trying to achieve it in the only way he knew how.

The air shimmered on the gallery, and a black-bladed sword flashed out, its point grazing against Edgar's throat.

'Cael?' Kyra cried, her eyes wide.

'Where is she?' said Cael, holding the Fated Blade in his right hand, while his left clutched a Quadrant.

Edgar raised his gaze, his features calm. He glanced at the sword blade resting against his throat, then he looked Cael in the eye.

'Where is who?' he said.

'Don't play games with me,' said Cael. 'I know you took her.'

'I have no idea what you are talking about,' said Edgar. 'Whom am I supposed to have taken?'

'Arrosa and Clova. Where are they? Speak, or die.'

'Arrosa's gone?' said Kyra.

'Ward snatched her from Colsbury, and he took Clova as well,' said Cael. 'Are you proud to work for a man who kidnaps a four-year-old girl?'

Edgar frowned. 'You just said that it was Ward who took them. Ward does not work for me.'

'You fucking liar,' said Cael. 'I saw Ward stealing three Quadrants from the university in Plateau City, and then I saw you hand three Quadrants over to Belfar.'

Kyra got to her feet. 'You got those Quadrants from Ward?'

Edgar nodded, as the black blade scored a line of blood on his neck. 'Yes.'

'You told me that you had exiled Ward,' she said.

'I did exile him. Ward approached me some days ago, wanting to talk. I was angry with the Empire for the death of Lord Ballatar, so I agreed to meet him. He gave me the Quadrants.'

'Why?' said Kyra.

'You would have to ask him,' said Edgar. 'I have given up trying to work out Ward's motives, but I knew it would be better if the Quadrants were with me rather than him. Perhaps he wishes the invasion of Na Sun Ka to be a success. He was wearing eye guards, but so was I, and so neither of us could read the other's thoughts.' He looked up at Cael. 'I am sorry if Ward has taken your wife and this Clova girl, but they are not here, and I had nothing to do with it.'

'He's telling the truth,' said Kyra. 'Listen to me, Cael; I would know if Arrosa or Clova were here. I can sense Gifts, and I would be able to sense Clova's self-healing powers. They aren't in Nom Karta.'

'You say Ward took them from Colsbury?' said Edgar. 'How could that be possible? Why didn't your mother prevent it?'

'My mother wasn't there,' said Cael.

Edgar narrowed his eyes. 'If you remove the sword from my throat, then perhaps I might be able to help you.'

'Why would you help me?'

'You have proved two things about yourself to me these past few months, Cael Holdfast,' he said. 'First, you have shown how resourceful and powerful you can be. You effortlessly escaped from the prison by the Tempest mine, capturing Lord Ballatar in the process; and, second, you have shown a willingness to negotiate. I want to help you, because I want you to remember that I helped you.'

'You wanted a hostage so you could threaten us.'

'Not true. I initially did want a hostage – that part is correct, but I wanted one so that I could bargain for Ballatar's life. And, had I wished to take a hostage, I would not have selected a four-year-old girl, nor would I have taken your wife.' He smiled. 'I might have captured you, or Corthie, but I draw the line at involving innocent bystanders. However, with Ballatar's death, I no longer want or need a hostage; that time has passed.'

'What kind of help could you give me?' said Cael.

'Sheath the sword and I will tell you.'

Cael remained where he was, the edge of the Fated Blade still resting against Edgar's throat.

'I believe him, brother,' said Kyra. 'Let him help you find Arrosa. If you kill him, you might never find her.'

Cael drew back the sword, then he slid it into the scabbard by his belt. 'I'm listening.'

The wound on Edgar's neck healed itself, and he wiped away the blood with his fingers.

'Ward has several old domains upon the Doomed Worlds,' he said. 'When I met him, it was in a castle upon a world by the name of Solitudus; that was where he handed over the three Quadrants. Solitudus is a barren wasteland, with very little fresh water, and its impoverished inhabitants are clustered around the few rivers and deep wells that exist. I do not know if this is the place Ward has taken Arrosa and Clova, but it is where I would look. The castle has many dungeons, dungeons that could probably fit the entire population of that world, for Solitudus was once green and fertile, and the castle was once at the centre of a vast city, now ruined and deserted. The population has plummeted since that time. I am now going to reach for my Quadrant. Do not be alarmed, Cael; all I intend to do is show you how to get to Solitudus.'

Cael's hand hovered over the hilt of the Fated Blade as Edgar slowly reached behind his Tempest breastplate. He withdrew his Quadrant, and then, with his free hand, he traced out the positions of three fingers over the copper surface.

'That will take you to Ward's castle,' Edgar said, placing the Quadrant back into its place behind the breastplate.

'What if you're lying?' said Cael. 'What if your instructions send me into the middle of a volcano?'

'Then you will die,' said Edgar. 'Your mother will discover what I have done, and then I will die, if Kyra doesn't kill me first. I recommend returning home before you travel there, to stock up on water and other supplies – Solitudus is a harsh place to be. The sandstorms can strip the skin from exposed flesh, and the heat is almost unbearable.'

'Greenhides?'

Edgar shook his head.

'Edgar knows what our mother is capable of doing,' said Kyra. 'He knows what would happen if you were harmed because of his advice. I know you must be worried about Arrosa, brother, but you can trust Edgar on this.'

'Helping you helps me,' said Edgar. 'There may come a time when you and I will sit down to discuss the future of the known worlds, Cael Holdfast. I want you to trust me; I need you to trust me. I hope you find Arrosa and the girl, and I hope you are able to bring them home.'

Cael took a step back, his eyes uncertain, then he triggered the Quadrant and vanished. Edgar got to his feet and strode towards the door.

'Where are you going?' said Kyra, as she hurried after him.

She followed Edgar back into the common room, where Bailey, Allura and Belfar were sitting.

'Lord Belfar,' said Edgar.

Belfar got to his feet. 'My lord?'

'Return to Gyle immediately. I want the invasion of Na Sun Ka launched as quickly as possible.'

'But, my lord,' said Belfar, 'we have only one and a half thousand dragons prepared and ready. I thought we needed two thousand?'

'One and a half thousand shall have to suffice. An opportunity has arisen to conduct the invasion while Cael Holdfast is busy elsewhere. We have no time to lose. Throw everything we have at Na Sun Ka.'

'Everything?' said Belfar.

'You heard me. Take Allura with you, as she is ready to return to active duty. Go.'

Belfar bowed. 'Yes, my lord.'

Allura got to her feet and stood next to Belfar. He removed a Quadrant from his robes, and both gods vanished.

'What's going on?' said Bailey. 'Why will Cael Holdfast be busy elsewhere?'

'It seems that Ward has inadvertently done us a favour,' said Edgar. He turned, and saw Kyra glaring at him.

'You utter bastard,' she said.

Edgar raised an eyebrow. 'Why?'

'All that talk about wanting to help Cael, when all you were trying to do was get him away from Dragon Eyre.'

'I do want to help Cael,' he said, 'and I also want to win this war. The two objectives are not mutually exclusive.'

He walked away, and Kyra went after him.

'Wait,' she said; 'I hadn't finished.'

Edgar carried on. They returned to the gallery, where Edgar picked up his glass of wine and took a sip.

'I could have killed Cael; do you know that?' he said. 'I could have killed your brother on several occasions; but each time I have spared him. I also genuinely hope that Arrosa is safe and well, and that Cael finds her. At the same time, I have an alliance with the Wystians, and I have pledged to help them conquer Na Sun Ka. I don't understand why you can't see that, Kyra.'

'It all seems so cynical, to take advantage of my brother like that. There's something you're keeping from me. What else did you and Ward cook up? How many times have you met him since his so-called *exile*?'

Edgar gazed out at the view of the dragon palaces of Nom Karta. 'More than once.'

Kyra took a step forward. 'You lie too easily, Edgar. You told me that you hadn't met Ward; that you had no interest in meeting him. How can I trust someone who lies like that?'

'I am sorry for lying.'

'Are you? What about all those things you were saying to me before Cael arrived? Were they all lies, too?'

'No. I knew you would be angry with me if I told you I had met with Ward; I was angry with myself for doing it. Sometimes... sometimes I am not in control of my emotions. A tide rises within me, and sweeps me away. My one hope is that I am still being affected by my time in the restrainer mask, and that these waves of anger will pass in time. I don't want to be like this, Kyra.'

'Let's go back to what happened,' she said. 'You stormed off when you learned that Ballatar was dead, yes?'

'Yes.'

'And you went to see Ward?'

'I did.'

'Did you ask him to capture a Holdfast in retaliation for the death of Ballatar?'

Edgar said nothing.

'Answer me,' she said. 'Answer me, or I'm leaving.'

'I knew Lord Ballatar for a very long time,' he said; 'not as long as I've known Bailey, but a considerable time, nonetheless. I doubt I would be able to describe to you how angry I was that the Empire so capriciously murdered him.'

'The Empire didn't murder him.'

'I don't believe it. I think Cael was told to deliver that message to me, and I hold your brother blameless; but I don't believe it. My rage fed deep into my blackest thoughts, and I wanted revenge. Had I not shown mercy to the Holdfasts? Had I not spared Cael, and Corthie? I was angry with myself, for being too kind to my enemies, when that kindness had been rewarded with the murder of my friend.'

He turned to her.

'So yes,' he said. 'The answer to your question is yes. I ordered Ward to lie in wait and to abduct the first Holdfast he could get his hands on. I ordered him to take his prisoner to his castle in Solitudus, and to keep them unharmed. I wanted the Empire to feel the pain of knowing that one of their own was in the same situation as Ballatar had been when he was being held captive; I wanted them to suffer the same fear and anguish. But, I told Ward not to harm anyone he captured. I even wrote out a short note, for Ward to leave behind; a note that would be found and read by whoever happened to be there. It was petty of me, but my anger needed an outlet.'

'What did the note say?'

'I can't remember. It was something along the lines of *You had better hope we treat our captives better than the way you treated Ballatar*; I cannot recall the precise wording. My anger faded as soon as I had left Ward's company, but then I reasoned with myself. I knew that Karalyn was in Colsbury; therefore, I could not bring myself to believe that Ward would have any success there. I assumed Colsbury was impregnable. Why would Karalyn leave it undefended?'

'I have no idea. Knowing my mother, it could have been anything. She might have wanted her children to visit Aunty Celine for all I know. The Empress doesn't control her actions; far from it. No one can control her. My mother does exactly as she pleases.'

'Ward must have been close by, waiting for an opportunity to strike.'

'Will he do as you ask? Will he keep Arrosa and Clova safe?'

'We had better hope so.'

'Arrosa has powerful Gifts; did you know that?'

'What can she do?'

'She can detect lies. More importantly, given the situation, she can turn people into glass.'

Edgar narrowed his eyes.

'It's true,' said Kyra. 'She can do it through physical touch. It's called the Gift of Vitrification. Ward might already be dead, especially if he doesn't know this.'

'Ward is like a mirror image of my darker thoughts,' he said. 'If Arrosa has a chance to kill him, I hope she takes it. I hope Cael arrives to find Ward dead.'

'And do you also hope that Na Sun Ka is overwhelmed by your Wystian allies?'

'I do. The Empire will have no choice but to negotiate if we force them to evacuate Dragon Eyre. A lasting peace will be one step closer.'

'At the cost of thousands of deaths.'

'But your brother won't be there. He will be on Solitudus when the invasion begins; he will be safe.'

'What about my cousin Cole? And my Uncle Corthie? They will be on Na Sun Ka.'

He looked into her eyes. 'I cannot save everyone, Kyra. No one can.'

CHAPTER 22
THE DAM BREAKS

Sun Ta, Na Sun Ka, Western Rim – 20th Abrinch 5266 (18th Gylean Year 17)

'And this one,' said Rosie Jackdaw, 'is balanced on your shoulder. It's probably best if you go down to one knee when you're aiming it, as the recoil could knock you off your feet.'

Nestorian picked up the long metal tube. He examined both ends, then Rosie lifted it and put it up onto his right shoulder. Nestorian went down to one knee next to her.

'The other person then...' she said.

'It needs two people?' said Drechtalang.

'Yes,' said Rosie. 'The other person loads a projectile into this end; then you go to the other end, pull the fuse cord through the little hole, and light it. Three seconds later, a small amount of Ectus powder at the rear of the projectile ignites, and the explosion sends the projectile whooshing out.'

Drechtalang laughed. 'It whooshes, eh?'

'Shut up,' said Corthie; 'I'm trying to pay attention.'

'Why, boss?' said the hedgewitch. 'You'll be too busy swinging your Clawhammer around to mess about with the Jackdaw lady's fancy weapons.'

'What's the range, ma'am?' said Nestorian.

'A hundred yards if the weapon is held horizontally,' she said; 'perhaps a hundred and fifty if it's held at an angle.'

Nestorian altered his position, and gazed along the metal sights attached to the far end of the tube.

'Does it have a name, ma'am?' he said. 'I'm not too keen on calling it a *tube*. And we can't call it a pipe, or Drechtalang might try to smoke it.'

'Professor Ravi is calling it the Battanara.'

'Why?' said Corthie.

'Because that's the second part of his name. Ravibattanara.'

'Is that his full name? I didn't know that.'

'We're working on a better firing mechanism,' Rosie went on; 'one that won't need a second person, but it's fiddly. Imagine a crossbow trigger on the underside of the Battanara. If we can make that ignite the Ectus powder, then it'll be more efficient.'

'And we'll be able to use it in the rain,' said Drechtalang.

'The improvements are coming along quickly,' said Nestorian, as he got to his feet.

'The Treasury is throwing gold at us,' said Rosie. 'Whatever we ask for – personnel, resources, equipment, production facilities – we get it; no questions asked.' She glanced at Corthie. 'That's your sister's doing. She's very keen on us making better weapons.'

'What would happen if I aimed a Battanara at a god's head?' said Nestorian.

'The god's head would evaporate, I guess,' said Rosie. 'No more god.'

Nestorian shook his head. 'I always wondered why Implacatus would never allow us to develop these weapons on Ectus. They insisted that we produced the same damn pisspots over and over; and they had a hundred rules about not exporting the technology to other worlds. It was instant execution if we talked to anyone about what went on in those factories.'

'They were scared,' said Cole, who had been sitting quietly. 'The last thing they wanted was mortals wielding powerful weapons. We were taught a bit about that in university. The gods of the City of Salve suppressed all study of new technologies, in order to keep the mortals subservient, and to stop them building weapons that could kill them.'

'The Battanara makes me feel obsolete,' said Corthie, 'so I can only imagine what the gods of Implacatus would think of it. Whoosh – there goes Edmond.'

'Are the coastal defences getting any of these, ma'am?' said Nestorian.

Rosie shook her head. 'We haven't made enough of them yet. Besides, nothing beats the Forty-Eighters if you want to destroy an invading force of dragons. Their rate of fire can fill the sky with a cloud of shrapnel so thick that nothing can get through.'

Claudian walked into the large hall. 'Have you finished your demonstration, Miss Jackdaw?'

'I think so,' said Rosie.

'Would you like me to take you back to Plateau City?'

'No, thanks,' she said. 'I have another demonstration to put on for the regular army this afternoon, and then I was hoping to see my sister this evening. I'll go back to Plateau City tomorrow, if that's all right with you?'

'That will be fine. I will collect you tomorrow.'

'Are there any updates on our missing team member?' said Corthie.

'None as yet,' said Claudian. 'However, we estimate that the Wystians won't be ready for another dozen days or so. I am certain that Cael will be back by then.'

'Can we say his name openly now?' said Corthie.

'Yes. The entire government, and the enemy, it seems, is aware that both Cael and Cole are working as imperial agents. Now, before I return to Colsbury, is there anything you need from me?'

'Aye,' said Corthie. 'A Quadrant would be nice, along with someone who knows how to use it.'

'Unfortunately, every Quadrant we possess is already assigned to someone,' said Claudian. 'There is no doubt that Cael will bring his back when he has returned from his operation. Was there anything else? No? Then I will see you all tomorrow.'

The air shimmered, and Claudian vanished.

'Are you married, Rosie?' said Drechtalang.

'Not that I recall,' she said.

'Then you might be open to a bit of Sanang loving?'

Rosie snorted. 'Uh, thanks, but, eh, no thanks.'

'I knew she had good taste,' said Nestorian, as he examined the four Battanaras they had been left.

Drechtalang shrugged. 'It was worth a try.'

Corthie glanced at Cole. 'Do you want to check the skies by the coast for me?'

'The Wystians won't be coming for a dozen days, boss,' said Drechtalang. 'You heard what the Adjutant told us. We should smoke weed and drink more of your whisky.'

'I'll do it, Uncle,' said Cole.

'Thanks,' said Corthie.

Cole gazed up at an open skylight, and his eyes glazed over. Corthie got up from his seat by the table and stretched his limbs. The team had been idle since Cael had left them the day before, and Corthie was bored. He walked over to the crates and picked up a Battanara. Rosie helped him sit it the right way round on his shoulder, and Corthie looked along the sights.

'Don't point that thing at me, boss,' said Drechtalang.

'So, what's Cael doing?' said Rosie. 'I heard he rushed off yesterday, like there was some kind of emergency.'

'Holdfast business,' said Corthie.

'He knows,' said Drechtalang, 'but he's not telling us. Isn't that right, boss?'

Corthie shrugged. In truth, he had no idea why Cael had grabbed his things and left in a hurry; except that his nephew had told him it was urgent, and that he wouldn't be long.

Cole's eyes cleared, and he shook his head. 'Nothing.'

'What did I tell you, eh?' said Drechtalang. 'Let's get so drunk we can't walk.'

'Is that what you boys do down here all day,' said Rosie, 'while there are crates of explosives lying about the place?'

'Not every day,' said Drechtalang.

'I want to,' said Corthie, 'but we're on duty.'

Maddie walked into the large hall. 'Hey, Rosie!'

Rosie smiled, and the two women embraced.

'I'm liking this new job of yours,' said Maddie. 'I've seen more of you in the past few days than I have in the last couple of years.'

'I have to work this afternoon, but is it all right if I stay the night?'

'Oh, I don't know about that... Only joking, it would be great. I've left the kids up in Ulna with Topaz, so we can have a proper night out. Now, when I say *a proper night out*, I really mean the bar in the army base next door, as we're not allowed to go out in the city after dark. Should we invite the boys?'

Rosie glanced at Corthie and his team. 'Hmm. All right, if they promise to behave themselves. And then, tomorrow morning, you can take me up to Ulna for five minutes so I can visit my niece and nephew, yeah?'

'If we aren't too hungover,' said Maddie. 'Right; I'd better get back to the big black dragon; we're going out on patrol.'

'I'll walk you out,' said Rosie.

Maddie glanced over at Corthie and the others. 'We'll see you in the bar this evening, yeah?'

'We'll be there,' said Corthie.

The four men watched as Maddie and Rosie left the large hall, then Drechtalang frowned.

'They didn't ask if we actually wanted to go out with them tonight,' he said. 'They just assumed we would.'

'You stay in, then,' said Nestorian. 'I'm looking forward to a night out with the Jackdaw sisters.'

'I think I'll go up to the roof to get some fresh air,' said Corthie.

'I'll come with you,' said Cole.

Corthie glanced at Nestorian and Drechtalang as he and Cole

walked towards the stairs. 'Don't blow each other up while we're away, lads.'

They ascended the spiral staircase to the roof of the mighty Temple of Ulna, and emerged into the mid-morning sunshine.

'The weather on Dragon Eyre is so predictable,' said Corthie. 'Light showers at night; glorious sunshine all day.'

'Simon designed it that way,' said Cole.

'Is that right?'

'That's what I was taught.'

'In Clackenbaird, you can experience sun, rain, wind, hail – all in the same day, regardless of the season. Do you remember the last time you were in Kell?' Corthie grimaced. 'Shit; sorry. I forgot for a moment.'

'That's all right,' said Cole. 'It was nine years ago.'

'Your mother was a good woman.'

'Your mother died that day, too.'

'Aye.'

They walked up to the edge of the roof and gazed out over Sun Ta. The city was still divided in two, with the districts inhabited by the former settlers from Implacatus separated from those where the natives from Dragon Eyre lived. Soldiers from the Sanang divisions were patrolling the roads that lay between the two opposing sides, who feared them more than they feared each other. A large, central square was host to a marketplace, and a fence had been built down the middle to keep the two sides apart, while soldiers watched from a wooden tower. In the distance, Corthie could see the masts of the ships docked in the harbour, while two dragons were in the air, scanning the surrounding areas for any sign of the impending invasion. A third dragon joined them, as Blackrose soared up into the sky from the forecourt of the temple complex. Maddie was strapped into the harness on the dragon's shoulders, and Corthie waved up to her.

'Do you ever wonder why we're fighting for a city that doesn't want us here?' said Cole.

'If we weren't here,' said Corthie, 'the settlers and the natives would be murdering each other.'

'What's that got to do with us?'

'Nothing, I suppose, but that's not why we're here. The whole point of occupying Na Sun Ka was to protect Blackrose's realm. If it falls, then we move back and defend Yearning. If Yearning falls... well, if Yearning falls, then I guess it's over.' He glanced at his nephew. 'And before you say, *Why should we defend Blackrose's realm?* do I have to remind you that she came to our aid when the Ascendants were attacking the Kell Pass? When we needed her, she was there.'

'And now she needs us?'

'Exactly.'

'Did you ever see my father fight?'

'I missed a few of his big battles, like Rainsby, and I was on Lostwell when he helped defend Colsbury from Agatha; but aye – I saw him fight. Keir and I worked for Sable during the war against the Ascendants, just like you and Cael are helping me.'

Cole nodded, but his eyes remained narrow. 'People keep telling me that I'm nothing like my father,' he said. 'Did you know that I've barely used my powers?'

'I heard you used them when you were trapped on Cael's world.'

'Yes. I killed dozens of townsfolk.'

'But they were going to kill you. It was self defence.'

'Maybe, but a rage came over me – a rage that I've been trying to suppress my whole life. What if the others are wrong, and I am exactly like my father? What if once I start killing, I can't stop?'

'I know that feeling,' said Corthie. 'Fighting and killing are among the few things I've ever been good at. I used to enjoy it far too much. But listen to me, Cole – there is nothing wrong with fighting to defend those who cannot defend themselves. That was the rule I always tried to follow. Don't be scared to use your powers if you need to. If nobody stood up to bullies, they would walk all over us.'

A scream came from somewhere in the city, and Corthie glanced down. A portal had opened in the middle of the divided marketplace, and ironhides were pouring through it, their claws tearing apart every civilian within their reach. One ironhide went for a squad of Sanang soldiers, and ripped them to shreds in seconds, then another tore down the fence that cut the market in two. The three patrolling dragons swooped down from the sky. Blackrose opened her jaws and aimed her fire at the portal, but the ironhides ignored the flames, and continued to rush through. The portal disappeared, leaving two dozen of the enormous beasts loose in the city. They began to scatter down the narrow alleyways leading off the large square, heading into settler and native areas. The dragons hovered overhead, unable to react, as the screams of terror rose up into the sky. A bell pealed from somewhere, and Sanang soldiers hurried out of their barracks by the Temple of Ulna, racing off in the direction of the city centre.

Corthie turned and ran for the stairs, Cole in pursuit. They descended as quickly as they were able, and emerged into a scene of chaos on the ground floor. Soldiers were pulling on their armour, while others were sprinting to their posts. Corthie rushed into the large hall where the remnants of his team were based, and ran into Drechtalang and Nestorian, who were hurrying in the other direction.

'Has the invasion begun, sir?' said Nestorian.

'I don't know,' said Corthie. 'It might be a raid to soften us up, or it might be the real thing. Get your armour on; you're both coming with me.'

'A raid?' said Drechtalang, as they gathered by the table, where their equipment was sitting. 'What kind of raid?'

'Ironhides,' said Corthie. 'Do you remember those beasts that attacked us on the dragon carriers? Them, but more, and they're loose in the city.'

'Won't the dragons get them, sir?' said Nestorian, as he buckled on his Tempest breastplate.

'They are impervious to fire,' said Corthie; 'and they can self-heal. We need to remove their heads. Bring a Battanara. Cole, you carry a crate of projectiles. Drechtalang, you can watch Nestorian's back.'

'Again?' said the hedgewitch.

'Aye, again. Cole, give me a hand with my armour straps.'

Cole hurried to Corthie's side, and fastened the buckles of his Tempest armour.

'I will keep the ironhides off us,' Corthie said, 'while Nestorian blows the shit out of them. But we'll have to find them first.'

'That should be easy, boss,' said Drechtalang; 'we'll just follow the trail of blood.'

Corthie picked up his Clawhammer, and waited for the rest of his team to get ready. He powered his battle-vision, and controlled his breathing. He had killed ironhides before, but never as many as had been let loose within the streets of Sun Ta.

A young officer ran into the hall. 'I have been sent to summon you, sir. An attack is underway in the centre of the city.'

'We know,' said Drechtalang.

'Tell your commanding officer that we'll be leaving the temple in the next few minutes,' said Corthie. 'Cole, make sure you've got plenty of matches, and carry as many projectiles as you can.'

The young officer watched them for a moment, then he turned and hurried away.

'You all ready?' said Corthie to his team.

They nodded.

'Follow me.'

They left the hall and walked towards the main gate. Imperial soldiers, most of them from the Holdings, parted for Corthie and his team, and a few shouted words of encouragement. Corthie reached the entrance, and stepped out into the bright sunshine. Several bells were pealing, and all nine dragons were in the sky. Smoke was rising from a few different locations around the city, but Corthie had no idea what was causing it.

An officer raced over, then he pointed towards the central district of Sun Ta.

'That way, sir – straight ahead. Several beasts have been seen north of here.'

Corthie nodded, then he broke into a run, the Clawhammer gripped in his right hand. He and his team left the large plaza that sat in front of the great temples, and entered the winding lanes of the central district of the city. A few civilians almost collided with him as they fled south, then screams intensified from ahead. Corthie and the others moved through the crowd of civilians, and carried on. They came to a wider road, lined on both sides with trees. Twenty yards in front of them, an ironhide was ripping its way through another large crowd of civilians.

'Load the Battanara,' said Corthie. 'I'll keep it distracted.'

He raced forward, powering his battle-vision. The ironhide seemed too busy to notice him, but then, at the last second, it turned to face Corthie, its claws extended. Corthie dodged a wild lunge of talons, rolling to the side, then he swung the Clawhammer, ripping through the flank of the beast. The ironhide howled in agony, then the wound on its side began to heal. Another ironhide charged down the street, coming to the aid of the one fighting Corthie. The first ironhide lunged at Corthie, and he fended its limbs away with the Clawhammer, then he turned, battering away an attack from the second. Corthie's battle-vision hummed with life, but fighting two ironhides at the same time reminded him of when he had faced two Ascendants in Fordamere. He dealt out wounds to both of the beasts, but couldn't get close enough to their heads to kill them. A blow from an ironhide struck Corthie's chest, and he flew backwards, hitting a tree. He dived to the side, as claws ripped through the trunk, then he slammed the Clawhammer down into the brain of the beast. At the same moment, something flew by his side, and an explosion blew the second ironhide apart.

Corthie gasped, and leaned on the Clawhammer. His body was aching from hitting the tree, and it took a moment for his battle-vision to dull the pain.

'Those things move as quickly as you, boss,' said Drechtalang, as his team raced forward.

Cole glanced at the dismembered bodies of the civilians scattered over the road. 'Twenty of these beasts are on the loose,' he said. 'They're going to kill thousands. I tried to get into their minds, even though Cael said it was impossible, but they have no eyes. No eyes, and fire does nothing to them; I'm completely useless out here.'

'You helped me load the Battanara, lad,' said Nestorian, who was standing with the weapon over one shoulder.

'We can't stop now,' said Corthie.

The survivors from the crowd of civilians staggered down the street towards the team. They stared at the bodies of the two dead ironhides, then Corthie gestured south.

'Run to the temples,' he cried. 'You'll be safe inside the temples.'

Drechtalang nudged Corthie. 'Boss – look!'

Corthie turned in the direction of the city harbour, and saw the sky light up and crackle with hundreds of small explosions.

'The Forty-Eighters,' said Nestorian.

Amid the explosions, over two hundred dragons were soaring down from the blue sky. One was being ripped apart every second by the Forty-Eighters, but the Wystians flew on, heedless of the casualties, and dozens got close enough to the harbour to unleash their flames. Fire streamed out over the harbour district, followed by a series of explosions as the Forty-Eighter batteries were hit. The artillery by the harbour fell silent, but the dragons continued to burn the district, and then a colossal explosion blasted through a large building on the quayside, sending smoke and rubble into the air.

Blackrose soared over the street from where Corthie and the others were watching the harbour burn, then the black dragon swooped down, disappearing from sight behind a tall steeple. When Blackrose next arose, she had an ironhide clutched in her forelimbs. Drechtalang let out a cheer, then the ironhide slashed out, its claws tearing through Blackrose's scales. The Queen of the Eastern Rim roared in anger and pain, then the ironhide sliced through the straps keeping the harness attached to the dragon's shoulders, and Maddie fell through the air, screaming. Blackrose ripped the ironhide apart with her claws, and dived down after her rider.

'With me,' cried Corthie, as he set off towards the back lanes where Maddie would have landed.

The rest of the team ran after Corthie, as more explosions rippled through the harbour district. They turned a corner, and saw Blackrose perched atop a low wall, her head peering down in a narrow alleyway. Lying on the ground by the dragon's face was Maddie. The rider was still strapped into the harness, and the leather padding had cushioned her fall. Corthie ran over to her.

'Malik's sweaty crotch,' Maddie muttered, as she sat up. 'That hurt a bit.'

'Are you injured, my rider?' said Blackrose.

'Just my pride, I think,' she said. 'Hello, Corthie.'

'Hello, Maddie,' he said as he crouched next to her. He unbuckled her straps, and helped her get disentangled from the harness.

'I shall not leave you down here on the ground, my rider,' said the dragon. 'Can anything be done, Corthie?'

Corthie gestured to his team. 'See what you can do about fixing the queen's harness, lads,' he said. 'It doesn't have to be pretty.'

Nestorian, Cole and Drechtalang hurried forward. They picked up the harness, and Blackrose remained low as they began fitting it back onto her shoulders.

'The day we knew would arrive is upon us, Corthie,' the black dragon said, as his team got to work. 'The invasion has begun earlier than we had expected. I have witnessed a dozen portals open up in quick succession all over Sun Ta. Without doubt, more will have opened in other parts of Na Sun Ka. Fifty Wystians here, twenty ironhides there, and a hundred of those vile undead dragons that we last encountered in the Kell Pass.'

'The Forty-Eighters blew the shit out of the ones over the harbour though, eh?' said Drechtalang, as he tied the ends of two cut straps together.

'Over a hundred Wystians sacrificed themselves to destroy the batteries defending the marine headquarters,' said Blackrose. 'The harbour is no longer able to defend itself from attack.'

'I can't do much about the dragons,' said Corthie, 'but I can hunt ironhides.'

Blackrose tilted her head, and Corthie realised from her expression that she was masking the pain she felt from the wounds on her flank that had been inflicted by the ironhide.

'This is a battle we cannot win,' she said. 'More Wystians appear with every passing second, and the ironhides have already destroyed entire companies of Sanang warriors. Three of my Eastern Rim dragons have fallen, ripped apart by those undead abominations.'

Nestorian raised a thumb in the air. 'The harness is secure again, sir.'

'You have my thanks,' said the black dragon. 'Climb back up, my rider.'

Cole helped Maddie grab onto the harness, and she scrambled up onto the dragon's back.

Blackrose turned to face Corthie again. 'I will do what I can from the air, if you remain on the ground, Edmond-slayer. Kill as many ironhides as you can, and I will slay whichever foe dares to confront me in the sky. Farewell, for now. If the city is overwhelmed, retreat to the Temple of Ulna.'

Blackrose checked that her rider was secure, then she ascended above the streets. She circled once, then she soared away in the direction of a cloud of black specks in the sky to the west of their position.

Drechtalang frowned. 'Did she say *undead dragons*?'

'Edgar released them from the Palace of the Almighty,' said Corthie. He gazed along the street. 'Stay close to me,' he went on. 'We can still win this. All we have to do is kill everything they throw at us. Come on.'

The day passed in a blur of battle-vision, smoke, terror and blood. Corpses littered the narrow lanes, and fires were raging in every part of the city. Undead dragons surrounded and picked off Blackrose's forces from the Eastern Rim, while the ironhides tore their way through the civilian population. The Forty-Eighter batteries filled the sky with explosions, destroying Wystians and undead dragons in their dozens, but slowly, one by one, the batteries were silenced by flames. Within the span of a few hours, much of Sun Ta was in smoking ruins, its streets flowing with blood; and still Corthie hunted the ironhides, his exhausted team trudging along behind him as he made his way through the carnage looking for more to kill.

'That's fifteen of the bastards,' said Drechtalang, as he gazed down at the remains of an ironhide destroyed by Nestorian's Battanara.

'How many projectiles are left?' said Corthie, his eyes on the warren of streets around them.

Cole dug through the straw in the crate he was carrying. 'Three.'

Corthie glanced up as four Wystian dragons soared overhead.

'Do you think they saw us?' said Nestorian. 'The longer we stay out on the streets, the more likely it is that the Wystians will see what we're doing.'

'They're turning,' said Cole. 'They're coming back!'

Corthie watched as the four dragons banked in the air – two soaring to the left, the other two to the right. They began to circle round towards the team's position, their jaws opening.

'Get off the road,' Corthie cried.

He ran towards the entrance of the nearest building, and kicked down the front door of an apartment block. The team raced in after him as flames flooded the street where they had been standing. Fire rushed up the hallway of the building as Corthie broke down another door and dived into an apartment. Nestorian cried out as flames enveloped him. Corthie and Drechtalang pulled the Banner sergeant into the apartment, and Cole slammed the door shut. The front windows of the room exploded as the flames from the dragons intensified, and Corthie dragged Nestorian deeper into the apartment. They sheltered in the kitchen – a small dark room where the flames didn't reach, and Drechtalang placed his hands onto Nestorian's scorched skin. The hedgewitch had already healed every member of the team at least once during the long day of running and fighting, and he slumped back against a wall, as Nestorian's injuries disappeared.

'I'm out,' muttered Drechtalang. 'Just make sure none of you get injured again, eh? Not for a couple of hours, anyway.'

Cole knelt by the kitchen door, which was open a crack, and his eyes glazed over.

'The four dragons are outside,' he said, 'and more are coming. I think they might have been looking for us.'

Nestorian joined Cole by the door, his uniform hanging in tatters.

'I can see a window in the front room from here,' Nestorian said; 'well, what's left of it.' He reached for the Battanara. 'Cole, check along my line of fire; tell me when a dragon is about to cross it.'

Corthie helped load the weapon as Cole's eyes remained glazed over. Nestorian balanced the Battanara on his right shoulder, with one end aimed through the gap in the kitchen doorway.

'Leave it,' said Drechtalang. 'Right now, they might think we're dead, but if you loose that thing at them...'

Corthie pulled the small fuse cord into place by the other end of the Battanara and readied the matches.

'Does no one ever listen to me?' said Drechtalang.

'We'll run for it as soon as we hit one of the big scaly bastards,' said Corthie. 'We'll head for the back of the building.'

'One of them's moving into range,' said Cole. 'Any moment... Now!'

Corthie struck a match and lit the end of the fuse. The flame ran quickly down the cord and disappeared into the rear of the Battanara. A second later, the weapon jolted back as the projectile shot through the air. An explosion rumbled and shook the building, then a dragon screamed in agony.

'Run!' cried Corthie.

The team piled out of the kitchen and raced towards the rear of the building. Drechtalang kicked a door open, and almost ran into a dragon's face, which was poised by the entrance. Corthie leapt forward, the Clawhammer swinging, and its talons connected with the dragon's face, ripping three deep, long gouges down through its right eye and green scales. The dragon roared in pain and shock, and Corthie went for its throat, his battle-vision thrumming. The Clawhammer bit through the dragon's neck, and its head lolled and swayed as blood poured from the wound. Above, two other Wystians had witnessed what had happened, and they soared down, their jaws opening.

Another dragon appeared, a large dark orange dragon. Gallantmorn slammed into the two Wystians racing towards Corthie, his jaws snapping out, and his claws ripping their wings to shreds. His jaws clamped round the neck of a Wystian, snapping it in two, then his rear limbs ripped out the throat of the other, and both Wystians plummeted to the ground.

'Climb onto my shoulders, Corthie!' Gallantmorn cried, as he lowered himself down by the rear of the building.

Corthie shoved Cole towards Gallantmorn's flank. More Wystians were coming, spotting the opportunity to kill both Corthie and an Eastern Rim dragon. Cole clambered into the harness upon Gallantmorn's shoulders and sat down to the left of Annu'tila, the dragon's rider; then Corthie pulled himself up after him. The dark orange dragon reached out and picked up Drechtalang and Nestorian, gripping one in each forelimb.

Three dragons attacked as Gallantmorn ascended, and he took blows to his flanks, underside and wings. He surged upwards, and broke free of the Wystians, but dozens more were on their way, and the sky seemed full of them. Gallantmorn's blood dripped from a dozen wounds, but his eyes burned with a fierce light, and he set off in a burst of speed, heading south over the ruins of the city centre.

Wystians dived and soared in their eagerness to catch the Eastern Rim dragon, but Gallantmorn's desperate speed outpaced them all. He descended like a lightning bolt from the heavens when they neared the great temples of Sun Ta. Four of them were in flames, and the bodies of thousands of dead Sanang soldiers were smouldering in the enormous forecourt. Gallantmorn pulled up from his dive at the last moment, and crashed through the open entrance of the Temple of Ulna. As soon as he was inside, soldiers from the Imperial Army closed the huge, iron-framed doors, and barred them.

Gallantmorn skidded to a halt on the scored marble floor of the temple's great hall, his wings ragged, and his face marked with claw wounds.

An army officer ran forward. 'My lord,' he said.

Gallantmorn raised his head from the floor. 'I am spent,' he said. 'I have slain more dragons this day than I believed possible, and I can do no more.'

Corthie, Cole and Annu'tila climbed down from the harness, as Gallantmorn opened his forelimbs to release Nestorian and Drechtalang.

'Is there any salve left?' Annu'tila cried. 'My dragon needs salve.'

'I'm afraid we have run out, sir,' said the army officer.

Several hundred soldiers were also in the great hall of the temple, and most were gazing at the wounded dragon.

'You saved us, Gallantmorn,' said Corthie. 'Thank you.'

'Perhaps I have now removed the stain of shame I felt from my part in the battle for the carriers,' he said. 'My wounds are grievous, and I will not be able to fight for some time; but they are not enough to kill me.'

Rosie appeared from a doorway, and ran over to Corthie.

'Praise Malik that you're back, Corthie,' she said, as her gaze went over Gallantmorn. 'I heard that a dragon had returned, but... where's Blackrose?'

'I don't know,' said Corthie. 'It's been a few hours since we saw her and your sister.'

'Should we go out to look for them?' said Rosie.

'I'm afraid that is impossible, ma'am,' said the army officer. 'The Temple of Ulna is now under siege. Hundreds of Wystian dragons are outside, but the walls are too thick for their flames to penetrate.'

'How many soldiers do we have inside?' said Corthie.

'Around three thousand, sir,' said the officer. 'We also have supplies of food and water that should see us through.'

'Until when?' said Corthie.

'Until Adjutant Claudian returns, sir. He is due back first thing tomorrow. He will be able to evacuate us.'

'Don't we have a spare Quadrant in here?'

'No, sir.'

'Maddie has a Quadrant,' said Rosie.

'The marines also have one,' said Nestorian. 'Their senior officers are permitted to use it.'

Gallantmorn eyed the Banner sergeant. 'Did you not see the explosion by the harbour that lit up the whole sky? That was the headquarters of the Imperial Marines.' With a struggle, he raised his head to survey the soldiers gathered in the hall. 'To survive,' he said, 'we must hold this temple until morning. Every entrance must be sealed, and every soldier must perform their duty.'

'I will remain by the front doors all night,' said Corthie, the Clawhammer in his hands as he gazed at the soldiers filling the hall. 'No one will pass.'

CHAPTER 23
SOLITUDUS

Hold Fast, Republic of the Holdings – 30th Day, First Third Summer 545

Cael crept into the white-tiled bathroom, walked up to a cabinet, and opened it, the ragged skin on his hands leaving bloody fingerprints all over the clean surfaces. More blood dripped into the sink from his neck and face, and he gasped with the pain from his burnt and damaged skin. He rummaged around in the cabinet, until he found a small glass vial.

'Who's in there?' cried Celine. She pushed the bathroom door opened and stared at Cael. 'What happened to you?'

Cael pulled the stopper from the vial and drank the small amount of salve held within. His body shook for a few seconds and the pain peaked, then a wave of healing and well-being surged through him. He exhaled, and sat on the side of the bath, his skin smooth again.

'Cael?' said Celine.

'I'll clean up the mess,' he said.

'I don't care about the mess,' she said; 'I want to know how you got injured in the first place.'

'I ignored someone's warning,' he said, 'and I got caught in a sandstorm.'

'A sandstorm that ripped your skin to shreds?' She walked closer to him, put a hand on his chin, and examined his face.

'The salve has healed the damage,' he said.

She turned to the sink and turned the hot water tap. She held a cloth under the running water for a few seconds, then began to wipe away the blood from Cael's face.

'Your mother isn't here,' she said, as she dabbed at his cheek.

'I wasn't looking for her.'

'No? She's doing the same thing that I imagine you were doing – looking for Arrosa.'

'How do you know about Arrosa?'

'Kelsey was here this morning. She said that she had already told you; then she told us. Your mother will find Arrosa with the Sextant.'

'My mother might take several days to find her,' said Cael. 'I know where Arrosa is; I've just been to the world where she was taken, but I was unprepared. The heat, Aunty – it made summer in the Holdings feel as cold as Kell. I need some desert clothes. I need to cover every inch of my body. That's why I'm back on the Hold Fast estate – I needed the salve, and I know we'll have desert clothes stored away somewhere.'

Celine rinsed the bloody cloth under the warm water, and began work on cleaning the blood from Cael's forearms and hands.

'I can sort you out with everything you need,' she said. 'We sometimes have to go into the desert in summer, to rescue horses that have strayed too far from the grazing grounds. Robes, goggles, gloves, and a pair of decent boots with soles that won't let your feet burn. You'll need water skins, too. However, I would rather you left it to your mother.'

'Arrosa is my wife.'

'Yes, I know that; but your mother is experienced at this sort of thing.'

'It'll take too long. My mother will be searching every world the Sextant can see.'

'Aren't you supposed to be on Dragon Eyre?'

'The invasion is days away, Aunty.'

'And how do you know where Arrosa is?'

'Edgar told me.'

'Do you trust him?'

'Not really, but Kyra was also there; and she trusts him.

'You saw your sister?'

'Aye.'

She rinsed the cloth again and eyed him. 'That's the blood off. How are the soles of your feet?'

'They were blistering, but they're fine now. I don't suppose Mother told you where she had hidden the Sextant before leaving?'

Celine smiled as she wiped down the tiled surfaces, clearing them of the blood that had fallen there.

'I'm sure you can guess the answer to that,' she said. 'Since when do any of the important Holdfasts tell little old me anything? Sometimes, I think they forget I'm up here. I mean, they took Cole away, right when I was in the middle of training him to run the estate. Before that, Keir also left. Am I supposed to manage the estate until I drop down dead from exhaustion? I've been doing it on my own for twenty years, ever since your grandfather Killop died. Do you think I will ever be allowed to train a replacement?' She frowned. 'Don't answer any of those questions. I love my job; I just hope I'm not getting too old for it. Right – stand up and follow me.'

Cael got to his feet and they walked out of the bathroom.

'Why are there no bloodstains out here?' said Celine.

'I used the Quadrant to appear in the bathroom, Aunty.'

'All the way from a sandstorm on another world, and with your fingers ripped to shreds?'

'Aye.'

'That sounds quite impressive,' she said, as they descended a flight of stairs.

'It is impressive, I suppose, but I can't take the credit for it. A god imprinted the knowledge into my mind, and using a Quadrant is as easy as breathing. I don't even have to think about it. It took Sable thirds of practise to be able to use a Quadrant one-handed, and I was doing it after a couple of days.'

'Now you sound as though you're bragging.'

'Sorry.'

They reached the ground floor of the mansion, and walked round a sparkling fountain that lay in the middle of a junction of marble-lined corridors. Cael gazed at the water, feeling his thirst rise, and he cupped his hands in the fountain and drank.

Celine rolled her eyes. 'You are not one of the estate dogs, Cael; you are a Holdfast. Remember your manners. Oh, and you will need to replace that salve. It was there for medical emergencies.'

'I was suffering from a medical emergency, Aunty.'

'Yes, but you will still need to replace it. Come on; the stores we need are in an outbuilding. We shall have to brave the weather for a few moments.'

They came to the rear porch, and Lahnos and Ora'lya glanced up from the long swing chair. Both had tall glasses of iced tea in their hands, and Cael's thirst grew again.

'Good morning, Cael,' said Lahnos. 'Kelsey told us what had happened – is there any news?'

'I've found out where she is,' he said. 'Aunty, could I get one of those iced teas?'

Celine pulled a cord, and a bell rang within the mansion. 'Order one when the servant arrives; I'll fetch what you need.'

'Thanks,' said Cael.

He sat down next to Lahnos as Celine walked down the steps and out into the scorching heat. The sun was burning down from the sky ahead of them, but the canopy over the porch was keeping the chairs in the shade.

'I can't believe how hot it is today,' said Ora'lya.

'You should try the world I was just on,' said Cael. 'Where's the baby?'

'He's inside with his grandparents,' said Lahnos. 'You can't bring him outside in this weather.'

A servant appeared by the door. 'Did someone ring?'

'Could I have an iced tea, a jug of cold water, and a packet of cigarettes, please?' said Cael.

'Of course, sir,' said the servant. 'I won't be a moment.'

Cael gazed out at the shimmering heat haze as the servant bowed and walked away.

'Imagine having servants,' said Ora'lya. 'Imagine being brought up here. The Holdfasts live like royalty.'

Cael shrugged.

'Lahnos and I had poor upbringings,' she went on. 'This life was something I thought only existed in stories.'

'I would rather have had my parents around,' said Cael. 'When I was about eight, my mother told me that she had originally planned to settle down in a tiny cottage in the Domm countryside. We would have been poor, but we would have been together. Instead, they went to Colsbury, where my father was killed, and my mother left to search for Corthie.'

'Where's Domm?' she said.

'At the opposite corner of the Star Continent,' Cael said. 'As far as you can travel without falling into the ocean.'

Ora'lya nudged Lahnos. 'Ask him; I know you want to.'

'Would you be all right with it?' he said.

'You've known Arrosa for years, Lahnos. She looks up to you like a big brother.'

Lahnos nodded, then he turned to Cael. 'I want to come with you. I can help.'

Cael eyed him. 'I thought you were supposed to remain on the estate.'

'I am; but who would know if I left for a while? Would you report me to the Empress, Cael? I'd need to let Sigum know. He might want to come, too.'

'It's not safe for dragons,' said Cael. 'The sandstorms would rip his wings to shreds.'

'All right; then we'll leave him here.'

'Celine is fetching desert clothes and equipment for me,' said Cael. 'You'd better tell her we'll need two sets.'

Lahnos nodded and got to his feet. 'I also need to speak to Sigum. I'll be back in a minute or two.'

He walked off the porch and through the blinding sunshine towards the little square where a large fountain sat.

'Thank you,' said Ora'lya.

'For what?' said Cael. 'I could do with his help.'

'I know, but he's been feeling useless ever since Kelsey was here. He asked Karalyn if she'd take him with her, but she refused.'

The servant returned and set down a tray onto a little table; then he bowed and retreated into the mansion.

Cael picked up the jug of water and drank down half of its contents in one long gulp, then he ripped open the packet of cigarettes and lit one.

'Thank Pyre for that,' he said, putting his feet up.

'You thanked Pyre, but not the servant, I noticed,' Ora'lya said.

'The servant gets paid; Pyre does it for free.'

'Being polite is also free. Little things like this matter, Cael Holdfast.'

He eyed her. 'Fair enough. I'll try to remember that.'

The porch drifted into silence as they waited for Celine and Lahnos to return. Cael had been putting on a brave face in front of everyone, but his insides were churning with a mixture of raw fear and helplessness. Every hour that Arrosa was missing was another hour in which she might have been hurt or killed. If Edgar had been telling the truth about not being responsible for the capture of Arrosa and Clova, then Ward might kill them both out of spite. Perhaps Ward was trying to inflame the war. Edgar said that he wanted peace, but what did Ward want? Then there was the possibility that Ward was already dead – transformed into a sculpture of green glass. Did he know about Arrosa's Gifts? But, if Ward was dead, then Arrosa and Clova would be stranded wherever they had been taken. Cael's nerves jangled and his stomach turned, but his exterior remained calm, as though he was confident that everything would turn out fine. That was another thing his grandmother Daphne had taught him, and she had taught him well.

Celine and Lahnos emerged from a whitewashed outbuilding close to the stables. Both were laden down with robes, boots, water skins and other equipment, so Cael got up and walked out into the glare of the sun to help them. He took a large pile of robes from Celine, and they went back up into the welcoming shade of the porch.

'I brought extra gloves,' said Celine, 'and two pairs of goggles. I'll fill up the water skins while you two boys get changed.'

'We'll need to cover every inch of flesh,' said Cael, as Celine walked into the mansion with the water skins. 'The sandstorm ripped the skin from my face and arms.'

Lahnos nodded.

Cael unfastened his belt, and laid it and his sword onto the low table.

Lahnos eyed the hilt. 'Is that Sable's Fated Blade?'

'Aye,' said Cael. 'She lost it in Nom Karta, and I stole it back. I've decided to keep a hold of it for now.'

Lahnos and Cael shed their outer garments and clad themselves in the long robes that had been in the store room. They wrapped the robes round their arms and legs, and then their faces, leaving only a space for the eyes, which they covered with the goggles. Belts kept the robes in place, and Cael began to sweat under the weight of the thick garments. He slid the scabbard containing the Fated Blade deep into his robes, and Lahnos did the same with a small war axe. Ora'lya helped them on with their boots and gloves, then Celine returned, and gave each man two full water skins. Cael eased one glove off, and placed the Quadrant within the fold of his robes; then he glanced at Lahnos, whose horns were poking through the robes at the top of his head.

'Did you find Lord Sigum?' said Ora'lya.

Lahnos nodded. 'He wanted to come, but I told him about the conditions we would be experiencing. I think he understood.' He glanced at Cael. 'Where will we arrive?'

'In the middle of a desert,' said Cael. 'We're looking for a castle.'

'Can't we use the Quadrant to arrive inside the castle?'

'We would if I knew where it was, but I couldn't see anything more than a few feet in front of me. I've searched several areas already, so we can skip those.'

'Take care, Lahnos,' said Ora'lya.

'If Karalyn comes back,' said Celine; 'what should I tell her? Where exactly are you going?'

'To a desert world called Solitudus,' said Cael. 'It's one of the seven Doomed Worlds.'

'Could you be more precise?'

'Hold on,' said Cael. He glanced into his aunt's eyes, and imprinted the instructions needed to travel to where they were going by Quadrant. 'Did you feel that?'

Celine nodded.

'Tell Mother to look into your mind, and she'll see how to reach the place I'm taking Lahnos. Tell her she's welcome to join us.'

'Maybe you should wait for her to get back.'

'If she hadn't hidden the Sextant, then we wouldn't need to wait. I can't sit around here while the lives of Arrosa and Clova are in danger.'

He positioned a glove inside his robes next to the Quadrant, then he nodded at Lahnos.

'Do it,' said Lahnos.

Cael traced his fingers over the copper surface, the air shimmered, then the two men appeared in the midst of a howling, blinding sandstorm. Cael shoved his hand into the glove before the sand could start to strip the flesh from it, then he ensured the Quadrant was safely tucked behind several layers of thick cloth. He glanced to his right, and saw Lahnos standing next to him. Cael shouted something, but his voice was lost to the roaring wind, so he pointed instead, and, heads down, they began to walk forwards, their boots sinking into the hot, golden sand.

Sweat was rolling down Cael's face, but the goggles were shielding his eyes, and he squinted out as they trudged along. He tried sending out his powers, but he got disorientated almost immediately. The sandstorm seemed to rise upwards for hundreds of feet, and was surrounding them in every direction. He felt Lahnos grab hold of his belt as visibility decreased further. The glass on the goggles was getting more scratched and blurred with every moment that passed, yet still they stumbled on, cocooned within their heavy robes.

They reached what must have been the edge of a tall dune, and tumbled down the other side, rolling and falling until they reached the bottom. Cael tried to stand, then he tripped over something solid, and fell back to the sand. Lahnos grabbed his arm, then he pointed at the ragged remains of what had once been a wall. He helped Cael get back to to his feet amid the raging storm, and they pressed on, ascending a gentle slope. They passed another ruined wall, then another – one high enough that they had to clamber over it. The next obstacle they reached was a steep bank of sand, too high to climb. Cael tried it anyway, but his boots kept slipping back down to the ground. Lahnos pulled him by the arm, and they began to work their way round the side of the steep bank. The bank seemed to turn to the left at a right angle, and the storm lessened a little as they followed it round, then Lahnos stopped. He pointed at something, and Cael squinted through the blizzard of sand.

Stairs. Worn steps cut from huge blocks of stone were set along the side of the steep bank. They were partly covered by sand, but still visible, and they began to ascend. The higher they climbed, the more it became apparent that the steep bank had been formed by sand drifting next to a massive wall, and, after a few minutes, the eroded sandstone blocks of the wall rose clear above the dunes. The storm was still raging around them, but Cael grew more confident that they had finally found the castle Edgar had mentioned. At the top of the steps, he and Lahnos climbed over a parapet, and gazed down into the interior courtyards of a vast fortress. Sand was piling up everywhere, blown into thick drifts, but the buildings were rising above it – tall towers, a domed hall, squat keeps, and a maze of interior walls. The exterior stonework was pocked with holes, the erosion biting deep, but not deep enough to penetrate the interior. They found another set of stairs that led down into an internal courtyard, and then they entered a covered arcade where, for the first time since they had arrived, the noise from the storm fell to a level where Cael could hear himself think.

They went deeper into the thick shadows of the long arcade, passing beneath some of the fortifications, and the wind lessened with every stride they took. The sand petered out, and they found themselves walking on large, worn flagstones. They removed their goggles and the robes covering their faces, then Lahnos pulled the stopper from a water skin and drank. He passed it to Cael, and he took a long drink of the warm water.

'And you walked through that with nothing covering your face or arms?' said Lahnos.

Cael nodded, then he retrieved his cigarettes and lit one.

'Is this an ideal time to be smoking?' said Lahnos.

'I'll be quick,' said Cael. 'I need something to calm my nerves.'

'You?' said Lahnos, as he freed his war axe from his robes. 'I thought you liked taking risks.'

'This is different. This is about Arrosa.'

'I heard that Ward stepped over Kelsey to get to Arrosa,' Lahnos said. 'Why? Wouldn't the Herald of the Empire have made a better hostage? Why did he specifically target Arrosa?'

'I don't know.'

'I've been thinking about it, and the only conclusion I can reach is that it has something to do with you.'

Cael stubbed out the cigarette.

'Ward wanted you distracted, but why?' Lahnos went on. 'Or maybe he was trying to lure you into a trap.'

Cael loosened the Fated Blade, keeping it in his robes where he could reach it easily.

'I'll check the way ahead,' he said, 'and look for a way inside.'

He sent out his powers, while, at the same time, he ignored the words Lahnos had spoken. He pushed his vision along through the arcade. It divided into several different tunnels that ran under the battlements and several of the castle buildings, then he found a doorway leading into a hall. He nodded to Lahnos, and they set off, moving through the shadows until they reached the entrance. The wooden door had long gone, leaving only the corroded iron frame and hinges. They stepped inside. Some light was filtering in from a high clerestory window, and the sound of the storm could be heard again. Cael and Lahnos walked towards another doorway, then Cael stopped, and glanced down. A flag stone to his left had a scuff mark on it, as though something had scraped over it.

'I think that's recent,' he said.

Lahnos nodded. 'What now?'

'We try to find stairs that will take us down to the dungeons.'

'There might not be any dungeons.'

'This castle is supposed to have extensive dungeons.'

'According to whom?'

'Edgar.'

'Did you read his mind?'

'No, he told me. I've already been through this with Celine. I don't trust Edgar, but he told me that he had nothing to do with what happened, and he told me that he had met Ward here – in this castle.'

The sound of rusted armour echoed through the doorway ahead of them, then another sound, of metal scraping against stone, came from behind. Four soldiers in armour walked through the doorway, then another four appeared in the entrance to their rear. All eight were fully clad in armour stained brown with rust, and each was holding a mace in the gauntleted hands.

Lahnos raised a hand, and Cael sensed him use the Gift of Pain, but none of the eight warriors responded. Cael shot his vision out, and slid it through the visor covering a warrior's face. He entered the man's mind through his eyes, then recoiled from what he found.

'My Gift isn't working,' said Lahnos.

'They're already dead,' said Cael. 'They no longer feel pain.'

'Shit,' said Lahnos. 'Where's Sable when we need her? Let me take the lead. I can heal myself; you can't.'

The eight warriors were lumbering towards them, but Lahnos didn't wait. He hefted his Tempest-edged war axe, and charged at the warriors blocking their retreat. Cael drew the Fated Blade and followed him.

Lahnos barrelled into one ungainly warrior, and they both fell to the ground. Another warrior aimed a blow at Lahnos, but Cael parried it, and the Fated Blade sliced through the handle of the corroded mace. Cael glanced down at the blade for a moment, then he swung it again, and it severed a warrior's hand, cutting cleanly through iron and bone.

On the ground, Lahnos pulled off the helmet of the warrior he had knocked over, revealing a face riddled with rotten flesh.

'I'll hold him down,' cried Lahnos; 'you cut the bastard's head off.'

It took twenty minutes for Cael and Lahnos to send the eight warriors back to their deaths. Lahnos had picked up a few injuries, but they had healed themselves within seconds; Cael hadn't been so lucky. Blood was seeping through his robes in two places, and he staggered then fell to the stone floor as Lahnos decapitated the last of the undead.

Lahnos rushed to his side and crouched next to him. He pulled aside the robes, and examined Cael's wounds.

'You'll live,' he said, as he pressed cloth against a long cut that ran down Cael's right side. 'You probably don't want to hear this, Cael, but you can't heal yourself, and you don't have battle-vision. Maybe you should avoid...'

'Now you fucking tell me,' groaned Cael.

'You have immense powers, Cael; but fighting isn't one of them.'

'I took down more than one of those bastards.'

'There are three dream mages in existence, and you are one of them. You need to protect yourself. What if that wound gets infected? What if there are another dozen of those creatures waiting for us in the next room?'

Cael said nothing as more cloth was wrapped round his abdomen, staunching the bleeding.

'Can you walk?' said Lahnos.

'I'm a damn good fighter,' he said.

'You're better than many,' Lahnos said, 'but you're no Sable, and you're no Corthie. Neither am I, but I can heal myself, so it doesn't matter. If you try to take on a god with eye shields and battle-vision, there will be only one winner.'

Cael sat up. 'Have you finished lecturing me?'

Lahnos got to his feet, and extended a hand. Cael took it, then he grimaced as Lahnos pulled him upright. Cael staggered, and Lahnos held him up by putting his left arm round his waist.

'Maybe we should go back,' Lahnos said. 'We could find some salve and try again.'

'Not yet,' said Cael. 'Let's keep going. I can manage.'

Cael straightened his back, despite the pain, then he flattened his features. Show no one how much pain you are feeling, his grandmother used to say. Your friends will pity you, and pity leads to scorn; while your enemies will take advantage. Lahnos eyed him, then they carried on. They went through the doorway, and came to a long hallway, with rooms branching off on either side. Halfway along, there were stairs going up and down, and they descended into the shadows of the basement. They came to a smaller hall at the bottom of the stairs and searched along the corridors that branched away. They found guard rooms and prison cells, but they had long been abandoned, leaving nothing but sand and dust. They paused for a short rest, and Cael leaned against a wall, and sent out his powers. As soon as his vision was released, he felt all pain recede, and he dreaded returning to his body. He scanned more hallways and passageways, his powers gliding through the dark dungeons. Perhaps Lahnos was right. If he triggered the Quadrant, he would be able to use the *Go back* command to return to the castle; and he was on the verge of giving up when he came to another stretch of subterranean dungeons, where the cells were in far better condition. He examined them, and in the third one along, he found Arrosa and Clova, still dressed in the same clothes they had been wearing on Colsbury. Aila's young daughter was sitting on Arrosa's knee, and the Gunstian was telling her stories about Chadura to keep her distracted. Without hesitating, Cael went into the mind of his wife.

Lahnos and I are close, he said.

Cael?

Aye. Hold on; we're coming.

Be very quiet. There are... creatures down here. Soldiers; dead soldiers. We've already encountered a few.

I knew you would come for us, Cael; I never gave up hope.

I'll use the Quadrant to get closer. See you in a moment.

He withdrew from Arrosa's mind and severed the connection. At once, the pain from his side hit him again, and he barely suppressed a cry.

'I found them,' he said, pulling out the Quadrant.

'Are they far from here?' said Lahnos, his gaze on the copper device.

'Not too far,' said Cael.

He stared down at the Quadrant, but the pain was making it difficult to concentrate. He should be able to take himself and Lahnos right into the same cell where Arrosa and Clova were being kept, but his fingers were shaking, and one tiny mistake would see them arrive in the middle of a wall, or worse, in the same space as the two people they were trying to reach. Cael decided to err on the side of caution, and swept his fingers over the device. The air shimmered, and they appeared in the wide corridor outside the cells. Clova cried out, and Arrosa got to her feet. She smiled, then her expression changed when she saw the pain on Cael's face.

'Stand back,' said Lahnos, the Tempest axe in his right hand. 'I'll break through the lock.'

A door opened before Lahnos was halfway to the cell, and a dozen undead warriors emerged, their rusted armour squealing, and their maces raised.

Lahnos turned, readying himself. 'Stand behind me, Cael. Open the cell and get us out of here.'

Cael staggered towards the cell door, then the agony surged, and he slipped to his knees, cracking them off the stone flag stones. He heard Lahnos's war axe strike the first warrior, then he looked up to see several more approaching him from the other direction.

The air crackled, and his mother appeared, the Weathervane grasped in her right hand. Without even glancing at Cael or Arrosa, she charged forward, Belinda's old sword cleaving the undead warriors apart in a blur of movement. Lahnos stepped back to get out of her way, and then the small audience of him, Cael, Arrosa and Clova watched as Karalyn carved her way through the lumbering undead warriors. Cael saw her dispatch the last of them, then he toppled to the floor. He heard footsteps, then he saw his mother's face looking down at him. She pressed her hand to his forehead, and a great wave of power passed through him as, for the second time that day, he was healed.

'Did Celine tell you where we were?' said Lahnos.

Karalyn eyed him. 'Celine? No. I was operating the Sextant, and I sensed two with Gifts, one with self-healing, and one dream mage on this world. I would have lifted you clear, but the sandstorms were interfering with the Sextant.' She turned back to Cael. 'Are you trying to get yourself killed, son? Why didn't you wait for me?'

She turned away before Cael could reply, then she went up to the cell door, and ripped it from its frame. She threw it to the side and scooped up Clova in her arms, while Arrosa ran over to Cael.

'Thank you for coming for us,' she said, taking his hand.

'Are you hurt?' he said, as he got to his feet.

'Ward didn't touch us. I think he knew I could turn him to glass. He sent us both to sleep as soon as we arrived here, and then we woke up in the cell. We haven't seen him since.'

Karalyn glanced at Lahnos. 'Thank you for protecting my son, but you should have dissuaded him from coming here in the first place. We'll go to the Hold Fast estate first, to drop you off.'

Lahnos gave Cael a wry smile, but said nothing. The air crackled, and they appeared on the rear porch of the mansion on the estate. Celine and Ora'lya were sitting on the long swing chair, and both stood.

'I will take Arrosa and Clova back to Colsbury now,' said Karalyn, who was still holding on to the little girl.

'Wait,' said Cael. 'Thank you for rescuing us, Mother, but I haven't seen my wife in days.'

'Aila will want her daughter back,' said Karalyn. Her frown subsided a little. 'Fine. I'll return to collect Arrosa in a couple of hours.'

Karalyn vanished, along with Clova.

Celine shook her head. 'Did you see that?' she said. 'She acts more like a god every time I see her.' She turned to the others. 'None of you move from this spot. I shall order lunch, and we shall sit and eat like civilised people.'

She walked into the mansion, and the four left behind sat down on the long swing. Cael put his arm round Arrosa, and they gazed out at the heat haze.

'How did it go?' said Ora'lya.

Lahnos tucked away the war axe and picked up the glass of iced tea that he had been drinking.

'Celine was right,' he said. 'We should have waited for Karalyn.'

CHAPTER 24
BEDRAGGLED

Colsbury Castle, Republic of the Holdings – 30th Day, First Third Summer 545

'It has certainly been an eventful few days,' said Jazi. 'At first I was nervous, then jubilant, then that horrible attack happened in the gardens...' He paused. 'The soldiers were very courageous. Two of them placed themselves between me and the explosion that ripped through the dining table. So brave. And I still don't really understand how or why Colsbury was attacked like that.'

'The Empire has its enemies,' said Kelsey, as they stood on the middle balcony of the Summer Palace.

'It was a dreadful, cowardly thing to do,' said Jazi. 'The government of Amatskouri... I mean Adorati, stands firm with the Empress. You have our unqualified support. If you need anything, please ask.'

'What I need from you is this – make Adorati a success. Make it prosperous, peaceful, resilient and secure. Build cities to rival anything the Rahain used to have, and cherish your freedom. That's how we win, by creating a better future for our children.'

'I will do my best, Kelsey. Before I go, let me say that I earnestly hope that Arrosa and Clova Holdfast are safely returned to you soon. I have no children of my own, as I felt it unfair to award my wife and I a spawning licence when so many have to do without, so I can barely comprehend how poor Aila is feeling.'

'Karalyn is working on it.' She glanced at him. 'You will need to issue many more spawning licences, now that you have an entire country to populate.'

Jazi smiled. 'Yes. I intend to issue ten thousand within the next year, as part of the first batch. My wife and I will wait for the second batch, though. I wouldn't want the electorate to think I was taking advantage.' He looked away. 'I will never be able to thank you enough, Kelsey.'

Claudian stepped forward. 'I am ready to return the Amatskourian delegates to their city, ma'am.'

Kelsey nodded. 'Don't linger there,' she said. 'You are due to return to Na Sun Ka this morning, Adjutant.'

Claudian tilted his head, then he escorted Jazi over to where the other Rakanese were waiting. Jazi waved at Kelsey, then the air shimmered, and they disappeared.

Kelsey turned, and walked over to where Cardova and Shella were standing.

'Her Majesty wanted to ask you something,' said Cardova.

'Aye?' said Kelsey. 'Where is she?'

'She's spending time with Aila,' said Cardova. 'Naxor and the children are also there.'

Shella raised an eyebrow. 'Naxor seems to be taking his role of uncle very seriously these days.'

'Maybe,' said Cardova. 'Anyway, Kelsey, Her Majesty wants your opinion on whether we should continue with the parties and festivities. We're due to have singers and musicians from Sanang take the stage this afternoon, but that might not be prudent under the circumstances.'

Kelsey leaned on the railing at the edge of the balcony. 'Is she worried about it looking bad, or is she concerned about security?'

'Both,' said Cardova. 'Can we guarantee that another attack won't take place? Karalyn has agreed to stay in Colsbury, but she has to find Arrosa and Clova first, and she has already been looking for an entire day. As for the other concern – would we risk looking as though we're callous and unfeeling, or should the parties continue, to show that we aren't intimidated?'

'We'll have our critics no matter what we do,' said Kelsey.

'I agree, but that doesn't answer the question.'

'I'm the wrong person to ask,' she said. 'We should see what Aila thinks, and take her lead. If Clova's mother thinks we should carry on, then we shall.'

They entered the palace, and walked into its well-lit interior. Cardova gestured towards a state room, and they passed the eight soldiers by the doorway and walked inside. The Empress was sitting with Aila, Naxor, Killop and Konna, while the other children were also in the grand room. Ceres was being cradled by her mother, while Cairney was glowering out of a window, his eyes tight.

The three arrivals bowed before the Empress.

'Any news?' said Thorn.

'None regarding those who were taken, Your Majesty,' said Kelsey, 'but the Amatskourian prime minister and his retinue have left Colsbury.'

'I want Corthie here,' said Aila.

'I can ask Claudian to collect him this morning,' said Kelsey.

'When you visited Sun Ta,' said Aila; 'did you tell my husband what had happened?'

'I told Cael, but Corthie was off speaking to Blackrose at the time. I can only assume that Cael broke the news to him.'

'You should have taken the time to make sure Corthie knew.'

'Perhaps, but my priority at that moment was to inform Karalyn. We should leave it to my sister; she will be able to use the Sextant to track them down. She set off as soon as I told her.'

Aila glared at her.

'Claudian will be back from Amatskouri soon,' Kelsey went on. 'I will tell him to waste no time in bringing Corthie back.'

'Don't you have a Quadrant? You could do it now. And why did Ward step over you? Why did he reach for Arrosa and Clova?'

'I don't know.'

'We are doing what we can,' said the Empress. 'My Herald is right; let's leave it to Karalyn.'

'Order Kelsey to collect Corthie now,' said Aila.

'I have already ordered my Herald to remain here,' said the Empress, 'at least until Karalyn returns. If Colsbury is under threat, then I need my Herald by my side to block the powers of the gods.'

Aila's face twisted with frustration.

Naxor stood. 'I shall go to Na Sun Ka. These children need their father.'

Aila gazed up at her cousin. 'Thank you, Naxor.'

The doors opened before Naxor could take his Quadrant from his robes, and Karalyn walked in with Clova in her arms. There was a collective gasp of relief from everyone in the room, and Aila got up and ran towards her daughter. Karalyn passed Clova to her, and Aila sobbed as she held her tight.

'Thank you, Karalyn,' said the Empress, standing. 'Is there also news of Arrosa?'

Karalyn nodded, her gaze steely. 'She's on the Hold Fast estate. Cael took it upon himself to search for his wife, and I had to rescue him as well. I left them there so they could spend some time together, but I will go back for her shortly.'

'I gave Cael permission to search for his wife,' said the Empress.

Karalyn shook her head. 'You should have left it to me.'

Thorn narrowed her eyes. 'Perhaps.'

'Regardless,' said Naxor; 'doesn't Karalyn's arrival mean that Kelsey is free to travel to Sun Ta to collect Corthie?'

'Is there any need, if Clova is back?' said Kelsey.

'I would like you to go,' said the Empress. 'I think Aila would appreciate seeing her husband again, even if only for a short time.'

Kelsey bowed her head, then she glanced at Karalyn.

'I'll be staying here,' said her sister. 'Colsbury will be safe.'

Kelsey took her Quadrant from her shoulder bag. 'I will be back with Corthie as soon as I've found him, Your Majesty. Lucius, please inform Claudian that I will deliver this morning's orders to the Sun Ta garrison. He can remain here to assist you. There's no point in both of us going.'

Cardova nodded. 'I'll pass on your message.'

Kelsey glanced down at the engravings on the copper surface of the Quadrant. If she was going to issue that day's orders, then it would make more sense to visit the marine headquarters in Sun Ta before going onwards to the army base in the Temple of Ulna to collect Corthie. She hovered her fingers over the device, then triggered it.

The air shimmered, and Kelsey began to fall. Her first thought was that she had made a mistake, then she saw the harbour of Sun Ta just before she struck the water. Her left leg collided with something solid, and she twisted. Her head went under the water, her feet slipping on the rocks. She panicked for a brief moment, but it was enough for her to let go of the Quadrant as she tried to scramble back to the surface.

It didn't make any sense. She should have arrived on the long quayside in front of the marine headquarters, and yet she was floundering in the murky depths of the harbour basin. Her hands gripped onto something, then she realised it was the leg of a dead marine. She tried to cry out, and a rush of bubbles escaped her open mouth. She let go of the leg and clawed her way along the smooth surface of a rock, her head rising back above the water. Gasping for breath, she forgot where she was for a moment, then she saw the wreckage of the imperial ships filling the harbour, the ruins along the waterfront, and the smoke in the air. She leaned up on a rock, and tried to still her breathing. As well as smoke, dragons were filling the skies above her, circling over the city, and swooping down here and there to incinerate something.

Sun Ta had fallen. Despite the intelligence reports, the Wystians had invaded and, somehow, they had broken the defences of the city. Kelsey moved closer to the shadows cast by the ruined quayside, her breathing calm, then she stared at her surroundings. Amid the sunken vessels in the harbour were dozens of dead dragons, and more could be seen along the battered shore, their wings ripped to shreds by the imperial Forty-Eighters. Kelsey counted forty at least that she could see. On the ground, nothing seemed to be moving, but the barricades that had sealed off the harbour district had been swept aside by something. A squat brick barrack block was burning, but the flames were low, and Kelsey judged that she was seeing the remnants of a great conflagration that must have taken place during the night. In the distance, a bell was pealing.

She needed to warn the Empress. Tens of thousands of imperial soldiers and marines were based in Na Sun Ka, and if the island's capital had been conquered, then an evacuation was required. Kelsey would need to open a portal...

She remembered the Quadrant, and cursed aloud. She gazed down at the opaque waters of the basin, and tried to recall where she had been when she had let go of the copper device. She took a long breath, then plunged down into the waters, her hands feeling their way over the solid blocks that had once lined the quayside. Deeper and deeper she went, until her lungs were aching, and she had to return to the surface, screaming silently in frustration. Sweeping aside all feelings of panic, she tried to think. Maddie had a Quadrant, and Blackrose should be somewhere in the city. The marine officers also had one of Elbannon's devices but, she reasoned, surely they would have used it to send word if they had been able to do so. She glanced over at the ruins of the marine headquarters. Unlike several harbour front buildings, the headquarters had not been burned by dragon fire, but it was in ruins, levelled to its ground floor, with piles of rubble and debris scattered around it, as though it had been demolished with explosives.

Blackrose, then, was her only option. It was either that or succumb to despair. Kelsey almost smiled at the thought. Despair? She was the daughter of Daphne Holdfast, and she was the Herald of the Empire. She might die, but she would never give up. She looked at the dragons circling overhead, then she turned, and began to swim towards one of the few surviving piers, keeping close to the shadows of the ruined quay. She ducked under the cover of the wooden supports of the long pier, and found a cluster of bodies bobbing up and down on the waves. Kelsey pushed her way past them, and found a set of stone steps climbing up to the quay by the base of the pier. She pulled herself out of the water, and it was only then that she felt the pain coming from her left leg. A long cut had opened up below the knee, and blood was flowing freely from the wound. She ripped off a lower length of her skirt, wrung it out, and tied it round her leg, her hands moving without too much conscious thought, then she sat back on the stone steps and tried to plan her next move.

It was around three miles to the great temples of Sun Ta – an hour's journey with a sore leg. The streets were narrow in the centre of the city, and there was a decent chance that she could make it as far as the Temple of Ulna without being seen by any dragons flying overhead. The same circumstances would apply to the city garrison; would there be soldiers also taking cover from the dragons? She longed for the sight of a familiar uniform. With an escort of soldiers or marines, her path to the Temple of Ulna would be considerably smoother; her brother would likely be there, along with Blackrose. Her spirits rose at the thought of Corthie, and she began to limp up the steps. She peered over the top of the quay. A few rows of burnt-out warehouses and boatsheds were on her left; a fifty-yard dash, and she would be out of sight of the dragons. Kelsey steeled her nerves. Don't over think it, she told herself, just do it.

Kelsey crept up onto the stone surface of the quay, and half-ran, half-limped towards the nearest burnt-out shell of a warehouse. She refused to look back over her shoulder. If a dragon noticed her and decided to burn her, then it would be over in an instant; and it was better not to know. Panting, and with her heart pounding, she reached the shadows of the warehouse. She limped along its outer flank, and smiled. The dragons of Wyst were still circling over the city, and none had swooped down to investigate. She adjusted the torn section of cloth round her left leg, and set off towards the centre of Sun Ta.

She slowed when she reached the remains of a barricade that had once blocked one of the narrow lanes leading to the harbour. Something had pushed the wooden beams aside with ease, and the cobbles were stained dark red with blood. Had a dragon descended? The street seemed too narrow to accommodate the bulk of a dragon; but what else could have ripped the barricade to pieces? She stepped past the wreckage, then froze, as a sound reached her ears. It seemed familiar, as though claws were scraping against stone, and her thoughts went to the greenhides of Jezra, and the way that they had hidden beneath the ancient ruins only to spring out and kill unsuspecting members of the Brigades, or soldiers from the Banner of the Lostwell Exiles. Had Edgar brought greenhides to Sun Ta? Kelsey discounted the possibility, even as her ears told her otherwise. If there were greenhides, then she would have seen them by that time, or else she would have seen a few of their corpses littering the streets. She turned a corner, and saw a pile of half-eaten marines, their bodies torn to pieces by claws and fangs. Kelsey's heart seemed to jolt, and she shivered as a base fear rippled through her.

Kelsey stayed where she was, making no sound as her eyes scanned the street ahead. The scraping sound arose again, closer than before, then an enormous creature emerged from an alleyway. It was eyeless, and she knew at once what it was. Edgar hadn't brought greenhides; he had brought ironhides, and one of them was moving towards her. Without any eyes, it couldn't see her, and she remained still, holding her breath as it moved its armoured bulk out of the alleyway. The creature opened its jaws, its head up as if alert to any sound. Somewhere off to the right, a stone rattled off the cobbles, and the ironhide turned, saliva dripping from the rows of stained teeth. A low growl came from the ironhide, then something else was thrown – an orange-sized spherical object. Kelsey threw herself to the ground as the explosion tore off one of the ironhide's limbs, then more bombs were thrown from a doorway, and the ironhide screamed. Kelsey held her hands to her ears as the ground rumbled and shook. Green blood spattered against the walls of the street, then figures ran from the shadows. They raced towards the half-dismembered ironhide, long axes in their hands, and set about the creature, swinging and hacking until the ironhide's head was severed from its body. One of the figures turned, reached out, and grabbed Kelsey by the arm.

'Move,' the marine cried. 'The dragons will be here any moment.'

Kelsey got to her feet and hurried after the marines as they sprinted down the alleyway. They went into a building and out through the back door, then they crossed another alley and entered a burnt-out apartment block. They piled into a room, and settled down, each becoming silent as they crouched by a wall. One of the marines stayed by a window, his hand raised as he scanned the skies, then, after a few long moments, he lowered his hand.

'Sky's clear, sir.'

The marines relaxed.

'Good job, lads and lasses,' said the officer. 'Now,' he went on, his eyes on Kelsey; 'who do we have here? You don't look local.'

'Well spotted, Lieutenant,' said Kelsey. 'Do you want to tell me what the fuck is going on? Actually, I think I can work it out for myself. Ironhides, dragons... what else is there to say? Sun Ta has been well and truly minced. How about you take me to the Temple of Ulna?'

The ten marines glanced at each other.

'Perhaps I should have introduced myself first, eh?' Kelsey went on. 'You're looking at the Herald of the Empire. Don't laugh. I may look wet and bedraggled, but I wasn't exactly expecting to arrive in the middle of... this. Why didn't the marine commanders send word?'

'They never had a chance, ma'am,' said the officer. 'The headquarters was the first place to be hit. Unk Tannic, we think. The entire building blew up before the Wystians had breached the perimeter.'

'Is it really the Herald?' said a marine.

Kelsey took out the imperial signet ring she kept attached to a silver chain around her neck, and the marines leaned forward to look at it.

'Are reinforcements coming, ma'am?' said the officer.

Kelsey shook her head. 'Right now, nobody on Colsbury has the first idea of what's happening here. I was supposed to be collecting Corthie, but the quayside where I arrived had been blown to shit; hence the wet clothes. And then I, uh... and then I lost my Quadrant in the harbour basin. I dived down to search for it, but there's rubble everywhere. It'll be quicker to get to the Temple of Ulna. If Blackrose is there, then she can begin the evacuation. When did the invasion start?'

'Yesterday, ma'am,' said the officer. 'Portals opened up all over the city. The Forty-Eighters took down dozens of Wystians, but the dragons kept coming... It was all over in hours.'

'But there must still be thousands of soldiers and marines stuck here.'

'The ironhides were let loose right next to the Sanang divisions... There might be a few of them left, but the rest of us will be scattered all over the place. A few ironhides smashed through the barricades; they carried off dozens of marines, then the dragons took care of anyone else who was out in the open.'

'What about my brother?'

'Your brother is the only reason any of us are still alive, ma'am. He and his team killed more than half of the ironhides, but we haven't seen him since yesterday evening. We had to hide from the last of the ironhides overnight; it was too risky to be on the streets, and we only emerged at dawn. That ironhide was the second we've killed today.'

'There can't be many left,' said another marine. 'Maybe one or two?'

'How many explosives have you got?' said Kelsey.

'A few,' said the officer. He glanced at her leg. 'Can you run, ma'am?'

Kelsey got to her feet. Her left leg was aching, but she refused to show any pain in front of the marines.

'The Temple of Ulna,' she said. 'Let's go.'

The marines led Kelsey along the back streets and alleyways in the centre of Sun Ta. Some roads were empty, their houses burned and in ruins, while others had remained untouched. The civilians of Sun Ta seemed to have vanished, though Kelsey knew that those who remained would be hiding in their cellars, praying that they would be spared by the ironhides and Wystians. Bodies littered many of the streets, along with the gargantuan bodies of decapitated ironhides, and a few fallen dragons. The marines slowed after half an hour, then they came to a halt as the officer gestured ahead. Kelsey peered through the shadows, and saw a great heap of dead Sanang blocking the road. Five dragons were perched on the roofs of the buildings just beyond the heap, and Kelsey could see the tops of two great temples on the far side of them. The officer signalled towards a door, and a marine eased it open.

'I suggest we take a look at what's happening in the plaza before we go any further, ma'am,' the officer whispered to Kelsey.

Kelsey said nothing, and followed the marines into the building. They ascended two flights of stairs, and came to a window overlooking the vast plaza that sat in front of the dozen temples. Four of the enormous edifices were in flames, while a fifth was surrounded by dragons. Rubble was blocking the entrances of the besieged Temple of Ulna, and Kelsey put a hand to her face. She watched as two dragons sent streams of fire into the ruined windows and skylights of the huge temple, while dozens of others observed from the nearby roofs. Down in the plaza, the bodies of the warriors from the Sanang divisions were carpeting the cobbles, and blood was flowing into the gutters that ran by the buildings.

'Pyre's crotch,' muttered a marine. 'The Sanang have been pasted.'

'There's no way across the plaza, ma'am,' said the officer. 'What now?'

'Sir,' said another marine. 'There's a woman down there.'

Kelsey and the marines looked down. Amid the carnage of the Sanang, a robed woman was talking to four Wystian dragons. From her gestures, and the pained expression on her face, it looked as though she was complaining about something. She raised her hand in the direction of the Temple of Ulna, then she shrugged.

'I think she might be one of Edgar's gods,' said Kelsey. 'If I'm right, then I am probably the cause of her displeasure.'

'You, ma'am?' said the officer.

'She's what? – sixty yards away? Well within range. I'm preventing her from using her powers.'

The marines said nothing as they watched the robed woman argue with the dragons. After a few moments, she withdrew a Quadrant from her robes and disappeared.

'It looks as though you were right, ma'am,' said the officer. 'Who else but a god on the enemy side would have a Quadrant?'

'She's back,' said another marine. 'The god's back, but she's on the far side of the plaza. No, wait; she's gone again.'

Kelsey frowned, then her eyes widened. 'We need to get out of here.'

'Ma'am?' said the officer.

'She's working out my location,' said Kelsey. 'They know about my blocking abilities. We have to move.'

The marines glanced at the officer, who narrowed his eyes.

'I have been chased by gods on more than one fucking world,' Kelsey said. 'If that god can...'

'Get down!' cried a marine, as a dragon's head approached the building where they were sitting.

The marines dived to the floor, then the officer pointed towards a door. They crawled along by the wall, then a dragon's forelimb tore across the window, sending debris falling onto them. The dragon's eye stared through the opening, and the marines bolted, running back down the stairs. Another dragon had landed by the rear of the building, and was staring in through the windows. It caught sight of the marines, and roared out a warning.

The air shimmered, and the robed god appeared in the hallway next to Kelsey and the marines. Without hesitating, the god swiped her fingers over her Quadrant. The air shimmered again, and Kelsey found herself standing in a bare chamber, the god next to her. The god clenched her fist and punched Kelsey in the face. Kelsey's head jerked back from the impact, and she fell to the cold stone floor. She groaned as blood came from her nose, then the god rolled her over, knelt on her back, and pulled Kelsey's arms behind her.

'Stop struggling, Holdfast,' hissed the god. 'I'm not going to kill you; yet.'

Kelsey felt a cord being wound round her wrists, then it was pulled tight. The god rolled her onto her back, and smiled down at her.

'I've heard all about you, Herald of the Empire,' she said. 'Blocking my powers is a clever trick, but one we were prepared for.'

'Who are you?' said Kelsey.

'My name is Allura, Holdfast.'

'What the fuck do you want with me?'

'Unfortunately, that's not up to me,' said Allura. 'If it were, you would already be dead. You are a feeble little mortal; it would be so easy to end your life, but Edgar has other plans.'

'Edgar?'

Allura nodded. 'Welcome to Nom Karta, Kelsey Holdfast.'

CHAPTER 25
FORESTALLED

Nom Karta, Inopei – 5th Lexinch 1597

Larron's knife sliced through the onion.

'So, if I have this right,' he said, 'then, at this very moment, thousands of imperial soldiers and marines are being slaughtered by the Wystians on Na Sun Ka?'

Kyra kept her gaze on the kitchen floor.

'In a way,' said Achan, 'this seems like justice, of a sort.'

Larron narrowed his eyes at the professor.

'Let me explain,' said Achan.

'I don't want to hear your explanation,' said Larron. 'You think the Empire deserves a good kicking. You think that, after the deaths of all those Rahain and Rakanese in last year's invasions, the imperialists are being punished, and the gods and the Wystians are merely balancing the scales. Have you forgotten about the ordinary men and women who serve in the army and marines? Do you think they all deserve to die?'

'Not necessarily, but...'

'My parents gave years to the Empire,' Larron went on, his temper rising. 'My mum was a soldier, and my dad was a marine.'

Achan raised his palms. 'I know that. Things were different back then – your parents were defending the Empire, not invading other worlds.'

'The Empire is defending the Eastern Rim,' cried Larron. 'What do you think the Wystians will do to the civilians living in Blackrose's realm? Do they also deserve to die, because the Empress made a few mistakes? The Eastern Rim has known peace for only ten years; before that, they were either occupied by Implacatus, or had their islands infested by greenhides.'

Achan's face paled a little. 'But...'

'I don't want to hear it,' said Larron. 'You criticise the Empire for being too aggressive – where is your condemnation of Edgar and the Wystians? I was opposed to the Empress's handling of the invasion of Rahain, and I am also opposed to the Wystians slaughtering their way through Dragon Eyre. You aren't a pacifist, Professor; you just want to see the Empire fall.'

'As did you,' said Achan. 'I can recall hearing you saying on more than one occasion that the Empire had to go; that the Empress was a warmonger. Have you changed your mind?'

Larron fell silent, then he nodded. 'Maybe I have. Maybe I had to see for myself what the alternative looked like. The Empire is far from perfect, but at least we are allowed to voice our opposition. Will the Wystians do the same?'

'The Empire placed me into a cell,' said Achan, getting to his feet. 'So much for freedom of speech.'

'How many prisons do the Wystians run?' said Larron.

Achan said nothing.

'I feel nothing but shame for helping Edgar,' Larron went on. 'Here I am, preparing his dinner like a good little servant, while he unleashes thousands of dragons upon the Empire and the Eastern Rim. My parents would disown me if they could see me.'

Kyra raised her head. 'Edgar wants peace.'

Larron eyed her. 'What happened to you, Kyra? If the Empress had told you that she wanted peace, but first she needed to slaughter half a world to get it, you would have told her to fuck off.'

'This is the only way to achieve a lasting peace,' she said.

'You make me sick,' he said. 'Why are you allowing Edgar to get away with things that you would have condemned the Empress for doing? You're as bad as Achan; you're a hypocrite.'

'Edgar is doing the best he can.'

Larron gave her a wry smile. 'He's got into your head, hasn't he? I've seen the way you look at him, when he's brooding in his shiny white armour. Oh, he's a good-looking guy; not my type, but pretty handsome all the same. Are you hoping to save him from his inner demons, or do you just want to fuck him?'

Kyra's eyes darkened as she got to her feet.

'That comment was a little off,' said Achan. 'You should apologise.'

Larron laughed. 'Off? It was the truth.' He shook his head. 'One of you is so blinded by his hatred of the Empire that he doesn't care how many are killed; while the other is besotted by the guy doing the killing.'

Kyra walked out of the kitchen, then she ascended the stairs to the apartments where the gods lived. She walked into the main common room to find Bailey heating a kettle of water on a stove, as Edgar sat in a chair, a grim expression on his face as he stared into the distance.

'Coffee?' said Bailey.

Kyra glanced over at the god, then she sat down and folded her arms across her chest.

'Is something wrong?' said Bailey. 'I would leave Edgar alone, if I were you. Lord Belfar is due here at any moment with news about Na Sun Ka, and I think Edgar might be feeling the pressure.'

'I cannot rid my mind of thoughts of the dead,' said Edgar. 'What have I done, Bailey? How many will die before I can pursue peace? I am sickened by my actions.'

'We have been over this,' said Bailey. 'There is little point in continuing to berate yourself.'

'You tried to warn me, didn't you, my old friend?' Edgar said.

Kyra frowned. 'What does that mean?'

Bailey shrugged. 'Nothing.'

'Bailey tried to dissuade me from allowing the Wystians free rein to invade Na Sun Ka,' Edgar said to Kyra; 'but I didn't listen. All I want is peace, Kyra; you have to believe me. And yet the burden of the dead weighs heavily upon my soul.'

The kettle boiled, and Bailey filled three cups with hot water.

'I, too, want peace,' he said, as he picked up a tray; 'but I might have gone about it a different way. In a century or so, if all goes to plan, then perhaps your way will prove to have been for the best, and I will admit I was wrong.'

'It will take longer than a century for my crimes to be assuaged,' said Edgar.

Bailey set the tray down onto a little table in front of Kyra. 'He's been like this all day,' Bailey said. 'Inconsolable.'

'My brother would have thought nothing of what I have done,' Edgar said. 'Neither would Allura or Ward, my brother's children. Am I weak, Bailey?'

Bailey picked up a cup. 'You have sent undead dragons, ironhides, two gods, and thousands of dragons into Na Sun Ka, Edgar. I hardly think that qualifies as weak.'

A door opened, and Lord Belfar entered the room, a smile on his face.

'We have won a resounding victory, my lord,' he cried. 'Na Sun Ka is ours.'

Edgar got to his feet. 'Tell me everything.'

Belfar grinned. 'All came to pass just as you had foreseen, my lord. With Cael Holdfast occupied elsewhere, the portals were opened without opposition. I did as you asked, and threw everything we had at the island. All along the western coast of Na Sun Ka, we sent dragons behind the enemy lines, and the artillery batteries were destroyed for little cost. In Sun Ta, things were a little more difficult, and over two hundred Wystians were slain by the enemy's Forty-Eighters, but the city has been wrested from the armed might of the Empire.'

'Has the Empire evacuated its forces?'

Belfar's grin slipped. 'Well, no, my lord. That fact has puzzled me, if

I am honest. Rather than fleeing, the defeated remnants of the Imperial Army have taken refuge in a few isolated strongholds. Even when the ironhides were cast among them, they still did not evacuate. At this precise moment, I estimate that there might be upwards of fifteen thousand imperial soldiers remaining in the city. Many are besieged within the Temple of Ulna, and resistance there has been strong; but the end is inevitable.'

Edgar said nothing, then he glanced at Kyra. 'Why haven't they evacuated?'

'I don't know,' said Kyra. 'Is there news of my uncle, Lord Belfar?'

'Corthie Holdfast has been a considerable thorn in my side, girl,' Belfar said. 'He killed a large number of ironhides, and then he retreated into the Temple of Ulna before the Wystians could surround him. Not even your renowned uncle can fight off multiple dragons at once, it seems. I have ordered the Wystians not to press home their attack on the temple with too much vigour; but Corthie remains inside, as far as I know.' He turned to Edgar. 'Corthie has one solitary dragon from the Eastern Rim in the temple with him, my lord.'

'Blackrose?' said Edgar.

'No, my lord; a lesser creature. The Queen of Ulna was last seen being attacked by over a score of our undead dragons. The queen, I suspect, is dead.'

'You suspect?' said Edgar.

'I have not seen her corpse, my lord, though reports claim that she was grievously wounded. Perhaps Lady Allura knows more; I left her in command on the ground, where she was overseeing the siege of the Temple of Ulna. Is that coffee fresh, Bailey? Pour me a cup.'

Bailey got up and walked back to the stove.

'I don't understand,' said Edgar, as he began to pace the floor. 'The Empire has dozens of Quadrants, and their commanding officers are in continuous contact with the Sun Ta garrison. Why haven't they pulled their forces out? Do they mean to martyr themselves? Are they hoping to make a futile last stand? Belfar, did you deliver our ultimatum to the imperial forces?'

'We tried, my lord, but conditions in Sun Ta are making communications difficult, and we all assumed that the imperials would have fled by now. Our attack was sudden, overwhelming and complete.'

'What was your ultimatum?' said Kyra.

'It was simple,' said Edgar. 'We would agree to stand off, if they agreed to evacuate. Does the Empress care so little for the lives of her soldiers?'

'Perhaps she is merely trying to defend her ally,' said Bailey.

The two other gods turned to the stove, where Bailey was filling a fourth cup with coffee.

'Presumably,' Bailey went on, 'Queen Blackrose and the Empress are well aware of what will occur if the Wystians reach the Eastern Rim. Did we really expect the Empire to abandon its friend and ally, and flee at the first sign of trouble?'

Edgar picked up his full cup of coffee and hurled it at the wall. 'Damn her! Damn the Empress. She has lost; why can't she accept it?'

A low laugh echoed from the doorway.

'Perhaps,' said Allura, 'the Empress cannot accept it, because she is blissfully unaware that the invasion has even begun.'

The room fell into silence as Allura walked into the room.

'Is that true?' said Edgar.

'So I believe,' said Allura. 'That is certainly what Kelsey Holdfast told me.'

'You have spoken to my aunt?' said Kyra.

'Spoken to her, captured her, and locked her up in a cosy little cell,' said Allura. 'The mortal witch claims that none of the Empress's inner circle have any idea of what is currently happening upon Dragon Eyre. It seems as though our surprise attack involved a little too much surprise.'

Allura sat, and rested her feet on the low table.

Edgar stared at her. 'But how? How could they not know?'

'I thought you would be pleased, Edgar,' she said. 'This will make our victory complete. By the time the Empress hears of it, we will have destroyed every imperial soldier upon Dragon Eyre. Thorn will be begging us for terms. Isn't that what you wanted?'

'I wanted to defeat them, not annihilate them.'

Allura shrugged. 'What's the difference? The outcome remains the same.'

'Where is my aunt?' said Kyra.

'Relax, little mortal girl; I haven't killed her.'

'Bring Kelsey Holdfast to me,' said Edgar.

'But I have only just sat down, and that coffee smells fresh.'

'Now, if you please,' said Edgar.

Allura exhaled, then she got back to her feet and walked out of the room.

'This might be our chance,' Edgar said. 'The Herald of the Empire is authorised to negotiate with us. There is still time to reach an agreement with her; an agreement that will save the lives of the imperial soldiers who remain upon Dragon Eyre.'

'Save them, my lord?' said Belfar. 'I thought we were fighting them.'

Edgar turned to Belfar with a raw fury in his eyes. 'Are you being wilfully stupid, Belfar? If we slaughter the garrison to its last soldier, and if we kill Corthie Holdfast, then the Empire will never treat with us. They will nurse a grievance that will endure for years to come. I am trying to walk upon a razor's edge without falling into the abyss that lies to either side.'

Belfar looked away, his eyes hardening.

Allura appeared at the door again, dragging Kelsey with her. She dropped Kyra's aunt onto the floor, then she reached out with a foot, and rolled her over.

Kelsey eyed Allura, then she struggled to her feet, her hands tied behind her back. She glowered at the gods, then her gaze fell upon Kyra.

'Ha,' said Kelsey. 'Who's the warmonger now, ya little bitch?'

Kyra's mouth went dry.

Kelsey turned to Bailey. 'And you, ya treacherous shitebag. To think that we trusted you. You make Naxor look reliable.' She spat on the floor. 'Well, Edgar? What the fuck do you want?'

Edgar stared back at her. 'Peace.'

Kelsey started to laugh.

Allura raised her hand to slap Kelsey, but Edgar was quicker, and blocked the god with an arm. He pushed Allura back, then he took a small knife from the table and cut through the bonds securing Kelsey's wrists. The Herald of the Empire rubbed her hands together, then she picked up a cup of coffee from the tray and downed it.

'Peace, eh?' said Kelsey.

'Yes, Herald; peace,' said Edgar. 'What will it take?'

'You want to hear my terms, do you?' said Kelsey. 'All right; here are my terms. You will pull back your forces from Sun Ta until every surviving citizen of the Empire has been evacuated; after that, you can have Na Sun Ka; it's nothing but rubble now, anyway. Then, you will transport the Wystians directly to Wyst, bypassing the rest of the Eastern Rim, and you will also transport the Riggans from Wyst back to Rigga. You will then commit to the defence of Blackrose's realm. If the Wystians attempt to leave Wyst, you will join with us to repel them. I also want a treaty; a treaty that sets out our two spheres of influence. You will swear not to attack us or our allies, and we will do the same. Yearning and Zamata remain with us. Olkis and Alef remain free and independent. You get the Dominion, but we get equal trading rights to the Tempest mine. If any of your gods attack the Star Continent again, you will hunt them down and hand them over to us. We will do the same if anyone attacks you.' She placed her hands on her hips. 'How does all that sound, ya big prick?'

'I accept your terms,' said Edgar. 'Do we have a deal?'

Kelsey frowned, as Allura's face contorted with rage.

Kyra turned her gaze to Edgar. Next to Kelsey, he seemed young and almost unsure of himself, and Kyra had to force herself to remember that he was thousands of years old. The darkness in his eyes had gone, but she knew it could return at any moment. Was Larron right – did she imagine that she could somehow save Edgar from himself?

'My lord,' said Belfar, 'shouldn't we discuss this in private before agreeing to anything? The Empire is in retreat, and we might never have a better opportunity to push them for more favourable terms.'

'I have made my decision,' said Edgar.

'But we have them by the throat,' said Allura, her eyes blazing with anger. 'The Holdfasts killed my father – your brother, my lord – and they have slaughtered countless numbers of other gods. We should crush them, and yet you wish to pander to their requests? Edmond would be ashamed.'

'Edmond was a monster,' cried Edgar. 'Do you think I want to be like him? My brother tortured me for millennia precisely because I didn't follow his lead. We have achieved what I set out to achieve, and we have forced the Empire to negotiate.'

'That wasn't a negotiation,' spat Allura. 'It was a craven capitulation.' She turned to Kelsey. 'We should cut her head off and send it to the Empress; that would signal our negotiating stance.'

Kelsey smiled. 'You seem a little upset, Allura. Maybe you should lie down in a dark room for a while.'

'Enough,' said Edgar. 'Allura and Belfar, I want you both to return to Na Sun Ka immediately. Order the Wystians to pull back from the city of Sun Ta until all imperial citizens have departed. Go.'

The two gods glanced at each other, then Belfar triggered his Quadrant, and they vanished.

Edgar sat down, leaving Kyra and Kelsey standing in front of him.

'You did the right thing, Edgar,' said Kyra.

'Aye?' said Kelsey. 'It's a pity he didn't try this approach before thousands of folk on Dragon Eyre were killed.'

Kyra lowered her gaze. 'Is Arrosa all right? And Clova? Did Cael find them?'

'Oh, so now you care about the family, eh?' said Kelsey. 'Don't think for one moment that you'll be easily forgiven for what you've done, Kyra. You picked a side that unleashed dozens of ironhides into the streets of Sun Ta. Then they kidnapped Cael's wife so that he wouldn't be there for the invasion. You used to say that I had blood on my hands – maybe it's time you looked in a fucking mirror.'

'But...'

'Not another word,' said Kelsey. She turned to Edgar. 'What now? How am I supposed to relay this deal to the Empress?'

Edgar glanced up. 'Kyra can take you home. And then... then I hope she returns here, to me.'

'I will,' said Kyra, 'as long as the Empire doesn't arrest me.'

'They won't arrest you if you are acting as my emissary,' said Edgar.

'Then I will return.'

Kelsey narrowed her eyes. 'Is something going on between you two? Is that it? Pyre's wonky tits, Kyra, have you fallen for this eejit? Well, I guess that explains it.'

'There is nothing going on, Herald,' said Edgar. 'Kyra has rejected my advances. She said that nothing could ever happen, and I have to accept that.'

Kelsey laughed. 'That restrainer mask must have really messed with your head, Edgar. However, our deal stands. I'll have the terms written up. The Empress might refuse to agree, but I think I can win her round.'

'There is another term that I wish to add to the agreement,' he said.

'Aye?'

'Salve,' he said. 'If the Empire retains trading rights with the Tempest mine, then we must have the same rights for the salve mine. Tempest for salve; do you accept this?'

Kelsey chewed her lip. 'All right. Again, it's the Empress who will have the last word on this, but I'll add it to the draft of the treaty. Then, we'll need to arrange another, more formal meeting to debate the details, before we sign and pledge our oaths.'

Bailey walked over. 'This is a momentous day,' he said, raising his palms. 'Lord Edgar and the Herald of the Empire, forging a lasting peace together.'

'Don't get ahead of yourself,' said Kelsey. 'We still have thousands of soldiers and civilians to evacuate from Na Sun Ka. And you'd better hope that my brother is still alive. If Corthie has fallen, then the Empress is likely to shove any treaty up your arse.'

Larron entered the room, wearing a long apron. 'Dinner is...' He paused when he saw Kelsey, and his eyes widened. 'Herald? Ma'am?'

'I remember you,' said Kelsey. 'How does it feel to be a traitor?'

'Are you... a prisoner?' he said.

Kelsey shook her head. 'Kyra is about to take me back to Colsbury.'

'Can I go with you, Herald?' Larron said. 'I don't want to be here.'

'You are free to leave,' said Edgar.

Larron glared at the god. 'I will never forgive you for what you did to Na Sun Ka. You are nothing but a murderer.'

'Steady,' said Kelsey. 'Edgar and I have reached an agreement on how to end the war.'

'Don't trust him,' said Larron. 'He's as changeable as the wind. He's not right in the head, Herald, and the other gods can barely hide the contempt they feel for him. He...'

The air shimmered in two different places within the room, and seven armed figures appeared. Ward plunged a sword into Edgar's back, while Allura slashed a knife across Bailey's throat. Edgar fell to his knees, then Belfar drove a dagger into his left ear, as Ward sheared off the god's right hand. Bailey clutched his throat and fell into Kelsey, knocking her to the floor. The Herald put her hands over her head as Allura leaned over Bailey and stabbed him repeatedly, puncturing the god's chest in over a dozen places, before leaving the blade embedded in Bailey's forehead.

'You treacherous coward!' Ward cried, as he forced Edgar to the floor. He drove his sword back into Edgar's chest, then ripped downwards, opening up the god from neck to waist.

The other four gods who had accompanied them moved to surround the three mortals. One swung his sword at Larron, and the blade ripped through his neck, decapitating him, and spraying the room with blood. Another lunged at Kyra, and drove his sword into her stomach. Kyra cried out in pain, and fell to her knees, as blood soaked the front of her dress.

'Do not kill the Holdfast women!' shouted Ward. 'They are far more valuable to us alive.' He snapped his fingers at Belfar. 'The masks; quickly.'

Kyra toppled onto the floor next to the headless body of Larron. She clutched her waist, unable to wrest her gaze from the sight of Edgar's wounded and bleeding form lying two yards from her on the blood-soaked rug. She felt hands grip her shoulders, then she was dragged across the floor until she was lying next to Kelsey, whose wrists had been bound, and whose mouth was being clamped shut by one of the others. Kyra tried to use her powers. If she could summon enough energy, then she might be able to transport herself and the others to a safe location, but the pain in her waist was consuming her.

Belfar produced a metal mask from his robes and hurried towards Bailey, who was being held down by Allura. Belfar positioned the mask over Bailey's face, with the two three-inch spikes pointing downwards; then Allura pulled the knife from Bailey's forehead. Belfar pushed down, ramming the mask into the god's face, as Allura fastened the buckle at the back of his head.

Bailey screamed, as Allura and Belfar stepped back. They watched Bailey writhe on the floor, as blood poured down his cheeks from under the mask.

'You damn fools!' cried Ward. 'Bailey was still wearing his eye guards. Those things are irreplaceable.'

'I'm sorry, my lord,' said Belfar, as he pulled another mask from his robes.

Kyra forced herself to watch as Ward and Allura held Edgar down. She knew what they were about to do, and she steeled herself, trying to focus on any powers that she might be able to summon. Belfar approached, then he set the mask down, and leaned over Edgar. He pushed the severed hand out of his way, then he reached out, and plucked a thin, transparent circular film from Edgar's left eye.

As soon as the eye guard had been removed, Kyra drove her vision powers into Edgar's mind. The god's thoughts were filled with impotent rage and excruciating agony; along with a base terror at the prospect of life in the mask. Kyra sent soothing thoughts into Edgar's mind, and he recognised her presence. At once, his emotions turned to her, and she felt the love he bore towards her, and the fear that she would die from the wound in her waist. She hid her pain from him, and continued to soothe his agony.

I am here for you, she whispered in his mind.

Belfar removed the other eye guard, and prepared the mask.

Kyra pushed Edgar's consciousness into a small corner of the god's mind, shielding it from pain, and isolating it from what was happening to his body.

You will be safe here, she whispered; *nothing can hurt you here.*

Belfar brought the mask down, driving the metal spikes into Edgar's eyes, and severing Kyra's connection to his mind. Edgar's body went limp, and the seven gods stared at what they had done for a few silent moments.

'Perhaps we should kill them both,' said Allura.

'We do not kill family,' said Ward, as he stood and wiped the blood from his hands. 'Edgar is our uncle, Allura; and even that pathetic oaf Bailey is related to us through Theodora. We shall give them a few centuries in their masks, and then we shall see if they are prepared to be more reasonable.'

Belfar held out his hand. Sitting on his palm were the two eye shields. Ward gazed at them, then he took them and slipped them into a pocket. He turned to Bailey, who was still writhing on the floor, then he walked over to where Kelsey and Kyra were being pinned to the rug. Ward crouched by Kyra's side. His gaze went from the blood pooling under her body, to the wound in her waist.

'I apologise for wounding the girl, my lord,' said one of the demigods. 'I did not know that we were to spare the mortals.'

'I am grateful that you didn't kill her,' said Ward, 'but I would rather she didn't bleed to death on the floor.' He placed a hand onto Kyra's forehead. 'You are like your brother, girl,' he said. 'I can affect you with my powers through touch.'

Kyra felt the wound in her waist close up, but there was no relief from the agony that was coursing through her body.

'There,' said Ward. 'Your life is no longer in danger, but I felt it prudent to keep you in a certain amount of pain. You are a powerful mage, Holdfast girl, and I wouldn't want you getting up to any tricks.' He turned to Kelsey. 'There will be no peace between us, Herald of the Empire,' he said. 'Our forces will take Dragon Eyre, and then we shall wrest the salve mine from your control. Imagine what thousands of Wystians could do to your beloved Star Continent. Your cities shall burn, and we gods shall dance on the ruins.'

Kelsey tried to speak, but one of the demigods was using his hand to cover her mouth.

'Let her talk,' said Ward. 'I wish to hear what the Herald has to say.'

The demigod removed his hand, and Kelsey gasped for air.

'You have collectively committed suicide,' she said. 'Our family killed the Ascendants; they will have no problem dealing with a few twats like you.'

Ward laughed. 'Oh yes? And who will even try to get close to us? Corthie? He is trapped inside the Temple of Ulna, and I have ordered the Wystians to mount a full assault on the building. Sable? Your niece took care of her, neutering her like a wild dog. Blackrose? Her bones are being picked clean by ironhides. It is over for the Holdfasts and their allies, Miss Herald; your reign of terror is at an end.' He glanced at Belfar. 'Inform Laverne of the change in leadership, and tell her to remain at her post in the Tempest mine. Then, travel to the Doomed Worlds and let Lord Elmhirst know that I am now in charge.'

Belfar bowed, then he triggered his Quadrant and vanished.

Allura crouched by Kelsey and Kyra. 'What shall we do with these two, my lord?'

'Don't call me that,' said Ward. 'I am your brother, not your lord. We are Edmond's heirs, the last of his children, and we shall rule together. Speak to Queen Famula. She will be relieved to know that Edgar's futile attempts to negotiate with the enemy have been forestalled.'

Allura tilted her head, then she sheathed her knife and walked from the room.

Ward gestured to the four demigods who had arrived with them. 'You can cease pointing your swords at them,' he said. 'They are going nowhere. I will let it be known that any attack upon our position by the Empire will result in their immediate execution.'

'We should execute them now, my lord,' said one. 'They are too dangerous to be allowed to live.'

'Dangerous?' said Ward. He laughed. 'They are nothing. I honestly fail to see what all the fuss is about. Kyra's abilities are being negated by the agony consuming her body, and, besides, like her brother, she is easily defeated by the mere presence of eye guards; while Kelsey has nothing but her blocking abilities. They are frail, and weak, and quite beneath my contempt. I want Edgar and Bailey wrapped in chains, and I want the two mortal women to be hooded and placed in the deepest chambers of this palace – far enough away so that our powers will be unaffected. Once that is done, we shall return to Dragon Eyre, to oversee the destruction of the last pockets of resistance upon Na Sun Ka.'

The four demigods bowed, then two picked up Bailey, and the other two lifted Edgar from the floor. Ward stepped over the body of Larron and sat down on a chair close to Kelsey and Kyra, as the demigods carried the masked gods out of the room.

'Do you know something, Holdfasts?' Ward said. 'I actually feel sorry for my deluded uncle. Thousands of years in a restrainer mask has clearly warped his sense of perspective, and addled his morality. I thought that, by killing his friend Ballatar, he would return to the way he was before, but I was wrong. I think perhaps that Edgar has forgotten that he is one of the oldest gods in existence; no, he is the oldest. He has watched mortal empires come and go for countless generations, and yet he believed that, this time, things would be different. Things are never different; that is what I have learned. Mortals are transient; we are eternal.'

'Edmond thought he was eternal,' said Kelsey; 'then my Uncle Corthie ripped him in half.'

'Your uncle has had a good, though brief, run. For a short time, Corthie was indeed the greatest mortal warrior upon the known worlds, and he shone like the brightest star; but, like all mortals, his life has passed in the blink of an eye. I will bring you his charred skull when the battle for Sun Ta is over, and then, perhaps, I will allow you to be my slave, Kelsey Holdfast.' He glanced at Kyra. 'You, however, will be executed as soon as the war has been brought to a successful conclusion, as I do not intend to wear eye guards until you expire of natural causes.'

Kyra started to cry, as pain overwhelmed her. Ward leaned forward and ran a finger over her cheek, wiping away her tears.

'That's right, mortal girl; weep,' he said. 'Weep for the death of all you hold dear. Your dream powers will not be passed on to another generation, Kyra Holdfast. They will end with you.'

CHAPTER 26
DAUNTLESS

Hold Fast, Republic of the Holdings – 30th Day, First Third Summer 545

Cael held on to Arrosa's hand as they walked among the buildings of the Hold Fast estate. The sun was blazing down upon them from a perfectly blue sky, and a heat haze lay upon the baked ground.

'I've been thinking about where we should live when this is all over,' Cael said.

'I thought we'd agreed on the townhouse in Plateau City?' said Arrosa.

'Do we have to choose one place?' said Cael. 'We could move around, season to season.'

Arrosa laughed. 'That's exactly what you used to complain about.'

'Aye, but this time it would be our choice. I guess summer on Colsbury is a given; so maybe spring in Kell, autumn in the Holdings, and winter in Plateau City?'

'Swap the last two about, and I could agree to that,' she said. 'Winter in the Holdings, so then we could get sunshine all year round. We should build our own house somewhere, though. In Kell, maybe?'

'Aye, somewhere with a view of the mountains, but close enough to Clackenbaird so that we can visit Corthie, Aila and our cousins.'

'What about work? The Empress might want me to stay close to her, so I can scratch my ear every time someone lies.'

They stopped by the stables, and slipped into the shade of the high wall.

'I think my career in the marines is over,' he said.

'Really?' she said. 'I would never have guessed.'

'Do I need to get a proper job?' he said. 'I could work on the estate when we're here, and help out with Corthie's family when we're in Kell.'

'Maybe you should be aiming for a place on the Imperial Court,' she said.

'Why, because I'm a Holdfast?'

'Not just for that reason. You proved yourself when you were in the marines, and when you were working with Sable and Corthie; even if you had a tendency to disregard orders.'

'Only if the orders were wrong.'

She gazed out in the direction of the fountain. 'Will the war end soon, do you think?'

'If I can prevent the invasion of Na Sun Ka,' he said, 'then it might be over sooner than anyone had expected. Edgar wants to negotiate; I believe that, but he also wants a victory. Did Ward say anything to you about what he wants?'

'He didn't say a single word to me. You know, I'm sweltering in this heat and that fountain looks inviting.' She leaned over and unfastened her sandals. 'I'm going in,' she said.

She picked her sandals up and ran towards the fountain. Cael watched her, then he went after her, and they jumped into the fountain. The water was cool, and they laughed as they splashed each other, their clothes drenched within seconds. A silvery-green dragon soared overhead, then Sigum landed in the square next to the fountain, his eyes on Arrosa and Cael. Arrosa splashed water into the dragon's face, and Sigum laughed.

'That feels good,' the dragon said. 'I have never experienced heat such as this, little Arrosa. I have to fly very high to escape it. I have visited the mountains far to the north of here, and I have also roamed a hundred miles to the east, to see the ocean crash against the ragged shore; but there is no escape from this furnace.'

'There's an easy answer to your troubles,' said Cael; 'persuade Lahnos to help the Empire.'

'And be sent to Na Sun Ka? I think not. Without the brave Bullan to cajole him, I fear that Lahnos will never serve this Empire again. Ask him when his infant son turns eighteen, and you might have better luck.'

Cael sank into the cool water, the spray hitting his face.

There was a sound from the rear porch of the mansion, and Cael turned to see his mother walking down the steps and into the hazy sunshine.

'Karalyn has returned,' said Sigum. 'Does this mean that it is time for you both to leave?'

Cael said nothing as Karalyn walked over to the fountain. She smiled at the sight of Arrosa and her son in the water, then she gestured for them to come out.

'Your clothes will dry in a few minutes,' she said. 'Did you have a relaxing afternoon?'

'It was wonderful,' said Arrosa. 'We had lunch on the porch, then we went for a walk.'

'In this weather?' said Karalyn. 'Do you notice anyone else outside?'

'It's different when you live here,' said Cael, as he clambered out of the fountain. He extended his hand, and helped Arrosa step onto the baked earth of the square.

'This felt like a holiday,' said Arrosa.

Karalyn nodded. 'You seem to have recovered well from being held prisoner, Arrosa.'

'It wasn't so bad. In truth, I was far more worried about Clova. How is she?'

'She is back with her mother and siblings,' said Karalyn. 'Are you ready to return to Colsbury?'

Arrosa gazed at Cael. 'If I have to. I would rather stay here with my husband.'

'Your husband is due to return to Na Sun Ka,' said Karalyn; 'though I would also prefer that he stayed.' She glanced at her son. 'You are under no obligation to fight in this war, Cael.'

Cael smiled. 'I knew you would say something like that. It makes no difference to me, Mother; I'm going back to Dragon Eyre. Cole is there, and so is Uncle Corthie, and I'm not going to let them down.'

'And I knew you would say something like that,' she said. 'You're a stubborn boy; you always have been.'

'Is there any news?'

'Regarding what?'

'The war?' he said.

Karalyn gave a gentle shrug. 'I haven't been paying any attention to what has been happening on Dragon Eyre. Kelsey went, though, to collect Corthie, so that he could see Clova. You did tell your uncle that Clova was missing, didn't you?'

Cael glanced away. 'I didn't want to worry him.'

Karalyn sighed. 'That wasn't your decision to make, son. You should have told him.'

'Does it matter now? Clova is safe. So, is Uncle Corthie back on Colsbury?'

'I didn't see him, but I was with Caitlyn and Carden for most of the afternoon.'

'I guess I should get my armour on,' he said. 'I doubt much is happening in Sun Ta, but you never know.'

'Don't do anything too reckless, young Cael,' said Sigum. 'Lahnos and I are very fond of you.'

'Thank you, Sigum,' said Cael. 'I'll see you next time I'm here.'

The three humans walked over to the mansion, and entered the shade of the porch. Cael had stacked his Tempest armour by a chair, and Arrosa helped him with the buckles as he pulled it on.

Karalyn frowned when she caught sight of Cael's sword. 'What are you doing with Sable's Fated Blade?'

'I had it with me when Lahnos and I were on Solitudus,' he said.

'That didn't answer my question.'

'Edgar stole it from Sable, so I stole it back.'

Karalyn nodded, though her eyes remained tight. 'You are too young to be taking so many risks.'

Cael laughed.

'It isn't funny,' his mother said. 'I have already lost a daughter; I do not wish to lose a son.'

'You haven't lost Kyra, Mother. She's doing perfectly well with Edgar. She's his Daimon.'

'Aye, and look what happened to him.'

'You could bring her back here any time you liked,' he said. 'Bring Edgar, too, and we'll sit him down and thrash out a deal between us.'

'I am not going to get...'

'Aye, I know,' he said. 'You're not getting involved. I don't agree with your stance, Mother; you should know that. You should remove Sable's blocks, and transport the Wystians to another world; and those are merely my opening suggestions.'

'I'm with Cael on this,' said Arrosa. 'You could end this war if you wanted to.'

'And what about the next war,' she said; 'and the one after that? And every famine, plague, riot, drought, and so on for all eternity.'

'Then tell me where the Sextant is,' said Cael, 'and I'll deal with the Wystians.'

'You have proved that you can't be trusted with the Sextant,' said Karalyn. 'You know, I didn't mind that you created a new world; it was the fact that you hid there for thirds that annoyed me.'

Cael smiled at her. 'But I've learned my lesson.'

Karalyn laughed. 'Aye, right. Come on, Arrosa; your clothes look dry enough.'

Arrosa leaned up and kissed Cael, then she stood next to Karalyn.

'Stay out of trouble, Cael,' said his mother, then she and Arrosa vanished.

Cael took out his cigarettes and lit one, then he turned and gazed out over the endless plains of the Holdings. The horizon was lost in the heat haze, and the grass had turned brown beneath the vast blue sky.

He strapped the Fated Blade to his waist, and picked up a bag of clothes. He waved to Sigum, then he stubbed out the cigarette, took out his Quadrant, and swiped his fingers over the copper surface.

The air shimmered, and Cael appeared in the middle of the large hall inside the Temple of Ulna where Corthie's team was based. Cael blinked. The entire hall was filled with injured soldiers lying in rows. Drechtalang was going from soldier to soldier, crouching by each as a lit stick of keenweed hung from his lips. The hedgewitch glanced up, and his eyes widened. The ground shook and rumbled, and dust fell from the high ceiling, then Drechtalang sprang to his feet and ran towards the door.

'Where are you going?' Cael cried. 'What's going on?'

The Sanang hedgewitch reached the open entrance, and lifted both hands to his mouth. 'Corthie!' he shouted. 'Corthie! Cael's back!'

Cael glanced down at the injured soldiers, then he wended his way between them and walked towards the entrance. He arrived by Drechtalang's side just as Corthie bounded into view, his armour battered and scorched, and dried blood coating the left side of his face.

Cael stared as Corthie ran up to him. He threw his arms round his nephew and squeezed, and Cael gasped for air.

'What took you?' Corthie said. 'We've been trapped in this damn temple since yesterday afternoon. Where is everyone? Where's Claudian?'

Cael tried to gather his thoughts. 'The invasion?'

'It started yesterday morning,' said Drechtalang; 'and it was pretty much over by the time the sun set. Portals everywhere. Ironhides, dead dragons, living dragons, you fucking name it.'

'Never mind that,' said Corthie. 'The Wystians are renewing their attempts to break into the temple, and I'll have to stand by the main entrance to stop them. Start the evacuation, Cael; start it now.'

Cael nodded. 'The evacuation. Aye. I'm on it.'

'Wounded first,' said Corthie, 'then the civilians.' His eyes welled as he gazed at his nephew. 'Pyre's arse, lad; it's good to see you. I thought we'd been abandoned.'

'No one knows, Uncle,' Cael said. 'Nobody on Colsbury knows what's happening.'

'Take the first batch of wounded there,' Corthie said; 'that ought to convince them. If you need me, I'll be next to Gallantmorn and Cole in the main entrance hall.'

Cael turned as Corthie raced away. He took in the sight of the rows of injured soldiers.

'I'll start here, and work my way round the hall,' he said to Drechtalang. 'Gather the other wounded, and the civilians. Bring them here, if you can; it'll be quicker.'

Cael swiped his fingers over the Quadrant, taking twenty injured soldiers with him. They appeared in the large forecourt between the Summer Palace and the two keeps on Colsbury, then Cael triggered the Quadrant again, and moved up to the middle balcony. Several of the tables were filled, and he saw his mother and Arrosa talking to Cardova and the Empress. Along from them, Aila and Naxor were sitting with her children, and Clova waved to him.

'Na Sun Ka was invaded yesterday,' Cael cried out. 'Sun Ta has fallen, and the Temple of Ulna is besieged. I've brought wounded from there, and there are plenty more to come.'

The balcony stilled into silence.

Claudian got to his feet, his eyes wild.

'Why didn't you go, Adjutant?' Cael said. 'Corthie told me he felt abandoned.'

'The Herald went in my stead,' said Claudian.

'Did you see Kelsey?' said Karalyn.

Cael shook his head. 'I was there for less than a minute. I have begun the evacuation, and there are twenty injured soldiers down in the forecourt. I'll take the next batch to the army base in Plateau City.'

Several voices spoke up, but Cael wasn't listening. He activated the Quadrant, and appeared back in the hall inside the temple. Without waiting, he transported another twenty injured soldiers to the Star Continent, depositing them outside the army hospital in the large garrison complex in Plateau City. Again and again, Cael went back and forth, until the large hall had been cleared. When he returned to Sun Ta for the ninth time, he saw soldiers leading a long line of civilians who had been working for the imperial armed forces. Cael went up to an officer.

'How many people are in the temple?' he said.

'Nearly four thousand,' said the lieutenant.

'I will take care of them,' said a loud voice.

Cael turned, and saw Claudian striding along the temple hallway.

'I arrived a few moments ago,' said the Adjutant, 'and I brought a spare Quadrant. I will open up a portal to evacuate the civilians and the rest of the forces from the Temple of Ulna. I need you, Cael, for something else.'

Flames ripped through the broken skylights high above them. Claudian glanced up, but the fires did not reach the ground where they were standing.

'Sir?' said Cael.

Claudian met his glance. 'We believe that there are thousands more of our people trapped within the city,' the Adjutant said. 'I want you to scout for them, locate them, and bring them home. Do not engage with the enemy unless absolutely necessary; is that understood?'

'Aye, sir.'

'And keep your eyes open for the Herald of the Empire,' Claudian went on; 'there has been no sign of her in the Temple of Ulna, so she may be hiding somewhere in Sun Ta.'

He turned away from Cael, activated a Quadrant, and a swirling black void formed in the hallway. The void settled, revealing an empty parade ground within the army base in Plateau City, then Claudian ordered the civilians to start crossing through.

Cael gazed down at his own Quadrant, then he swiped his fingers over it, and appeared on the roof of the Temple of Olkis, a quarter of a mile from where he had been standing. He crouched low next to the stone parapet, and looked back at the Temple of Ulna. Over two dozen dragons were attempting to break into the huge building. Some were using their forelimbs to rip open side doors or skylights, while others were blasting fire into any available opening. Cael turned away from the sight, and began to scan the rest of the city. In under a minute, he had found a stranded batch of over two hundred Imperial Marines, who were taking shelter in a row of half-burnt apartment blocks on the road to the harbour. Cael activated his Quadrant, and arrived in their midst.

A dishevelled captain stared at him. 'Cael Holdfast?'

'That's right, sir,' he said. 'I'm here to get you marines out of Sun Ta.'

'I thought you had deserted, lad.'

Cael gazed at the expectant marines. Several were injured, and the rest looked exhausted.

'Wounded first,' said Cael, then he triggered the Quadrant.

For over an hour, Cael scoured the city of Sun Ta, moving from location to location to transport stray units of soldiers, marines and civilian personnel to Plateau City, as the Wystians concentrated their attacks on the Temple of Ulna. After the largest batches had been found and taken home, Cael turned to the smaller groups, targeting isolated squads, and even individuals who had been separated from their units. He surprised a grizzled old sergeant who had been hiding in an attic, but Cael asked no questions about how he had got there, or what had happened to the men and women he had been leading. The army base in Plateau City had been put on alert, and the hospital staff were out on the parade grounds, tending to the thousands rescued by Cael, and the thousands who were still coming through Claudian's portal. The other end of the portal was being operated by an army major, and he was urging the civilians through. Cael crossed in the opposite direction, and arrived back inside the besieged temple. He pushed his way past the heaving crowds queuing up to reach Plateau City, and came into the enormous entrance hall. The main gates had been blockaded with a giant mound of rubble, upon which Gallantmorn was standing, his jaws blasting fire towards the dragons on the far side. By the feet of the dark orange dragon stood Corthie, his Clawhammer fending off the dragons trying to reach through the entrance. The Wystians were trying to pull down the mound of rubble, but between Gallantmorn and Corthie, they were having little success. Cole was standing a few yards behind them, his arms raised as he used his fire powers to keep the Wystians' flames from striking Corthie; while Claudian and a few senior officers were to the rear, discussing the next stage of the evacuation.

Cael nodded to Cole as he hurried forwards, then he approached Claudian.

'I have cleared the harbour district and the city centre, sir,' he said.

Claudian and the other officers turned to him.

'What is this deserter doing here?' said a marine colonel.

'He's been working with Corthie Holdfast,' said an army officer.

'Cael is not a deserter,' said Claudian. 'He is an agent of the Empire. Cael, I want you to start scanning the outlying garrisons to the south of the city. We have had reports that several have been destroyed by the enemy, but there may be survivors.' He lowered his voice. 'Have you seen any sign of the Herald?'

'No, sir.'

'What about the Queen of Ulna? Blackrose is also missing. Eye witnesses claim to have seen her being attacked by undead dragons.'

'I will look for the queen while I search the south, sir.'

'Good lad; get to it.'

A loud crashing noise came from the entrance, as part of the archway supporting it fell. Huge blocks of masonry tumbled down into the hall, and several hit Gallantmorn. The dragon moved his body to shield Corthie, and took the blows, as the rubble rained down. The floor of the temple shook, and Cole staggered backwards, retreating from the mound blocking the entrance. Gallantmorn's head and neck emerged from the pile of rubble, then he dragged himself out, Corthie clutched in his forelimbs. He set Corthie down onto the marble floor, and Cael's uncle laughed and shook the dust from his head. He caught sight of Cole, and ushered him towards Cael and the officers.

'The Wystians will take a while to get through all that,' Corthie said. 'How's the evacuation going?'

'The civilians are out,' said Claudian. 'The soldiers will be next.'

Cole swayed, and Corthie put a hand on the shoulder of his nephew to keep him upright.

'I think Cole could do with a rest,' Corthie said. 'He's been using his fire powers for hours.'

'I'm fine,' said Cole. 'Ten minutes; just give me ten minutes.'

Claudian produced a vial of salve from a pocket, and handed it to Cole. 'Take a small dose of that. We need you here to shield us from the flames of the Wystians. Cael – get out of here; you have your orders.'

Cael glanced at his exhausted cousin, then at the grim defiance shining in the eyes of his uncle. He tilted his head towards Claudian, then triggered his Quadrant.

He appeared atop a tall tower to the south of the temples, a location he had used during his search of the city centre. To the north, dragons were swarming all over the Temple of Ulna, tearing the outer fabric of the building to pieces with their claws. One of them was enlarging a hole by a skylight in the roof, and was close to getting inside. Cael crouched by the parapet of the tower, and sent out his powers. He shot his vision across the distance between him and the dragon, and penetrated its mind.

Greetings, dragon, he said.

The dragon lifted his head from the skylight and glanced around, looking for the source of the voice.

Have you seen Blackrose? said Cael.

The dragon began to resist Cael's presence in his mind, but his memories flashed to a scene in which over a dozen undead dragons were mauling the Queen of Ulna in a midair battle over the city. Blackrose's wings were being torn to shreds as she defended herself with fire, teeth and claws, then an undead creature fastened its jaws round her throat, and she began to fall. The memory ended, and all Cael sensed from the dragon was anger.

Get out of my thoughts, god, the dragon cried.

I'm not a god, said Cael. *I'm better than that; I'm a Holdfast.*

Cael drove his full powers through the dragon's mind, obliterating his memories and consciousness. The dragon's head lolled, then he collapsed onto the roof of the temple, blocking the skylights he had been trying to access. A headache pounded behind Cael's eyes, and he turned away from the north. He began to search the southern outskirts of the city, racing his vision over large areas of Sun Ta that had been untouched by the attack. He came to a fort by a major road junction, but it was a burnt-out shell, filled with the charred and smouldering bodies of hundreds of Sanang soldiers. The next fort along was in the same condition, but the third was still in flames. Two Wystians were circling over it, spraying fire down into the fort's interior, as its garrison tried to fight back with crossbows. The fort's small battery of Forty-Eighters was lying in broken ruins on the top of the keep, its crew dead, while the surviving garrison was being picked off one by one.

Cael activated the Quadrant, and appeared on the roof of the fort's keep. The two dragons were keeping their flames away from the roof, to avoid setting off the munitions that lay next to the broken Forty-Eighters. Cael kept low as he ran to a full basket of the orange-sized explosive devices, then he took shelter behind a low wall. He picked up one of the small bombs, twisted the upper half, and hurled it up at the closest dragon. The bomb bounced off the dragon's right flank, then exploded, the shrapnel ripping through the dragon's flesh. The dragon roared out, then he stared down at the roof and opened his jaws. Cael threw a bomb into the dragon's open mouth as sparks raced over the beast's jaws. The device ignited, and the lower half of the dragon's face was blown apart, its jaws disintegrating in a flash of smoke and blood. The other dragon wheeled back, banking over the keep, as its wounded companion crashed onto the outer wall of the fort, its weight and bulk causing it to collapse in a grinding roar of rubble and dust.

Cael narrowed his eyes and sent his powers into the mind of the surviving dragon.

I am Cael Holdfast, he said; *and you are about to die.*

Cael drove fear and panic into the dragon, overwhelming his thoughts and battering his consciousness. The dragon screamed, his eyes burning red with terror.

Come closer, Cael said, *and open your mouth.*

The dragon tried to resist, but Cael's powers were gripping its mind like a vice. The dragon hovered over the fort, as the Sanang garrison watched from the ground, then it opened its jaws. Cael jumped up onto the parapet, in full view of the garrison, then he dropped two bombs down the dragon's throat. They went off at the same time, and the dragon's head evaporated in a red cloud of blood, brains and bone, coating Cael's armour and uniform.

Below, the Sanang soldiers were staring upwards, then they ran for cover as the dead dragon fell into the forecourt, crashing into the outbuildings and smashing through the flag stones.

Cael triggered his Quadrant, and appeared next to the headless dragon.

'Gather round,' he cried. 'It's time to go.'

The Sanang soldiers rushed out from the shadows of the outer walls.

'The city has fallen,' Cael went on. 'Who wants to go home?'

The soldiers crowded round Cael, many slapping him on the back. A few picked up fragments of the dead dragon's skull or fangs to take as souvenirs, then Cael activated the Quadrant, and transported the first batch of two dozen to the army base in Plateau City.

The Sanang roared in relief as they arrived on the crowded parade ground, their arms in the air. A medical officer saw them, then she eyed the gore and blood on Cael's uniform.

'Is any of that blood yours, lad?' she said.

'None of it,' said Cael.

'The boy killed two dragons!' shouted a Sanang. 'He blew their fucking heads off.'

Cael said nothing, then he returned to the fort. It took him seven trips to evacuate the rest of the Sanang from the garrison. When the last of them were standing on the parade ground, he walked into their midst.

'Has anyone seen the Queen of Ulna?' he shouted. 'Has anyone here seen Blackrose?'

'We saw her, boy,' said an older Sanang warrior. 'She was hunting those undead bastards in the skies near our fort. She took out over a dozen, but there were too many.'

'She went down by the banks of the river,' said another, 'then the undead were all over her. Wystians also flew by, heading for her direction.'

'The queen is dead,' said the older warrior. 'There was fuck all we could do.'

Cael said nothing, then he triggered the Quadrant, and arrived back inside the Temple of Ulna. The evacuation of the garrison was underway, and soldiers were filing through the portal, as Corthie sat next to Gallantmorn on the heap of rubble, Cole a few yards from them. A woman in civilian clothing was also there, talking to Cole as she sat next to him.

Cael clambered up the mound of rubble blocking the wide entrance.

'Rosie Jackdaw?' he said. 'Why are you still here?'

Rosie turned to him. 'I'm not leaving without my sister,' she said. 'Cole is searching for Blackrose.'

Cael glanced at his cousin, whose eyes had glazed over.

'Is he looking for the Queen of Ulna?' said Gallantmorn, raising his bloody and battered head.

Cael shook Cole's shoulder, and his cousin's vision cleared.

'Search by the banks of the river,' Cael said, 'to the south of the only intact fort along the city's outskirts. The Sanang claim to have seen her go down there.' He pushed the location of the fort into Cole's head. 'South of that location.'

Cole nodded, then his eyes glazed over.

'What did the Sanang say?' said Rosie.

Cael said nothing.

'Is she alive?' said Corthie.

'Give Cole a moment,' said Cael. He took out his cigarettes, lit one, and sat on the heap of rubble. He gazed at his hands, but they were steady. He should be terrified, but he felt drained of all emotion. He would feel it later, he knew.

Claudian walked over. 'Five minutes,' he called out. 'The last of the garrison will be out of here in five minutes. Lord Gallantmorn, you and Corthie will be the last to leave. When I blow the whistle, you will proceed to the portal.'

Corthie raised a hand. 'Wait. If Maddie or Blackrose are still alive, then we have one last thing to do before we leave Na Sun Ka.'

'I cannot keep the portal open indefinitely,' said Claudian.

'I have a Quadrant,' said Cael.

Claudian glanced at the blood covering the front of Cael's armour, and his eyes tightened.

Cole gasped, his sight clearing.

'I've found Blackrose,' he said. 'She's surrounded by the bodies of undead dragons, but over a dozen Wystians are circling overhead, ready to finish her off.'

'She's alive?' said Rosie.

'Only just,' said Cole.

'And my sister?'

'Maddie's there, too,' said Cole; 'sheltering behind Blackrose's forelimbs.'

Corthie got to his feet. 'Let's get them. You up for it, Cael?'

Cael threw away his cigarette. 'Do you need to ask?'

'I'm coming, too,' said Rosie.

'And I,' said Gallantmorn. 'I did not come all this way to leave my queen to die alone.'

Cole muttered something, and stood. 'Count me in.'

'We'll take up positions around Gallantmorn,' said Corthie. 'Rosie, stay close to the dragon's flank. Cael – get us in and out again as quickly as you can.'

'I don't know if it's a good idea to risk three Holdfasts like this,' said Claudian.

Corthie smiled. 'Then it's lucky no one's asking you.'

CHAPTER 27
CARELESS

Sun Ta, Na Sun Ka, Western Rim – 21st Abrinch 5266 (18th Gylean Year 17)

'Everyone take a single sip of salve before we go,' Corthie said; 'and where's my hedgewitch?'

'I'm right here, boss,' said Drechtalang, as Cole sipped from the vial and passed it on.

'And Nestorian?'

Drechtalang pointed at the heap of rubble blocking the temple entrance. 'He's in there, somewhere, rigging up a little surprise for the Wystians.'

'Get your arse out here, Nestorian,' Corthie shouted.

The Banner sergeant emerged from the thick shadows to the left of the mound, and hurried toward Gallantmorn and Corthie.

'The first dragon to make it through that gateway is in for a shock,' he said. 'I've set up enough explosives to bring down the front wing of the temple.' He glanced at the others, and then at the portal, where only a handful of soldiers were still waiting to leave. 'Are we evacuating?'

'We're pulling out of the temple,' said Corthie, 'but we're not leaving Dragon Eyre; not yet. Cael is going to take us to a location south of the city. We're going to protect Blackrose and Maddie, but only until Cael takes us to the Star Continent.'

'Will the Quadrant be able to transport two dragons and the rest of us at the same time?' said Gallantmorn.

'That won't be a problem,' said Cael. 'I just need to get close enough to Blackrose to trigger it.'

'Has everyone had some salve?' said Corthie.

The others nodded, except for Rosie.

'I don't need any,' she said, passing the vial back to Corthie.

Corthie raised the vial to his lips and took a tiny sip of the silver liquid. A warm sense of well-being rippled through his body, and he felt his injuries and tiredness vanish. He pushed the stopper back into the vial, and slipped it behind his Tempest breastplate. Over to his left, Nestorian shouldered his loaded Battanara, and Drechtalang picked up a bag of projectiles for the weapon. Claudian watched the last of the soldiers evacuate to Plateau City, then he dissolved the portal.

'I shall be returning to Colsbury now,' he said to Corthie. 'What should I tell the others?'

'The truth,' said Corthie.

'Aila was insistent that I bring you home immediately.'

Corthie nodded. 'She'll understand when she finds out what we're doing.'

'Clova is desperate to see her father,' Claudian went on.

Corthie narrowed his eyes. 'Why would you single out Clova?'

Claudian glanced at Cael. 'I assume you told Corthie that his daughter was abducted?'

Cael shook his head.

'Clova was abducted?' Corthie cried.

'She's back; she's safe,' said Claudian. 'Karalyn, Lahnos and Cael rescued her and Arrosa.'

Corthie glared at his nephew. 'So that's where you went, you sly little bastard? Did you not think that I might have wanted to help?'

'It was a trick,' said Cael, 'to lure us away from Na Sun Ka so that

Edgar could order the invasion. If we'd both gone, things would have been even worse.'

Corthie laughed, but it wasn't a joyful sound. 'Worse? How could it possibly have been worse? I should have gone, and you should have stayed.' He exhaled, then he turned to Claudian. 'Tell Clova that I will be home as quickly as I can. Tell her I love her.'

Claudian tilted his head. 'I shall do as you ask. Good luck, and I shall see you on Colsbury.'

The air shimmered, and Claudian disappeared, leaving the temple deserted.

'Get ready, Cael,' said Corthie. 'Everyone – stay close together, and we'll get this done with as much speed as we can manage.'

Cael took out his Quadrant, then he swept his bloodstained fingers over its surface. The air in the temple crackled, then they appeared near a wide river, the banks of which were littered with the dismembered bodies of over twenty undead dragons. Their flesh was rotting in the late afternoon sunlight, and a malignant odour was filling the air. To the north, Corthie saw the outskirts of Sun Ta, then his eyes glanced up. A dozen Wystians were circling overhead. They were swooping down in pairs, aiming for part of the riverside choked with the corpses of the undead dragons.

'I see the queen,' said Gallantmorn. 'She is lying amidst the fallen.'

'We have also been seen,' said Cole, pointing upwards.

Three dragons were peeling away from the others. They banked, then plummeted downwards. Drechtalang lit the fuse by the rear of the Battanara, and a projectile shot out. At the same time, Cael raised a hand, and one of the dragons screamed and fell away. The projectile slammed into the side of another dragon, and the explosion tore the beast in half. Of the three dragons, only one made it as far as the group. Gallantmorn raised his claws as flames came down, and the descending dragon veered away as though it was about to flee, then it darted to the side, seeing the Quadrant clutched in Cael's left hand. The dragon grabbed hold of Cael by the waist, and began to ascend. Gallantmorn sprang up, his forelimbs raised. His claws dug into the flank of the ascending dragon, and pulled him back down. The dragon screamed, then it drew back its forelimb, and hurled Cael through the air. His body flew over the river, the Quadrant falling from his grasp and splashing into the dark waters, then Cael smacked into the side of a headless undead dragon on the far bank and lay still.

'Cael!' shouted Cole.

Corthie turned to Gallantmorn, who was wrestling with the dragon who had picked up Cael. He raised the Clawhammer to go to the aid of the dark orange dragon, then two other Wystians began descending towards the Queen of Ulna. Blackrose was on her side, her scales covered in wounds, and her eyes closed. The two dragons hovered over her for a moment, as though they were wary of approaching the mighty queen, then they opened their jaws, and went for her neck.

'To the queen!' Corthie cried. 'Cover me, Cole.'

Corthie raced over the ground, his Clawhammer in both hands, as the others followed him. One of the dragons glanced up, and sent a burst of flames in Corthie's direction, but Cole deflected the fires to the left, where they incinerated the remains of an undead creature. Corthie reached Blackrose, and jumped, landing on the shoulders of the huge black dragon. He swung the Clawhammer, and its three greenhide talons tore a great wound down the dragon's face, gouging out its left eye. It lunged out with its forelimbs, and Corthie rolled to miss them, then he rammed the spiked butt of the Clawhammer up into the underside of the dragon's jaws. Something shot past his shoulder, then an explosion ripped the right wing from the other dragon hovering over Blackrose. More flames came down, but Cole was ready, and he pushed them to the side. Corthie ripped the Clawhammer from the jaws of the dragon above him, then he fended off another wild swing, the dragon's claws glancing off the Tempest breastplate. The two wounded dragons retreated. One was crawling along the ground, its right wing in ragged ruins, as the other tried to fly off, half blind and with blood covering its head.

'That's right, ya scaly bastards!' shouted Corthie, as he stood upon the shoulders of Blackrose. 'Did you like that?'

Rosie was rooting around down by the black dragon's forelimbs, then she cried out. Nestorian and Drechtalang ran to help her, and they pulled the body of a woman from behind Blackrose's claws, where the dragon had been shielding her.

'The salve, Corthie!' Rosie cried.

Corthie reached behind his armour, and threw the small vial down to Rosie, who caught it one-handed. Another two dragons plummeted downwards, their jaws blasting the area with flames. Cole grunted, and the flames were pushed back to all sides around them. The bodies of the undead dragons erupted in flames, their rotten flesh burning in a wide ring around Blackrose. A dragon soared through the acrid smoke and flames, and rushed at Corthie, both forelimbs reaching out for him. The Clawhammer tore through the dragon's left forelimb, severing it, but the right battered Corthie across the chest, with only the Tempest armour saving his life from the long claws. Corthie fell back, winded and in agony, but his body kept moving, and he lunged out again, closing with the dragon and ripping the Clawhammer down its face. The dragon screamed, and Corthie swung again. The Clawhammer ripped through the dragon's neck, and its head swayed then fell. Flames exploded above Corthie, getting closer as Cole started to tire. Another dragon snapped at Corthie, its jaws gleaming in the red light of the fires, then Nestorian shouted a warning as a projectile flew out of the Battanara. Corthie put his hands over his head as the projectile struck the dragon's shoulders. The roar of the explosion deafened Corthie, then blood and gore rained down upon him from above. He glanced up, and saw the dragon topple backwards. It crashed into the ground, and lay still.

Corthie staggered back to his feet, still upon the shoulders of Blackrose. Around the Queen of Ulna, three Wystians lay dead, with a further two grievously wounded, while seven others continued to circle overhead, their eyes on Corthie.

Corthie laughed, and raised the Clawhammer into the air.

'I am Corthie Holdfast,' he shouted up to the dragons. 'If you want me, come and get me!'

Gallantmorn approached from the north, dragging an injured limb, and with long rips down his left wing. There was no sign of his rider Annu'tila upon his shoulders, but his harness was streaked in blood. He stood next to Blackrose, his gaze going from Corthie to the Wystians above them. Corthie met his gaze, but it was clear to him that Gallantmorn was nearly spent.

Blackrose moved under Corthie's feet. He glanced down, and saw that Rosie had emptied the vial of salve into the mouth of the black dragon. Maddie was on her feet next to her sister, her injuries gone, and they were watching as Blackrose groaned. Some of the queen's wounds had started to heal, but many remained open.

'We need more salve,' Rosie cried. 'It wasn't enough.'

'It was enough to save her life,' said Maddie. 'How did you get here? Did you fly on Gallantmorn's shoulders?'

'Cael had a Quadrant with him,' said Rosie.

'Had?' said Maddie.

'I saw it fall into the river,' said Rosie.

Maddie glanced around the broken, smouldering landscape. 'Where is he? Where's Cael?'

Rosie pointed. 'A dragon threw him over there.'

Maddie's eyes widened. 'Is he dead? Is Cael dead?'

'I can see his chest rise and fall from here,' said Corthie. 'He's alive, but I don't know how we're going to get him.'

'I shall fetch him,' said Gallantmorn.

Maddie frowned at the dragon's wounds. 'Can you fly?'

'I will not be taking to the air again for some time, Maddie Jackdaw,' said Gallantmorn, 'but I can still walk.'

'We can't let him go,' said Maddie. 'The Wystians will kill him if he wanders off by himself.'

'Use your Quadrant to get Cael,' said Rosie. 'Bring him back here, and then we can all leave.'

'Do you think Blackrose and I would have been driven to the ground if I still had my damn Quadrant?' said Maddie. 'I lost it when I fell into an alleyway somewhere in Sun Ta. A dragon cut through the harness straps.'

'You lost it?' cried Rosie. 'You dozy cow!'

'This is getting us nowhere,' said Gallantmorn. 'I shall retrieve Cael, unless Corthie forbids it.'

Corthie tore his gaze from the seven Wystians circling overhead, and he glanced down at Gallantmorn and the others. Gallantmorn looked exhausted, but how else were they going to be able to rescue Cael?

'Let me do this,' said Gallantmorn. 'I shall bring Cael back to you, and then we can search the river for his Quadrant.'

'I can cover his journey with the Battanara, sir,' said Nestorian.

'And I can try to heal Cael when he gets back,' said Drechtalang.

'You're a healer?' said Maddie. 'Get over here and heal Blackrose.'

The hedgewitch shook his head. 'I have been using my powers ever since the Wystians invaded, and I barely possess enough reserves to keep myself alive. Nothing I have would make any difference to a dragon, but I might be able to save Cael.'

'If we split up, we will be attacked again,' said Corthie, 'but I can't see any other way. Do what you can, Gallantmorn, while we protect the queen.'

The dark orange dragon tilted his injured head, then he turned to gaze at Cael's body. He was lying next to the dismembered corpse of an undead dragon on the far bank of the river, about a hundred yards from where Corthie was standing. Gallantmorn took one last look up at the Wystians, then he set off, dragging his wounded limb as he limped towards the river.

'Malik's ass,' cried Maddie. 'I can't watch.'

The Wystians continued to circle for a few moments, then three of them peeled off and soared towards the river, while the other four opened their jaws and began to descend. Cole raised his arms to shield Blackrose from the four attacking from above, but his protective powers could do nothing to help Gallantmorn, who was bathed in flames from the three descending by the river. A projectile whistled through the air, but the three dragons had been expecting it, and they swerved aside, allowing it to pass, and it exploded in an empty field off to their right.

Corthie swung the Clawhammer as the first of the four dragons got into range, and the greenhide talons smashed against the dragon's teeth, dislodging several. The dragon bundled into him, knocking Corthie off his feet. A massive forelimb came hurtling downwards, but Corthie rolled before it could trap him, then he leapt up, and raked the Clawhammer across the dragon's flank. As that one retreated, another approached, its head emerging through the smoke and flames. Corthie fended off an attack by the dragon's teeth and claws, as Cole deflected more flames. Another dragon approached from the side, then a clawed forelimb swept across Corthie's chest, sending him flying through the air. He landed on Blackrose's tattered left wing and rolled down it, stopping just yards from Rosie and Maddie. Rosie pulled a projectile out of the bag over Drechtalang's shoulder, as the two dragons edged closer to Corthie. Rosie did something to the upper part of the projectile, then she raced forward and pushed it into Corthie's left hand.

'Ten seconds!' she cried.

Corthie stared at the long, cylindrical projectile, as a dragon opened its jaws to devour him. He rammed it upwards and into the dragon's mouth. The dragon pulled back in surprise, then its head exploded, showering Corthie with flesh and blood as the other dragons retreated back into the sky. Corthie lay still for a long moment, every inch of him covered in dragon blood. He felt a hand on his shoulder, and he opened his eyes to see Cole gazing down at him.

'Gallantmorn is dead,' Cole said. 'He didn't make it halfway to Cael.'

Corthie pulled himself upright, then he swayed and staggered from the bruises and aches all over his body. He stared up, and saw six Wystians overhead, then his gaze went to where the body of Gallantmorn was lying next to the near bank of the river, his throat ripped out and his neck broken. In the sky above Gallantmorn, the sun was beginning to set over the mountains of Na Sun Ka. Corthie gazed at his team. Cole looked exhausted, and sweat had formed little channels through the grime on his face. How long would he be able to deflect the flames of the dragons, when they renewed their assault? Rosie and Maddie looked fine, but neither was armed, and neither had any powers. Nestorian was busy reloading his Battanara, and Drechtalang handed him the last projectile from the bag.

'I will go for Cael,' said Corthie, 'and then I will see if I can find his Quadrant. It's probably still at the bottom of the river.'

'What?' said Maddie. 'No way. If you leave, then we're all dead, and that means Cole's dead, too. And if Cole's dead, then the dragons will burn you into a crisp. I'll go. I'm the only one here who knows how to use a Quadrant. If I can find it, then we'll be out of here in no time.'

'If Gallantmorn couldn't even make it to the river,' said Rosie, 'then what makes you think that you can? You'll be dead in seconds.'

'But I'm smaller than a dragon,' said Maddie. 'I can sneak about. I'm pretty good at sneaking about.'

Rosie grabbed hold of her sister's arm. 'No. I'm not losing you in this awful place.'

'What choice do we have?' said Maddie. 'If we stay here, then we'll all die. You're a good little sister, Rosie, but you have to let me try.'

Cole frowned. 'Where's Drechtalang?'

Nestorian cursed, then he gestured towards the near bank of the river. The hedgewitch was creeping along by the charred bones of an undead dragon, heading towards the water's edge. He glanced over his shoulder at Corthie and the others, gave a thumbs-up, then he started to wade out into the river, keeping his head down.

'That stupid bastard,' said Nestorian.

'He might make it,' said Rosie. 'The Wystians haven't seen him yet.'

'Then we need to keep them distracted,' said Corthie. 'Nestorian, fire the last projectile at the dragons overhead; keep their attention on us.'

Nestorian nodded, then he gestured for Rosie to stand by his shoulder to light the fuse, as he pointed the Battanara up at the Wystians.

'Wait for it,' Nestorian whispered, as Rosie readied her matches. 'Now.'

Rosie lit a match, and touched the flame to the fuse. It sizzled its way into the end of the Battanara, and the last projectile spat out, jolting Nestorian's shoulder back. The missile flew through the air, and exploded as it struck the flank of a black and yellow dragon, lighting up the darkening sky for a brief moment. The dragon screamed, then it fell, plummeting down from the sky and crashing into a neighbouring field.

'Fucking shot,' said Cole. 'Here they come.'

Corthie climbed back up onto Blackrose's shoulders and readied the Clawhammer, but the surviving Wystians made no move to descend.

'What are they waiting for?' said Maddie. 'Do they know we've run out of bombs?'

'If they knew that, they'd already be down here,' said Nestorian, keeping the Battanara on his shoulder.

The Wystians continued to circle above them.

'Come on!' Corthie shouted at them. 'Are you too scared to fight me?'

The air shimmered over to his left, and five men appeared, all armed with Tempest weapons.

Corthie stared at them for a moment, thinking that imperial reinforcements had arrived to rescue them, then one of the figures raised a hand, and Maddie, Rosie and Nestorian collapsed to the ground.

'I also tried to send the two Holdfasts to sleep, my lord,' said the man who had raised his arm, 'but they are resistant to my powers.'

'Good,' said the leader of the five men. 'I don't want Corthie asleep; I want him to be conscious when I kill him.'

Cole raised his own arm, but two of the dragons dived from the sky, and sent flames at him. Cole reacted, deflecting the raging fires, and keeping them from the area surrounding Blackrose.

'Do you know who I am, Corthie Holdfast?' said the leader of the five men.

'A soon-to-be-dead god, by any chance?' said Corthie, jumping down from Blackrose's shoulders.

'My name is Ward,' the man said. 'I have relieved Lord Edgar of his command. Under my regime, there will be no mercy shown to the Holdfasts.' He gestured to the dragons, and they closed their jaws and pulled back.

Cole sank to his knees as the flames ceased, panting and gasping for air.

'Your nephew seems to have exhausted himself, Corthie,' Ward went on. 'If I wished, I could now command the Wystians to tear you limb from limb, but I want to be the one who takes the head of the greatest mortal warrior in existence.'

Corthie laughed. 'You're making it too easy for me, god. I'll carve you up in seconds.'

'These four demigods all have battle-vision,' said Ward; 'as do I.'

'All at once, or one at a time,' said Corthie. 'Bring it on.'

Cole staggered to his feet and drew his sword.

'It might be best if you stay behind me,' said Corthie; 'but not too close. You don't want to get caught out when I'm swinging the Clawhammer.'

'I'll watch your back, Uncle,' he said.

'You're a good lad, Cole, but leave this to me.'

Ward gestured to the four demigods, who fanned out.

'I will keep you alive long enough for you to watch me kill the Queen of Ulna,' said Ward.

'You're pretty good at talking, god,' said Corthie. 'Have you got anything else?'

The four demigods rushed him, each raising their Tempest swords. Corthie powered his battle-vision. He was tired after spending two whole days and a night fighting, but he had enough left in him to handle a few gods. He charged at them. They were fast, but he was faster, and the Clawhammer ripped the first demigod in half without Corthie breaking sweat.

'That's one,' said Corthie, as the other three backed off.

Blackrose stirred, and her forelimbs twitched. Two of the demigods stared at the huge black dragon, but her eyes remained closed.

'Forget her,' cried Ward. 'Blackrose is dying. Kill Corthie and Cole; think of nothing else.'

The three demigods charged again, but one of them went for Cole. Corthie fended off the two attacking him, then the third demigod got through Cole's defences, and his Tempest sword hacked through Cole's armour and sliced across his stomach. Cole fell backwards, blood staining the hole in his breastplate. Corthie punched one of the demigods with his free hand, and the man was sent flying back, then he severed the right arm of another with a downward stroke of the Clawhammer. He raced to defend Cole, and Ward attacked him from behind. Corthie parried the attacks from both directions, but he could sense how good Ward was. The punched demigod returned to the fray, and Corthie was attacked again – the two demigods from one side, and Ward from the other. Corthie feinted to the left, then lunged out at Ward, and the Clawhammer battered off the god's armour, but did not penetrate it. Corthie swung again, evading a lunge by a demigod, and the tip of one of the Clawhammer's talons sliced across Ward's face. Ward screamed in pain, his nose and upper lip gone, then he gestured to the sky. Three dragons soared down, their claws extended. Corthie fended off one, but the second batted a forelimb that Corthie was unable to dodge. The weight of the dragon's blow broke several of his ribs as Corthie was slammed back against the ground. The third dragon opened its jaws to bite Corthie, and he rammed the Clawhammer into its mouth, forcing the jaws to remain open. The dragon roared and backed off, unable to dislodge the weapon from its mouth. Corthie rolled and got back to his feet, unarmed.

Ward stared at Corthie through his mask of blood. The lower half of his face was starting to heal, but bone was showing through the wound. The noise coming from the dragon with the Clawhammer lodged upright in its jaws was so loud that Corthie could barely think. A demigod rushed at him from the left. Corthie ducked the swing, and gripped the man by the throat, squeezing until he heard the neck break. He ripped the Tempest sword from his grasp, forced him down, and hacked his head off.

'That's two,' Corthie said, swaying. He smiled. 'Two and a half, if you count the guy who lost his arm.'

Ward pointed at the dragon with the Clawhammer in its jaws. The giant beast collapsed to the ground, unconscious, its screams ceasing.

'That's better,' said Ward, his words slurred as they came from his lipless mouth.

The other two dragons swooped again, and Ward sprang forward as Corthie turned to fend off the claws. The god's sword found a gap in Corthie's armour, and the blade plunged into his side. Corthie staggered back, blood pouring from the wound, then the last demigod attacked from his right. Corthie felt the blow batter off his breastplate, then he rammed his sword into the side of the demigod's head, and twisted. The demigod fell to the ground, and Corthie backed up until he reached Blackrose.

'Three and a half,' said Corthie.

'It is over,' said Ward, his face still healing. 'I, the last son of Edmond, shall find vengeance for the murder of my father. How does it feel to be beaten, Corthie?'

'I wouldn't know,' said Corthie.

Ward approached, while the two dragons remained overhead.

'Let me kill him, god,' cried one of the dragons. 'He has slain many of my kin this day.'

'You may kill the others,' said Ward, 'but Corthie is mine.'

Corthie started to feel light-headed. His battle-vision was suppressing some of the pain from the broken ribs and the wound in his side, but most was getting through. He blinked, then surged all that he had left. He charged forward, his Tempest sword cleaving through Ward's armour, and wounding him from shoulder to waist. Corthie raised his sword to deliver the killing blow, then a dragon swung at him from behind, ripping the back plate from his armour, the claws cutting three deep lines through Corthie's flesh.

'Get back!' Ward shouted at the dragon, as Corthie sank to his knees.

Ward staggered, the wound across his chest healing, then he

raised his sword and raced forward, his movements a blur. He rammed the sword down, the Tempest blade meeting Tempest armour, and Ward's strength forced it through the sheet of black metal, and he drove it deep into Corthie's chest. Corthie pushed himself to his feet, the sword penetrating deeper, then he reached out with his hands and gripped the sides of Ward's head. Ward pushed the sword in further, and Corthie felt his life start to drain away. He pushed his thumbs into Ward's eyes, then beyond them into the god's brain. Ward screamed, then Corthie pulled his hands apart, and tore Ward's skull in two.

Corthie looked down as Ward's body collapsed onto the ground. The god's Tempest sword was still in his chest, almost up to the hilt. The last surviving demigod stared up at him from the ground, his right arm severed near the shoulder.

'Do you fancy another go, wee man?' Corthie said. 'I wouldn't want you to feel left out.' He laughed, then he fell to the ground.

His eyes were still open, and he watched as the wounded demigod crawled over the bloody and broken ground, pulling himself along with his remaining arm. The demigod approached Ward's corpse, then he reached out for something hidden beneath the god's armour. The air shimmered, and the demigod disappeared.

'You cheeky little bastard,' Corthie said. He rolled onto his side, and pulled the Tempest sword from his chest. He shuddered with pain as blood flowed from the wound, then he fell onto his back and stared up at the two dragons circling overhead.

The two dragons began to descend, then both screamed at the same time. Their eyes rolled up, and they crashed to the ground, landing either side of Blackrose. One ploughed into a pile of dismembered undead dragons, and the other slammed into the river bank, breaking its neck in the fall. Corthie laughed at the sight, then the pain began to consume him.

'Aila,' he whispered.

He felt hands cradle his head, and he managed to see Cael crouching over him.

'Stay with me, Uncle,' Cael cried, as tears streamed down his cheeks.

'Cole is hurt,' Corthie gasped. 'Get him home, Cael; get them all home. It's up to you now.'

'I'll do my best, Uncle,' said Cael.

Corthie laughed for the last time. 'I know you will. What a fucking place to die.'

Corthie closed his eyes, feeling Cael's hands on his face, and hearing the sound of his nephew's tears. He had died before, in the cavern of Fordamere on Lostwell. He had been alone then, but he wasn't alone now. It wasn't much of a difference, or maybe it was everything. He pictured the faces of his wife and children, then he smiled and slipped away.

CHAPTER 28
HARMLESS

Udall, Ulna, Eastern Rim – 22nd Abrinch 5266 (18th Gylean Year 17)

Sable gazed at her six-year-old son clambering up the rigging of the *Giddy Gull*, her eyes tight. The crew on the deck of the brigantine cheered when the boy reached the top of the main mast, as though they already considered him to be a seasoned sailor, but Sable always felt her nerves go taut whenever she watched him. If he fell, then he could break a limb, or even die, and she sometimes wished she had chosen a god to be his father, just as she had done with her daughter. He was a strong boy, that was clear, and he was going to have the height and build of a Kellach man, but he was definitely mortal.

Topaz laughed, a cigarette hanging from his lips. 'Look at him go, ma'am.'

'I can hardly bear to watch,' said Sable.

'Little Joss is doing fine, ma'am,' said Topaz. 'With all the practice he's getting up there, he's going to fit right in with the crew.'

'What if I don't want him to be a sailor?'

Topaz narrowed his eyes, as though he had never considered the question before.

Lara appeared to their left, carrying Lindi in her arms as she walked along the scrubbed deck. She passed the two-year-old girl to Sable.

'Hold the tiddler for a minute, babe,' Lara said. 'I need to go below and check that everything's ready for a fast escape to Olkis.'

'Are we sure that we want to go to Olkis?' said Sable.

'Well, we ain't hanging around here if the damn Wystians come.'

'Yes, but Olkis? What about somewhere... not on Dragon Eyre?'

Lara snorted. 'Don't you be suggesting the bleeding Star Continent, not with its pathetic little Inner Sea. I'd be bored of sailing around that in days. Nah, we'll be safe in Langbeg; we could even take back Befallen Castle for the family. Ann's in Langbeg, and don't forget that Tilly will be taking the *Sow's Revenge* in that direction. The Osso sisters need to stick together.'

Sable wasn't sure that she agreed, but she kept her thoughts to herself. Without the ability to fight anyone, she doubted that she would be of any assistance in the re-taking of a castle, and despite having lived with Lara for years, she was still lacking the basic seafaring skills the others took for granted. Without her ability to fight, she was starting to feel useless; harmless. Ordinary.

Was it so bad? She had Lara, and they had Joss and Lindi. They also had many friends, loyal friends upon whom they could depend. Many would be envious of her position, but Sable felt bereft, as though a large part of who she was had vanished.

'All right; Olkis,' she said, as she kept her eyes on Joss up in the rigging, then she noticed that Lara had already gone.

Topaz nudged her with an elbow, and pointed towards the bridge palace. Sable turned, and saw dozens of dragons swooping and descending over the huge building, as though they were gathering.

'What does that mean, do you think, ma'am?' said Topaz.

'I should probably check,' Sable said. 'There might be news from Na Sun Ka. Could you take Lindi for me while I find out?'

Topaz nodded, then he put his fingers to his mouth and whistled. A nine-year-old girl with brown hair ran down from the quarter deck, and came to a halt in front of her father.

'Hey, Beth,' Topaz said. 'Take Lindi for ten minutes, would you? Sable needs to pop up to the palace.'

'Is mum home?' the girl said.

'That's one of the things I'll be finding out,' said Sable, as she passed the infant to the girl. 'Thank you, Beth.'

'That's all right, Aunty,' said the girl; 'but I want to see my mum if she's back with Blackrose.'

'I'll fetch you if that's the case,' said Sable. She took out her Quadrant, nodded to Topaz, then she swiped the copper surface and appeared in the centre of the bridge palace, just outside the main entrance to the largest audience chamber. She gazed through the doorway. Dozens of dragons were cramming into the hall and, in their midst, she saw the form of Blackrose, lying on the floor as though she was wounded. A handful of humans were also there, gathered by the queen's head.

Sable weaved her way among the dragons, and hurried to where Maddie was standing. Her sister Rosie was next to her, and the Jackdaw sisters were embracing each other; and both were in tears. Sable frowned as she saw Nestorian and Drechtalang from her old team in Sun Ta, then her eyes fell upon her two nephews – Cael and Cole, who were standing apart with their eyes lowered. Adjutant Claudian was also present, and he was crouching by Blackrose, talking to the wounded queen as he pulled a vial of salve from a pocket.

'Stand back!' Claudian shouted, then he tipped the contents of the vial into Blackrose's mouth.

The Queen of Ulna convulsed on the floor for a few moments, then her eyes opened wider, and she got to her feet, her injuries gone. She gazed around the hall, saying nothing, then she raised her head and emitted a great cry of anguish. The audience chamber stilled, as Blackrose's lament filled the air, a sound so mournful and full of pain that Sable felt her heart almost break.

Blackrose fell silent, and she lowered her head, her eyes dim with grief.

'Corthie Holdfast is no more,' she said. 'He gave his life to save mine.'

Sable took a step back, her fists clenching as she tried to deny the words the dragon had spoken.

'My beloved friend is dead,' Blackrose went on, her voice ragged; 'his wife has lost a husband, seven children their father, and two sisters their brother. Next to their grief, my pain is insignificant; and yet this loss has torn my heart to pieces. Corthie was the bringer of hope; a defender of the weak; a friend loyal and true; a great warrior who held no hatred within his heart, and his passing shall be mourned on Ulna for as long I breathe.'

'No,' said Sable.

The queen gazed down at her.

'I refuse to believe it,' said Sable.

'Alas, my dear Sable; I saw him with my own eyes,' said Blackrose. 'I am sorry; I wish it were not so.'

Sable started to weep, and her two nephews approached to flank her.

'Who did it?' cried Sable. 'Who is responsible?'

'It was Ward,' said Cael. 'Ward and the Wystians.'

'Ward is dead,' said Cole. 'Uncle Corthie killed him just before he died.'

Grief consumed Sable's mind. Without any conscious thought, she put her hand in her pocket, triggered her Quadrant, and vanished. She appeared high up in the rocky mountains of Ectus, next to Meader's tomb. She sank to her knees by the cairn, surrounded by wild flowers in bloom.

Not Corthie. Anyone but Corthie.

She raised her head and screamed into the blue sky.

It took a while for a plan to form amid the stifling haze of grief and anger clouding Sable's mind as she lay by the mountain tomb. If she couldn't fight, then she would need others to become her instruments of revenge. Gods and dragons were going to die, even if it wouldn't be Sable herself wielding the weapon.

She needed Cael before she could do anything else, and that meant having to return to Udall. She got to her feet, and gazed out at the ocean. Of course it had been Dragon Eyre that had claimed the life of her nephew; it was a place of great beauty, but also one of death, loss and violence. Sable went through a list of people to blame. Was Sable herself responsible? Hadn't she encouraged Corthie to fight for Na Sun Ka? What about Karalyn, the one woman with the power to remove the Wystians from Dragon Eyre forever? The Empress and Kelsey, for following the path to war in the first place; or Blackrose, for tricking the Empire into defending the southern borders of her realm? Or Kyra, for placing the blocks into Sable's mind, which had meant she hadn't been there to fight alongside her nephew? Or Cael, for sparing Allura, which had caused their team to disintegrate? Each had played their role, and each would have to live with what they had done. Corthie had been treated as a weapon, when he had just been a man; a good man. The best of the Holdfasts.

Sable dipped her hand into her pocket, and appeared back in the bridge palace. The audience hall was still packed with mourning dragons, and Topaz was there with Beth and Lindi, sitting next to Maddie and Rosie Jackdaw. Sable wondered how long she had been gone for, then she noticed Cael and Cole, who were sitting by themselves. Cole's cheeks were streaked with tears, but Cael looked as though he wanted to kill someone.

Sable walked over to Topaz. 'Tell Lara I might be gone for a while,' she said.

Topaz glanced up at her.

'We'll tell her,' said Maddie.

Sable tilted her head, then she went up to her two young nephews.

'On your feet, boys,' she said.

Cael glanced up, and stood. 'Whatever you are planning to do,' he said, 'I will be part of it.'

Sable nodded. 'I'd hoped you would say that. Cole, do you wish to stay here?'

Cole shook his head.

'Then get up. We have a lot to do.'

Cole got to his feet, and wiped the tears from his eyes.

'I have one question before we go,' Sable said. 'Is there any realistic possibility that you might be able to loosen the blocks in my head?'

'I wish I could,' said Cael. 'The only way I could remove them is if I were to scour your mind.'

Sable noticed the sword hanging from Cael's belt.

'You have my Fated Blade?' she said. 'Good; you hold on to it for now. You're going to need it.'

She triggered the Quadrant, and they arrived in the dark attic at the top of the Summer Palace on Colsbury. Sable glanced at the spot where the Sextant had been stored for years, then she turned to Cael.

'We're going to need both of our Quadrants for what I have planned,' Sable began.

'I lost mine on Na Sun Ka,' said Cael. 'We searched the river it fell into, but we couldn't find it.'

'That's why we couldn't take Corthie to someone who could bring him back from the dead,' said Cole.

'Wasn't Drechtalang there?'

'He was,' said Cael, 'but he was exhausted after healing me and Cole, and he's no soulwitch. He couldn't have done anything for Corthie, even if he had been fit and well. We had to wait for hours before Claudian arrived to collect us.'

'Where is Corthie now?'

'Here,' said Cole. 'Claudian brought us to Colsbury first, before he took the rest of us to Ulna. Aunty Aila has the body.'

'Then everyone on Colsbury knows?'

Cael and Cole glanced at each other.

'Things are worse than you imagine, Aunty,' said Cole.

'How could they possibly be worse?'

'Kelsey is missing,' Cole went on. 'She went to Na Sun Ka yesterday morning, and she hasn't been seen since.'

'Kelsey's gone?' said Sable. 'What is Karalyn doing about it?'

'I don't know,' said Cael. 'She wasn't here when Claudian brought us back from Sun Ta. Should we wait for her help?'

'No,' said Sable. 'Your mother would try to stop me from doing what I am about to do. If either of you have any qualms about taking revenge for Corthie, then now is the time to back out.'

'What... kind of revenge?' said Cole.

'Utter, and absolute,' said Sable; 'the kind no one comes back from.'

'I am prepared to do whatever it takes,' said Cael. 'Though...'

'Though what?' said Sable.

'I want to see Arrosa,' he said. 'She's downstairs, somewhere, and I'd like to see her before we go.'

'That will have to wait,' said Sable. 'You need to stay angry; you need to cut yourself off from anything that might soften your heart. There will be time for love later; now is the time for death and vengeance.'

'How do you intend to fight?' said Cole.

'You'll see. Perhaps you should stay here, Cole. You're a good lad, maybe too good for this type of work.'

'Will there be dragons where we're going?' he said.

'There will be several.'

'Then you're going to need me,' said Cole. 'Who else will be able to shield you from dragon fire?'

Sable chewed her lip. 'All right.'

'There's no need to worry about Cole, Aunty,' said Cael. 'I've seen my cousin in battle, and I want him by my side.'

'I said all right. Now, we need to select one more member of our little team. Give me a moment.'

She sent out her vision, and began to search through the Summer Palace. Within a few moments, she had located the person she was looking for, and she severed the connection. She triggered the Quadrant, and they appeared in a dark room, where all of the shutters had been closed.

The sound of someone weeping was coming from the shadows on the other side of the room, then it stopped.

'Who's there?' came a voice.

'Cael, Cole and myself, Your Majesty,' said Sable.

'Sable? Open a shutter. Just a little.'

Cole walked over to a window and eased open one of the shutters, allowing a shaft of sunlight to penetrate the chamber. The Empress blinked in the light, and Sable saw the grief on her face.

'Your Majesty,' Sable said, 'I intend to strike back at our enemies; I intend to obliterate them. By this day's end, I shall be wading in their blood. Will you help me?'

'What do you need, Sable? An army? Soldiers?'

'No, Your Majesty. I need one more person to join me and my nephews. A partner to help us carry out a slaughter.'

'Who?' said the Empress. 'Give me their name, and I will release them from my service so that they can assist you.'

Sable stared into her eyes. 'You. I need you. I don't need the Empress; I need Thorn of Greyfalls Deepen. I need a soulwitch.'

The Empress got to her feet. 'Me?'

'Don't you feel your powers burning through your body with rage, Your Majesty?' said Sable. 'Don't you want to use those powers to punish those who took Corthie from us? Come with us, and I will set you free.'

Thorn's eyes hardened.

'Is this wise?' said Cole. 'We cannot risk the life of Her Majesty.'

'Why not?' said Thorn. 'For years, I have sat by and sent countless young men and women to fight on my behalf. Take me with you, Sable. Let me prove to the Empire that I am prepared to do what must be done. Let me prove my love for Corthie. My mistakes led to his death... Let me do this.'

'I have one condition,' said Sable.

'Name it.'

'You will obey my orders until we return.'

Thorn said nothing for a moment, then she tilted her head. 'Had anyone else asked, I would refuse; but for you, Sable, I acquiesce. Lead us. Bring me the vengeance I desire.'

Sable nodded.

Thorn walked over to a desk, and sat. She wiped the tears from her eyes, and began to write something on a sheet of paper.

'We shall tell no one of our intentions,' the Empress said, as she wrote, 'but, for the sake of the Empire, I need to leave a note, in case anyone thinks I have been abducted. I am leaving the government in the hands of Lucius and Shella until we return. Cole, could you please open the second wardrobe along? Inside, you will find a breastplate and a sword.'

Cole bowed his head, then he walked over to the wardrobe and opened it. He removed a hardened leather breastplate, dyed a sapphire blue, and a sheathed sword.

'Give the sword to Sable,' the Empress went on, her eyes on the paper as she continued to write.

Cole did so, then he walked towards the Empress with the armour. She signed her name at the bottom of the sheet, then she straightened her back and held her arms out to the side. Cole slid the armour over the upper part of her blue dress, and tightened the buckles and laces.

Cael narrowed his eyes. 'Do you intend to fight in a dress, Your Majesty?' he said.

'I do,' said Thorn. 'The armour is my one concession to the preservation of my safety. If I die, then the succession laws are clear. Burn my body if that happens, Cole; leave nothing for our enemies.' She turned to Cael. 'In the letter that I have written, I have named you as my favoured successor, should I not return.'

'Me, Your Majesty?' said Cael. 'But... what about...? There are others better qualified than I.'

'I happen to disagree. One of our priorities is to rescue Kelsey, if she can be found. I suggest that you retain her as Herald; she has the greatest mind in the Empire.'

'We must be prepared for the worst,' said Sable. 'Kelsey might be dead.'

'I will not believe it until I see it with my own eyes,' said Thorn. 'Let us go.'

Sable drew the sword that Cole had given her. She glanced at the gleaming blade for a moment.

'Get ready to arrive in the midst of several hundred dragons,' she said. 'Act immediately, without waiting for me to spell it out.'

'I am ready,' said Thorn. 'Give us our orders.'

'Cael will render us invisible,' said Sable. 'Cole will shield us from dragon fire. I will protect us, as my blocks allow me to defend my family if they are attacked, and you are all my family. And you, Your Majesty, shall be my bringer of death.'

She placed her left hand into a pocket and activated the Quadrant. The air crackled, and they appeared in the great plaza in front of the huge temples of Sun Ta. Swarms of Wystian dragons were circling overhead, calling out to each other in victory, as smoke rose from the burnt-out Temple of Ulna.

'We are invisible,' said Cael.

Thorn raised her right hand. 'For Corthie,' she whispered, then she unleashed her powers.

Sable felt the great wave of death leave Thorn's fingers, the force of it causing her to take a step back. Directly above them, dozens of dragons began to scream in pain, as the flesh and scales fell from their heads. Those out of Thorn's range veered and banked, searching for the cause of their fellows' suffering, then the first dead dragons started to fall from the blue sky, a deadly hail of plummeting bodies. They crashed into the houses and streets lining the plaza, then more fell into the great open space that was carpeted with thousands of dead Sanang warriors. By the time each dragon hit the ground, their heads were nothing more than bare skulls, and a wild panic arose among those on the periphery. Some of the terrified Wystians began sending random bursts of flame down into the plaza, and Cole deflected one that came a little too close to Thorn's location; but most of the dragons were fleeing the area. The last dragon to fall was still alive. It gasped and choked as it struck the plaza, then it rolled to a halt, and Thorn began walking towards it.

The wounded dragon raised its head, its eye sockets bleeding, as Thorn approached. Cael, Sable and Cole kept up with the Empress, following her as she made her way past over a hundred dead Wystians. Thorn reached the injured dragon, and placed an invisible hand onto its left flank. Thorn closed her eyes, and the body of the dragon began to wither and shrink. It cried out a last scream of agony, then its eyes closed, its body nothing but a lifeless, dried-up husk. Thorn stepped back, swaying and giddy with power. She opened her eyes, and they shone dark with all she had taken from the dragon. She raised a hand and pointed at a dragon over two hundred yards from them, and its head exploded in a crescendo of blood and bone.

'Take me closer, Sable,' she said. 'There are many more Wystians to kill this day.'

Sable took them to the top of the Temple of Haurn, and Thorn got to work, bringing down every Wystian brave enough to venture into the skies over central Sun Ta, until their corpses were piled high in the streets of the city. Several fires broke out, some caused by panicking dragons, the others from when they had crashed into rows of houses. Sable then took them to the highest tower overlooking the harbour, and the Wystians sheltering there were the next to die, their death screams filling the perfect blue sky. Sable felt out with her own powers while Thorn slaughtered every dragon in sight, and she searched for any areas of the city where normal mage powers were being blocked, but it was in vain. If Kelsey was still alive, then she was not in the city.

'I cannot sense Kelsey anywhere,' she said to Cael and Cole, who were watching the carnage.

Cole raised an arm to deflect another random burst of dragon fire.

'I have also looked for her,' said Cael. 'We are using so many powers that she would sense us if she was here.'

'What about gods?' said Sable. 'Can you sense any of those?'

'Only one,' said Cael. He pointed over to the west of the city centre.

'There is a god in one of those buildings. He is aware of us, but he can't see exactly where we are.'

Thorn lowered her hands, as the last of the dragons in the harbour crashed into the waters of the basin.

'A god?' she said.

'Aye,' said Cael.

'Take us to him, Sable,' said the Empress. 'Apologies. I keep forgetting that you are in charge.' She glanced at Cael and Cole. 'Is anyone keeping count?'

'Over six hundred, so far,' said Cole.

'It's not enough,' said Thorn. 'I want more.'

'You shall have them,' said Sable. 'Let's deal with the god first, before he can flee back to Nom Karta.'

She activated the Quadrant, and they appeared on the roof of a building in the west end of the city centre. Thorn cleared the area of over two dozen dragons who had been flying in a wild panic overhead, and their bodies plummeted to the ground, smashing through the apartment blocks and into the narrow streets.

'Find me the god, Cael,' said Sable; 'then make us visible again.'

Cael's eyes glazed over for a second, then he pointed at a neighbouring building. 'In there. Third floor.'

Sable felt Cael place the exact location into her mind, and she triggered the Quadrant again. They appeared in a plush hallway, next to an open door. Inside was a grand reception room, where seven men and women were standing. Six were wearing the black robes of the Unk Tannic, and Thorn felled five of them with a sweep of her left hand, while she left the sixth gasping on his knees, his hands on his throat.

The seventh man was in the robes of a god, and he stared at Thorn. Sable walked forwards. She sent out her powers, but the god was wearing eye guards. His hand started to reach for his robes, and Cael ran over and punched him in the face. He reached into the god's robes and pulled out his Quadrant, then backed away.

'What are you waiting for, god?' said Sable. 'Try to kill us.'

The god narrowed his eyes.

'I think this one is Belfar,' said Cael, as he tucked the god's Quadrant behind his breastplate.

'Holdfasts?' said Belfar.

'That's right,' said Thorn. 'Four of us.'

She placed a hand onto the forehead of the sole Unk Tannic survivor and drained him dry. She rolled her shoulders, and advanced towards Belfar.

'None of this is my fault,' said Belfar, his hands trembling. 'Lord Ward is in charge now.'

'Did Ward order the invasion of Na Sun Ka?' said Thorn.

'No, that was Edgar,' said Belfar, 'but Edgar was ready to negotiate. He came to a deal with Kelsey Holdfast, but Ward stopped him.'

'Where is Kelsey?' said Sable.

'In Nom Karta, I think,' said Belfar. 'As Edgar spared the Holdfasts, will you now spare me?' He glanced at Cael. 'You spared Allura, did you not, boy?'

'The time for mercy is over,' said Cael.

Sable threw a knife at Belfar's feet. 'Pick it up.'

'What?' said the god.

'Pick it up.'

Belfar leaned over, and grasped the knife in his left hand.

'Attack one of us,' said Sable.

'But...'

'Do it, or the Empress of the Sapphire Throne will flay the flesh from your body.'

Belfar stared at Thorn. 'She is... the Empress? The Empress is here?'

'You are all going to die today,' said Thorn. 'You, the gods, the Wystians. Wouldn't you rather go down fighting?'

Belfar stared at the knife, then at the Empress, then he cried out and lunged forward. Sable swung her sword and cleaved the god's head from his shoulders. The body fell to the carpet, while the head rolled into the corner of the room. Sable walked over and picked it up by the hair.

'I want to drain the next god we come across,' said Thorn.

Sable nodded. She had proved that she could still kill, despite the blocks, but it felt hollow.

'Take me to more Wystians,' the Empress went on. 'Where will they be gathered?'

'They are fleeing all over Na Sun Ka,' said Cael. 'Many are flying towards the west.'

'Maybe they're going to try to fly back to Gyle,' said Cole.

'Then we should block their escape,' said Thorn. 'Sable?'

Sable dropped the head, and glanced up. She activated the Quadrant, and they appeared amid a volcanic landscape. The western coast of Na Sun Ka was a little to their right, and broken Forty-Eighter batteries were lying in heaps along the tops of the cliffs, along with the bodies of hundreds of Holdings soldiers. Thorn gazed at the bodies, then she turned and raised her right hand, as Cael made them invisible. Dozens of Wystian dragons were circling by the coast. The news from Sun Ta had yet to reach them, and many were celebrating their triumph.

Thorn sent out her powers, and annihilated them, their screams echoing off the flanks of the dormant volcanoes, and the bodies falling into the lifeless desert.

'We'll work our way east from here,' said Sable. 'We'll catch the others as they retreat from the city.'

She triggered the Quadrant, and they got to work.

The sun was halfway down the western sky behind them when Thorn sat down by the edge of a ridge. She gazed into the valley, where the dead bodies of over a hundred Wystians were lying. The Empress had been killing for hours, and yet to Sable she looked relaxed and ready for more, with only her eyes betraying the grief she held within her.

'That's all of the large groups dealt with,' said Cael, 'but there are isolated pockets of more Wystians scattered all over the island.'

'What's the count?' said Thorn.

'Well over a thousand,' said Cole. 'I don't have the exact number.'

'Then we should make Gyle our next stop,' said the Empress. 'Let us bring death to the heart of the Wystians. Let us ensure that they never trouble Dragon Eyre again.'

'With all due respect, Your Majesty,' said Cole; 'shouldn't we spare some time to rescue Kelsey? If the gods discover what we have done here, they might kill her.'

'And there are gods to kill in Nom Karta,' said Sable. 'Gods and dragons.'

'Dominion dragons?' said Thorn.

'They are allied to our enemies,' said Sable. 'They are legitimate targets. We don't have to kill them all; just the royal family.'

'And then we go to Gyle?' said Thorn. 'I will not leave this task unfinished. There are still around six thousand Wystians on Gyle; what will stop them invading again?'

Sable nodded. 'Inopei first, then Gyle. We'll rescue Kelsey, if she is still alive, and slaughter everyone in Nom Karta.'

'Not everyone,' said Cael. 'My sister is there.'

The others fell into silence.

'I will not allow anyone to harm her,' said Cael. 'Kyra has made mistakes, but she thought she was doing the right thing.'

'No one will hurt your sister,' said Thorn. 'Kyra's betrayal wounded me deeply, but she remains one of us.'

Sable sat down next to Thorn on the edge of the ridge.

'I don't feel any better,' said the Empress. 'I thought I might obtain some measure of relief, or even joy from taking revenge upon our enemies, but I don't. I feel nothing but loss.'

Sable lowered her gaze. 'I filled this world with death when Badblood died,' she said. 'I killed and killed, but none of it could ever bring him back to me. It is the same with Corthie. We take vengeance not to make us feel any better, but because we all loved him so much.'

'I hope he knew that,' said Thorn. 'I hope he knew what he meant to us.'

'I hope so, too.'

A tear rolled down Sable's cheek, and Thorn took her hand.

'Take us to Nom Karta, Sable,' she said. 'Let's end this war.'

CHAPTER 29
FROM THE MACHINE

Nom Karta, Inopei – 6th Lexinch 1597

'Stop crying,' said Kelsey. 'It's starting to get on my nerves.'

'Shut up,' cried Kyra, from the other side of the dark cell. She rolled onto her other side, trying to get comfortable, but the pain coming from her waist was excruciating.

'What are you even weeping about?' Kelsey went on. 'Don't tell me that you feel sad about the Empire getting its arse kicked on Na Sun Ka – you helped the gods carry out the invasion. Are you crying for poor old Edgar, the man who unleashed ironhides onto the streets of Sun Ta?'

'We were so close,' Kyra said. 'If Ward hadn't appeared, then there would be peace. Don't you understand? Peace. Of course you don't understand; peace was never your priority.'

'Pyre's tits,' muttered Kelsey. 'I should have asked for separate cells. Maybe one day, if you are ever in a position of power, you might start to comprehend the kinds of compromises that rulers have to make. I don't wish death on anyone, least of all our own soldiers. Have the Empress and I made mistakes? Aye, clearly. Did we do it out of a bloodthirsty greed for all-consuming power? Hardly.'

'Your mistakes have cost countless lives.'

'And so have yours. Still, you needn't worry about the Sanang divisions any more; the ironhides and Wystians took care of them for you. They won't be terrorising any more Rahain civilians. They won't be able to defend the Star Continent from Ward, either, but I don't suppose you care about that.'

'You're wrong about me, Aunty; I care. Every death fills me with horror and pain.'

'And yet you continued to assist Edgar.'

'You spoke to Edgar; you agreed to make a deal with him. Thousands of years in a restrainer mask hurt him more than you can imagine. All he wanted was a safe place to live; a place where he could settle everyone trapped on the Doomed Worlds. He was doing it for them.'

'Then why didn't he just ask?'

Kyra snorted. 'And what would the Empire have said? You and the Empress would have refused to cooperate with him.'

'He attacked us first. His forces massacred the garrison defending the Tempest mine.'

'You stole that mine from the Dominion; do you deny it? The Empire had no business sending soldiers to Athumia. You perceived the Dominion to be weak, so you took from them, just as you took the salve mine from the City. You are a bully, Aunty. You and the Empress are bullies, preying on the weak.'

Kelsey fell silent for a few moments.

'I suppose you might have a point,' she said after a while. 'We did perceive the Dominion to be too weak to forcibly take the Tempest mine back from us. All right; I concede that. We were wrong to invade Inopei.'

'Then why did you?'

'Because we wanted a source of Tempest, and the Dominion refused to negotiate with us. They wanted to keep it all for themselves, and they wouldn't grant us access to the mine.'

'What about the salve mine?' said Kyra.

'That's different. The salve mine lies two hundred miles outside the City's territory. It doesn't belong to them; it just happens to be on the same world. They would have a plentiful supply, if they hadn't already exhausted their own mines. They *do* have a plentiful supply, because they are now part of the Empire. Everyone wins.'

Kyra rolled her eyes from behind her hood.

'Now,' Kelsey went on; 'how are you going to get us out of here, Kyra?'

'What?'

'Cael was able to escape from prison, when he was being held close to the Tempest mine; and he had a bag over his head, too. Surely you can match the achievements of your brother?'

'I can't persuade people, Aunty; I lost that ability years ago. And I can't make myself invisible, either.'

'No, but you can travel without a Quadrant,' said Kelsey. 'Could you not drain some power from a dragon and transport us both out of here?'

'I'm in too much pain, Aunty,' she said. 'Ward didn't heal me properly. He closed the wound, but left the pain. In my current condition, any dragon would be able to stop me from taking their strength.'

'Oh. You're in pain? You should have said. Can you still use your dream powers, aye? Even from behind a hood?'

'I've tried. Allura is the only god in Nom Karta at the moment, but she's wearing eye guards, so not even Cael would be able to get into her mind. She's talking to the Dominion dragons about Ward's new regime.'

'Can you go into the dragons' minds and find out what they're planning?'

'What's the point? We're stuck in the deepest cellar of a dragon palace; there's nothing we can do.'

'You know, Kyra, sometimes I wonder if you're a real Holdfast. We don't give up – ever; not until we breathe our last.'

Kyra ignored the comment, but she sent out her powers all the same, despite the agony in her waist. She pushed her vision out of the dingy basement cell, and up a flight of old, stone stairs to a higher level. She passed the two rooms where Edgar and Bailey were being held, and stopped to take a quick look at both. Bailey was thrashing around on the stone floor, groaning and mumbling; while

Edgar's body was still. Kyra kept her gaze on Edgar, longing to free him from the mask nailed on to his face. Blood was seeping out from under the metal edges of the mask, and pooling beneath his dark hair. Kelsey assumed that the god was evil; but she was wrong. Edgar had made mistakes, but he had been trying his best to reach a peaceful settlement, and the war would already be over if Ward hadn't intervened.

She sensed something coming from a distant part of the palace, and hesitated. It had been a flash of vision powers, tinged with dream, and she recognised the signal instantly.

Cael. Her brother had entered the palace.

Kyra raced her vision up to the ground floor, and soared it through the long hallways of the vast dragon palace. She felt her brother use his vision again, and she surged towards his position. He was scanning that area of the building, looking for something, or someone, and she met his vision stream and intertwined with it.

Brother.

Sister. Do not try to resist us.

Us? Who are you with?

Cole and Sable. And the Empress.

The Empress is here? What does she want? Edgar is no longer in control; Ward placed him and Bailey into restrainer masks, and Kelsey and I are being held prisoner in the cellars.

We have come to end the war.

Ward will refuse to negotiate.

Who said anything about negotiating, sister? We have already obliterated the Wystians on Na Sun Ka. The gods are next.

You did what? she said.

Show me your location, and we will release you and Aunty Kelsey.

Wait. You killed the Wystians? But that's impossible. There are thousands of them.

There are now one thousand fewer than there were this morning. Show me your location.

Kyra paused. A thousand Wystians were dead? A slaughter of that magnitude appalled her, despite all the Wystians had done. She felt sick, and almost severed the connection.

I can feel your anger, sister, Cael said, *but you should feel no pity for those who killed Uncle Corthie.*

Corthie isn't dead. You're lying.

He died in my arms, after Ward and the Wystians cut him down. He died saving Blackrose. My thoughts are open to you – read them if you doubt my words.

Kyra hesitated, unable to believe her brother, but dreading to discover the truth. Could Corthie really be dead? How could the mightiest warrior on any world possibly fall to a god like Ward?

It was the Wystians, too, said Cael, in answer to her question. *Had it been Ward alone, Uncle Corthie would still be alive. Ward is also dead, you should know that. Corthie's last act was to kill him.*

No.

I'm sorry, sister. Show me your location, and we will come to you.

Kyra felt her spirit crumble, and she led Cael's vision down to the deep cellar where she and Kelsey were hooded and bound.

We will see you soon, said Cael, then he broke off the connection.

Kyra sobbed aloud, as grief enveloped her.

'Not again,' said Kelsey. 'What is it this time?'

'Uncle Corthie's dead.'

There was a long silence, then Kyra realised that she could hear Kelsey crying behind her hood.

'It was Ward,' Kyra whispered, 'but Uncle Corthie killed him before he died. I know this because Cael told me. Cael is in the palace with Cole, Sable and... and the Empress.'

'The Empress?' said Kelsey.

'Aye. They've come to free us, and to kill the gods.'

Kelsey fell into silence again.

'They'll be here soon,' Kyra went on. 'And I almost forgot to say – they killed a thousand Wystians on Na Sun Ka, for revenge.'

Kyra stopped talking, and bowed her head. Her brother and the others had also come to Nom Karta for revenge. Was that how it worked? It was fine to massacre gods, soldiers and dragons, but kill a single Holdfast, and all sense of morality collapsed? Kyra had loved Corthie, but how many were going to die in his name? They would be coming for Edgar, she realised. The avenging Holdfasts would rightly place the blame for the invasion of Na Sun Ka on to his shoulders, and their wrath would be implacable.

Her thoughts spiralled into despair. If her brother was the one to kill Edgar, she would never forgive him. Edgar had his dark thoughts, but he was trying to be better – his attempt to broker a treaty with Kelsey had proved that. Why should he be condemned for the invasion of Na Sun Ka when the Empire had already invaded the same island? It was a double standard – one rule for the Holdfasts, and another for everyone else.

She waited in silence. Kelsey did not utter another word, as Kyra listened for the sound of footsteps in the stone corridor outside their makeshift cell.

At last, she heard voices talking outside the door. Kyra used her powers to see what was happening, and she watched as the tip of a Tempest sword was rammed into the lock, and the door opened. Cael stood in the entrance, silhouetted by the dim lamplight coming from the corridor, a Fated Blade in his right hand. He sheathed it, then he walked over to Kyra, and removed her hood. Sable went over to Kelsey, and did the same, then the prisoners' bonds were cut, and their hands were freed. Kelsey reached out and embraced Sable, who held her close.

'My Herald,' said the Empress, as she approached Kelsey from the doorway. 'I cannot tell you how relieved I am to see you alive.'

Kelsey broke away from Sable and wiped the tears from her face. Thorn walked up to her and placed a hand onto her shoulder.

'Is it true?' said Kelsey. 'Is my brother dead?'

'It is true,' said the Empress, 'and I would have succumbed to despair if you had also been taken from us.'

Kelsey got to her feet. 'And the thousand Wystians?'

'Also true,' said Thorn. 'I intend to kill the rest once we have dealt with the gods and dragons of Nom Karta.'

'It was you, wasn't it, Your Majesty? You killed the Wystians.'

'It was I.'

Kelsey nodded. 'I'm glad.'

Kyra got to her feet. The pain flared in her abdomen and she staggered, but, in the shadows of the dark cell, none of the others seemed to notice.

'Does the death of a thousand dragons make you glad, Aunty?' she said.

'Those dragons slaughtered tens of thousands of people on Na Sun Ka,' said Kelsey, 'and then they helped Ward kill my brother. Damn fucking right I'm glad.' She turned back to Thorn. 'Thank you for rescuing me, but now I am nothing but a liability. My blocking abilities will stop you from killing Allura, who is the only god currently in Nom Karta.'

'I can kill Allura,' said Sable, 'if Kyra removes the blocks in my mind.'

Kyra said nothing, a hand leaning against a wall of the cell to support her.

'Will you do it, sister?' said Cael.

Kelsey eyed her. 'Allura helped Ward place the restrainer mask onto Edgar's face, Kyra. Let Sable be Sable again. Let her take care of Allura.'

'I have conditions,' said Kyra.

'Go on,' said Thorn.

'If I do this, then you must promise to release Edgar and Bailey from their masks, and you must promise not to hurt them in any way. Edgar had negotiated a peace treaty with Kelsey, just before Ward's coup.'

'Is this true, Herald?' said Thorn.

'Aye, Your Majesty. I recited a list of conditions that I didn't think Edgar would accept, but... he agreed to them all. I was about to bring those terms to you when Ward intervened. The other gods took great exception to what Edgar was proposing; well, apart from Bailey.'

'You don't have the authority to sign any peace treaty, Kelsey,' said Sable.

'And I told Edgar that,' she said. 'I told him that the Empress would have to agree; but I also told him that I would present the terms in good faith. Edgar is... an odd character. I think his mind was seriously damaged by so many millennia in a mask. I also think that Kyra and Edgar might have fallen for each other.'

'I do not love Edgar,' said Kyra.

'But you have feelings for him?' said Thorn.

'I... I don't know. There is something in him, something good. I can sense it. He's not insane, no matter what Kelsey says, but he is... troubled.'

'I accept your terms,' said Thorn. 'We will release Edgar and Bailey, and we shall not execute them. As for the terms of any treaty, I reserve the right to make up my own mind about that. Now, remove Sable's blocks.'

Kyra glanced at the others. Of all who stood before her, only Cole had remained silent. Instead of talking, her cousin had stood listening in silence. Cole had always been the voice of moderation and reason, and she wondered if he might prove to be an ally to her.

'What do you think, Cole?' she said.

'I think you should remove Sable's blocks,' he said, 'and then I think you and Kelsey should remain down here, while we go back upstairs and kill everyone in Nom Karta apart from Edgar and Bailey.'

Kyra's spirits fell further. Was everyone so consumed by vengeance that they had lost sight of their humanity? She glanced at Sable, went into her mind, and dissolved the blocks.

'It's done,' she said.

Sable took a slow breath, then she unbuckled her sword and offered it to Cael.

'My Fated Blade, if you please,' she said.

Cael nodded, and they exchanged weapons.

Kyra walked out of the cell, and the others followed her along the passageway. The pain in her waist flared, and she placed a hand against a wall to stop herself from falling.

'Are you injured?' said Cael. 'Why didn't you say?'

'She was stabbed by a demigod while Edgar was being overthrown,' said Kelsey.

'If you are in pain,' said the Empress, 'then will you allow me to heal you, Kyra?'

Kyra glanced up and met the Empress's gaze. Part of her wanted to refuse the offer of assistance, but if she did so, then she wasn't sure that she would be able to climb the stairs to Edgar's cell.

'I would be grateful if you could heal me, Your Majesty,' she said.

Thorn placed a hand onto her arm, and Kyra's felt a sudden rush of well-being surge through her body and, within seconds, the pain had gone. Kyra closed her eyes for a moment, panting in relief.

'Thank you,' she said. 'Follow me.'

Kyra led them up a flight of stairs, and into a long hallway with storerooms running down one side. She pointed at two doors.

'Edgar and Bailey are in there,' she said. 'I warn you – if either of them are harmed, I will place blocks into each of your heads; blocks that I shall never remove.'

The other Holdfasts looked at her, and Kyra sensed that even Cael no longer respected her.

Cole glanced along the deserted corridor, as Sable approached the first cell door. 'Where is everyone?' he said. 'Is the palace deserted?'

'There are humans in the other wings of the palace,' said Kyra, 'but many fled or were killed in the recent civil war among the Dominion dragons.'

'What about the Dominion soldiers?' said Cole.

'There are Bullan regiments up on the outer walls of Nom Karta,' said Kyra, 'but few enter the palaces. Why? Do you want to kill all of them, too?'

Sable opened the door leading into a cell and walked inside, as the others watched from the entrance. Sable crouched by the body of Bailey, and removed the restrainer mask from his face. Bailey flailed around in agony, and Sable held him down as she disconnected the metal pins keeping his chains in place.

When Bailey had been freed, Sable got to her feet and went to the other door. It, too, had not been locked, and she opened it. Kyra pushed past her and entered the makeshift cell. She knelt down by Edgar's still form. He looked at peace, despite the blood trickling down each side of his face. She reached behind his head, her fingers moving through Edgar's blood-coated hair, and unbuckled the mask's thick leather strap. She gripped on to the front of the mask, and pulled it from his face. She gazed down at the two bloody eye sockets, and felt a mixture of sympathy and revulsion. She wiped some of the blood from the god's cheeks, then Sable came in and started to remove Edgar's shackles.

'What will we do with them?' said Cael.

'Nothing,' said Thorn. 'We have given our word to your sister.'

'How long will it take for them to recover?' said Cole.

'A few days, maybe,' said Sable, as she loosened the chains. 'It depends if we give them any salve, or if we use healing powers on them.'

'We have no salve with us,' said Thorn, 'and I shall not be using my powers on them. They are gods; their self-healing will preserve them. I will need all of my powers for what we are about to do when we meet Allura and the Dominion dragons.'

'Your powers will be useless if I'm with you,' said Kelsey. 'Sable won't be able to deal with several dragons, even with her blocks removed.'

'We will not leave you alone down here, Herald,' said Thorn.

'I have the Quadrant I took from Belfar,' said Cael.

'Take it, Kelsey,' said the Empress. 'Take it, and return to Colsbury. Your children will be happy to see you, and you can inform Lucius and Shella of what has been happening here. We shall follow you, after we have destroyed the Dominion leadership.'

Cael held out his Quadrant, and Kelsey stared at it.

'I don't want to abandon you all,' she said.

'You won't be abandoning us,' said Thorn. 'You will be holding the reins of the Empire until we return. Ensure that Yearning remains strong and resolute – it is now the front line against the Wystians.'

Kelsey took the Quadrant. 'Maybe I should take Kyra with me.'

Kyra glanced up from Edgar's side. 'I'm not leaving Nom Karta,' she said. 'If you take me back, I shall flee. I don't need a Quadrant to travel, not now that the pain has gone.'

'Return alone, Kelsey,' said Thorn. 'Rule in my stead until we have finished our work here.'

Kelsey nodded. She wiped a tear from her face, triggered the Quadrant, and vanished.

Kyra got to her feet. She gazed down at Edgar, then she walked out of the cell.

'I beg you, Your Majesty,' she said, 'do not wantonly destroy the dragons of the Dominion. They were acting to defend their land – land that was taken from them by the Empire. Instead, I ask that you accept the treaty negotiated by Edgar and Kelsey – a treaty that would lead to a lasting peace.'

'Our enemies threw away any chance of peace when they killed Corthie,' said Thorn. 'The dragons of the Dominion allied themselves to those who massacred tens of thousands upon Na Sun Ka; they chose their own course, and now they shall pay.'

The others began to move towards the stairs, and Kyra kept up with them.

'The dragons will burn you all,' she said.

'They won't,' said Sable. 'Cole will deflect their flames. Besides, we will be invisible.'

'Scout ahead, Cael,' said the Empress. 'Find out where the queen of the Dominion is, and tell us how many dragons are in her company.'

Cael nodded, then his eyes glazed over as they walked.

'This is wrong,' said Kyra. 'Please don't do this. Kill Allura if you must; she was one of those who helped place Edgar and Bailey into the restrainer masks, but spare the dragons. The Dominion has just recovered from an awful civil war; there will be chaos if the royal family is wiped out.'

The others ignored her, then Cael's eyes cleared.

'Queen Famula is in the main audience chamber,' he said, 'along with Allura and around two dozen other dragons and a handful of human servants.'

'Take us there,' said Thorn.

Cael tilted his head, and they ascended another flight of stairs. Kyra caught up with her brother as they reached a dragon-sized hallway.

'You know this is wrong, Cael,' she said. 'What happened to Uncle Corthie was terrible, but this is revenge for the sake of revenge, and nothing good will come of it. All you are doing is adding to the misery and suffering of the known worlds. The Aucterians are not too different from us; they were only trying to defend their lands from the Empress. They are ready for peace, but if you do this, the war will never end.'

Cael shook his head. 'The Wystians...'

'The Dominion aren't the Wystians, brother,' she said. 'Not a single Dominion dragon has even met a damn Wystian.'

'They sheltered the gods who planned and carried out the invasion of Na Sun Ka.'

'And for that they must all die?' said Kyra.

Cael came to a halt, then he gestured towards a large, arched opening. 'The audience chamber is through there, Your Majesty,' he said.

The group quietened as they gazed at the tall entrance. The sound of dragons talking echoed through, along with the voice of a woman.

'Make us invisible, Cael,' said Thorn.

Cael nodded. 'It is done.'

Thorn turned to Kyra. 'Do not try to stop us,' she said. 'If you do, then I will consider our agreement to be at an end, and Edgar and Bailey will die.'

'Please, Your Majesty,' said Kyra. 'You have already destroyed the Wystian invasion forces; how much vengeance is enough?'

'For Corthie,' she said, 'there is no limit to what I am prepared to do. We loved, and we have lost. I, the Empress, the Holder of the Worlds, will bathe this day in the blood of our fallen enemies; and I shall relent only when the safety of the Empire has been secured. Love is guiding my actions, not hate; love for Corthie, and love for the people over whom I rule.' She glanced at the others. 'Are you ready to follow your Empress into the abyss?'

Cael and Cole nodded, and Sable drew her Fated Blade. Thorn led the way towards the opening, and Kyra followed them. She knew she could attempt to interfere in Cael's invisibility powers; she could make Famula and the others immune from her brother's vision, and from Thorn's soulwitch abilities, but then it would be her family dying, instead of the dragons of the Dominion. Those dragons were cruel and arrogant, and they governed the Dominion as though they were infallible gods, but did that make them worthy of death? Were they irredeemable? And what price would the Holdfasts pay if they carried out another massacre? Annihilating the Wystians on Na Sun Ka could be seen as an act of war, but the slaughter of the Dominion leadership would be nothing more than an atrocity, one that would stain the name of the Holdfasts for all time.

They entered the great audience chamber. Queen Famula was sitting on a massive heap of cushions and blankets, while Abda and Saphben, her chief advisors, were flanking her. Twenty other dragons were assembled in the hall, including the purple dragon who had escorted Kyra, Larron and Achan to Nom Karta. Lady Sigra Min Sigmund, the granddaughter of Lord Sigel, was keeping to the shadows at the rear of the hall, sidelined and ignored by the royal family. Allura was also present, and she was going over Lord Ward's plans for the continuation of the war.

'The invasion of the Star Continent is now our main aim,' Allura was saying. 'As soon as Dragon Eyre has been pacified, we shall move into the heart of the Empire. For this, we shall require foot soldiers, and the Dominion can supply them, Your Majesty.'

Famula's eyes glowed. 'You wish us to send Aucterian soldiers to another world, god?'

'There are several divisions of Banner soldiers upon the Doomed Worlds, Your Majesty,' said Allura, 'but not enough to conquer and occupy the Star Continent. Besides, Lord Ward wishes to use the

Banner forces to seize the salve mine, which lies upon another world. Could the Dominion spare one hundred thousand soldiers? What about the Bullan?'

'The Bullan are engaged in a great rebellion,' said Abda, 'and many no longer obey our orders. The Dominion cannot afford to divert so many soldiers, not while we face threats from the Bullan and the Gunstian Empire. We would be left undefended.'

Invisible to their sight, Thorn walked up to Allura, and placed an unseen hand on to the god's arm. Allura screamed, and fell to her knees, as her flesh began to wither.

'What is this?' cried Saphben 'Who is doing this?'

Thorn stepped back, her eyes lit with the power she had taken from Allura, and the god's lifeless body collapsed to the floor. Thorn raised her right hand, her gaze upon the queen of the Dominion. Several dragons reared up, their jaws opening. They couldn't see Thorn or the others, but they could sense that someone was there. One of the dragons unleashed her flames upon the general area where Thorn was standing, and Cole raised his hand, and the fires were deflected to the side.

'The Holdfasts are here!' shouted another dragon. 'Flee!'

Thorn pointed at Queen Famula, but nothing happened, then every dragon in the hall closed their eyes and collapsed to the ground, unconscious. The floor of the hall trembled and shook, then Thorn turned to Kyra.

'It wasn't me!' Kyra cried. 'I did nothing.'

The air crackled, and Karalyn appeared in front of them, her eyes wet with tears, and with a barely-controlled rage written on her features.

She stared at Thorn. 'You have done enough.'

'Don't stop me,' said the Empress.

'I am not stopping you,' said Karalyn; 'I am saving you from yourself.'

'But, Mother...' said Cael.

'Silence,' said Karalyn. 'You asked me to intervene, and here I am.

Look at what your wars have done. My brother is dead, and for what? In the name of Corthie, I am bringing this conflict to an end. There shall be peace, and I shall enforce it.' She glanced at Sable. 'You, I forgive. You know no other way to act, Sable, and I have another job that I am entrusting to you. Go.'

Karalyn pointed at Sable, and she vanished.

'As for the rest of you,' Karalyn went on, 'I am disappointed, but not surprised.' She gestured to the floor by her left, and Bailey and Edgar appeared, still unconscious. Karalyn raised her hand, and the wounds on the faces of the gods began to heal. She gestured to her right, and Kelsey appeared, along with Laverne and Elmhirst. The two gods stared at their new surroundings, and raised their hands in panic.

'I have blocked your powers,' said Karalyn; 'just as I have blocked the powers of everyone else in this hall.' She pointed ahead of her, and Queen Blackrose appeared with Maddie standing next to her. 'Now, Sable; do it now,' she said, then she turned to the Dominion dragons, and Famula, Abda and Saphben opened their eyes.

'I compel you all to listen to my words,' Karalyn said, as the assembled crowd stared at her. 'I have removed your powers, and rendered you all unable to attack each other. I have also commanded Sable to use the Sextant to transfer every last Wystian to World Three, where they will be safe, and where Dragon Eyre will be safe from them. Sable has done so. I shall give you one hour to negotiate an end to this war. If you are unable to reach an agreement in that time, I will exile you all to a world from which there will be no return, and you can kill each other there.'

Karalyn steadied her gaze, her eyes piercing everyone gathered around her. 'Long have I tried to stay out of the affairs of the known worlds; long have I resisted the temptation to interfere in the lives of others, but you have pushed me too far. My brother did not die for nothing. His sacrifice shall be the foundation upon which I shall build a lasting peace. You have one hour – use it well.'

The air crackled, and Karalyn disappeared.

'The Demon Witch,' gasped Saphben. 'The Demon Witch has returned.'

'She has gone,' cried Abda, 'but our enemies remain.'

She lifted her claws to strike Thorn, and Blackrose raised her own forelimbs to defend the Empress. Abda lashed out, then she screamed in agony and rolled on to her side.

The others in the hall watched as Abda's pain began to subside.

'Did you not hear my mother?' cried Cael. 'None of us are able to attack each other, and none of our powers will work. She is watching us; I can feel it.'

'Then we had better get to work,' said Kelsey, walking into the centre of the hall. She reached Thorn, whose eyes remained defiant. 'Your Majesty,' Kelsey went on, 'do I have your permission to negotiate a treaty with Edgar and the Dominion, on behalf of the Empire?'

Thorn said nothing. Kyra ran over to Edgar, whose eyes had healed.

'You did something to my head, Kyra,' he said; 'something that shielded my mind from the horrors of the mask. I shall never forget it.'

She gazed back at him. 'Will you now help end this war, Edgar?'

He nodded, then she held out her hand and helped him stand.

'I am ready to negotiate with the Empire,' Edgar said.

'You are not in charge of us,' said Elmhirst.

'Ward is dead,' said Kelsey, 'as are Allura and Belfar. You two are only alive because you didn't help Ward overthrow Edgar.'

'And the Wystians?' said Blackrose. 'Have they gone; have they been exiled from Dragon Eyre?'

'If that's what Karalyn told us,' said Kelsey, 'then it's true.'

'The Demon Witch is a Holdfast,' said Famula. 'We cannot trust any agreement brokered by her. The murderer of King Gahad my father is treacherous and wicked.'

'My mother just saved your life, Queen of the Dominion,' said Kyra, 'and I plead with you to take heed of her words. If we fail to come together to make peace, none of us will see our homes again.'

'Let us negotiate,' said Blackrose, as she eyed the dragons from the Dominion. 'Queen to queen; Empress to god.'

Kelsey turned back to Thorn. 'Your Majesty?

Thorn lowered her gaze.

'How can we agree to something that will satisfy everyone?' said Saphben.

'I have a few ideas about that,' said Kelsey; 'ideas that Edgar and I have already discussed. This is what Corthie would have wanted. Let's do it for him. My sister was right – let his death mean more than revenge and retribution; let it also lead us to peace.'

Thorn gazed at her hands.

'I have killed over a thousand dragons today,' she said, 'and yet the pain of losing Corthie has not lessened. Karalyn did not save only the Queen of the Dominion; by stopping me, I have also been saved. Herald, negotiate a peace with our enemies, a peace that leaves the Empire secure; a peace that ends the killing; and a peace that honours the name of your brother.'

Kelsey tilted her head, then she walked up to Edgar and extended her hand. Edgar stared at it for a moment, then he took it.

'For your brother,' he said.

Kelsey held his gaze. 'For all of us.'

CHAPTER 30
A PLACE TO REST

Marchside, Kell – 4th Day, Second Third Summer 545

Cael and Arrosa waited their turn, as blustery rain swept across the hillside next to Clackenbaird Farm. The sun was shining down through a gap in the clouds, and the wet, green landscape was glistening in its light. Ahead of Cael, Kelsey was leading Calpurnia and Caelius to the top of the slope, where each deposited a stone onto the large cairn. Kelsey bowed her head and whispered a few words, then she escorted her children away, their hair blowing in the wind.

Cael and Arrosa moved to let them pass, then they climbed the rough track to the summit. The hill chosen for Corthie's tomb had a view that encompassed the surrounding slopes and glens. To the right, the farmhouse was visible, and then the large buildings that were clustered by the hill of Marchbrae, while, in the distance, lay the town of Marchside, capital of Kell. Cael gazed at the view, then he placed his stone onto the large cairn. Arrosa did the same, and they took each other's hand.

'What were his last words?' said Arrosa.

Cael didn't need to look into his memories to find the answer. He had replayed the death of his uncle hundreds of times since the battle, and every detail had been inscribed into his mind.

'He said, *What a fucking place to die.*'

'And what a place to be laid to rest,' said Arrosa. 'His children will see this cairn every time they step outside.'

They turned, and gave way to Chief Kallie, who looked strong despite her advancing years. The old chief of the Kell placed her stone onto the cairn, then she walked down the slope with Cael and Arrosa, as Maddie and Rosie made their way up. Over a hundred people were gathered at the base of the hill. Aila was there, with her seven children, and Karalyn was next to her with her two youngest children. King Daniel and Queen Emily were with Van Logos, while the Empress was standing close by, flanked by the members of her Imperial Court. Aila and the Empress had exchanged barely a word since the imperial party had arrived in Clackenbaird for the funeral of Corthie, and, from the dark glances of some of her children, it was clear that more than one of them blamed the Empress for their father's death. Four dragons were in attendance – Blackrose, Frostback, Halfclaw and Sigum, and Lahnos had also made the journey, bringing Ora'lya and his infant son. The Empress had released him from her service. The wars were over, and Lahnos was once more a free man.

Cael and Arrosa went to stand next to the Empress and Kelsey, and Cairney looked over from Aila's side to give them a glance that was filled with anger and disdain. Cael didn't mind; the boy had lost his father – he was entitled to be angry about it.

Naxor and Caelius Logos returned down the slope after placing their stones upon the cairn. Caelius retook his place with the rest of the Imperial Court, but Naxor held back a little. The demigod glanced at Aila, then he bowed in front of the Empress.

'With your permission, Your Majesty,' Naxor said, 'I hereby resign as Chamberlain of the Empire. I intend to remain here, in Kell, to help my cousin raise her children.'

'I thank you for your service,' said Thorn, 'and I accept your resignation. You have chosen an honourable course, and I am sure that you will be a great help to Lady Aila, as well as a source of comfort.'

Naxor bowed again, then he walked over to stand with the Marchbrae Holdfasts.

The Empress nodded to Kelsey. 'You know what to do.'

Kelsey bowed, then she eyed Cael. 'With me,' she said.

Cael followed Kelsey into the crowd of onlookers and mourners, then they stopped when they reached Brogan and Bedig, who were standing amid a large group of Kellach.

'Lady Brogan,' said Kelsey.

Brogan's eyes tightened.

'You and your brother have served the Imperial Court for many years,' Kelsey went on, 'and your brother continues to serve as Lord Marshal.'

'What do you want, Kelsey?' said Brogan. 'Are you here to apologise for taking my role as Herald?'

'I am here to offer you the role of Chamberlain of the Empire,' said Kelsey. 'We have missed your presence in the court, Brogan. Perhaps the role of Herald was unsuited to your talents, but I think you would make a great chamberlain.'

'But Naxor...'

'Naxor has resigned. He plans to remain here, in Clackenbaird.'

'You should accept, sister,' said Bedig. 'Kelsey had nothing to do with your dismissal.'

'I would also like you to train Cael in the workings of the imperial government,' Kelsey went on. 'He has proved himself.'

Brogan glanced at Cael, then she took a long breath and nodded. 'Thank you, Kelsey. I would be honoured and proud to serve.'

Kelsey tilted her head, then she led Cael back towards the Empress.

'I'm to be trained?' Cael said.

'Aye,' said Kelsey. 'One day, you might earn a position in the court. I read the Empress's letter, the one she left in case she died while fighting the Wystians. Your name featured prominently.'

'The Empress is wrong about me,' he said. 'I'm not the right person to ever become an emperor. I'm stubborn, and I have a tendency to disregard orders.'

'I am well aware of that,' Kelsey said. 'Do you know who else was stubborn, and who often disobeyed the commands of her Empress? Daphne, my mother. You remind me of her, in a way that I occasionally find a little disconcerting. You are as ruthless as Sable, and as brave as Corthie, and I can think of no better successor. That's all in the future, but. We have a long way to go before then.'

They reached the Empress, and Kelsey gave her a slight nod.

'Will you speak, Kelsey?' said Thorn. 'I fear my words will only be divisive. I think Aila and her children hold me responsible for Corthie's death.'

'Their emotions are still raw, Your Majesty,' Kelsey said.

'Nevertheless, I do not wish to exacerbate their suffering.'

Kelsey glanced at the hillside. The last of the mourners had returned down the slope, and there was no one left to ascend. She tilted her head, then she took a few steps forward. The crowd turned to look at her, and Kelsey waited until the silence was complete.

'There was no one like my brother,' Kelsey said, as the rain started again. 'No one more loved; no one more feared. He was also forgiving. I was cruel to Corthie when we were children. He was too good, too pure, and I hurt him as a way to hurt my father. I am ashamed of how I behaved, but that is not the reason I am telling you this. When I went to Lostwell to find Corthie, I wanted to speak to him, to tell him that I was sorry. I had no right to expect anything from him, but you all know what he was like. He forgave me, and a friendship grew between us that was worth more to me than I can put into words. Rest in peace, little brother; I miss you.'

Kelsey bowed her head and Karalyn stepped forward, as the rain intensified.

'I want to say something,' Karalyn said. 'I echo my sister's words, but I wish to add to them. Each one of us knows that Corthie yearned for a peaceful life. We all know that he wanted to live out his days here, with Aila and their children. Corthie was a warrior, but he was also a farmer, a husband, and a father. If Ward hadn't attacked Clackenbaird, then Corthie would still be here, but I do not wish to apportion any blame.'

Her glance passed over the Empress for the briefest of moments. 'Instead, I want to remind everyone that Corthie's death has been avenged in the best way possible – by the agreement of a treaty between the Empire and the Dominion; an agreement that will ensure peace between the two sides, and an agreement that I hereby pledge to enforce. If either side breaks their oaths, I shall descend in wrath to deliver just punishment – I swear this by the memory of my brother, and in his name I shall keep the peace, for now and evermore.'

Thunder rumbled in the distance, as the crowd stared at Karalyn through the rain. Cael looked into his mother's eyes, and saw the pain and the determination within her, and, for the first time in his life, he feared her.

The crowd began to disperse. Aila was holding a wake in the huge, sprawling farmhouse of Clackenbaird, and many of the mourners began to make their way up the gentle slope towards it. Aila glanced at the Empress, and approached her, her children and Naxor following.

'Empress,' said Aila.

'Lady Aila,' said Thorn.

'There are many things I wish to say,' Aila went on, 'but I shall not utter them. I suspect you already know what is in my heart, Your Majesty. I always knew my time with Corthie would be short. In the centuries to come, I might even be glad that I did not have to witness his decline into old age; that, in my memories of him, he will always be young; but that time lies far into the future. Right now, all I feel is anger.' She glanced down, and placed a hand on to her waist. 'Our eighth child lives within me, a child that will never see their father, and for that child I shall have to be strong.'

'You're pregnant?' said Arrosa, her eyes widening.

Aila's gaze flickered over to Cael and Arrosa, but she ignored them.

'I will not bring my children up to hate you, Thorn,' she said to the Empress; 'for it is pointless for immortal gods to hate those doomed to die; but know this – when you mortals have all passed from this world, my children and I will still be here, and we will never forget.'

Aila turned, and led her children up the track towards the farmhouse. Naxor eyed the Empress for a moment, then he bowed his head and went after his cousin.

'That was uncalled for,' said Caelius Logos.

'Aila has every right to be angry,' said Thorn. 'I think we should take our leave and return to Colsbury. We shall achieve nothing by attending the wake; let them mourn their loss without reminding them of how their loss came to pass.'

'I think that would be wise,' said Karalyn. 'I shall let Aila know.' She glanced at Cardova, who was carrying Caitlyn, and holding on to Carden's hand. 'Take the children to Colsbury, Lucius. I shall return after the wake.'

'I shall travel with the Empress,' said Blackrose. 'There is no room in the farmhouse for dragons, and I wish to speak to Edgar.'

'Then let us depart,' said the Empress.

Sable took out her Quadrant, and Kelsey did the same. They both swiped at the same time, and the imperial party appeared in the bright sunshine of Colsbury Castle, between the keeps and the Summer Palace. The two Quadrants had brought all four dragons back, along with every member of the Imperial Court, and a few others who had been with them. Cael shook the rain from his hair, then he glanced up and saw Edgar, Bailey and Kyra looking down at them from the middle balcony of the palace.

'Let's meet up one hour from now,' said Kelsey, 'so we can get dried and changed into fresh clothes. The Empress requires all members of the Imperial Court to attend the signing. Cael and Arrosa – you will also be there. Dismissed.'

Cael watched as Thorn and Kelsey walked towards the palace together. The Empress's head was bowed after the confrontation with Aila, and Cael could almost feel the heavy burden that she was carrying.

'Aila spoke no lies,' said Arrosa.

'Of course she didn't,' said Sable, 'but she was wrong to blame the Empress. Many of us were at fault, myself included.'

'Where did you put the Wystians?' said Cael.

'On to World Three.'

'I know that, but where? There are humans living on that world.'

'I chose an uninhabited location,' Sable said, 'with forests, rivers and mountains. It's a far nicer place than Rigga. The Wystians will be fine.'

They started to walk towards the palace.

'Where is the Sextant?' said Cael.

Sable smiled. 'Do you think your mother would have left that knowledge in my head, Cael? I arrived, somewhere, did as she asked, and then Karalyn removed my memories of where I had been. For a few brief moments, I had every world under my power. I almost felt like a god.'

'There is only one god now,' said Arrosa; 'and her name is Karalyn Holdfast.'

An hour later, Cael and Arrosa walked out on to the middle balcony, where a long table had been placed. Cael had half-expected to see most of the Imperial Court there, but, apart from Kyra, Bailey and Edgar, the balcony was deserted.

Kyra turned, her hands clasped by her waist. 'How was it?'

'We each climbed a hill, and laid a stone upon Uncle Corthie's cairn,' said Cael. 'It's a shame that you couldn't be there.'

'I was visiting Larron's parents in Plateau City,' she said.

'You could have done that afterwards.'

Kyra said nothing.

'I am very sorry for your loss, Cael,' said Edgar. 'We saw the Empress and the others arrive with you. Does this mean that the Empire is ready to confirm the treaty?'

'The Empress is ready, and I am ready,' came a great voice from the forecourt.

They turned, and were faced with Blackrose, whose height allowed her to peer down at the humans on the balcony.

Edgar tilted his head. 'Greetings, Queen of the Eastern Rim.'

'Greetings, Lord of the Doomed Worlds and of the Dominion,' said Blackrose. 'Once, we were foes; now, we are at peace. While we stood by the cairn, Karalyn issued a warning to us all. She swore to bring down retribution on any who break the terms of our agreement.'

'We fully intend to keep our side of the bargain,' said Bailey. 'The Empire will sell us salve in return for Tempest, and we will each have our separate spheres of influence.'

'What about you, sister?' said Cael.

Kyra narrowed her eyes. 'What about me?'

'I was hoping to persuade you to stay here,' Cael said. 'The wars are over, and you could rebuild your life upon the Star Continent.'

'I doubt the Empress would agree.'

'She would, if you asked her,' said Cael. 'Just think – you could return to university.'

Kyra lowered her gaze, then she shook her head. 'No, brother,' she said. 'I want to stay with Edgar on Inopei. I... we... I want to try a life with Edgar; he...'

'I am in love with your sister, Cael,' said Edgar.

Cael narrowed his eyes. 'She is a mortal, and you are a god.'

'Did not Aila love Corthie?' said Edgar. 'I am aware of the price I will pay, but we want to try. I am no longer the god I once was. I feel... born again, as though I were young. Perhaps it is the salve that has changed me, or perhaps it was the millennia trapped within Edmond's mask.'

'He spoke no lies, Cael,' said Arrosa. 'He loves her.'

'There is a certain balance to this,' said Blackrose. 'Each of Karalyn's dream mage children has picked a different side, while their mother watches from above.'

'And what of the Eastern Rim?' said Edgar.

Blackrose gazed off into the distance for a moment. 'We shall join the Empire,' she said. 'I shall remain queen, and the Eastern Rim will continue to run its own affairs, but I now accept that my realm cannot defend itself against a determined enemy, such have been our losses. Only within the embrace of the Empire will my people be allowed to flourish in peace. As for the Western Rim, it is too early to say. Without the Wystians, the Unk Tannic will shrivel and die. In time, perhaps, all of Dragon Eyre might join with the Sapphire Throne.'

'Then the Empress has truly won,' said Kyra. 'She wanted the Star Continent united; she wanted the City of Salve and Dragon Eyre – and now she has it all.'

'She doesn't have everything,' said Edgar. 'The Dominion and the Doomed Worlds are ours, forever. The entire eastern half of Athumia falls into our new domains, a place where the gods and mortals from the Doomed Worlds might at last find somewhere to settle.'

'Are you going to pull out of the Doomed Worlds?' said Cael.

'Not entirely,' said Edgar. 'There are many productive mines on several of the worlds, but we shall maintain the smallest of presences. The vast majority of those living there will be resettled in Aucteran.'

Bailey smiled. 'While I get to hold on to my house on Zamata.'

'It's not a house; it's a monastery,' said Kelsey, as she led the others from the Imperial Court out on to the balcony.

The Empress was wearing a sapphire dress, and a slender crown sat upon her brow. Edgar and Blackrose tilted their heads in Thorn's direction, then the Empress sat by the long table, while the others gathered round. Kelsey gestured to Shella, and the Imperial Chancellor unrolled a large document, which she laid down onto the table in front of the Empress.

'Some of the ink is still wet,' Shella said, 'but everything we agreed has been inscribed upon this treaty. Bailey's home upon Zamata shall be the designated location to sort out any squabbles we might have; the island shall remain neutral and independent, and under the protection of both the Dominion and the Empire. As custodian of Zamata Gataza, Bailey will be responsible for distributing Serpent Eye jewels to both sides, as long as the terms of the treaty are being met. Agreed?'

Edgar nodded. 'Agreed.'

'The treaty has also been amended,' Shella went on, 'to mark the fact that the Eastern Rim will be joining the Empire.' She glanced at Blackrose, who tilted her head.

'I have no objections,' said Edgar.

'I think that was the last of the changes,' said Shella.

'What about Professor Achan?' said Kelsey. 'He is a wanted fugitive, and I believe he is hiding in a palace in Nom Karta.'

'Achan has expressed a desire to remain in the Dominion,' said Edgar.

'Then I pardon him,' said the Empress. 'I shall not allow one misguided man to disrupt our agreement. You may keep Achan.'

Edgar tilted his head. 'And the Sextant?'

'That remains with Karalyn,' said Kelsey. 'My sister has made it clear that she will allow neither side to use it, or to learn of its location. We are also to stay clear of World Three. Karalyn will not permit any interference in the lives of the Wystian dragons now dwelling there.'

'And the other dragons?' said Bailey. 'The dragons of the Dominion and the dragons of the Eastern and Western Rims have suffered grievous losses over the last few decades. I am already being asked by some in Nom Karta if there might be opportunities for marriages of alliance to be formed between the two worlds. There are great-grandchildren of King Gahad who are struggling to find mates.'

'I shall consider this,' said Blackrose. 'In truth, the dragons of my realm are also curious to meet those from the Dominion, despite the differences in our habits and traditions. Tell the dragons of the Dominion that I am not opposed to a future where our two kinds might meet without rancour.'

'Thank you, Your Majesty,' said Bailey.

'If that is all,' said Kelsey, 'then I think we are ready to sign.'

When it was all over, Bailey withdrew a Quadrant, while Edgar and Kyra moved to stand next to him.

'Will I see you again, sister?' said Cael.

'Our lives have diverged, brother,' she said, 'and each of us is where they are meant to be. Think of me on our birthday, and I will think of you.'

Cael looked away as Bailey swiped the Quadrant, taking Edgar and Kyra with him. He put a hand to his eyes.

'My mother was right,' he said. 'Kyra is lost to us.'

'She was lost to us a long time ago,' said Kelsey, 'but things change. You were once lost to us, and now you are the Empress's favoured successor.'

Cael glanced up, and saw the faces looking at him. Despite his heartache at the sight of his sister leaving the Star Continent, he controlled his emotions. For some reason he couldn't quite fathom, the Imperial Court and the Holdfasts had decided to place their faith in him. To them, he was the hope for the future; but he had no desire for power and the responsibility that came with it; no desire to do anything but find somewhere quiet to be with his wife.

Kelsey smiled at him. 'Give the idea some time to bed in,' she said. 'The Empress shall be on the Sapphire Throne for a long time to come.'

Thorn gazed at her court. 'And you will ensure that I continue to earn my position,' she said; 'for there is no greater honour than to serve the people of the Empire.' She stood. 'There is much to be done, but I shall excuse Cael and Arrosa for a few days. Go, and enjoy yourselves, and return when you are ready to start work. Claudian, give Cael his new Quadrant, if you please.'

Cael and Arrosa bowed, then Claudian stepped forward, and handed a Quadrant to Cael.

'Don't do anything too reckless with it,' he said.

Cael smiled. 'When would I ever do anything reckless, Adjutant?'

Claudian narrowed his eyes, then Cael swiped the Quadrant, and the air shimmered. Cael and Arrosa appeared on the rear porch of the mansion on the Hold Fast estate. Cole, Celine, Lahnos and Ora'lya were already there, sitting in the shade of the unrelenting sun.

'Look who it is,' said Lahnos, 'the future Emperor and Empress of the Allied Worlds.'

'Empress?' said Arrosa, her eyes narrowing.

'Are you claiming that it's never occurred to you, Arrosa?' said

Lahnos. 'The wife of an Emperor is the Empress. Who will be your Herald?'

'This is all hypothetical,' said Cael, as he and Arrosa sat. 'We're talking about something that lies decades into the future. A thousand things could happen between now and then. And, need I remind you, Lahnos, that the next Emperor or Empress has to be voted for by the Council of Electors? An endorsement from the current Empress means nothing.'

Lahnos laughed. 'If you say so. Who will be your Herald?'

Cael laughed back at him. 'That's easy – it'll be Cole.'

'Yeah, right,' said Cole.

'Iced tea?' said Celine.

'In a minute, thanks,' said Cael, getting back to his feet. 'I have something I want to show Arrosa first.' He glanced at Cole. 'Did you arrange it for me?'

'I did,' said Cole. 'Go into the old cloakroom by the fountain.'

Cael smiled at him. 'You see? Excellent Herald material.'

Cael led Arrosa off the porch, and they entered the cool hallways of the mansion.

'What are you going to show me?' she said.

'You'll have to wait and see,' said Cael. 'So, winter here, summer on Colsbury, and the rest of the time in Plateau City?'

'What about Kell?'

'I'm not sure that would be a good idea any more,' he said. 'I am one of those that Aila and her children blame for Uncle Corthie's death.'

'That's not fair,' said Arrosa. 'It wasn't your fault.'

'It's difficult to argue with grief,' he said. 'Let's take it slowly with the Marchbrae Holdfasts.'

'Is that what we're calling them? What are we?'

'I don't know. The Colsbury Holdfasts? It's going to take time to heal the wounds that have divided us.'

They came to the fountain that sat in the centre of a junction of corridors, and Arrosa waited next to it as Cael looked for the cloak-room. He opened a door, and gestured for Arrosa to join him. They went into the dark interior, and Cael noticed a large box on the floor. He crouched down by it, as Arrosa stood by his shoulder.

'What is it?' she said.

'Take a look.'

Arrosa knelt down and opened the box.

Inside, three black and tan puppies gazed up at her. One jumped up, and put her front paws on the edge of the box, then she licked Arrosa's nose.

Arrosa's face broke out into a smile. 'You remembered.'

Cael reached into the box and scratched one of the puppies behind the ear. 'They might be small now,' he said, 'but they are going to grow up to be big; as tall as your waist. All three are girls. Do you like them?'

Arrosa took his hand. 'I think I already love them.'

EPILOGUE

Marchside, Kell – 22nd Day, Second Third Summer 545

'Uncle Naxor,' said Carter, 'will the gods attack our home again?'

Naxor sipped from his glass of fine whisky, and gazed at the five children sitting in front of him. Their faces were reflecting the glow of the roaring fire in the hearth of the large study, while shadows shrouded the rest of the room. The shutters were closed against a night squall that was passing over the hills around Clackenbaird, and the wind outside was howling.

'What are gods?' said Naxor.

The children said nothing. Twenty-one days had passed since the death of their father at the young age of thirty-three; and it had been eighteen days since Naxor had decided to live permanently in Clackenbaird. It had been hard work, harder than Naxor was used to. He had maintained the large house, worked long hours to oversee the Marchbrae businesses, organised meals and supplies, and kept the children company while Aila mourned the loss of her husband. Hard work, but it would all be worth it.

'Konna,' he went on, 'tell me – what defines a god?'

The girl glanced up at him. She was two days past her eleventh birthday, and she was already taller than Naxor. All of Aila's children had the Kellach build of their father's side of the family. A horde of little giants, Naxor thought, as he gazed down at them.

'It is someone who lives forever,' the girl said.

'Close, but not entirely accurate, Konna,' said Naxor. 'It is true that, left to their own devices, gods will indeed live on forever but, alas, we have seen that this does not always happen. Gods can be slain, if they lose their heads or if they are reduced to ash in a fire. I hope you have noticed that this definition says nothing about morality. Gods are not intrinsically good or evil. Some are certainly evil, but so are many mortals, are they not? The difference between immortals and mortals lies not in their capacity for good or evil – no, it is defined by their perspective upon life.'

He sipped from his glass, savouring the whisky.

'Gods measure their lives in centuries and millennia,' he went on, 'not in mere years or decades. Things that seem important to mortal creatures are useless or irrelevant to the gods. When every single mortal you know is dead and buried, you will have aged not a day. Think on that. The Empress, the Herald, every soldier in the great Imperial Army – they will die, and you will not. Eternal life brings its obvious rewards, but there is also a price we must pay.'

'What price, Uncle?' said Killop.

'The price your poor mother is paying right now,' said Naxor. 'If you befriend or fall in love with a mortal, then you must harden your heart, for their life-spans pass in the twinkling of an eye. You will live to see the great-great-great-great-great grandchildren of Kelsey Holdfast. After a few generations, you might start to muddle up their names, for they will come and go so quickly. Therefore, I caution you – try not to become too attached to any mortal, lest your heart be broken over and over again. To shield your emotions, you must keep a little distance between yourselves and the mortals of this world. Now, can anyone tell me the difference between a god and a demigod?'

'A demigod is the child of a god,' said Konna.

'Again, you are very close, Konna,' said Naxor, 'but there is one little aspect you have neglected to mention. The children of true gods are ever-living, even if that god mated with a mortal. With demigods, however, like you and I, and your mother – if we mate with mortals, then our children will also be mortal. But – and listen carefully to this part – if you were to mate with other gods or demigods, then your children would live forever.'

He gazed at them all in turn.

'This might all seem complicated and silly, but it is, in fact, at the heart of everything. Do you want to see your children grow old and die in front of you? I had children in the City of Salve.'

'You have children, Uncle?' said Cairney.

'I *had* children,' said Naxor. 'Because every god in the City was born of the same family, we could not have children together; therefore, I was forced to seek partners among the mortals. As a consequence, all of my children were mortal, and each one of them has long since passed away. Can you imagine the heartache and pain that caused? If I hadn't taken steps to protect myself, I would have become too sad to carry on. It may sound cruel and heartless, but it is the only way our kind can survive. If I could give you all two pieces of advice, they would be these: keep an emotional distance from the mortals; and marry among other gods, to ensure that your own children are also immortal.'

'But there are no other gods in Kell,' said Konna.

'Gods still exist upon other worlds,' said Naxor. 'Lord Edgar is moving all of the gods and demigods out of the Doomed Worlds, and he is settling them on Athumia. Lord Edgar, in my humble opinion, was acting primarily to secure a future for his fellow immortals. Did he go about it the right way? No, he did not. But, did he act for a noble cause? Some might say that he did. Thanks to Edgar, the gods and demigods of the Doomed Worlds are now safe and free. Furthermore, the truly evil ones among them – Ward, say, and Allura, have been weeded out. Edgar himself, of course, comes from a very prestigious lineage, being, as he is, the younger brother of the Second Ascendant.'

He smiled at the children.

'You, too, come from a most noble lineage,' he said. 'Your mother's grandmother was the mighty and royal God-Queen Amalia of the City, the greatest ruler my world has seen; but her husband was yet more powerful. Your great grandfather Malik. Have you heard of him? In his prime, there was no one stronger, no one more courageous and gallant. Through him, you are also related to the Ascendants, for Malik was the younger brother of none other than King Nathaniel, the Fourth Ascendant, and the creator of this world. For thousands of years, King Nathaniel had the Sextant in his possession. He was the last great world-builder, and the ruler of an empire that spanned several worlds, and you are his descendants. You are the true royalty of this world, not that silly woman in a blue frock who sits upon her little throne in Plateau City.'

The children laughed.

'Of course,' said Naxor, 'I am just teasing about our beloved Empress. Thorn is an adopted Holdfast, but I am sure you already knew that. She has no Holdfast blood in her, but it runs strong within you, my nephews and nieces. And what an inheritance! What great heroes have emerged from the Holdfasts – your grandmother Daphne; your great-aunt Sable, and, of course, your renowned father, the greatest mortal warrior who has ever lived. You children are doubly-blessed, because it is only in you that both bloodlines converge – that of the Holdfasts, and that of the Ascendants. Can you imagine a more noble inheritance? Can you picture, for a moment, where this inheritance might one day lead us? When the other Holdfasts are dead and gone, you will remain. Power awaits. Power, glory, riches and the Empire itself lie at your feet. Will you walk past them, or will you seize your birthright with both hands?'

'I hate the Empire,' said Cairney. 'The Empire took our father from us.'

Naxor eyed the nine-year-old boy. Out of all of the children, Cairney held the most promise. He was going to be a formidable warrior, that was clear, but he was also headstrong and defiant. He could be moulded into a great leader, an immortal ruler. All Naxor needed was time, and he had it in abundance.

'I understand your pain,' said Naxor, 'and I understand why you would blame the Empire; but the Empire itself is not good or bad. The acts of an Empire depend upon its rulers. Badly led, any Empire will do evil things, even if its intentions are good; but well-led? If well-led by immortals, those who see events with the perspective of centuries, then an Empire can become a truly majestic institution. Wise, noble, and eternal. It is the natural place for gods and demigods to rule, while the natural place for mortals is to serve those who evince a wisdom and experience that is quite beyond their feeble life spans. Your mother and I served the governments of the City for close to a thousand years. Nathaniel ruled Lostwell for five millennia. Compare that to Thorn, who has been Empress for a little over ten years. Do you see the difference? Even if Thorn ruled for another forty years, her reign would amount to nothing more than the blink of an eye to a god. Therefore, the third piece of advice I would offer you is this: be patient. You have no need to rush into anything. Sometimes, all you need to do is wait. I have been waiting, waiting for an opportunity such as this – an opportunity to guide and mentor the next generation of immortal rulers; the next royal family of gods. I may not be a Holdfast, but I share with you the immortal blood of Amalia, Malik and Nathaniel. You are my kin, my family, and I will do whatever it takes to see you all flourish.' His eyes pierced them, as they gazed up at their uncle. 'Whatever it takes.'

The door swung open and Aila walked in, holding three-year-old Carron by the hand.

'Ceres has finally gone to sleep,' she said, her eyes heavy. 'Thanks for making dinner and for taking care of the laundry, Naxor.'

Naxor smiled at her. 'It was no trouble at all, my dear cousin. I am at your service.'

'Are you meeting with the Lach distillers tomorrow?' she said. 'We have important orders that need to be arranged, and...'

'Please don't worry about any of that,' said Naxor. 'It is all in hand. That is why I am here, to share some of your burdens.'

A tear rolled down Aila's face, then she wiped it away. She leaned over, and kissed Naxor's cheek.

'My beloved Aila,' he said; 'you have always been there for me, and it is an honour to do the same for you. Take a seat. Relax and join me for a small whisky.'

Aila shook her head. 'I just want to lie down and sleep.'

'Then go to bed, my dearest cousin,' he said. 'I will take care of everything.'

'Thank you, Naxor,' she said. 'I don't know what I'd do without you. Goodnight, everyone. I will see you in the morning.'

She led Carron back out of the room and closed the door.

Naxor turned back to the five oldest children of Corthie and Aila.

'Now,' he said, as a gentle smile returned to his features; 'where were we?'

AUTHOR'S NOTES

MARCH 2025

Thank you for reading ***Sapphire Throne***, the third and final book of the Twins Trilogy. With only four more books to follow ***Sapphire Throne***, the end of the entire Magelands arc is approaching, and I could feel the weight upon my shoulders as I wrote. In some ways, ***Sapphire Throne*** marks the end of an era, in others, it points the way to the conclusion. Not since ***Holdfast Imperium*** has the ending of a book almost broken me as much as writing ***Sapphire Throne*** did. **Epic** dealt with the first generation of Holdfasts, **Eternal Siege** the second, and **Empire** now homes in on the third – the generation of Cael, Arrosa and Cole.

I hope you enjoyed it.

RECEIVE A FREE MAGELANDS DOMINION SHORT STORY

Building a relationship with my readers is very important to me.

Join my newsletter for information on new books and deals and you will also receive a Magelands Dominion short story that is currently EXCLUSIVE to my Readers' Group for FREE.

www.ChristopherMitchellBooks.com/dominion

ABOUT THE AUTHOR

Christopher Mitchell is the author of the Magelands epic fantasy series.

For more information:
www.christophermitchellbooks.com
info@christophermitchellbooks.com

Printed in Great Britain
by Amazon

60660954R00274